Good to a Fault

Good to a Fault

Marina Endicott

Library and Archives Canada Cataloguing in Publication

Endicott, Marina, 1958-

    Good to a fault / Marina Endicott.

ISBN 978-1-55111-929-8

    I. Title.

PS8559.N475G66 2008   C813'.6   C2008-903537-2

Freehand Books
412 – 815 1ˢᵗ Street SW
Calgary, Alberta
Canada   T2P 1N3
www.freehand-books.com

Book orders
Broadview Press Inc.
280 Perry Street, Unit 5
Peterborough, Ontario
Canada   K9J 7H5
phone: 705-743-8990
fax: 705-743-8353
customerservice@broadviewpress.com
www.broadviewpress.com

"Away Melancholy" (excerpts): from *Collected Poems of Stevie Smith*, copyright © 1972 by Stevie Smith. Reprinted by permission of New Directions Publishing Corp.

Printed in Canada on chlorine-free paper using 100% post-consumer waste.

Freehand Books, an imprint of Broadview Press Inc., acknowledges the financial support for its publishing program from the Government of Canada through the Book Publishing Industry Development Program (BPIDP).

for Peter

You that are in love and charity
with your neighbours,
and intend to lead
a new life

1. Left turn

*T*hinking about herself and the state of her soul, Clara Purdy drove to the bank one hot Friday in July. The other car came from nowhere, speeding through on the yellow, going so fast it was almost safely past when Clara's car caught it. She was pushing on the brake, a ballet move, graceful—pulling back on the wheel with both arms as she rose, her foot standing on the brake—and then a terrible crash, a painful extended rending sound, when the metals met. The sound kept on longer than you'd expect, Clara thought, having time to think as the cars scraped sides and changed each other's direction, as the metal ripped open and bent and assumed new shapes.

They stopped. The motion stopped. Then the people from the other car came spilling out. The doors opened and like milk boiling over on the stove, bursting to the boil, they all frothed out onto the pavement. It seemed they came out the windows, but it was only the doors.

An old woman was last, prying herself out stiffly. Her lap was covered with redness, roses growing there and swelling downwards, and she began to screech on one note. The man, the driver, was already shouting. The line of curses streaming out of his mouth hung visible in the heavy air. Their car was the colour of butterscotch pudding, burnt pudding crusted on it in rust. The whole driver's side had crumpled inward, like pudding-skin when it is disturbed.

Clara's ears were not working properly. There was a vacuum around her where no sound could ring. She could see all the mouths moving. She swallowed to clear her ears, but pressure was not the problem. What had she done? All of this.

The membrane of silence burst. There was the noise—Clara felt it hit. Her body vibrated like a tuning fork. She kept her mouth shut. She put her hands up to her lips and held them closed with her fingers.

The man was flailing his arms in big circles, his head jutted forward to threaten her. "What kind of a driver are you?" he was yelling, for the benefit of everyone nearby. "My fucking *kids* can drive better than that! My *kids*!"

The little girl sitting on the pavement looked almost happy, as if her pinched face had relaxed now that some dangerous thing had actually happened. Clara sat down beside her. Strange to be sitting down right on the street, she thought. The road was warm. Cars whipped by, their wheels huge from this low down.

The man strode over, almost prancing. "You fucking *hit* us! What were you doing?"

"I'm sorry," Clara said.

It was out, the whole thing was her fault. In the case of a disputed left-hand turn, the turning party is always at fault. The man's face was blotched with red stuff. His hair was dusty. He might be thirty, or forty. She should be getting his insurance information, giving him hers.

She got up, trembling knees making her slow. The women kept wailing. The younger one, a baby clutched to her breast, came rushing at Clara—to strike her, Clara thought, flinching away.

"My baby! You could of killed us!" The woman's shirt flapped open, Clara saw her pale breast, there in the middle of the street. And then her eyes, glaring dark in her shocked face. Shreds of skin stuck to her shirt. Whose— the baby's? He lolled in her arms, maybe unconscious, his blue sleeper stained with matter, redness. Clara reached out to touch the poor little creature's forehead, but the mother leaped back, crying, "Get away! Get away from us!"

The old woman was stupidly plucking her bloody skirt away from her body, bits of flesh falling. Wherever Clara turned there were more. A boy, bleeding, holding his head. His clothes were dirty, he must have been knocked out onto the road. Where was the other one? Clara caught at the girl's shirt and hauled her back from the other lane of traffic.

"Get your hands off her," the mother shouted. "What are you trying to do now?" There was no way to speak, to tell what she had meant. She had been driving to the bank on her lunch hour. The bank would be going on without her—how tenderly she longed for the line-up, and herself standing there, safe.

The younger child sat down on the road, feeling his head. He seemed to be poking into his skull, his finger buried in blood. Clara was afraid that this was hell, that she had died when the cars hit; that maybe there was no such thing as death, that she would be living this way from now on, in hell. Then the police came, and there was a siren winding closer, so the ambulance was coming.

Clara knelt down on the black street beside the boy and took his hand, pulling it gently away from his scalp. "I think you've got a cut there," she whispered. "Give me your hand. Let the doctors look at it, you don't want to make it worse."

He stared up at her, eyes flickering over her face, trying to read her like a book, it seemed.

"They'll be here to help us in a minute," she said. "I'm sorry, I'm so sorry."

A paramedic, clean and young, leaned in the window to say they were taking the grandmother away, and the nursing mother. The police officer nodded, signalling something, so that the paramedic grunted and stood upright. He banged once on the door to say goodbye. Another ambulance arrived. The children and the man were packed into it. In the cramped back seat of the police cruiser, Clara was left to the last. The paramedics insisted that she go too, although she said she was all right. The second tow-truck was there already, taking her car.

They bundled her up onto the bench in the back, and she sat down on the edge.

"What will they do with the Dart?" the girl asked. "All our stuff is in it."

"We were living in our car," the man said, accusing Clara.

The paramedic asked him to be quiet, so he could check his pulse, or to stop the quarrel. They were all silent, after that.

It was cherry juice on the grandmother. Mrs. Pell, she was called. She'd been eating a big bag of Okanagan cherries. There was a little blood, from the children, but most of the frightening mess was juice and pulp. The baby was all right. The little boy, Trevor, had a bandage on his head, but it was only a scalp wound, no concussion; instead of using stitches they had glued it shut with blue space-age glue. The girl's scraped arm had been cleaned. The father was fine.

But the mother was not well. She had a fever, and there were clusters of tiny bruises. Not from the accident. The emergency nurse stared at them, touching with her fingers.

The father roamed the halls. The mother was put into a room, the baby lying beside her on the narrow hospital bed. The children sat silent beside their mother. Not knowing what else to do, Clara arranged for the TV to be connected, whenever the technician next came round.

Clara Purdy had been drifting for some time in a state of mild despair, forty-three and nothing to show for it. Her racing heart woke her from dreams at three each morning to fling the covers away, angry with herself for this sad-ness, this terror. Six billion people were worse off. She had all the money she needed, no burdens—she was nothing, a comfortable speck in the universe. She felt smothered, or buried alive, or already dead.

Her mother had died two years before, leaving her the plain bungalow in a quiet area of town. Whether she wanted it or not. There she lived, like someone's widow, all alone. She worked in insurance, at the same firm for— it would be twenty years next winter. The time seemed too gauzy to bear the weight of twenty years.

Clara imagined that people saw her as pleasant enough, intelligent, kind. A bit stuck-up, she got that from her mother. But sad, that she'd never had children; never gotten over her short, stupid marriage; never travelled or gone back to school and made something of herself.

Her self was an abandoned sampler, half the letters unstitched, the picture in the middle still vague. Looking after elderly parents had made her elderly. The eight months of her stillborn marriage might have been her whole life. She had returned home to care for her father as he died, and then stayed for her mother's long illness, and nothing had pried her out again. She was too reserved, maybe; she'd made a mess of her few brief attachments since the divorce.

Instead of the heavy work of being with people, she gardened, read books on spirituality, and kept the house trim. She missed her beautiful, exasperating mother. When she was sad, she bought expensive clothes, or went to a movie by herself—two movies in a row sometimes. Anyway, she had no excuse for sadness. A grown woman doesn't pine away because her difficult mother died, because her father had died long before—or because she'd trickled her life away on an old tragedy that now seemed overblown.

She went to the Anglican church, to the early service, Book of Common Prayer first and third Sundays. Not *in the church* the way her mother had been, managing and holding court. Clara was not on the coffee list, and did not read the lesson: she was shy in a certain way, not to make an issue of it, and did not find it easy to speak in public loudly enough to be heard, even with that high-tech tiny microphone on the long black stalk. She did the flowers when her turn came round in the rotation, but after church, and in the dark when she awoke at 3 a.m., she thought continually about how useless she was in the world.

One Saturday a twisted woman stood in line ahead of her at the grocery store. Old but undaunted, this woman had complicated aluminum crutches and a large backpack. All business. The clerk helped load her grocery bags into the backpack, and eased it up onto her back—they must have done this before. Driving home, Clara saw the old woman moving along, spiderly with her crutches and pack. Clara slowed down, wanting to offer her a lift, but she had seemed very proud in the grocery store. It would be miserable to be rebuffed. Clara let her foot fall more firmly on the accelerator. The radio was spouting some story about a mother who had drowned her two children in the bathtub. The neighbour, on the radio, was saying she had heard the children crying, and that at the time she'd been grateful when the crying had stopped, but now she wished she'd—Clara snapped it off.

The world was full of people struggling along with heavy suitcases, poor men dawdling in doorways until they could get their eyes to focus on the sidewalk, children with bloody noses darting past on skateboards—it was laughable, when you began to watch for who needed help. She saw an elderly gentleman fall painfully to his knees, getting off a bus, and that time she almost made herself take action; but a boy got there before her. He helped the old man up and dusted off his trousers, shaking his head at the state of the streets. A native boy, skinny and bruised, fit for care himself.

There was some barrier between Clara and the world that she couldn't budge. Sometimes she thought she would have to go and work in Calcutta with the Sisters of Charity. Everything was wrong with the world—she could not keep on doing nothing.

In Emergency, Clara was the last to be examined and let go. She phoned her office to say she wouldn't be back that afternoon, then bought magazines and puzzle books and went upstairs to 3C, the multi-purpose ward where the mother had been put. The whole family was huddled around her on the bed closest to the door. Old Mrs. Pell was sitting on the orange leatherette chair. It would recline, Clara knew from the months her father had spent in hospital, but the grandmother was sitting up, staring at the door. She must have seen Clara, but she said nothing, didn't even blink her turtle eyes.

The husband turned his head from where he sat on the bed, then stood abruptly, dislodging the baby from its comfort and startling the older children.

"You've got a nerve coming up here," he said, sullen rather than aggressive. Clara understood: she should have brought more than magazines. There was a machine in the elevator alcove. But when Clara returned with five cans of juice, only the mother was left in the room.

"They went outside for a smoke," she said.

"The children too?"

"Well, what was he supposed to do with them? I've got my hands full here."

The baby lay still beside her, mouth open, in a calm stupor. Two empty formula bottles on the bed table. Clara added the cans of juice, shifting them around to make room.

"It wasn't your fault," the mother said. Lying there pale and skinny, she said that. But it wasn't true. Clara was an insurance adjuster, and knew about fault.

"My name is Clara," she said, as if that was the correct thing to do, introduce yourself to the person you've put in hospital.

"Lorraine Gage."

"Purdy, sorry. I'm Clara Purdy."

"My husband is Clayton. And the kids are Darlene and Trevor," Lorraine said formally. "And this is Pearce."

"What a nice name, Pearce. Have they—do they know what's—" *Wrong* seemed like the wrong word to use. She sat in the orange chair, so Lorraine didn't have to crane her neck uncomfortably. "What's going on with you?"

"They're doing tests. They took some blood already. They'll be back to get me pretty soon, some scan or other. It won't hurt."

"No, that's good."

"There's something—I haven't been too good for a while. The crash just made me notice."

The baby stirred. Lorraine folded her arm more gently around him where she had been tightening her hold. "All right, it's all right," she said to him, softer than Clara had yet heard her. "This is one good baby," Lorraine said. "My others were good too, but this one! So easy! Hardly know he's there except he holds your hand. Look."

She lifted a corner of the sheet, showing the baby's fist wrapped around her thumb. Tiny, even fingers, tiny fingernails.

"Even in his sleep," Clara said, shaking her head as if it was a miracle. Anything was a miracle, any moment of ordinary time just then.

The husband stuck his head around the corner. "Found the TV," he said. "Lounge down the hall."

"Okay," Lorraine said. "I know where you're at."

"Yeah. Button up your overcoat," he said, to Clara's surprise. He let go of the door handle and disappeared.

Lorraine smiled. Her teeth were jumbled and not in good shape, the two eye teeth sharply jabbing over the others, but the smile warmed her face.

"You belong to me," she said, and it took Clara a minute to realize that she was filling in the line of the song, not telling Clara that her life was no longer her own.

While their dad was buying cigarettes, not paying attention to them, Darlene tugged Trevor's hand and pulled him into the stairwell. Flights of grimy metal steps wheeled endlessly upward and downward, making her dizzy. But they were going to get in trouble if they were always hanging around in the lounge by themselves. If they stayed out of sight they would not be kicked out, they could stay close to their mom.

"You be Peter and I'll be Penny," she said. "If anybody asks us."

This was 3. They climbed up to 7, and then up the single longer flight to a dead end, with one door. That probably led to the roof.

Quiet up there. The stairs were not too dirty. Somebody had tossed a brown paper bag with a banana skin and a whole apple in it. Darlene washed the apple carefully with spit and polished it on her T-shirt. Trevor's legs were shaking. Darlene pushed up against him, anchoring him to the cool concrete wall so he could calm down. She and Trevor ate the apple, bite for bite, and sat without talking.

Lorraine and Clara were still alone, reading magazines, when an orderly arrived. There was some small inconvenience getting Lorraine onto the gurney. Clara helped by holding the baby's head away from the belt. He had downy hair, and a pale red birthmark almost faded at his nape. His neck was small. The skin was smooth there; her fingers traced the mark.

"You come too," Lorraine said.

The attendant seemed to think that was normal. Clara hesitated, but someone would have to hold the baby during the test, and the grandmother had vanished. They wheeled along corridors and into a different elevator, down a few floors, more halls. The orderly left them parked outside an unmarked door and went inside. He came out, and left.

14

There was a considerable wait.

"Jesus, I could use a cigarette," Lorraine said, her voice distorted from lying flat.

"I'm afraid you—" Clara stopped, hearing herself sounding like her mother, sweetly domineering.

"Well, I know that! They don't let you smoke in hospitals, I know that. I don't let them smoke around the baby anyways. It's no good for them, second-hand smoke."

"Smokers in my office building have to go around the back now. There's a dirty overhang where they leave the trash, and you'll see six or seven people huddled under there in a snowstorm."

"Got to have their smokes, though."

"I smoked myself," Clara said. "Then my father had cancer, and it was easier to quit."

Smoke seemed to be winding around them in vapourish tendrils. The possibility of a long drag, breath you could see. Proof of life. Clara had not wanted a cigarette so badly for years. She could feel her fingers falling into place as if they held one.

"I don't smoke much any more," Lorraine said. "Late at night I'll have one of Clayton's."

"Well, if I could do that, one or two a day, I'd still be smoking," Clara said.

"Yeah, lots of people can't."

They fell into silence.

A few minutes later the baby woke. He did not cry, but he moved restlessly, his mouth pursing and his fist searching. He gnawed on his curled fingers till they were wet, until Clara asked if she should run and find another bottle.

"Don't go," Lorraine said. "I can nurse him, it's okay." Her eyes stayed on Clara, rather than straying to the baby. She knew where he was.

"I'll stay," Clara said to reassure her.

The door finally opened, and a technician in a lead apron came out to steer the gurney through. She gave Clara the baby to hold and said it would be a few minutes.

Clara stood there in the hall, suddenly alone. No nurses, no station.

She began to walk back and forth along the windowed hallway near the closed door, jiggling the baby slightly up and down. He liked up and down better than side to side, she found. She found it astonishing that the baby did not cry, or find her frightening or frustrating. He seemed to have forgotten his hunger. His fist closed around her fingers and he brought her hand close to his mouth and then stared, transfixed, at the size or shape or texture of her skin. The smell, she thought. Probably mostly soap. Different from his mother, at any rate.

At the end of the hall a low windowsill looked like a good place to sit. She let him stare, first at the glass, and then, his focus visibly altering, out at the courtyard garden below. He held on to her blouse with one hand, his perfect miniature fingers clutching the silk into even gathers.

No one came down the hall, no one disturbed them. Far in the distance, Clara could hear machinery rumbling and whirring. She could imagine the scan moving over Lorraine, and Lorraine trying to lie still, trying not to be afraid. Pearce put one hand on the glass, looking at the empty garden.

Darlene left Trevor sleeping on the stairs and went down alone. At each landing shiny linoleum halls ran away in every direction. Picking a floor, she wandered quietly along. Every room she passed held people in flimsy gowns coughing or lying suspiciously still. On TV when they knew people were dead a blue light flashed on and off. *Code Blue.*

She was mostly invisible, but one nurse at a desk asked her, "Are you lost?"

"No," Darlene said, not quite stopping. "My dad is having an operation to his heart, I'm just waiting to see how it turns out."

The nurse looked at her. "What's your name?"

"Melody Fairchild," Darlene said. "I'll go back and wait with my mom. She's pretty upset. I was looking for a place to get juice for my baby brother."

The nurse rolled her chair backwards to the little fridge for a couple of boxes of apple juice and handed them over the counter, then added a pack of cookies from her drawer. A bell rang somewhere so she stopped paying attention to Darlene. Maybe it was a blue light going off.

The lobby? She could check the payphones for quarters and look in the shop. But she should go back for Trevor. She found the stairwell and ran up all those spiralling, echoing metal steps. But the landing was empty, he was gone. Or this was the wrong set of stairs.

A doctor—too young and pretty to be real—arrived to talk to Lorraine. The husband had come back from the lounge with the little boy trailing cautiously after him, wanting to see Lorraine, but when the doctor entered the husband edged toward the door, an awkward beetle trying to scuttle away without being seen.

"Why don't I take the children downstairs for some supper?" Clara asked Lorraine. It was after six.

Lorraine said, "Clay?"

"I'll give the baby to Mom," the husband said, taking him, and out he went.

They couldn't all leave her, Clara thought, but the doctor must have been used to avoidance. "We just have a few questions," she said, making it mild. "Dr. Porteous will come by too, in a few minutes. He's the consultant."

Lorraine's eyes were slightly too wide open, the whites of her eyes showing. But to the little boy she said calmly enough, "Go get some supper with Clara, that's a great idea. You'll be fine with her."

The little girl hung at the door, a shadow. She glared at the boy like he'd done something wrong.

Clara did not try to take their hands. She went to the door and let them follow. In the elevator she said, as if she knew what to do with children, "Darlene, can you push the one marked L? Trevor can push the button on the way back up."

In the cafeteria line-up the little girl snaked out her hand to Clara's wrist. Without volition, Clara's hand pulled back. The girl's eyes rose sidelong, diamond-edged, to check what she was thinking.

"Where did you get this?" she asked, almost accusing. It was a bracelet, six or seven strands of beads in different colours, pretty.

"I got it—oh, in some store, I can't remember which," Clara said, forcing herself not to turn away, not to be cruel.

17

"In the Saan store, I bet," the girl said, triumphant. "I saw it there!"

Clara wanted to give it to her, but couldn't find a way to do it that would make up for having pulled her hand back. Suddenly everything made her so tired! She must have a vitamin deficiency. Or it was the trauma. She never shopped at Saan. *Shoddy goods*—her mother's voice rang in her ears.

"Yes," she said. "I think it was Saan."

The children ate their French fries. She had to go back to the counter three times for ketchup: twice for Trevor and once, separately, for Darlene. Trevor put mustard on his, too, but he had already filled his pockets with mustard packs himself.

"It's a pity to waste those chicken nuggets," Clara said.

"Oh, we won't *waste* them!" Trevor said, his voice squeakier than she'd expected.

"We'll take them up for Dad and Gran," Darlene said, patient with her rich ignorance.

Clara jumped up and went back for roast chicken dinners for the husband and the grandmother. The children loved the stainless steel hats meant to keep the dinners warm. They begged to carry one plate each, so she let them. Trevor dropped his right in front of the elevators.

"Better than dropping it *in* the elevator," Clara said, pleased with how calmly she took it. They told the morose kitchen helper about the spill, and got another dinner.

Upstairs, Lorraine was alone in the room. The lights were out, except a small bulb over the sink. Red from the sun's low angle streamed in the window.

Clara said, "Trevor, will you carry it very carefully?" He nodded, glad to be given a second chance. "Take these down to the lounge to your father and your grandmother, then." Darlene walked behind Trevor so he would not be distracted.

Lorraine was lying on her side in a fresh hospital gown, with the bed lowered.

"The doctor came in," she told Clara. Forgetting that Clara had been there, or maybe having no other way to begin telling it. "They think, they're pretty sure, I've got cancer."

She had the fortitude to say it right out like that, no hesitation. What kind, was all Clara could think to ask. "I'm sorry," she said, instead.

"It's not your fault," Lorraine said, and almost laughed.

It was the second time she'd said that to Clara.

Down in the lobby the booth selling stuffed animals was closing for the evening. A little cat caught Clara's eye, with a beaded collar like her bracelet, for Darlene, and a small mottled-green pterodactyl for Trevor. She didn't have the gall to go back up and disturb the family again, so she shoved the toys into the bottom of her bag.

At home, Clara called Evie, the office manager. Easier to deal with Evie than Barrett, the Regional Director, whose petty vanity required constant coddling. "I'm sorry to bother you in the evening like this, but I'm going to be away for a few more days," she said.

"Are you hurt? Is it worse than you thought?" Evie asked, relishing catastrophe.

"It's not—I'm fine, but—" Rather than explain the whole thing, and have Evie talking it over with Mat and the others, Clara said, "I am a little shaken up. I think I'll need a few days. The Curloe inspection was put off till the nineteenth anyway, and otherwise…"

"Oh, no, you stay home. You get some good rest. You're no good to us if you're a nervous wreck, are you? What a thing to happen. How are the other people?"

"Oh, they're fine, they're fine, no one was badly hurt."

"But it could have been. A baby, too, you said?"

Had she said that? Why go into any detail at all? Because she had been buzzing from the accident still, frantic with dreadful possibilities, words spilling over.

"Evie, I've got to go, I'm going to lie down now."

She lay in bed wakeful, the accident replaying in her mind. She said her prayers, naming each of them, and prayed that Lorraine's cancer would be healed, as far as she could reach to God, knowing that it would be no use.

2. In clover

*E*arly Saturday morning, Clara gave up on sleep and went back to the hospital. The husband and the children and Mrs. Pell must have slept in the visitors' lounge. Clara had brought a box of muffins, and juice for the children. Underneath a stack of magazines she'd packed some puzzle books and an old etch-a-sketch from the hall closet, which Trevor was happy to see.

The children were grubby. Clara offered to wash their faces, but Clayton declined. In a huff with her, or in some permanent state of huff he lived in.

He took Trevor off to the men's room. Darlene went by herself to the women's. Ten minutes later Clara found her there, sitting on the sink counter with her legs folded under her, ferociously reading a home decorating magazine. Clara backed out—but then, remembering the toys in her purse, pushed the bathroom door open again, and set the little white cat on the counter beside Darlene.

"This cat reminded me of you," she said, shy about giving a present.

Darlene looked at it but did not touch it.

"I thought you might like the bead collar," Clara said. So Darlene

20

wouldn't have to speak, she held out the other toy, Trevor's. "And will you give this one to Trevor?"

Darlene unfolded her stick-thin legs. She put the magazine down, carefully away from the splashes by the sink. "It's a pterodactyl," she said. "I'll tell him what it is." She got down, sliding the cat along the counter, and took the pterodactyl. Clara held the door open for her, and Darlene ran down to the lounge, her bare feet making no noise, the hospital already home.

Lorraine's bed was rumpled and she looked ugly and uncomfortable. A nurse was settling an older woman back into the bed to the left of the door. Lorraine strained herself upwards, trying to get into a half-sitting position.

"Some kind of lymphoma is what they think," she said.

Clara nodded.

"It's weird to say it out loud," Lorraine said.

"I know."

"It's a shock. They tried to tell me about it last night, they sent in an older doctor in the evening. The little bruises, those are petechiae. I just thought they looked kind of pretty, like a brooch of moles."

They were pretty. Little constellations, a sweet dark splatter of paint on Lorraine's arm, another patch on her leg just above the knee. Now they seemed hostile as snake bites.

"I hadn't heard of them before," Clara said.

"Me neither. Or I'd have known to go get looked at." Lorraine moved fretfully in the bed, tugged at her pillow. "These are lumps of dough. I wish I had my little pillow out of the car."

They were silent.

"I've got this fever," Lorraine said, after a moment. "They left me a bunch of pamphlets. *Your Cancer and You.*" The stack of papers sat, radioactive, on the night table.

"You look a little flushed," Clara said, hating the sound of her own voice so falsely, unspontaneously cheerful.

"They want me to stay in till they can get it down. There's—a bunch of more tests to do, there's—" Lorraine stopped talking.

The woman in the other bed moaned behind the curtain. Then she was silent too.

"Ovarian," Lorraine whispered. "She had a rough night."

Clara's head was aching badly. She couldn't seem to stop hearing her own words, and Lorraine's too, repeated in her mind during the silences. Fever, *fever*, fever, *more tests*, more, a little flushed, *a little flushed*.

"I think they'll probably let us stay here—them, I mean—one more night, but it isn't too good for the kids, in the lounge. I want them to go. There's some kind of a—some accommodation, Clayton's getting the details, if there's room."

Clara murmured something, one of those noises which encourage further conversation without committing the speaker to an exact opinion.

"They shouldn't of seen any of this."

No. Clara could see the dark circles under Trevor's eyes. Even the baby Pearce seemed lethargic, less comfortable and safe than right after the accident. Lorraine's distress infected them all, she thought. And nothing to do all day but wander from the TV lounge to the room.

"It's hard on everyone," she said. Innocuous enough, but the husband, coming in, took exception to it anyway.

"Hard on you?" he sneered. "Hard to sit and watch the results of what you did?"

Lorraine pushed him with her pale hand. "Quit it, Clay," she said. "She didn't give it to me."

"This whole thing," he began, and then petered out, his face pulling down in the chin. He had a sharp face, almost good-looking, with smooth beige skin. His chin was as small and rounded as a girl's, and he could look defeated in an instant. It must make him seem vulnerable, Clara thought, trying to make out what Lorraine had seen in him. He was not big, but had a springy build with muscles stretched over his bones. He looked strong but unhealthy, surly and eager at the same instant. A dog who's been badly treated, and has gone vicious, but wants you to fuss over him anyway.

The minutes stretched by in a silence that Lorraine seemed to want.

He sat quietly enough on the end of her bed, but couldn't settle. He shifted and re-crossed his legs every few seconds, until Clara found her own legs tensing, watching him. His eyes darted too quickly, checking Lorraine, checking the clock, the window, Clara—to see what mischief she was making?—back to his own hands, flexing and fisting on whichever pant leg

22

was uppermost at the time. He didn't wear a wedding ring, Clara noticed, but many men did not. Lorraine had one, and an engagement ring, nestled close together as they were made to do. People's Jewellers, Clara thought, before she could stop herself. Or Wal-Mart.

But just when she had dismissed their marriage and their whole lives this way, Clayton leaned forward on the bed and grasped Lorraine's hand. He bent his mouth to her curled fingers, and then bent his head farther forward, over her sheeted lap, and said, "No."

Lorraine brought her other hand to curve over his head through his dirty hair. She said it too. "No, I know. It can't be."

Clara got up without making a sound, and left the room.

The landing at the top of the stairwell was cold, the second evening. She should go steal Trevor a blanket from an empty bed, Darlene thought. It was probably warmer out on the roof. The big metal door had one of those release bars. She leaned on the bar, feeling it give. If she pushed it all the way down the alarm might go off. There was no sign, though.

She pushed it anyway. No sound. The heavy door swung open. She nudged Trevor with her toe and took his little springy fingers, and they stepped out into the evening darkness, and the warmth. Tarry black gel oozing up through the pebble coat of the wide expanse of roof. The wall all around was too low, be careful!

Darlene got Trevor to hold her waist while she leaned over to see cars and people like ants, toy ambulances going into the garage door down there. If she fell, someone would scoop her up and put her in bed next to her mom, her legs strung up to the ceiling in white casts.

She was going to throw up. She twisted up and backwards and grabbed Trevor's arm, almost yanking them both over, *whoo!* But not quite.

They were okay. They sat there. The soft black tar smelled good. And it was warmer out in the air.

On Sunday morning, after a second sleepless night, Clara found herself in tears during the Hosanna. She hated crying in church and had stayed away

23

for months after her mother's death. But here she was again, eyes raised up to the wooden rafters of the roof. No heaven visible up there. Some water spilled over, before she got angry enough to stop.

After coffee hour, not knowing what else to do, Clara stayed to talk to the priest, Paul Tippett. His own life seemed to be a shambles; she didn't know how he could help, sitting in his poky office with a cup of weak coffee in front of him. Clara held hers on her lap.

"What is the worst of it?" he asked her, when she had explained about the accident. His large-boned, unworldly face was kind.

"The worst? Oh!" Clara had to look away, her eyes half-filling again.

"Take your time," he said, his gentle expression undisturbed. He must be used to tears, of course; but not from her, she'd hardly spoken to him before now.

He listened.

"I see what they need," she finally said, "But I am unwilling to help." But that was not it, she was not unwilling—she was somehow stupidly ashamed of wanting to help.

It was probably part of his training not to speak, to let people go on.

"The mother, Lorraine, is very ill. From before the accident, nobody knew about it. It's cancer, lymphoma. Advanced. Her family has nowhere to go. They were living in their car, and the two older children are—and the baby, ten months old, too young to be without his mother—how will they cope with a baby in a shelter? The grandmother, I suppose, because the father is not a—but she's not—"

Clara stopped babbling.

She had worked in shelters, serving supper, making beds, setting up the cardboard dividers that shut each person off from the next, two feet away. It was not possible for her to send them to a shelter. During the Hosanna, in the high cascading descant, she'd known what she had to do. If any of this was true, if there was God. She had wanted useful work; this was it. And if there was no God, then even more, she had to do it.

"I don't want them in my house," she said. But maybe she did.

"No one could plausibly expect you to take them in," the priest said. "There are agencies…"

"It's not what's plausible, it's what I ought to do."

"You've visited them," he commended her. "Many would not think to do as much."

Many would not think to do as much, she thought, almost laughing. What a convoluted construction. A life in the pulpit. Except there was no pulpit in their church, he just stepped forward, with his tiny chest-hung microphone waiting to catch every word as it dripped from his lips. She stood up, needing to move, and put her coffee cup down on his overflowing desk.

"Visiting the hospital is—nothing! My life does not seem very worthwhile," she said. "Or even real." And that just sounded stupid and self-involved.

He looked thoughtful. Or was honest enough not to argue with her assessment.

With a sudden welling of defeat, Clara left.

The priest shifted her cup to a more stable spot, and rubbed his thumb along his smooth desk-drawer ledge. Her dress, deep indigo or iris purple, seemed to stay hovering in the room, filled his eyes still.

Clara Purdy: single, childless of course, took care with her appearance; fortyish, and not in good spirits for some time since her mother's death. He'd never had to deal with the mother. English, some cousin of an earl's, wasn't she? A piece of work, by all accounts. (*"They fuck you up, your mum and dad."*) Her funeral had been his first duty at St. Anne's, the week he and Lisanne had arrived. In parish archive photos the mother was aloof, fine-boned, with a 30s filmstar glamour even in old age. Clara must take after her father. Odd to think of a middle-aged woman chiefly as a daughter. Pleasant enough, quiet, careful. Insurance, at Gilman-Stott—but then the contradiction of that flower-petal colour. Lisanne admired her clothes, or envied them, depending on the mood of the day. Almost-Easter, true violet, perfect purple. Porphyry, periphery, preface… He drew back from the precipice.

Carnelian, or more than red—true coral for Lisanne, who would be waiting for him at home, fretful muscles sharp behind her black-wire eyebrows. The hospital chaplain was away all summer in England, locum at a parish in the Lake District. Maybe Lisanne would have liked that. Cerulean. Paul wondered how he could bear another hospital visit.

He took both cups and emptied them in the meeting hall sink. All the other cups had been bleached and dried and put away. He rinsed these last two and stacked them in the cupboard damp—rebellion.

Clara walked through her three-bedroom bungalow, working out where to put everyone. The grandmother in the guest room, the baby with her, in a wicker laundry basket padded and lined with a flannel sheet. The father: the pull-out couch in the small bedroom that had been her own father's den. The grandmother couldn't sleep on that thing. Nowhere left to put the children but her own bed. She cleared the soul-help books off the bedside table and piled them in the garage; she pulled off the linen cover and replaced it with a striped one, made up the other beds, and found towels for everyone, as if they were guests.

She looked around at her light, orderly house. Then she went back to the hospital to pick up the family. What was left of them.

Trevor was not in the lounge, but Darlene knew where to find him. She ran up all the stairs and let herself out onto the roof. Where was he? There, around the side of the little hut. She ran across the melty roof floor, pebbles oozing sideways under her feet.

"Look," Trevor said when she caught him. "This door's open."

He slid his fingers into the crack and pulled it open. Black inside there, and a glimmer of light. A bare bulb on the wall inside. They stepped through onto a metal cage floor, suspended over darkness. A chain ran across, blocking steep metal stairs.

Then they heard a grinding noise. "Down there," she said. "It's the elevators."

Their eyes adjusted to see that they were right on top of the elevators, a huge hole, with metal cables going down, down, seven floors. One elevator was coming up. Trevor craned out to watch, holding on with one hand and leaning out under the railing.

"Don't!" Darlene said. "It will come up and cut your head off."

"No," he said. "It has to stop down there."

It cranked and cranked and cranked, until with a sigh and a jerk it stopped.

In the silence, Darlene said, "We're going to the woman's house."

"Mom too?"

"Of course not." She did not say, "Stupid."

The father came into the kitchen while Clara was making a bedtime snack for the children. They were safe, sitting in front of the television in the den, blankly watching *The Jungle Book* with Mrs. Pell the grandmother.

"I'm going to need some cash," he said, hovering between threat and casual assumption.

"No," she said. Easy enough to open her wallet, give him a twenty. No.

"Can't get by on nothing, we got nothing left now."

"No cash." She looked up at the calendar. It was still Sunday. She'd sat in church today, deciding to do this, or realizing that it was not a decision.

"Tomorrow I'll get you an appointment at Manpower, we'll find you some temporary work."

"Fine!" His hands went flinging palm-up in submission, as if she'd won some fight. "Fine help you are."

He left, shouldering past her closer than he needed to, but she stood still. She was a little frightened, but only for a moment, because she was doing the right thing. She was surprised at herself, and again thought that she was doing the right thing—but maybe a foolish thing.

Listening in the den, Darlene ran her fingernails along the carpet. Her mom had clipped them when they cleaned up before they left her at the hospital, and the skin on Darlene's fingertips was frayed-up, nervous. She was having a hard time seeing with her eyes but her fingers were working overtime. She closed her eyes and combed along the carpet, and listened to the evil snake sssinging: *Trust in me, just in me, Sleep safe and sound, Knowing I am around...*

While the bathwater ran, Clara pulled off Trevor's shirt and shorts. His ribs were sharp under his bluish skin, but he did not look malnourished. A sore on the left side, probably a mosquito bite he'd scratched. She popped him in.

27

"Hot! Hot!" His little body squirmed away from the water, almost levitating.

She grabbed him out again, with a rush of fear in her throat, and put her hand into the water to check—she was sure she had checked—yes, it was only warm.

"It's not hot," she said. "Put your foot in first, and see. It's warm."

He tried his foot, obediently, and said *hmm*. He brought the other foot in, and stood there letting the water get used to him. Then he squatted, his pointy bottom submerged, but kept his arms wrapped around his large-boned knees.

"How old are you?" she asked. She imagined six or seven.

"I'm five!" he told her. He was big. Or her ideas of size were wrong.

"Sing," he ordered. She wanted to comfort him—he was only five. As she lathered up the soap she started off on a winding minor tune, the sad pig song her own mother had sung for her.

> *Betty Pringle, she had a pig.*
> *Not too little, not very big.*
> *While he lived, he lived in clover*
> *Now he's dead, and that's all over.*

Clara held each hand in turn and washed his thin arms, trying not to tickle him. With his free hand he crowned his kneecaps with bubbles.

> *Billy Pringle lay down and cried.*
> *Betty Pringle lay down and died.*
> *That's the end of one, two, three:*
> *Billy, Betty, poor piggy.*

"Like my mom," she heard a voice behind her say. It was Darlene standing in the bathroom doorway. Her long eyes sharp as diamonds again, her arms trembling.

"Like my mom, laid down and died."

"She's not dead yet," Clara said, rattled. Stupid thing to say! Her hands were soapy. "She's ill, Darlene, but Jesus will look after her. Jesus died for us, you know." Oh, how had that come out of her mouth?

"Like the pig," said Trevor in the bathtub.

It wasn't until ten o'clock that night, when the children had finally gone to sleep, that Clara realized she had not left a place for herself. She got a blanket and a pillow and lay on the sofa in the living room. She startled awake all night at every noise, then lay planning and thinking what to do: how much vacation time she had left, what files she needed to clear up at work, what to feed them all. The grandmother went to the bathroom many, many times. At least the baby didn't cry. The father got up and ate noisily about 2 a.m. But she could deal with him, and the children needed help. About dawn, she fell into a deep sleep.

The children were staring at her, in broad daylight.

"My dad's gone," Darlene said.

"He took your stuff," Trevor told her sadly.

Her nightgown was awry. She pulled it straight and rolled off the couch, wrapped in the afghan, and went to check. He had taken her mother's old car, which she had been using since the accident. The stereo from the den, the silver clock from her dresser. The silver teapot, but not the Spode cups and saucers, which were worth far more. Nothing she couldn't spare. A loaf of bread and some ham. The money from her wallet, but not the credit cards.

"He'll be back when that runs out," Mrs. Pell said, coming to join the party. She hadn't spoken since coming to Clara's house—Clara couldn't remember ever having heard her deep voice, rasping like a plumber's snake scraping the side of the pipe.

Darlene stood beside Clara looking out the front door at the empty driveway. Trevor held on to Darlene's T-shirt at the back.

"Will we have to go to the shelter now?" he asked her.

"No," Darlene answered.

She looked up at Clara.

The baby started to wail in the bedroom, and Mrs. Pell showed no signs of going to attend to him. Clara was thinking what to do.

She could report Clayton, they'd probably catch him quickly. But what would she report—a missing person or a car thief? She could choose to say she'd lent him the car, she could get him to come back.

Instead she went into the bedroom and picked up the little baby, the new one, the morning dew. The baby quieted immediately, holding her hand, his other arm clinging to Clara's neck, his body conforming to hers, his head warm against Clara's face.

Mine, she thought.

3. Spilt milk

*W*hen Clara got to Lorraine's room in the afternoon, after picking up a loaner car at the garage, Lorraine was too tired to talk. The tests had worn her out, or just the discovery of her illness. Clara put the flowers in a vase the freckly nurse found for her, and left a box of shortbread cookies from her neighbour Mrs. Zenko on the window ledge.

Clara didn't know whether to tell Lorraine that Clayton was gone. It would upset her, but it was hardly Clara's secret to keep, and she dreaded Lorraine finding out somehow and blaming her—or shrieking at her again. Lorraine's face screaming, her finger pointing, Pearce at her bare breast on the street: these images returned to Clara's mind too often already. She prickled with guilt for not telling her, but Lorraine didn't even ask about him. Perhaps he had told her he was going, had said he *wouldn't stay in that house,* some bluster like that. Clara sat in the straight blue chair, not the orange recliner, and talked about the children, how they were settling in. She asked if Lorraine was able to express (proud of herself for pulling that unfamiliar word from memory), and if she should bring Pearce in later.

"No, keep on with the formula. I can't nurse him now, all this stuff they're putting in me. It was about time to stop him anyways, he's nine

31

months old. He'll be a year, September 10th. But it was such a pleasure, why stop? Easier, too, when we were moving around all the time. Didn't have to clean bottles or buy those plastic baggies…"

Lorraine's voice threaded out, as if she'd gone to sleep on the thought of travelling, safe in their seashell car, her whole family close around her and her baby at her breast.

Clara watched her for a while, until she was sure she was either asleep or tired of company. She went home, stopping on the way to get fried chicken for supper, which was a great hit and made her believe she might almost be able to manage them.

On Tuesday morning Darlene waited until Clara had been gone ten minutes before she got up from the living room and went down the hall. Gran was watching TV, propped back on one elbow with her old potato feet on the table, in the little bedroom where their dad had slept that one night. Darlene could imagine him going around the house, the look on his face, walking past Clara out in the living room, finding the car keys in her handbag. She did not want to have to tell her mom about him being gone. In Gran's room Pearce lay sleeping in the basket, with a bottle drooling out of his mouth. Gran had dumped her stuff out onto the floor, as usual. It smelled like her in there: old teeth and hair.

Darlene had already gone through the desk in the living room: bills all tidy, and a cheque-book: $5,230 in the balance place, that was a *lot*. She had put it back carefully at the same angle.

No reason she shouldn't go in Clara's room. It was hers and Trevor's for now; maybe she felt like a nap. Their pyjamas were folded on the bed. The other furniture all matched, but it was all old. The chair by the window was covered with faded cloth. There were dents in the carpet where other chairs or dressers must have been before. Green walls, like her mother's sweater that Darwin gave her. Darlene loved the smell in there—like flowers, and maybe a long time ago someone had smoked a cigarette. It was lucky that she and Trevor got to sleep in here. For now. In the night-table drawers she found almost nothing: a nail-clipper and file and some flat blood-coloured cough drops. She tasted one, but it was disgusting. She spat it out, dried it off and put it back in the package. The dresser held a hundred sweaters, it looked like, smelling of clean wool and perfume. She was tempted to pull one out and rub her face in it, but she did not think she could fold it back properly, and then Clara would know.

Where was anything good? Darlene didn't even know what she was looking for. Not candy or money, they wouldn't be in here. The closet: she dragged the armchair over and pulled boxes off the top shelf. Old cream-coloured satin shoes, with a sway-backed heel and a button. They couldn't have ever fitted Clara, they were about her own size. She put them on, liking the ladylike arch in her foot, but didn't dare button the stiff strap, or take a step in them.

In a yellow box she found government stuff and old browned photo-copies, little pictures with wavy edges of guys in uniform. A bunch of letters tied up in string might be good, but Darlene was too chicken to open the string. If she couldn't get it tied right it would be like that time in Espanola.

In another yellow box, a marriage license for Clara Purdy and Dominic Raskin, 1982. Why wasn't she Clara Raskin, then? Some photos, a few letters, all jumbled together.

There was a noise in the front hall—Clara coming back?

Darlene had half-scrambled the yellow box back to the top shelf when she realized it was her grandmother banging the screen door, going out for a smoke. She could hear her yelling to Trevor, "You put the channel back when I get back!" and Trevor saying yes, yes.

She put the box on the shelf anyway. Another time, when she knew how long she'd have. She fluffed the clothes to make them look ordinary, fitted the chair back into its dents in the carpet by the window, and scuffed her sock feet over the drag-lines made by the chair. Trevor was shrieking in the living room. Gran yelled at him to shut up, and then Pearce was crying. She could do the bathroom any time—but there was still the kitchen.

The nurse must have just been in. Lorraine sat propped up, flipping channels, the sheets tucked tight around her. She looked sick, and Clara said so.

"It's the fever," Lorraine said. "They can't get it to stay down. Is Trevor okay?"

"He's happy outside. He likes the old birch tree that my father planted when I was born."

"A tree planted when you were born? How big is it?"

"It's not *that* big, I'm only forty-three."

"I didn't mean that," Lorraine said, coming close to a laugh. It seemed to hurt her chest. "How about Darlene?"

"She can tell me what they're used to, now—" Now that Clayton was gone. Clara steered away from that. "She's very good with Pearce, too. If he cries she can calm him better than any of us."

"He crying a lot?"

"Oh no, I didn't mean— Just when once in a while he makes a murmur."

"Because he's a good baby, he doesn't cry."

"He's a perfect baby. You must be missing him."

Lorraine began to sob. Clara sat watching, in an agony of guilt. After a moment, though, Lorraine stopped. As if crying took more energy than she was prepared to expend. "Spilt milk," she said. "They took that other lady out—the ovarian one. She went in for surgery, but when they opened her up they couldn't do anything. They sewed her back up and sent her home to Wilkie."

Difficult to respond to that.

"That's the bad part," Lorraine said. She patted the bed restlessly, and fumbled with the small flowered pillow that Clara had remembered to bring in for her.

"Can I fix it?" Clara slid her arm under Lorraine's neck, lifting her head gently. In one quick motion Clara slipped the flowered pillow out, shook it into softness again, and smoothed it into a double fold to fit nicely beneath Lorraine's ear.

"You're good at that."

"I had practice with pillows, looking after my mother for many years while she was ill."

They sat together in silence for a while but Lorraine was still restless. "We were on our way to Fort McMurray. Clayton's got a job lined up there. His cousin has an RV dealership, used, and now that so many people can't find any place to live up there, there's lots of people buying. Clayton was go-

34

ing to help Kenny fix up trailers, there was one on the lot that we could use while we figured out where to live. It would have been okay for a while, until we found something better."

"Lots of work up in Fort McMurray, they say."

"He can do a lot of things you wouldn't expect," Lorraine said. "He's a good cabinet-maker. He upholsters furniture, too, and that's hard work. That's what his cousin wanted him for, to reupholster the trailer fittings. He'd surprise you, how good he is."

Maybe he'd gone on without them, Clara thought.

Lorraine stopped talking, and twisted her head from side to side. "My neck hurts."

"Do you want me to see if they can give you something?"

"I don't want to take anything. I'm already taking stuff. I don't know."

Clara thought the fever was increasing.

"It's hard," Lorraine said.

"Yes," Clara said. Not knowing what else to say.

On the very top shelf of the last kitchen cupboard Darlene found a brown envelope taped down on a glass pedestal thing. Tons of money in it. It added up to seven hundred and something, counting pretty quick, one ear open for Clara coming back from the store. But it was no good to her, it was strange pink money from England. The car! She jumped down from the counter. Too far, so the balls of her feet hurt, but she didn't get caught.

Finding the house in surprising disarray, Clara tidied the living room and the TV room, and the hall, and the back steps—Trevor had made a fort there with blankets and pillows—before making lunch. Mrs. Pell went to her bedroom and shut the door, and they all left her alone. Clara gave Pearce a bottle. He stared into her eyes thoughtfully while he drank, his fingers splayed against her chest.

When he fell asleep she did three loads of laundry. She remembered to phone and extend the insurance on her mother's car, thinking she might be liable if Clayton got into another accident. She made cookies and started a list of necessities on the door of the fridge: formula, diapers, chicken soup from an envelope. They did not like canned. She wrote down everything the children asked for. It seemed like they were all in cotton wool, or that same smothering membrane which had been bothering Clara herself lately.

After supper Clara walked them to the park in the darkening evening. The children played on the flat merry-go-round, Trevor standing in the middle and Darlene running it around and around, faster and faster, until she could jump up too and they went spinning on and on through the indigo night air.

Clara stood a little distance away from their orbit, letting Pearce rest against her chest, feeling the weight and the balance of his body against hers. It wasn't so hard, being with children.

4. Counting money

At ten that night Clara went back through the hospital to Lorraine's silent room. The window was a dark rectangle in the white wall. She turned off the overhead fluorescent light, left on the small yellow bulb over the sink, and pulled the alcove curtain partway across so it wouldn't glare in Lorraine's eyes. Now they could see the lights of the city across the river, the pretty bridges, the night sky. Deep shadowy blue, not black, even so late.

"I'm worried about the kids," Lorraine said. Easier to talk in the darkness. "I'm worried about Clayton too, but not as much. He can take care of himself, more or less."

Now would be the time to mention Clayton's departure.

But Lorraine said, "I'm afraid."

All Clara could think of was, "Don't be." An unforgivable, asinine thing to say. She did not want to remember her father dying, or the horrors her mother went through. "I'm sorry. Of course you are afraid. I guess I mean, don't let superstition trap you into pretending to be positive all the time. There is no jinxing, and being blindly optimistic doesn't help."

"What does help then?"

"I pray, but it does not always—" She could think of no word but *suffice,* which would sound pompous. "It's hard to know what to pray for."

Lorraine snorted, and flapped her hands onto the sheet. "I know what to pray for! That my, this, *thing* will go away. That I will have my kids back with me. That everything will go on the way it was the day before we came to Saskatoon, when I was worrying about how to find work and a place to live, not how to *live.*"

It was not a tirade, but a considered statement.

"I had enough worry before. I'm not going to worry now. I'm not going to pray either. I'm going to be patient and wait for this to happen." She corrected herself. "Wait for this to go away."

There were blue marks under her eyes, and her skin was puffy. The steroids, affecting her already. If her fever could be brought down they were assessing her for chemo in the morning, Clara knew, and then would come a bad time. For a moment she was glad she had been with her mother during that long struggle, so she knew a little about it, to be able to help Lorraine.

"Is there anything you like to read? Magazines? *People?* Or something more serious while you've got some quiet time?"

"Some of each," Lorraine said. Her pointy smile was very tired.

One more thing, though. "I don't know what to do about Darlene. She wants to see you, of course. Should I put her off, or bring her in?"

"Don't bring Trevor, not right now. But you could bring Darlene. I need her to get some stuff from the car, now that I think of it. Good thing you said."

Clara had forgotten their car, in the impound lot. "They gave us the knapsacks, that first day… I've got the children's things."

"Yeah, but I got some stuff hidden in there, in the Dart. We were living in there for the last couple weeks. You know how it is. You have to keep your stuff somewhere."

From her tone Clara supposed it was money, or even drugs. But she would not be a good judge. Maybe papers, that kind of treasure. "I'll bring Darlene tomorrow. I meant to ask if there is anyone that I should call for you. I'm not sure if Clayton has had a chance to do that."

"Nice way of putting it," Lorraine said. "No, there's no one. No one that I know where they are, anyways."

This time Clara stopped herself from saying she was sorry. She decided again not to get into Clayton's absence. "You look like you could sleep," she said. "I'll bring books tomorrow."

"Yeah," Lorraine said. "I'll catch up on that summer reading I've been meaning to get to. Don't bring Pearce. That would be hard on him."

"All right," Clara said. "I'll keep him at home. He's good, he's doing well."

"Thank you." Lorraine closed her eyes and turned her head away from Clara before she opened them again. The window looked out on all the lights across the river, a million glinting sparks.

Walking down the hall, thinking ahead to breakfast for the children, Clara did not see Paul Tippett until he took her arm, right beside her. She jumped, and he apologized, both of them speaking in whispers because it seemed so late. The hospital was closing down around them, patients being put into storage for the night.

"How is your family?" he asked.

"The mother, Lorraine, is not doing very well," Clara said. It felt disloyal, to say it out loud. Superstition. She was as bad as anyone.

Paul Tippett looked sad, the clear lines of his face blurred. She was sorry, because she liked him, as far as she knew him. He seemed crippled by diffidence, but always kind.

"Will you do something for me?" she asked. "Will you visit her?" She could see him pull away involuntarily, like she had pulled away from Darlene's snatching hand. "Tomorrow, I mean, or—not as a parishioner, to comfort her—but I've got her children, and her husband's gone—oh, but don't tell her that. Just to ease her mind, that I'm not a monster, because she has no choice, she has to put them somewhere, and I'm the only—" Clara stopped. She was making a fool of herself.

He stared at her, in the lowered light of the night hall. "The husband has gone?"

"Yes," she said, not mentioning the car, or the teapot, or his weak threat. "But he might come back."

Paul thought Clara Purdy had experienced a radical change since he'd

39

last seen her. She seemed charged with energy. *The force that through the green fuse drives the flower.* It was involvement that put you into time, perhaps. He shook his head, astonished at the brightness of her face, then saw that she thought he was refusing her request.

"No, no—I will," he said quickly. "I will visit her. Sorry, I was thinking of something else. I'll tell her how fortunate her family is, to be with you."

He couldn't remember her house. A bungalow. "You have enough room for all of them, do you? What's her last name?"

"Gage. Lorraine Gage—in this ward."

He wrote it in his little calendar book and gave her a quick apologetic smile, for his reluctance. She could not help smiling back. She did like him. Too bad about Mrs. Tippett, that cold fish.

Lorraine lay in bed counting money. Seventy-seven dollars in the glove compartment. Lucky sevens. Three twenties, a ten, a five, the $2 bill saved for years. Whore's money, Clayton would call that. Not loose, for anyone to find (meaning Clayton, of course), but stuck between the back two pages of the map book. They were not going to get to Newfoundland or Labrador. $189 left in the bank, but she thought Clayton probably had her bank card, and he knew her PIN. A hundred dollars—one $100 bill—hidden, taped inside a box of tampons in the cardboard box in the trunk. He would not have found that, but the worry was that someone might throw out the box.

She could hardly stand to think about money. What would Clayton do? He had $300 and some left on the Husky Gas card before it maxed out. But no car, so gas wasn't going to do him much good. They could eat, though, at Husky station restaurants. If he decided to take the kids on to Fort McMurray, which she wondered if he was planning on doing, since he was obviously not at Clara's any more.

$189, $300, how long would that last?

At a certain point every time in all this figuring, Lorraine would feel her neck stiffen and swell from tension, and she'd fling the whole thing out of her mind.

She lay still, mostly. Moving made her feel weird, and whatever drugs she was pumped full of seemed to make it easier to be still. If things were ordinary, she'd be in the car, Pearce nestled in her elbow, worrying about money and thinking ahead to what work she could get in Fort McMurray. Worrying about who would look after the kids while she waitressed or cleaned houses again; about gas and how much a bunch of bananas and some fig newtons had taken out of the purse. She moved her feet under the pale green sheet and stared with torn-open eyes around the room. Here she was.

The moon made bars of yellow light that gradually drifted across the room. She could tell she must have slept when she saw the moonlight farther advanced on her sheets, on the end of the bed, on the wall. The moon rose in the east and set in the west, just like the sun. Sometimes with the sun. She'd sat nursing Pearce in the car while the others ate outside in the sun at a Taco Bell, last week. His mouth pulling, pulling, his eyes staring at her in a trance of happiness, and the white moon visible in the blue day sky.

She could not die on them. $77, $189, $100. It took her a few minutes to work it out in her foggy head. $366. Well, that was a lucky number. She liked threes and sixes. Clayton couldn't feed them all on that for long. He'd have to go to the food bank. Mom Pell had money somewhere, but she wouldn't give it up for food, at least not for the kids. Lorraine let herself hate Mom Pell for the cherries she'd insisted on buying, that huge six-dollar bag of BC cherries that had probably caused the whole thing, anyways. Making Clayton drive too fast to make up for stopping. Bits of red pulp clinging to everything after the crash, like your own body and brains turned inside out, like one of the children had been badly hurt. Lorraine's chest ached, the breasts and the inside too, wanting to have Pearce and the others there with her. She was filled with panicky rage just thinking about Clay and Mom Pell, but the children were so sweet. Except there was no money.

$77, $189, $100. How long did it take for welfare to kick in last time? But they weren't residents of Saskatchewan, they'd get sent back to Winnipeg on the bus. They couldn't leave her, though, and she was entitled to health care anywhere in Canada, they were always saying.

They needed $1200. Six for an apartment, another six for the damage deposit. First and last months' rent. Who knew how long it would take for Clayton to get paid, no matter how fast he found a job. There was no way. They'd be in housing, if there was room. Or a shelter. Clayton would not be good at looking after the kids on his own in a shelter, and Mom Pell was worse than useless. She would have to talk to the kids. They'd need some kind of—the thought of a weapon for them: a nail file, a pin—

Lorraine sat up and vomited neatly into a green plastic kidney basin. She lay back down. It might all be a dream. The moon had floated off, leaving the room dark and deserted. In a while, she slept.

5. The Dart

*I*t was impossible, being with these children. After four days of it Clara was exhausted by their clatter and the grime that attended them, and their easy assumption that she would do everything for them. The cooking alone never seemed to end. The perpetual low-grade noise started at dawn with Pearce waking up, and might have been the worst thing—but Clara wasn't sleeping anyway, too conscious of everyone else, of the new disturbing mass of people surrounding her. There was far too much to do in the house, keeping any kind of order, but they had to deal with the car, too, and she'd promised.

Darlene was eager to press the elevator buttons and fly up to her mother's room. But as they came closer she seemed to be repelled, as if the poles had suddenly reversed on her interior magnet. She took Clara's hand, three or four doors away, and whispered, "Wait."

Clara stopped. Darlene didn't look at her. She stared at the wooden rail that ran along the wall.

"I guess this is for people who are walking but might fall down?"

"I think so." Clara was frightened by how dire everything seemed, when she thought of things from Darlene's perspective. Or Lorraine's. "It'll be all right," she said, inanely.

Darlene let go of Clara's hand, and walked past the last few doors to Lorraine's room.

Lorraine was sitting up in bed when they went in. "Hey, sugar plum," she said. Her eyes were over-bright, her skin palely glowing.

"Mama," Darlene said. She was across the room instantly, leaning up on the bed, close to Lorraine's face. Their two faces pressed together, cheeks and noses, their whole faces, not just kisses. Lorraine's arms met around Darlene's back, and she lifted her up onto the high bed with her as if she didn't weigh anything.

"Oh, I'm so glad to see you!" she said, as well as Clara could make out, the words muffled in Darlene's hair.

Darlene did not speak, she only lay curled against her mother on the green sheets, her arm over her mother's waist.

"You look good," Clara told Lorraine, when she looked up and noticed her.

"I better look good, I'm on twenty different pills." Lorraine waved at the rolling table, where three or four paper cups held an assortment of coloured pills. "Six, seventeen, everything I need right here."

She bent again, curling lightly over Darlene's tense back. "Mmm, you smell good. Clean laundry, I love that smell."

Watching the hard work Lorraine was having to do, to be as healthy as possible for Darlene, Clara felt a painful tension herself. And Darlene was so quick to pick up on things.

"Hey, Clara brought me this nice nightie, gives me a little colour, don't you think?"

Darlene looked up at her mother's face, still not speaking. No colour in Lorraine's face, only the brilliant darkness of her eyes. She hugged Darlene close, rocking in a narrow range, back, forth, back, forth.

Clara went outside and stood to the right of the door where they could not see her. She studied the wooden handrail, remembering her own mother—for some reason remembering her as a young woman in a grey dress with

44

a white collar. Standing at the foot of the front porch steps, waiting for Clara's father to come down and take them to church. A hat on her head, one of those little bands you had to pin on, grey velvet. Her dimpling cheek, smiling at Clara's father, her wide, childish, heartbreaking mouth. She missed her mother so badly. Impossible as she was.

When Clara went back into the room they both looked at her sideways. They'd been talking in low voices, and for the first time she saw a resemblance between Darlene and her mother. The broad planes of their cheeks, and their eyes, with well-defined corners and dark line of brows. Their bodies, too, their strong open shoulders and the same narrowness across the back.

"I'll go down and get some juice," she offered, but Lorraine said not to leave.

"I'm just telling her where things are—it's no big secret any more, we got to get the stuff out before they crush it or whatever."

"Oh, I'm sure they won't do that until…" Until the insurance investigators were through with it, she meant, but Lorraine ran over her words.

"I want Darlene to get the stuff, it'll ease my mind." Her voice was flat, almost rude—fever burning civility away.

Clara took a notebook from her purse and wrote down: *pillow.*

Lorraine talked directly to Darlene, giving her the job. "In the glove compartment, I want the map book. The registration and insurance. My box from the trunk. The kitchen box and the duffle bags—you can take those to Clara's place, if she's got a garage or somewhere to stash them?" Clara nodded. Lorraine turned her gaze back to Darlene. "Okay, for a while, until we figure out where you guys are going next, while we're working on first and last month's rent."

Darlene looked at Clara. Clara did not know exactly how to interpret the look. Was she asking Clara not to tell about Clayton being gone? Or considering whether, or when, Clara planned to throw them out of the house?

Lorraine nodded, and Darlene slid down off the bed, obedient to some understood command. She went into the bathroom and shut the door.

"I wanted to ask you about that," Lorraine said, making an effort to sit up straighter. The debt racking up was too much to bear, she wanted to scream and throw Clara out of the room. "About the next few days…"

She couldn't get it out properly, and it seemed like time was speeding, contracting.

"I know we've got to get the kids out of your hair."

"I'm happy to keep the children," Clara said. "The family. As long as they need a place to stay."

"I don't have enough money to pay you," Lorraine said as baldly as she could, to cut through all those words of Clara's.

"No, no! Don't—" Clara said.

"We're lucky to have the chance, lucky you're being so kind." Lorraine said. She could not bring herself to mention the shelter, the nail file, the need to train Darlene to fend people off of both her and Trevor—she pressed her fingers into her eye sockets, under the brow bone, to get rid of those thoughts.

"It's not *kind*," Clara was saying. Lorraine could hear her getting all chokey.

"You might be doing it from guilt or something, but it's kind, you're good," Lorraine said, dismissing all that bullshit. "Darlene, you finished in there?"

The door popped open, and Darlene came in her quick, sidling way back to the bed. She didn't meet Clara's eyes.

Clara felt weighed down by the burden of obligation that all this was putting on everyone. If she was a better person she would be able to lift all that, say how happy she was to have company in the house, to have them. Her mother could have done it. All she could do was stop herself from false joviality. She closed her notebook and picked up her purse.

"We'd better get going, then."

"Good," Lorraine said. She closed her eyes. Not interested, for the moment, in obligation or gratitude or convention.

Darlene put her cold fingers on her mother's eyelids, and went with Clara to the hall.

Before heading for the impound lot Clara stopped for lunch at a little run-down café, because Darlene said "How about there?" Darlene had chicken soup and Clara sat watching, unable to eat for the great lump that pity had jammed into her throat. Darlene's arms were trembling by the time the soup came, her hand shaking her spoon. It looked like good soup, at least. Darlene's arms were too thin. That tank top was not fit to wear. She needed sleeves to stay warm, even in July. The sharp bones were almost visible under her skin, making her seem insubstantial, but also strong. Clara hoped that was how children looked who were naturally thin. Lorraine was thin, but was that natural, or because of her illness? Mrs. Pell was built like a propane tank, a little head and a big squat body. Darlene did not look like she could ever become that. She'll have to be strong, Clara thought. She asked, "Is the soup good?"

Darlene nodded. She said, as if further to the soup, "There's a girl in Trimalo, where we lived, whose mother died. She was run over by a car, so it wasn't the same."

"Oh, no—I'm sorry for the girl, it must have been hard to lose her mother so suddenly." Why say such stupid things? No easier to lose her slowly.

"She had to do all the work when they moved. Her father couldn't do anything, like get the phone hooked up or anything, he was too sad." Darlene's voice was flat and quick, almost mocking, as if she thought she'd sound older that way.

"How old was the girl?"

"Twelve. She babysat us when my mom worked. She had to go down to see her mother at the place. The police place. She felt her mom's face. It was all cold."

Still the quick words without proper feeling attached. Too risky to let deep feeling loose, maybe especially in childhood. "Darlene, do you want to talk about something a little less sad?"

"Everything is sad."

"Yes, you feel that, don't you?" Clara could remember that so clearly, how there was nothing in the world that was not sad. "What a heavy feeling. Do you need some dessert to lighten you up? Ice cream?"

Distracting a child with food—a recipe for obesity, Clara thought. But ice cream appeared to be just the ticket. Darlene's sundae came in a tulip glass, with whipped cream and a cherry. It made them both happy, briefly, and when they went back to the car the sun seemed to have come out, or a breeze had picked up. The air was clearer.

The impound lot was at the end of a paved road with so much dust and dirt packed over it that it looked like gravel. Driving along with the windows up, Clara tried not to think about the end of this malevolent cancer, of all these people who would be so sad. But she couldn't pretend to herself that she expected Lorraine to recover, because it was clear to her that Lorraine would not. Although she hoped that she was mistaken.

The high fence had outward-jutting barbed wire at the top. Clara felt she should have come alone to this depressing junkyard. But Darlene yelled, "There it is! There's the Dart!" Threading her narrow hand through the fence, straining her finger to make Clara see.

The attendant let them in, and gave Clara an envelope and a clipboard with a form on it to sign. He didn't offer to come back to the car with them. He was what her mother would have called "rough"—grizzle-haired with strong-smelling clothes. She smiled at the man to make up for her mother's opinion, as she had so often done in her company.

Darlene dashed ahead through the warren of paths, around the corpses and ghosts of cars. How much life we pack into our cars, Clara thought, missing her own. And missing her mother's car, that Clayton had now. Who knows in what town he's selling it, she thought. Good riddance. Time to get rid of some of her mother's baggage.

The Dart had keeled over to the left, both wheels gone on the crumpled driver's side. Darlene was already around on the passenger side, yanking on the front door.

"Wait!" Clara said. "I've got the key here, I think..." Yes, in the envelope. On a Playboy Bunny keychain. How could any man?

Darlene slipped it from her hand and into the lock, jiggled it as if she knew the secret, and it opened for her. It was a heavy door. The car smelled stale, smoky, of rubber and burning. Darlene leaned forward and up onto the seat, to flip open the glove compartment. But it stayed shut.

"It won't—it won't *open*!" she said, too loudly, pulling harder to show Clara. Her sharp young voice sliced through the still air.

The man at the gate called something, and Clara turned, letting the door slip out of her hand. Just in time she turned back and caught it, before it slammed shut.

48

"Oh!" Clara pushed the door wide open again and leaned on it, her stomach leaping. She could have broken Darlene's hand.

"Yikes," Darlene said, not particularly worried. "The thing's broken, the thing that makes the door stay open."

The gate man, beside Clara, had brought a short crowbar and a rubber mallet.

"Times things're stuck," he said. "Might need these."

"Thanks," Darlene said.

She took the crowbar and pried the sharp end in at one edge of the glove compartment.

"Should you?" Clara was saying, when the little door popped open.

"Okay," Darlene said, giving the gate man as big a smile as her mouth would make. "Go now."

He grinned back at her, ignoring Clara's hand-flap of apology. Off he went.

"You can't be so—" Clara hesitated to say rude. "He might have been insulted."

"Why?"

Clara decided it would be stupid to try to explain. Darlene had pulled out the maps, four or five separate provinces and the one larger book of all Canada. She flipped through it, but quickly, as if she didn't want Clara to see. Clara made a business of looking for her notebook in her purse, to find the list. "Map book, yes, registration folder."

The interior of the car was a mess, but no worse than any vacation trip. A garbage bag must have gone flying in the crash, full of wrappers and orange peels. Clara was shocked to see a burned patch on the back seat, blurred by cherry juice.

Darlene looked past her. "That's not from the accident, that's from the laundromat. We were doing the laundry in Yorkton, and Gran was smoking in the car."

"She burned the car?"

"She fell asleep. No more smoking in the car *ever*, my mom said. Pearce was in the front seat sleeping, and my mom freaked when she saw smoke coming out of the window. And you should of seen Gran jumping around in the parking lot, putting out her skirt!" Darlene laughed out loud, with a mean gleam in her eye.

Clara was suddenly worn out with all this eventful life.

After laughing Darlene was quiet, her hand on the warm gold vinyl of the front door. Then she slid into the front seat and pried out a small orange corduroy log, the size of a doll bed pillow.

"My mom likes this little one under her neck," she said, stroking the corduroy with the welt, the velvety way, and then back, her fingernails dragging the pile up. "It's not dirty, look." She scrubbed her cheek against it, then climbed out and handed it to Clara, who tucked it in her bag and carefully crossed out *Pillow* on her list. Darlene slammed the car door as hard as she could. A huge sound in the silent impound lot.

The trunk was packed like a jigsaw puzzle, boxes of every shape. The kitchen box was crammed with pots and an old plastic jug filled with cutlery. Other boxes, shoes and boots were stuck here and there: the whole thing given a hard shake by the accident and the tow. When they'd pulled out the duffle bags, and her mother's little box, Darlene balanced the kitchen box on them.

"You don't have to open these," she said. "You have enough stuff."

"Of course," Clara said, unmiffed. She put the Playboy Bunny key back in its envelope.

Darlene stared out the back window even after she could not see the Dart any more. It had not been bad, being in the car, even though Gran complained. Better than some of the places they'd lived—better than Espanola, last winter. She didn't have to come, anyway, Darlene thought. She could have stayed in Winnipeg, if she hadn't fought with Mrs. Lyne. Who wouldn't fight with Mrs. Lyne, though, and who could stand her stinky trailer?

She did not want to think about where her dad might be. Instead, she thought about going to sleep in the back of the Dart while they drove through the darkness, Trevor and her lying on each other's laps, twisting around to get more comfortable. Her dad whistling for a while in the mornings, or his face pressed against the window pretending to scare them when he came back with doughnuts—but she wasn't thinking about him. She loved sitting on the floor of the back seat, with the vibrations humming in her bones, and the ticking the motor made when they'd finally stopped late at night, the heavy feeling of stillness after moving for so long. Like the night in the parking lot, with the big moon, when they all lay out on the hood of the car, staring up at the sky, looking for satellites and shooting stars. Except that was the night that her dad was gone for a long time, and they woke up in the middle of the night when those scary guys rocked the car, looking for him. Her mom locked all the doors and whispered to stay still, not talk, not breathe, until they went away.

That was a long trip, to Saskatoon. They had stopped ten miles outside town so her mom could try to tidy everybody up, and then Pearce spat up on her last clean top, so they went to the Saan store to buy a new top so they could go see Darwin at her mom's cousin Rose's house. But Darwin was not at the house any more. The people who lived there now had never heard of her, or Darwin, so they'd lost him. Her mother had cried when they came out of the house, because she missed him. And then was the crash, and now here they were, parked at the hospital again, the parking lot that Darlene was getting to know very, very well. She tried to focus her eyes on Clara but it was too hard. She walked beside her, not even trying any more, carrying her mother's box and the orange pillow.

Lorraine was asleep. Darlene slid the box into the bedside table cupboard carefully, not making any noise. She put the orange corduroy pillow on the bed beside her mother's arm and looked at Clara—what should they do?

Clara had managed office staff for twenty years, but she found it strange to be the authority for a child. She tore a page from her notebook. "We'll write her a note," she said.

Dear Lorraine, she wrote. *We've left what you asked for in your bedside cupboard, and the nurse will have the key. Please don't worry about the things in the car, they'll be keeping the car in the lot for a few months. I've asked my parish priest to come by when he's in for his visits, and he can tell you that I'm a good citizen. I've got a couple of weeks off work, anyway, and I promise I'll look after the children. So you don't have to worry*

What a stupid thing to say. She added, *about them.* Leaving Lorraine free to worry about herself as much as she might like. Clara usually had nice clear handwriting, but for some reason the pen was not co-operating, and the letter looked scrawly and irresponsible.

I'll be back to see you later, she put. *Clara Purdy.*

When they got home, they found the baby trapped in a cage made of dining room chairs. Trevor was trying to keep Pearce happy by feeding him crusts of bread between the bars. A soap opera blared through the house from where Mrs. Pell snored on the couch in the TV room. The boys had been crying, but they'd worn out their tears. Pearce had smears of gummy bread crusted on his cheeks. Clara caught him up and soothed him, his arm gripping fiercely around her neck in his relief.

She washed everyone's face, gave Pearce a bottle to calm him down, and made grilled cheese sandwiches. Mrs. Pell managed to stay sleeping even when Clara snapped off the television, and didn't wake, or allow herself to be seen to be awake, till Clara brought her a sandwich and a cup of coffee. She took them with an ill grace and shut her door tight.

Clara took the children out to the back garden in the bright summer evening, asked Mrs. Zenko next door to watch them for half an hour, and raced over to the mall. She bought new shorts and running shoes for Trevor and Darlene, in a frenzy of efficiency, and a folding playpen for Pearce. The diapers would last a few more days. The groceries would hold till tomorrow. She found a case of formula on the way to the checkout, and was back within forty minutes. Mrs. Zenko and Trevor were watering the flowerbeds while Darlene lay on the grass with Pearce, tickling his knees with a long thread of grass. He was kicking, exercising, not laughing but calmly pleased to be fussed over. He reached his arms out for Clara, his huge face smiling, glowing in the lowering light. What a beauty he was.

Mrs. Zenko had brought over a large plastic container of the plain cookies she called angel cookies and a pretty wooden high chair, in perfect condition. "None of my children want this old thing," she said, as if she was embarrassed to offer something so slight.

Clara thanked her gratefully.

"Not the easiest thing to do," Mrs. Zenko said. "Taking on a family like this. I heard them yesterday, and this afternoon—I nearly came over to help, but I thought she wouldn't take it too kindly, so I just listened."

The noise must have been very bad, Clara thought. She and Mrs. Zenko knew each other well enough. "I'm not going to be able to leave the children with her," she said quietly. "Not for any length of time."

"No."

"I like their mother, Lorraine," Clara said. "He's deserted her." She leaned her cheek against the bird-feeder pipe her father had put up. It needed seed. Tomorrow she'd let Trevor climb the stepladder and fill it. "I'm going to need a book on looking after babies."

"You can read up, but most of it's just good sense. It's only ordinary to be with babies, after all. I've got a jar of chicken soup for you to take her tomorrow," Mrs. Zenko said. She coiled the hose neatly and went back to her own garden.

6. *Opposite action*

*P*aul Tippett hated hospital visiting. Clara Purdy, talking quickly to persuade him because she saw that it was against his will, had seen that—he must hide his will better. The corridors had been quiet around them in the relief of the evening. The blanket of the dark, or at least the dimmed fluorescent lights.

He pulled a notepad from the paper towers on his desk. Lorraine Gage. Well. Three children, according to Clara. Nothing he'd said had spurred her to the generous action she had taken. Except by opposite action, an effect he believed he often had on people. Not a flattering thought, but worth examining, while not examining Lorraine Gage. If he had said to Clara, "Open your house to these people, you must take Christian action in the world!"—what would she have done? Found a hundred reasons not to. But he had tried to comfort her, to say she was already doing enough… It was not enough. As a running continuo underneath conversation, louder when he was alone, Paul heard his wife's voice saying things to him, short sentences which were hard to bear. *Not enough. Not good enough. Hopeless.*

He was having a bad few days, that was all. Poetry could sometimes keep it at bay.

Foolish and ineffectual. Hypocrite. Priest. An example of similar action, he thought. Lisanne told him he was foolish, and he told himself the same. He was, after all, professionally opposed to opposition. He moved the papers cluttering his desk to one side. It was simpler than that, of course. Not opposite, or similar—it was the truth. Clara was right: visiting the hospital sympathetically was not enough. Lisanne was right: he was a fool. *Divine Spinoza, forgive me, I have become a fool...* Divine Lisanne, forgive me.

He had a sudden flashing memory of their third anniversary party: his sister Binnie, twelve years old, with tears in her eyes, listening as Lisanne mocked him for some failure. "He's not *stupid,* you know," Binnie had called, too loud, from her chair far down the table. Daring to enter the lists for him.

The children, that's where he'd come un-railed. He made a note at the top of the yellow pad. *Three children.* The proximity of death makes us remember our own insignificance, that no one will remember us, that we are animate atoms, at most; our lives don't matter. But the children do. If there are any children. A chicken: an egg's way of making more eggs.

He was tired, and confused. A woman lives, and then she no longer lives. Easy enough. The part before "and then" is the difficulty, those long days and nights where people stagger in twilight, dying at different lengths, hard or easy. It would not be easy in this case, as he understood from Clara and from his own knowledge. Dear Binnie. If only it was diabetes, or lupus, or something else. *She lost the fight. Cancer not being a gentle decline, but a ravaging, an invasion.* Phrases from the homily he had given at Binnie's funeral, because his mother had asked him to, and it was his profession. He did not want to do another funeral homily as long as he lived, and he wanted none at his own funeral. No tea, no baked meats, either. Let them find their own supper, all people who on earth do eat.

He did not want to come to this poor woman carrying the baggage of death. *We are not worthy to come to this Thy table, but Thou art the same Lord, whose property is always to have mercy.* When Binnie shifted, uneasy beneath the sheet, he had seen her naked to the waist, had been unable not to see her. Pearly skin. Not disturbing, it was only death. ("There is no God, no God," she raged.) Turn it aside. *Hopeless.* (And in her next breath, "Jesus, Mary, Joseph.")

He would have to telephone Clara and find out what she knew, at least. Not to put it off any longer, Paul pulled the phone from under a stack of bulletins and found Clara's number on the parish sheet pinned to the wall. Patchett, Prentice, Purdy.

He dialed and waited, unable to keep himself from hoping that she was not in.

"Hello?" It was a child.

"May I please speak to your—" He paused, at a loss.

"Gran?" A helpful guess from the high voice.

"No, no, I'm sorry. I'd like to speak to Clara Purdy, please."

"Clary!" The phone clattered down. He could hear the boy bellowing off into the distance. "Clary! There's a phone for you!"

A moment passed, and Paul heard footsteps towards the phone.

"Hello?"

"This is Paul Tippett. About the woman you asked me to visit?"

"Of course, Paul." She was distracted, having left Pearce standing in the newly assembled playpen. Paul was silent so long that she wondered if she'd said the wrong thing, if with his over-sensitivity he'd heard her impatience.

"I'm sorry," he said. "I was organizing what passes for my thoughts." He meant her to laugh, so she obliged. "I thought I should get some information from you before I go up to the hospital. The chaplain is away, and I won't have the usual form. But I thought I should have the children's names. And any details of her ordinary life would help. Could her mother—?"

"Mrs. Pell is not—" Oh, too much to explain. "She's not communicative," Clara said.

"No, I understand, certainly."

Did he? Clara was tired of talking. She wanted to lie down. She should never have taken this on, it was ridiculous. She had to find some way to get out of it. But that would mean finding Clayton, and that would probably mean charging him with car theft, and then he'd be in jail and the children would have nowhere to go. She was stuck. The clock clicked over to 5:00, bedtime was hours away.

"Will you be in your office for a little while?"

"I'll be here," he agreed. No urgency toward his home that she could hear. But maybe that was just professional patience.

56

Clara found Darlene washing her face in the bathroom, which she seemed to be doing too often. Perhaps it was a phobia, or some kind of obsessive-compulsive—Clara knew nothing. She must read up. In the mirror Darlene's narrow face looked like a flower, emerging from the green towel, one of the Flower Fairies from childhood books. She must be too old for those.

"Come into my—your bedroom for a moment," Clara said. But Trevor was lying on the bed on his stomach, colouring with washable markers. How washable were they, exactly?

Darlene led Clara instead to Clayton's room, where Mrs. Pell glowered in the recliner, watching a soap opera with the earphones plugged in. They sat on the sofa, Darlene taking charge and patting for Clara to sit beside her.

"The priest needs to know a few things about your mother," Clara said. "So he can talk to her in the hospital. Anything you can think of, really."

"Okay," Darlene said.

She seemed older this afternoon than this morning. Clara's hand went out to smooth back her hair, but she stopped herself, and waited.

"She's a good skater. She used to clean houses for people when we lived in Trimalo, when my dad was in the mine. It was, like, her own business."

"That's hard work," Clara said.

"She used to take me and Trevor with her when we were babies, she'd take the playpen and sit us in there while she worked. And she would give us a glass of juice from their fridges."

Clara remembered her own mother taking her along on a visit. She remembered sitting on polished wood in some strange English house, playing with broken toys. A tall girl taking a bite out of an orange, right through the bitter skin—the spray of orange oil misting up as her teeth bit down, and the bright smell breaking into the air. Ages ago.

"What does your mother like, that would make her feel happier?"

"She likes to draw. When we're driving along she draws pictures of us, or of things we see. She draws us a story."

"Do you have any of her drawings? Maybe in the things from the car?"

"I don't have anything that's hers." Darlene began to cry, as easily as she might have laughed in another situation. Tears spouted from her eyes and ran down her face, and instead of wiping them she let them fall.

"I know," Clara said, terribly sorry for her, not knowing what to say or do. "But you have Trevor, and Pearce, and your granny, and..." She could hardly say Clayton. And she could not bring herself to say that Lorraine would be home soon, or be better soon.

Darlene nodded. No Kleenex nearby—Clara wiped the tears away with her bare fingers.

Mrs. Pell looked up and saw Darlene crying, and made as if to take out her earphones. But the program changed, the ad she liked came on. That cat. She pushed the clicker at it for more volume... more.

Unlike the other mountains around him, Paul's reluctance toward the hospital seemed possible to conquer. He left the church, grimly glad to have somewhere to go other than home. There was a parking spot by the entrance generous enough for his old Pontiac. It was a sign, he told himself. He shook reluctance off as he got out of the car, literally shaking his shoulders in his concentration. He had to watch that. Lisanne was good for him, she caught him when the tip of his tongue was sticking out, or as he was about to walk into a parking meter, or when his physical actions betrayed his internal struggles. He was lucky to have an objective eye to catch his idiosyncrasies before he made a complete fool of himself.

He could hear the doggish submission in his thoughts, so he shook that off, too. He decided to go without Lisanne today, just for a holiday. The elevator came smartly to his touch, and soared up without stopping. God, he thought. Or bounden duty.

In the afternoon room the woman in the bed looked far away, like a boat drifted off its moorings.

"You're the priest," she said. "I thought only Catholics had priests."

"In the Anglican tradition we are called priests too—we don't depart as far from the Roman Catholics as some other denominations, although we do not require clergy to be celibate, and there are doctrinal..." *Quiet.* He needed a quick answer for that question, one that would serve over and over, but he never could think of one.

"Are you a Catholic?" he asked.

"Not me," she said. "I'm nothing."

She had a sharpness behind her staring eyes. An ironic understanding of her position, he thought.

"*Are you—Nobody—too?*"

"That's in a poem." Her pointed teeth slid over her bottom lip as her mouth dragged into something approaching a smile.

"Good ear. I'm sorry. I have a bad habit," he said, bobbing his head like a turtle—he could feel himself doing it. He stopped, and rubbed his ear. "Verse. Too good a memory of that one kind. Not good enough of every other kind."

"It's the frog one. We had it in school."

"Right, the admiring bog." He advanced into the room. "I'm Paul Tippett, Mrs. Gage," he said.

"Lorraine," she said.

He sat in the blue chair at her bedside. "Clara Purdy wanted me to reassure you that your children will be safe with her."

"And will they be?"

"Yes."

"Okay then."

They sat in silence for a minute.

Lorraine said, "Not that I have any choice, anyway."

He did not think she was self-pitying. That was one of the consolations of hospital visits, the good behaviour of the sick. *Weak,* to need consoling. It's proximity, proxy death that appalls. His sister's face came into his mind so vividly that tears sprang up to the gate of his eyes. Two years after her death, now, he was able to hold them back.

"I don't know her well," Paul said, taking himself back to duty. "She is shy, I think. But I know her reputation in the community, and her family is respected."

"She's kind of frozen up," Lorraine said, nodding. "It's a big deal, her taking them, though. I'd be hooped without her."

"Well, people seem to like her very much. She's younger than the way she lives, 'one foot in her mother's grave,' as my warden says. She's kind, she has energy and intelligence."

Lorraine lay still.

"Maybe you'll help her," Paul said, and felt Lorraine's withdrawal from the conversation. To suggest her cancer had a mawkish, mysterious-purposes side to it—yammering fool. *Priest*: the most contemptuous thing his wife could say.

He was silent.

From side to side on the bed, Lorraine turned her head. Looking past the walls to find some answer. Like her head was all she could move.

"May I pray with you?" he asked.

Her eyes fixed on him, her head stalled towards him. "No."

He waited.

"Yes," she said. "Pray for my kids."

He crossed himself. "Father, I commend your daughter Lorraine and her children to your care. Be with her. Give her courage and stamina and have her children in mind always, as she does. Keep them safe and well in the house of your servant Clara Purdy."

Lorraine was unable to recognize this dream her life had become. She thought, if I am God's daughter, are my kids God's grandchildren? She could not stop thinking those words, stupid as they were.

"We ask it in Jesus's name," Paul said. "Amen."

Lorraine's breath was coming higher in her chest, right under her collarbone, and her whole body felt flooded with heat. Racing, desperate blood, or fury, or some effect of the drugs: she couldn't tell.

"Thanks," she said. "I'll go to sleep, now." Lying.

Paul touched her arm before he left. His hand was warm as toast.

7. Dolly

Grace and Moreland came in from Davina to inspect the children. Clara's older cousin, her father's sister's daughter, Grace looked in on her from time to time, checking up on her. Davina was only an hour's drive, close enough to come for errands, if they felt like it. They arrived first thing in the morning, while Clara was clearing up breakfast.

"What are you going to do with *three* of them?" Grace asked Clara. Unfriendly to this new wrinkle.

"I don't know! The best I can, I guess. It's only for—a while."

"It's not like volunteering for the Humane Society, taking in a few pups over the Christmas vacation," Grace said. Moreland was dandling Pearce on his knee as if he had nothing else in the world to do. Which he hadn't, truth be known, beyond a quick trip to Early's for a bag of the larger dog chews.

"You must have lost your mind, if you don't mind me saying so. Beyond the fact that you've never had anything to do with kids, you have no idea what these ones are like! Who knows how long you might be saddled with them. Don't talk about causing the accident, we're no-fault here, and that's what insurance is for, anyway, you of all people know that—and where's the father run away to? You can't take this on."

"I like Lorraine, and she's alone. She needs help."

Darlene ran through the living room between them. She gave Grace one of her sharp glares, and Grace gave her one right back.

"Are they safe, do you think?"

Clara watched Darlene going around the kitchen corner. Was Trevor still in the back yard? She got up and looked out the dining room window. Peeling bark off the birch.

"I think they're okay, Grace. Safer here than wherever else they would be right now."

"I meant safe for you," Grace said.

"I know what you meant. I'm answering what you should have asked."

They were silent for a minute. Then Grace laughed, her temper repaired. "You've been quiet long enough, maybe you can stand the racket. You were so good with your mom, we've been wondering how you'd keep yourself occupied."

"Well, she's gone."

"I know. That's hard to get used to."

"Not for me, Grace. She was not herself any more. And really, she couldn't have got out any easier." Out through the door to death, that heavy door that sticks on its hinges and doesn't want to push open. "I've got different concerns now," Clara said.

Trevor raced through this time.

Grace's look trailed after Trevor. "You sure do," she said.

"I can see what's happening to their mother, and I like her, and I'd like to help her."

"That's all it is, then?"

"It's true, that I've wished for—I've missed—having children."

"You're not old, I'm not saying that."

"I'm only forty-three! They're better off with me, and I'm better off with them."

Grace looked at Moreland, but did not allow her eyes to roll. The baby crawled to Clara across the berber carpet, new eight years ago, still creamy and clean in this spinsterish house.

"What's the little one's name?"

"Pearce."

"Pierce your heart," said Moreland. "Sweet boy."

While Grace and Moreland were still there, Clara ran over to the hospital to see Lorraine.

"Your priest came," Lorraine said. "He had a lot to say about you."

Clara was wary about that. "Did he?"

"That you've been lonely since your mom died."

"Well, that was two years ago now. I'm not really lonely. I just haven't wanted to go back to church, to be honest." Clara sat beside the bed, taking the upright blue chair.

Lorraine was sitting upright herself. She looked very tired, her wide face stretched taut around her nose and eyes, with purplish shadows. Her eyes were staring, a look that Clara knew from other people who were ill, not open to easy comfort. Her legs moved restlessly beneath the yellow sheets.

"He said I should be glad to have you for the kids. So that's my plan," Lorraine said abruptly. It was too much. She could hardly bear to speak. Her body was aching, and her head felt like a large glass ball she had been trusted to carry, that she was bound to drop.

"I brought you some soup from my neighbour, Mrs. Zenko, the best cook I know. It'll do you good," Clara said. She went to find the microwave down the hall.

Lorraine lay back, not at all wanting soup. She didn't seem to be able to cry, but she had sometimes found herself sobbing, noise without tears, and she didn't want to do that in front of Clara. She was tired in her chest and deep in each arm, in a way she found very frightening. Knowing herself to be really sick, knowing it from inside.

She wanted her brother Darwin. It had been hard to find the house occupied by a stranger, someone who'd never heard of him or Rose. She should have looked after Rose better in her last years, made her come live with them instead of Mom Pell. But now Clara had Mom Pell. Lorraine almost smiled. The tender unfamiliar feeling in her cheeks made her laugh, especially because it was about something kind of mean.

Coming back, Clara smiled too; relieved, probably, to see her more cheerful.

Lorraine slapped herself mentally and sat up. "Thanks," she said, reaching for the bowl. It was homemade, invalid soup: pale gold, a few tiny noodles, shreds of chicken and delicate slivers of carrot and green onion.

Clara sat and watched her eat.

"How are they?"

Arranging her mind to tell what could be told, Clara said, "Trevor is happy, except for missing you, but he's an easy, good-natured boy. Darlene is sad, but not complaining. Harder to tell with Pearce."

"Eating lots?"

"Oh, like a monster. I'll have to weigh him for you." Clara paused. "I thought I might take him to the doctor, just to—"

"He's sick?"

"In case you hadn't been able to take him lately, to get him weighed, and so on."

Lorraine looked at her for a minute. Clara felt like she had stones in her stomach, but she didn't look away. *Nothing to be worried about,* she was saying to Lorraine's eyes. Behind, she was thinking *Don't ask about Clayton.* But Lorraine did not.

"Yeah," Lorraine said, finally. "The health cards are in my wallet, in the cupboard."

Clara unlocked the cupboard for her, and saw Lorraine's scuffed shoulder-bag on top of the box and maps. Lorraine went through the skinny wallet to find the health cards. She pulled out a photo, not Clayton.

"My brother," she said. "Darwin."

Clara took the photo, a broad smiling face under dark hair.

"We thought he was in Saskatoon, but we couldn't find him. The last place he was, they couldn't tell me anything," Lorraine said, searching for the health cards. "It seems like I'm all alone."

"Well," Clara began. "You've got your mother, and the children…"

Lorraine laughed. "That's Clay's mother. She's sure as hell not *my* mother. Thanks a lot." She handed three health cards to Clara.

"Oh!" That made more sense. "But her name is Pell, not Gage."

"Husband three, Dougie Pell. He wasn't around long, anyway. She's had a rough life."

Clara couldn't think of anything to say to that that wasn't rude.

"My mother's dead," Lorraine said. "She died when Darwin was little. My cousin Rose brought us up. Darwin's got a different dad. My dad died before I was born, he was a long-haul trucker. After that my mom got married again."

Clara wished she could respond, other than reciting the deaths on her own family tree. "I always wanted a brother or a sister."

"That's why I wanted to have lots, because it's good for kids to have each other. They get along so good, it's great to have them all, I'm glad I did."

Lorraine stopped talking and looked away, overcome suddenly by the unpayable, unbearable cost of Clara looking after her kids. And no word from Clayton, so probably he'd skipped town. Shit. She just had to let go of all this for now.

Clara thought maybe Lorraine was trying to spare her feelings for not having children.

"They're kind to each other," she said. "And to Pearce, always."

Lorraine nodded and lay back on the pillow. Clara knew she should go back and relieve Grace and Moreland, so they'd have time to shop. Only she didn't want to leave Lorraine alone. She put the health cards in her purse, wondering what to talk about next, but when she looked up Lorraine had fallen asleep. Her mouth had fallen slightly open, relaxed, and her hand lying nearest to Clara had opened too. Long fingers, nicely shaped. She was worth helping.

At home, Moreland was lying on the floor in the living room, building block towers for Pearce. Grace had taken the older two children downstairs to look for sealer jars, since it was almost time for saskatoons.

"I know your mom had extra in boxes," Grace called to Clara as she came down the basement stairs. "You ought to have a sale, get this basement cleared out. Looks like the Davina Museum shed down here."

Being told what to do by Grace was a constant hazard. Clara murmured

65

at her, nodding. Her mother had refused to do anything about the basement, and Clara had grown blind to it, but it was a horrible dark cave. She ought to get it done, Grace was right.

She found the children bickering behind the furnace, Darlene telling Trevor to stop, and Trevor on the verge of tears, yelling, "*Make me!*"

"Children!" she said sharply, embarrassed in front of Grace. They stared up at her from the floor, where they'd been pawing through a box of oddments. "My old toys!" she said, setting irritation aside to peer into the box. "Let's take them up and see if there's anything you would still enjoy. They're going to waste down here. But don't fight over them."

Trevor looked at her, crouching down by them. The soft round corner of her jawbone with the little hairs on it, and her eyebrows like brushes. He wondered if she was more beautiful than his mother, but even after this short a time he could not make his eyes remember exactly what his mother looked like, so he stared at Clara's pretty brown shoe until she took his arm to pull him up.

"You help me carry the box, will you, Trevor?"

He would help. His chest uncramped, and he could breathe.

By Friday night they were more at home, watching TV in the room with the pullout couch, which in Clara's mind was now Clayton's room. She did not call it that to the children. She was careful not to shrink from speaking of him if they brought him up, but they hardly did. They let him go, he was gone.

Maybe it was always like that with fathers, Clara thought, picturing her own father dimly. But then the slide fell properly into focus in her mind: her bright-eyed father rootling in the drainpipe one fall afternoon when she came home from school, calling down from the ladder to say, "Don't let your mother see you chewing your braid like that, County Clare." No one ever gave her a nickname but Dad. She could see his kind, creased face another time, installing a new radiator in the guest room. He called her in to watch a bead of mercury slipping away from him along the shiny floorboards. You remember a thing and reach to pluck it closer, but it slides off as if it's heard you coming. Only it leaves a residue on your fingers, mercury, much as you might think it did not. Dangerous, her father had said, even as he casually chased the bead across the floor. Don't lick your fingers after that! Clara shook her

head, not sure how she'd gotten to licked fingers. She was like that these evenings, after a day of learning how to deal with the baby and the children, and
the visits to the hospital—drifty, tending to trains of thought that stretched
out too far to be traced.

Darlene settled better under Clara's arm, not liking to be shifted when
Clara moved. Trevor looked up from his puzzle, but saw that everything was
still okay and bent his head back down to business. Soon he would have only
the sky left to do.

The movie was almost over. The mice would bring Cinderella the key to
open that locked door... Mrs. Pell had fallen asleep, stiff in the recliner, her
thick socked toes pointing straight up. Almost over, almost bedtime. Clara
hugged Darlene closer. The house was not warm enough, she thought, for
children and old women. She should get out the blankets and cover the tomato cages. In a minute. The cat was going to spoil it all, that obnoxious cat.
But the birds would help. A mouse cowered in a teacup, a drop of boiling tea
trembling on the end of the spout...

On Friday evenings she went to a movie by herself, in her usual life.
How could it be ordinary, so quickly, to stay in and be with three children
and an old woman? Clara missed her mother—she would have enjoyed all
this arranging and organizing.

They were getting married, the gold coach rode away.

Mrs. Pell sat up, wide awake again. "Darlene!" she said. "Get my purse."
She was not going to relax into this place. *Purse close*, was what woke her from
her dream. The bones in her butt felt sharp and sore. No place to sit quiet
here, and it was cold. Nobody helps you when you're old. Her crooked old
hand fussed irritably back and forth for a moment. She twitched the blanket
and said "Darlene!" Shrill and disappointed.

Darlene put the purse close by her thigh, and she covered it with a
corner of blanket.

"My mom calls me Dolly," Darlene said in Clara's ear, bending Clara's
head down fondly with her hands so it was farther away from her grandmother. Clara was not sure whether she did this to spare the old woman's feelings
or because it was a lie.

It didn't matter which, she told herself, and she called Darlene *Dolly*
from then on.

8. Maraschino

*A*ching hip. The clock showed 5:04 a.m. Banjo eyes on the ceiling all night long. The room was blazing bright already, too far north here.

Mrs. Pell lay in bed, furious, and thought about Clayton. Thief. Abandoning them, no surprise there. Liar. The minutes chased through her mind: buying cherries, Clayton cursing—then the crash, and the ambulance and the hospital, blood everywhere, that snippy Chinese-or-whatever bitch sneering at her, being poked at by that teenage doctor with his busy hands, Clayton yelling, Lorraine lying there looking like a fresh corpse. Chicken dinner in the TV room. Clayton crying, the kids crying, Lorraine lying there, cherry juice on her sweater over the chair. A snake eating its own tail.

Well, none of it was her fault, they couldn't pin any of it on her. Mrs. Pell stalked the border of sleep, huffing from time to time and rearranging her pillows. Her hip hurt, even lying still. Her chest felt tight—she wasn't breathing too good. She flexed her foot sharply to relieve a cramp; flexed again. It was cold. The sheets were smooth and clean, give her that, her house was clean. Not for long, though, she wouldn't be able to cope with all of them. Mrs. Pell saw her sister Janet, angry with her, making their bed the morning after their mother died, snapping the sheet, black look on her face. Sour. Her purse. There.

In his corner, Pearce breathed, eyes clamped shut and mouth open. *Sleeping like a baby,* Mrs. Pell thought. *The sleep of the just.*

Clara slipped in at 6:30 and lifted Pearce out of his crib, took him off to wash and dress and feed him. Mrs. Pell didn't bother to speak. Nothing to say. Out in the hall she could hear the kids getting up, Trevor running around. What a place to end up.

Clara fed the children breakfast, explaining to Trevor why there was no Count Chocula.

"My mom lets us eat it," he told her. "My dad lets us."

"Maybe that's because you're travelling, Trevor," Clara said, pulling the edge of the empty spoon over Pearce's mouth to clear off the extra baby cereal. Pearce was fastidious, he liked to have his mouth clean. He turned his face to meet the spoon. "I'm sure when you get to Fort McMurray you'll be..." She checked the Shreddies box while Trevor was campaigning. Sure enough, sugar was the second ingredient there too. She ought to be making Red River cereal for them.

Darlene's—Dolly's—eyes were glued to the kitchen television. She looked hollow and blanched. The sound was off because Clara could not tolerate it this early, but the silent cartoon people cavorted, wheeled, double-took and slammed into new scenes.

"Here, Dolly," Clara leaned over to give her another piece of honey toast. "Eat up."

Trevor put two Shreddies on a spoon, his face as sad as if his mother was dying.

"Trevor," Clara said, "I think I'm going to reconsider on the Count Chocula. I think when I go for groceries this morning I'll pick up a box so you can show me how good it is."

"Yay!" Trevor said, kicking Dolly. "She reconsidered!"

"Yay," she said to please him, leaning to the right to watch the coyote flutter off the cliff, anvil tied to his ankle. A little sign popped into his fist: *Goodbye, cruel world.*

Mrs. Pell was already wearing her coat when Clara went to tell her she was going for groceries. There was no real reason they couldn't all go. Clara had never shopped with children, but Mrs. Pell would be there; how bad could it be?

They got the special grocery cart with the red baby seat. Secretly, Clara supposed, she must always have longed to use this cart. And now she had every right to pop Pearce into the vinyl seat and wrestle with the knotted straps and bent buckles.

"You don't have to pay for this one," Trevor said, jumping on only the black squares. Dolly put her hand on the front of the cart, not pushing but connected.

Mrs. Pell peeled off to the chairs banked along the wall by the take-it-or-leave-it bookcase. "I'll sit for a while," she said, her voice old and tired.

Fine, fine, Clara thought. They started in the bread aisles, and the things that Trevor wanted to buy gave Clara waves of shock. White doughnuts—she had never heard of them. He found some to show her: twenty-four knobbly little knots packed in cellophane, chocked with chemical icing sugar. "No," Clara said. Wagon Wheels! Joe Louis cakes! She should have started at the fruit aisle. Whole grain bread, two loaves.

"Granny likes white," Dolly said. Almost a warning.

Clara resisted. "Whole wheat is much better for you." Grilled cheese sandwiches for lunch, Clara thought, dreaming of meals… A frowzy woman pushed past, her cart filled with young children wearing dirty pyjamas. Pyjamas! It's not *that* early in the morning, Clara thought. Maybe that would have been their life, living in the car. The smell of old rubber, those butterscotch vinyl seats. Dolly almost pointed. Perogies? Clara tried to check without prying. "Shall we get some perogies, Dolly? Mrs. Zenko makes the best—why don't we ask for some of hers?"

Dolly nodded. She smiled, first time that day. Her eyes darted up to Clara's, and Clara was glad to see any spontaneous movement at all in her.

In the pharmacy aisles Mrs. Pell ranged in front of the Aspirin. Children's Benadryl, there, she needed more of that, almost out. And somewhere here… 222s, but she didn't want those, too expensive, they watched them. Maybe nighttime stuff would help. She blew her nose in disgust. A person needs a little help to sleep but they can't get it, not here. The Kleenex fit nicely around the bottle of NyQuil and the Benadryl when she put it back into her pocket.

Pearce had fallen asleep. Trevor was hopping. *This?* he would say, *This?* popping things into the cart. Clara's reins loosened. Lettuce, maybe the bland iceberg for the children, a good dark green today.

"Get me a lettuce, Trevor," she said, turning away to the carrots.

Behind her she heard a yelp, and she turned in time to see the whole cannonball pile of lettuces tumbling off the tilted shelf, round and firm enough to roll all over. Trevor shook. "Sorry, sorry, sorry, sorry," he said. His thin arms milled to grab lettuces, clutched three—two escaped. He tripped on the tiles to avoid the lettuces rolling beneath him, and when Dolly tried to help he hit her by mistake.

"They're wrapped in plastic," Clara said, to calm him. "No harm done. Look, under the potato table. You can get in more easily than Dolly or me. Hand those ones out to me."

It was dark under there. Under the heavy potatoes—Trevor did not like being under things. He felt bad. He was all wobbling.

"Trevor! Come out," Dolly said. She hauled on his arm. "Don't pee!"

But it was too late. Trevor clambered in, farther under. His underpants were warm with pee, and then his leg was cold. Oh no. Clary would be so mad.

Clara stood with her hand over her mouth. A small fjord flowed out from under the potato table. How could she have forgotten to make everyone go to the bathroom before they left the house? Painful awareness of her own incompetence flooded through her body.

Dolly pulled on her hand. "I should take him to the bathroom," she said. "Where is it?"

Clara had no idea. Did they even have a public washroom in a grocery store? The vegetable manager came out with a rolling table of apples.

"Need help?" He was a shy man, with a port wine stain covering most of his face. Clara had never met his eyes before.

"We've had—a small accident," she said. "Is there a washroom?"

"Through the double steel doors, turn right right away," he said. "Not the cleanest, but it'll do in a pinch." He leaned down. "Hey, son," he said. "Come on out, you'll be okay. Whole place gets hosed down twice a day, we don't worry about accidents."

Trevor could see the double doors from where he squatted. He thought he could make it there. Dolly leaned down and said, "I'll go with you, Trev."

Clara opened the multi-pack of paper towels, and handed a big swath down to Trevor. "You mop yourself up, Trevor, and this kind man will get the rest. I'll go find you a new pair of pants in the clothing aisle. What colour do you like best?" She prayed he would not say yellow or some unlikely pants colour.

"I like blue," he said. Surely to God there would be blue.

Trevor crouched along under the table, awkwardly mopping with the bunch of towels, until he could crawl out the other end and take Dolly's hand. They went up to the double doors with dignity. Clara saw them into the grimy bathroom; an unpleasant place to spend ten minutes, but she thought they would be safe. "I'll be quick," she said, and she went off.

Dolly locked the door. "Never mind," she said. "Clary's not mad."

One good thing about Trevor—when awful things happened he didn't mind for very long. He could put them out of his mind. She would be still blushing three years later, when she thought of any of the times she had embarrassed herself, but she wouldn't think of them now. "I'll sing for you," she said. She started in on the pig song, and Trevor joined in, while he sadly hauled off his wet pants.

There was that Clara going too fast with the baby in the cart. He'd start screaming the place down. Four big chocolate bars in her basket; four up the sleeve. Those cameras were everywhere these days. A comforting weight banged against her leg from her coat pocket. Now she would not go hungry in the middle of the night. Now, salt. Sardines, she could put those in Clara's cart. She steamed off toward the canned fish aisle. Smoked oysters, too.

Trevor liked the Spider-Man underwear Clara brought. And he couldn't stop running his hands up and down his fleecy pants; it was beginning to bug Dolly. They were in line behind two other carts, and this was the shortest line.

Pearce had woken up fretful, but Clara didn't want to take him out of the seat if she'd have to put him back in screaming. Where was Mrs. Pell? She must be roaming around the store.

"Can I have a doughnut?"

Clara stared at Dolly for a minute before she could get her mind back to doughnuts.

"The apple fritters, can I have one?"

"Me too," Trevor said. Pearce started to cry.

"Oh, children, can't you wait for ten minutes? We have to go through the cash."

"You could just tell her we ate two of them," Dolly said.

It was sensible enough. But her mouth formed to say no.

"Please reconsider?" Trevor asked her.

Pearce was squalling, Mrs. Pell was missing. She laughed anyway. "Okay, Trevor, I have reconsidered."

Done shopping, Mrs. Pell left her basket in the aisle. Her pockets were too full, cookies would make a bulge. Wait, cherries, she needed some of those. She picked up the bright bottle and shuffled toward the checkout, where that woman had set the baby crying again. Typical.

The cart was already bumping up against the conveyor belt. Clara unloaded, shepherding the children through in front of her. She said no, no, not today, to gum, chocolate bars, and a picnic cookbook. She remembered to tell the cashier they'd eaten two fritters. It all mounted up, up, and Clara was shocked to see $127.62 on the window.

She got out her bank card, but Mrs. Pell's grimy fist came slap on the conveyor belt.

"And these," she said to the cashier, putting a large jar of maraschino cherries on the belt.

"$134.43," the cashier said, and Clara didn't have the strength of character to say no, or even to protest—seven dollars for cherries!

Bags in the cart, Pearce quieter, they processed out of the store, Mrs. Pell clanking gently with every step. One of the grocery managers followed them for a little while, trying to catch Clara's eye.

"Thank you, I don't need help," she said, smiling, recognizing him—Jeff Fisher from church. Her good humour was restored by kind service. "I've got lots of helpers today!"

Mrs. Pell, too, gave him a big smile. Row after row of dirty teeth.

9. A million billion trillion

*I*n the afternoon, just as Clara was thinking about going to see Lorraine, Clayton phoned. It never crossed Clara's mind that it might be him—she expected her cousin Grace, calling to talk some sense into her.

"It's me," Clayton said. She knew his voice immediately.

There was a pause.

"You didn't think you'd hear from me."

She couldn't speak.

"How're the kids?"

Was he drunk? She had to answer. "They're well," she said, her stomach jumping, quick blood flooding her legs. She leaned against the kitchen counter. A week since he left—it seemed like a year.

"What's happening with Lorraine?"

Trevor was going past the kitchen doorway. She didn't want the children to hear. She said nothing for a moment.

"I've got a right to know," he said, louder.

"Of course," she said. "They've told us it's non-Hodgkins lymphoma. They are going to start chemo on Monday, if they can keep her fever down.

You could phone the hospital, they would tell you." She didn't want him phoning Lorraine, though.

"I don't have time for that. You tell me."

"Well, this kind of chemo is very strong, so she will stay in the hospital. If the chemo does what it's supposed to do—I don't really know what's next. There are different kinds of bone marrow transplants... They're worried, because she's younger than most people who have non-Hodgkins lymphoma, but that means they'll try harder for her."

"Yeah." He was quiet for a minute.

"That's really all we know, we're waiting for them to find out more." *Don't let him phone Lorraine,* she was praying, so Lorraine wouldn't be worried that he was not with the children. Or so she wouldn't find out that Clara had lied.

Clara's fingers were clammy on the receiver. She changed hands.

"Okay, well, I got a line on a job. I'm moving around now, I needed the vehicle to get the work."

What could she say to that? "Yes," she said. Whatever he would think she meant: *yes, that's fine, have my mother's car...*

"Tell the kids I called."

She nodded, and then said "Yes," again. She could hear traffic going by behind him.

"I've been doing things for Lorraine, too," he said. As if he had to justify himself to Clara. When she didn't speak, he said loudly, "Fuck you." He hung up.

Dolly's new pink running shoe flashed in at the back door, and Clara dodged backwards and fled down to the bathroom. She scrubbed at her hands, managing not to catch a glimpse of herself in the mirror. He hadn't inquired after his mother, she noticed.

She longed for bedtime. After the dishes she took the children to the park, hoping to tire them out, but they were alone in the playground and their own company was wearing thin. She jounced Pearce up and down to console him for not riding the merry-go-round, and cheered at their speed or prowess when requested. She had to find them some friends.

Except that then Clayton would come and take them away, and all her work would be wasted, and then they'd have to miss the friends, as well as everything else.

At home Clara tried to put the sleeping baby down, slow as a river of lava flowing into his basket, but he felt the change and woke, crying.

Mrs. Pell jumped up from the TV to catch Clara at fault. She would have let Pearce cry, any other time. "You leave him with me," she croaked, in a mixture of impatience and triumph. "He'll behave for me, he needs his special soother."

Sure enough, the crying did not continue for long.

After the children were in bed Clara went through the house turning off lights and checking the stove, trying to bring order and safety back into her house. By the time she had put away the toys and tidied up the bedtime snack and folded the clothes from the dryer she expected to fall asleep at once, but she lay wide awake, her mind playing ridiculous scenes of Trevor drowning in the bathtub, or Mrs. Pell poisoning the baby. Clayton stealing into the house, taking his children. After midnight she remembered: she had not gone to the hospital to see Lorraine. She cried, then, and had to go to the kitchen for Kleenex to blow her nose.

Her life had been turned upside down and violently shaken, like the peaceful winter scene in a snowglobe, and she was some poor flake of snow twisting and hurtling in the demented storm. Imagine how Lorraine must feel, she told herself.

At 6 a.m., too early for the hospital, she went out to pull weeds from the front beds for an hour. Mrs. Zenko came over from her garden to have a look at the John Cabot rose bush, and Clara remembered to ask if she had any perogies in her freezer.

"I made cracked wheat buns for her last night," Mrs. Zenko said. She cheered Clara up, joining in the caretaking work as if it was only natural. "Yes, perogies, oh my yes."

"Their father called yesterday," Clara told her. "He scares me."

"He's an angry fellow," Mrs. Zenko said, without judgement. "Is he bringing back the car?" Clara had not mentioned the car, but of course Mrs. Zenko knew.

"He said he needed a vehicle for getting work."

"Well, that would be good. He's going to need something steady."

Clara found it hard to imagine Clayton in anything steady.

The neighbour from the other side of Clara's house, a large, pale-beige man who had moved in a few months before, came down his front steps. His difficult name was either Bradley Brent or Brent Bradley.

"I don't know what you're doing over there," he shouted over, when he caught sight of her. As if he'd been trying to get hold of her for days, to get this off his chest. "But if you're renting rooms, there's a bylaw for that. You could find yourself in hot water."

Clara and Mrs. Zenko stared at him.

"One call to the city," he said. "That's all it would take."

He got into his truck and backed loudly out of the driveway.

His plump little hen-wife scrambled out their front door and ran down to the truck, carrying a covered dish. She climbed up and in, and they drove off in a tearing of loose stones over the asphalt.

"What's with him?" Clara asked Mrs. Zenko.

"They're off to church. An awful lot of these men are impatient nowadays," she said, sad for them. "My John was a great one for keeping his temper. Your father, too."

"I feel sorry for Mrs. Bradley. Mrs. Brent."

"I can never remember either," Mrs. Zenko said, with her deep little laugh.

To give herself a clear mind, or else to delay, Clara went to church before going to the hospital. She slipped in late to the early service and did not genuflect, but crossed herself quickly. She always felt slightly snooty crossing herself, but her mother had ingrained it in her. All this ritual was so complicated: whether to stand for communion or kneel, stand or kneel for prayer, fold hands or adopt the charismatic pose, swaying and open-palmed. Many of the older women, surprisingly, swayed.

It was all superstition, anyway. Just sitting there, being there, was the essential thing, she had come to believe. But of course she could be wrong.

The Gospel was Mary choosing the better part, to let the dishes go and listen to Jesus talking in the living room—a reading that always annoyed Clara,

78

although she'd never considered herself a Martha. What would happen if she let go of the dishes now? It would be all right, because Mrs. Zenko would do them for her, popping in and out of the kitchen with her bright glance catching everything, tidy little ears pricked for the conversation while she got supper cleared up without a wasted movement or a sigh or a fuss. Occupied with Mrs. Zenko's holiness, Clara had trouble keeping her mind on the sermon. Paul Tippett was telling an anecdote. She wondered if he made them up, since so many were apropos, but that was ungenerous. Anyone's life is full of meaning. She should have phoned to thank him for visiting Lorraine.

He was contrasting Mary and Martha with last week's Gospel on the Good Samaritan—she hadn't consciously heard a word of it, as she sat fretting and deciding.

"A man no one would think of as saintly, a dirty Samaritan, took practical action to save the life of someone left to die by the side of the road. Today, Jesus scolds Martha for her brand of practicality, and insists that spiritual discussion is more important than putting the supper on. Why is practicality praised in one case, and in the other, reviled? I don't think that's too strong a word, *reviled*, for the way we call women Marthas with an edge of contempt, because they are busy in the kitchen feeding the masses. Jesus himself was good at feeding the masses. And staying under budget."

Paul seemed so pleased with this loaves-and-fishes nudge that Clara couldn't help laughing. She hoped she hadn't been too loud.

"The Samaritan acts in a moment of genuine crisis, when no one can see his goodness. But the flavour of self-importance in Martha's actions, and her peevishness toward her sister, may be uncomfortably familiar to us when we think of our own acts of goodness and how we look for recognition of our work."

Clara wondered whether Lisanne Tippett scolded Paul for idleness or lounged at the feet of bishops while he did the dishes. Or both. Then she erased that, mean-spirited.

"These stories remind me of Hebrews 13: *Be not forgetful to entertain strangers: for thereby some have entertained angels unawares.* I've been inspired this week by an instance of practical charity, one of our own parishioners— I'll let her remain anonymous—who has opened her house to strangers." He did not look at her. Clara felt hot and ashamed anyway, and hoped her face

79

was not flushed. Or maybe he was not talking about her, she thought, hare-brainedly.

"Her ordinary, private action reminds me that as humans together in the world we are essential to the purposes of God."

It felt like lying, to be called essential to the purposes of God when she was doing exactly what she wanted to do. It was only luck that her purposes and God's coincided this time.

The others sang while Clara stood silent, acidly aware of her own false-ness in being there at all. None of the words of church made sense to her. The Creed—what part of that could she say she believed? Resurrection of the body, life everlasting, not those... She thought of her mother and father falling to shreds in their graves, and then, sharply, of Lorraine. But Lorraine would get better.

But she did not think so.

The long communion prayers wore on, and Paul lifted the cup. A slight commotion rose in the back of the church: a man came in, walking too loud-ly. Frank Rich, the doe-eyed sidesman, helped him to a leaflet out of habit. From the corner of her eye Clara could see that it was a stumbling drunk. She was glad the children were at home.

The man wore a big black felt hat. He veered slowly up the aisle, work-ing against gravity, but advancing—an oil tanker, inexorable toward the coast. When he passed Clara his hand fell heavily on the arched end of the pew in front of her: large, oddly clean, long-fingered, with veins standing out, like the close-up of a surgeon's hand in an old movie. She glanced up to see his face under the shadow of his hat. Pock-marked skin, squinting eyes still aim-ing for the altar. He was not very old for a wino.

The congregation was still and silent, waiting.

Paul found drunks difficult, and braced himself to leap over his fear and distaste. But it was right that the man should come to church, and somehow strengthening that the congregation would be worried and ashamed. *Brush-ing from whom the stiffened puke / i put him all into my arms / and staggered banged with terror through / a million billion trillion stars...* The man held out his cupped hands at the rail and Paul gave him communion—the wine too— then let Frank Rich usher him down to the front pew. But he stood again, very tall, and came back up to the rail.

"Are you in trouble?" Paul asked.

The man's head lifted. His eyes stared into Paul's, their focus coming slowly home, resolving into human sense and pain.

Down in the pews the congregation shifted. Clara could feel the cowardly anxiety of well-off people in the presence of disaster. And felt it herself. Paul was talking so quietly that no one could hear the words. The man answered, louder but unintelligible. He was swaying now. He bent down to hold the rail. Paul lifted the movable section, took the man's arm and helped him out the side door to the vestry. Paul's murmur covered the man's ramblings as they went so that Clara could not hear anything but a noise of confusion and sorrow. He is good, Clara thought, a little surprised.

Paul was gone a long time. The congregation sat meditating on communion, or on alcoholism, or the homeless, or the poor whom we have always with us, Clara thought; or just aimlessly, peacefully, passing the time. Remembering her own responsibility, she prayed for Lorraine, the words wooden and empty.

Dolly slid her thin body between the sharp-twigged hedge and the fencepole, into the back yard of the house beside Clary's. She needed something to do, to stop from thinking all the time. The next-door guy had yelled at his wife for a while, *Come on, come on, come on,* and when she went scurrying through she slammed the front door to lock it. But Dolly was betting she had not locked the back door. Yes, it opened.

The back landing was the same inside as Clary's, but switched over, reversed. It was dark and smelled of stinky meat. Dolly slipped between piles of newspapers lining the steps, up the wrong side into the kitchen. Brown and gold linoleum, the same as Mrs. Lyne's trailer in Winnipeg, dark brown cupboards. The counters under the cupboards were stacked with old magazines. No cookie jars. Dolly checked the fridge—no cake. Leftover casserole with crusty macaroni around the edges. In the pantry she found a bag of pretzels with an elastic band around it. She unrolled the bag and ate a few, walking around the wrong-way circle of kitchen, dining room, living room. It was weird to be in a backwards house, like folding your fingers with your other hand on top. In here, shiny maple country furniture crowded in bunches.

The chairs had plastic wraps on the arms. The dining room table was piled with paper and files and newspaper clippings, all their edges straight as if that made it okay.

On the hall divider shelf sat three ugly teddy bears, one dressed in baby clothes. That one stuck out over the edge and Dolly nearly knocked it off. She stopped it wobbling. The clock in the hall made a really loud ticking. The mail was there: *Mr. B. Bunt, Mr. & Mrs. Bunt, Occupant.* Nothing interesting. She put the pretzels back in the pantry and went down the hall, peeking into two little bedrooms packed tight with boxes and papers: too hard to search. Their bathroom was pink and black, a woolly swan on the shower curtain. Dusty razor blades and pill bottles stuffed in the medicine chest. Nothing was very clean.

The main bedroom was full of bears, like a collection on TV: shelves of them, a hundred teddy bears sitting all over a giant bed covered with drooping pink satin, like icing. Dolly sat on the slippery bed and played with some of the bears, the less-pink ones. One lying close by the pillow had a nightcap on and a candle in his paw, and a zipper pocket on his butt to hold pyjamas. He crinkled. Dolly unzipped his pocket, and there was a lot of money. A *lot* of money, all sharp-edged brown hundred dollar bills.

She sat looking at it. First and last month's rent, right there.

A rush of air gasped down the hall, as the front door opened.

She'd never gotten caught before. Clary would be really mad. Dolly darted into the closet and pulled the half-door shut, then thought, *stupid!* Maybe it was clothes they'd forgotten.

She dodged out of the closet, but there was nowhere else to hide in this bear-filled room. Mrs. Bunt trotted down the hall murmuring, "Where, now where?" She was coming to the bedroom. Dolly slid gently back into the closet behind the folding door, squeezing Mr. Bunt's suits to the end. Her head filled with his old aftershave stink. She could see Mrs. Bunt's beigey-grey chickenhead through the crack of the door, rummaging on the dresser. Next she would look in the closet. Mr. Bunt yelled from the front door: he'd had enough, he was sick of waiting for her, she was disorganized and sloppy and a waste of air. Mrs. Bunt ran to the bathroom.

Dolly heard her crying, "Oh! I found them! Don't be mad! I left them on the sink!"

The front door slammed shut again and the blinds on the bedroom window clapped as the air in the house settled back. Dolly stayed still until she heard the truck fade away, then climbed out. She zipped up the bear's butt with the hundreds still inside. She knew where they were, and she could get in here any time. She put him back on the bed exactly where he had been, then went out to the living room and ran her fingers down the yellowy sheer curtains, staring out at what the world looked like from the Bunts' house. She was tempted to cut those curtains up with a big pair of scissors. But they might notice that.

Time to go. As she passed, she knocked the baby bear off the hall divider, but she picked it up and put it back carefully. Then she went back and flushed a pair of Mr. Bunt's socks down the toilet, and skipped out the back door.

Clara took the elevator to the fifth floor, tossing over possible lies. She couldn't very well say she'd been upset by a call from Clayton. She had stopped downstairs to get flowers. But up in the room, Lorraine's face was already shining, and bouquets ranged all along the window ledge on the opposite side of the bed.

"Hi!" she said. "More flowers! Must be my horoscope today, hey?"

"My goodness," Clara said. "How lovely."

Lorraine had been eating her lunch with a good appetite, but she pushed the rolling table aside. "My brother! And look what else he brought." She shuffled her feet beside the bed for a pair of moccasins, beaded all over the top in an intricate pattern. "He was here all night. And he'd driven seven hours before that, he was bushed. He laid down on the other bed for a while, till a nurse came and chased him out, I don't know, maybe five in the morning?"

"This is very good, that he could get away to come and see you," Clara said.

Lorraine laughed. "Darwin can always get away! That's Darwin!"

"What does he do?"

"Moves people, drives truck, paints houses—anything portable. Sometimes he works with a guy, this artist, who does big murals on the side of buildings in towns all over. Darwin sets up the scaffolding and helps with finishing, you know, setting the picture out. He builds houses sometimes but he's not like a trade or anything, just temporary help. He'll be back later, you'll get to meet him. And he wants to see the kids."

The bloodwork nurse came to the door, and Lorraine stuck out her arm patiently.

"They already took blood this morning," she said.

"Well, they need more," the nurse said. Clipped, busy. Not in this for her health.

Clara stepped back out of the room while the nurse got on with it. Darwin, the brother. She tried to remember the picture Lorraine had shown her, but was distracted, worrying about the children—she'd been out too long. She went to the pay-phone and dialed Mrs. Zenko's number.

"It's Clara," she said. "I'm sorry to ask, but would you mind checking on the children for me? I left them with—"

"I've just come back from your place," Mrs. Zenko said. "I brought the children with me and gave them some lunch, because I wondered if she would be too busy."

"Thank you."

"She was sleeping, actually," Mrs. Zenko said.

They sat on the phone in silence together for a moment, no comment necessary between them.

"And Dolly was out roaming. But they're happy now, they're washing dishes for me."

"You had dirty dishes in the sink?"

"They're washing my plastic containers. From time to time, you know, it's good to wash them all out and start fresh. They'll have a good time. Don't you hurry."

"Is Pearce okay?"

"He was sleeping too. That's a sleepy baby," Mrs. Zenko said. "I think I'd be looking into that."

Clara felt hot blood crashing through her shoulders and chest—what had she missed?

"You could take him to Dr. Hughes, but I don't need to tell you what to do."

"I don't— You can tell me what to do any time," Clara told her.

"Well. I never gave you the buns I'd made, this morning. You can take them tonight."

Clara hung up and went back to Lorraine's room, bracing herself to be friendly. The brother was sitting in the blue chair, his black felt hat on the end of Lorraine's bed, against the footboard where the charts hung. Mrs. Zenko would not like that, a hat on the bed. Clara picked it up quickly, fanning the bad luck away, before she recognized the hat.

"Here's Darwin, Clara," Lorraine said. "My brother Darwin!"

It was the drunk from church.

This was too much. Would she be expected to look after a drunk, as well? Grace would have a field-day with that.

He looked up and nodded, and then stood, very tall. He grinned with his teeth showing higgledy-piggledy and his pocked cheeks bunched, so amiable that she could not help but smile back. He raised a long-fingered hand to Clara in a kind of salute, as if they were in a secret society together.

"We met in church this morning," she said, putting out her hand to shake his, giving him the dignity of an ordinary person. She kept her voice carefully unjudgmental, not to betray to Lorraine how drunk he had been. He reached forward and took her hand, his big brown hand swallowing up hers.

"Church?" Lorraine said, and Darwin raised his eyebrows high.

"Me?" he asked.

She blinked. At the sound of his easy voice she realized that it could not have been him, how could she have thought so? It was the same kind of hat, a black rumpled jacket. Not surprising, if he'd been here all night. But she could have sworn—she felt a blush flood up from her neck to her hair. She had been so cool and gracious and proud of her compassion. She tried to let his hand go, but he held on little longer, smiling, and gave her the orange chair.

"I'm sorry," she said. "I thought…" She couldn't go on. *I thought you were a derelict, I thought I would keep your shabby secret.* Her scalp was hot.

"Everybody always knows me," he said. "I have Face Number 3." He was younger than Lorraine. He had the biggest head she'd ever seen on a human being.

Lorraine was overflowing with happiness. "You kill me," she said.

"Church!" She pulled her eyes away from Darwin and turned to Clara. "How're the kids doing?"

"Trevor and Dolly are well." She hoped it was it all right to say Dolly, if that was Lorraine's own pet name for her.

Lorraine didn't seem to care. "What about Pearce?"

"Happy enough—he's too young to tell us that he's missing you," Clara said.

"Clayton found Darwin, you know. How many places did he have to try, Darwin?"

Darwin had tipped back in his chair, looking out the big window. "He must have called all over," he said.

Still off balance, Clara tried not to stare at him. Had it been him?

"He caught me up at Fort Smith, I'd been up there working a couple weeks."

"Too long, Darwin," Lorraine said. "I missed you too much."

He kissed her hand. Clayton had done that too, Clara remembered. Clayton had darted down and stabbed at her fingers with his lips; Darwin brought her hand up and met it, kissing the heel of her palm and holding it to his cheek for a moment. Clara had always wished for a brother.

"You enjoying the kids?" Darwin asked.

She nodded, and tried to be more sociable. "We all went to the grocery store, it was an adventure for me."

"This is such a good day!" Lorraine said, rearranging herself in the bed. "First time you ever had three kids in a grocery store, eh? You don't need to say another thing."

"Well, Mrs. Pell came too."

Lorraine looked alarmed. "Did you check her pockets?"

Clara didn't understand.

"She shoplifts," Lorraine said. "Three convictions in Winnipeg. Her case worker was so mad."

Clara said nothing. I am such a fool, she thought.

"She's off probation now, or we wouldn't have taken her out of the province. The lady she was living with, Mrs. Lyne, she kind of threw her out."

Darwin groaned.

"Well, Clayton couldn't just leave her."

Clara nearly laughed at that, but her stomach was too unsettled. She remembered the clanking in Mrs. Pell's coat climbing into the car after the grocery store. She could see the manager following them—Fisher Jr., from church. Oh God.

She looked up, and thought she saw in Darwin's face that he was laughing at her. Enough. She stood quickly. "The children—my neighbour is too kind already, and I've left them with her."

Darwin said, "I'll walk out with you." The last thing she wanted. He was already kissing Lorraine, and at the door.

"Thanks," he said, as they reached the lobby.

For what? She pressed the button for the elevator. She couldn't meet his eyes, having mistaken him for a drunk.

"You're doing a great thing, here. Big job, taking on three kids."

Clara nodded. She was still smarting too much about Mrs. Pell to cover his thanks with mannerly protests.

"I haven't been much help to her these last few years. Been moving around a lot."

The elevator was taking forever.

"She's bad, isn't she?"

Clara looked up. "Have you talked to the doctor? Or did she tell you?"

"I talked to the nurse while she was asleep, and Clayton. He must have spent a bundle on phone calls. He says she's dying. Couldn't handle it, he said." No censure in Darwin's face about that. Clayton couldn't take cancer, like other people couldn't take the sight of blood.

"Where is he?" she asked.

"He wouldn't say. Around, I guess. He phone you?"

She nodded. The fear from that call was draining away. Had to, she thought, to make room for Mrs. Pell's shoplifting. Her hands dewed with sweat again at the image of Mrs. Pell getting caught, with all the children standing there, and everyone so surprised that it would be Clara Purdy—George Purdy's daughter!—in charge of her.

Darwin got into the elevator with her. "She needs a sleep. I'd like to see the kids."

"Oh," Clara said. "Of course."

The elevator sank to the ground, and they sank too.

10. Bunk beds

*T*revor was shy of Darwin until Dolly ran past him and got twirled in the air and pulled Darwin to show him Mrs. Zenko's kitchen, plastic containers everywhere from their bath. Trevor had been looking forward to fitting them back into their intricate nests in the bottom drawer.

"You can finish these after supper," Mrs. Zenko whispered to him. She picked up his kangaroo jacket from the chair, slipped it on *swoop, there, done,* the tidy way she did everything, and zipped it up for him. "You go enjoy your uncle, he looks like good fun to me."

She nipped his earlobe with her two first fingers and gave him a big container of tarts, like the witch with the gingerbread house, only not wicked. She was so little and compact, like a grandmother in a book. He wanted to carry her in his pocket.

His own Gran was more of the bad witch, or the wolf. "Nobody saw fit to tell me where you'd all gone," she was complaining to Clary when they went through to their yard. Darwin gave her a hug and said Clayton wanted to know was she okay, but she went off in a bad mood to watch TV.

After Trevor and Dolly took him for a quick tour round the house, Darwin offered to make scrambled eggs, his specialty, while Clara bathed the baby. Especially after Clayton's hostility, Darwin's undemanding friendliness was a relief. And Dolly was so happy to see him.

"We can make a bed for you here too," Clara said, when she brought Pearce into the kitchen for supper. "There's the basement but I'm afraid it's only roughed-in down there, and a bit cold."

"I'm going back to the hospital," he said. "The nurse said she'd give me a cot. I think Lorraine could use someone there overnight."

Clara was ashamed. She should have thought of that herself.

"You couldn't," he said. "You're looking after the kids so Lorraine doesn't worry about them. But can I have a nap here tomorrow? A good dark basement—I can catch some sleep in the afternoon."

While the others were finishing supper, Clara took Pearce to Mrs. Pell's room to find that special soother she was always boasting of. The room was a pigsty.

Holding Pearce up against her chest with one arm, she rummaged through the mess on the dresser and the bedside table. Nothing. Fallen into the wastebasket? She squatted down in one smooth slide, keeping Pearce vertical, and sifted through the basket gingerly. No soother. But two empty bottles of Benadryl. Three. In a wastebasket that had been empty last Sunday. Clara stood up, her head pounding with the effort, clutching the third bottle. 0-6 mos., ½ teaspoon. 7-12 mos., 1 teaspoon. She knew perfectly well what Mrs. Pell had been doing, and she wanted to kill the old harpy.

Mrs. Pell croaked from the doorway, "You take him in with you, see how you like it."

"Yes," Clara said. "I will."

"You'd be amazed at how many people do it," Dr. Hughes said, his tone calm enough to reassure Clara. "I've been tempted myself, on a long night. You check the dosage, you think how nice a little sleep would be... No real harm to the baby, but let's change the arrangements, no?"

"I kept him with me last night. I can look after him."

She felt her whole head hot and swollen, her neck swelling like it might burst, with the shame and horror of not having noticed this before. And it had been a long night out there in the living room with a wide-awake baby. Things would have to change.

Pearce batted the stethoscope dangling in his view. He was a good weight and size for his age. His birthday was on the health card—September 10th. Dr. Hughes admired his sturdy legs, and the way he stood holding onto the desk chair, joggling slightly as if there was music they couldn't hear and grinning at them with his wide, drooling mouth.

"More teeth coming there," the doctor said. "You may be using that special soother after all." But he was joking. She knew him well enough to smile and shake her head. Pearce grabbed the stethoscope again, but Dr. Hughes caught it in time.

Dolly and Trevor would be all right with Mrs. Zenko for another hour. Clara stopped at the mall, where the BUNK BED SALE sign had been up for a month. Strange, she thought, to have noticed that sign long before she could ever conceivably have had a use for bunk beds.

They cost more than she thought they should, even on sale. But she had money lying useless in the bank, and something had to be done. Duvet covers were two-for-one. She popped Pearce into a handy crib to keep him happy while she flipped through the colours. When she turned back, he was tracing the outline of a bear with one finger, singing to it. So she bought the crib, too, and paid extra to have the whole shebang delivered right away.

Darwin came back from the hospital in time to help Clara move the pull-out couch out of the TV room, and the single bed into it. It wouldn't be Clayton's room any more. They abandoned the heavy couch in the kitchen doorway till they could think how to get it down the stairs. Mrs. Pell sat stony in the living room through the upheaval. Clara had moved the television in there, onto the carpet. How horrified she would have been, even last week, to think of the TV in the living room—but it was only pretension to hide it, as if they were too cultured to watch.

This was going to be much better! Clara had a bubble of joy in her chest, even in the middle of the chaos, because now the children would be across the hall from her, and she'd be in her bed again. The crib would fit under the window in her room, close enough that she could reach out and touch Pearce's hand through the bars, to reassure him.

And Mrs. Pell would be safely stashed in the little room, farther away. She was easy to dislike: surly, criminal, sly; but Clara could not be bothered.

New things! Since her mother's death Clara had been clearing things out, not bringing things in.

Mrs. Zenko came across before noon, just as the delivery truck pulled up, and led the children out the back and through the hedge to give them some lunch at her place. Darwin talked the delivery guys into carrying the couch to the basement, and then Clara asked them to bring the small bureau in from the garage, for the television to sit on. She tipped them $20 each and they walked out, slapping Darwin on the back.

And of all the days, Paul Tippett drove up as the delivery van pulled away.

"I thought I should render an account of my visit to your friend," he told Clara in his shy, stilted way, climbing the steps. "But perhaps this is not a good time…"

Dusty and giddy, Clara couldn't stop herself from repeating, "*Render an account?*"

He laughed at himself, dutifully. "Well. I thought you'd like to hear how it went."

"I would," she said, sorry to have mocked him. "Come in, we're moving furniture, please come in. Oh, this is Lorraine's brother, Darwin."

Paul shook Darwin's hand. "Of course," he said.

Darwin gave him a grin and a thumbs-up and went down to sleep on the demoted pull-out couch.

Clara drew Paul down the hall to see the bunk beds, still in pieces. He unfolded the cryptic instructions and squatted down in the middle of the rubble as if he was finally home. She offered to make coffee and he nodded, immersed already. But he called her back to hold the first headboard steady while he fit the supports into slot B, and by the time they had managed to put the beds together properly and went back for it, the coffee was stone cold. Paul put it in the microwave without even asking her.

"I'll make fresh," she said, shocked at the idea of microwaved coffee.

"It's the way I like it," he said. "I make a pot in the morning in the church office, but I'm the only one there most of the time, so I reheat it all day."

Clara was about to ask why he didn't go to the good coffee place beside the church, but remembered in time that of course he didn't make enough money for lattes and Americanos.

"Good thing you happened to come over today," she said, instead.

He took his cup out of the microwave and went back down the hall to the new children's room. She thought he had not heard her, and she followed to say again, "Good that you chose today—"

"My wife left this morning," he said.

He put his cup down carefully on the dresser and opened the exacto knife to slit the plastic on the first mattress. It made a satisfying zipping sound as it ripped.

"Where's she off to?" Clara asked, before she realized that it could not be a trip. "Oh, I'm sorry," she said, idiotically.

Paul laughed slightly again, that deprecating, priestly laugh he used to make people more comfortable. Clara was sorry to have occasioned it twice in one visit.

"No—yes, she's left me," he said. "Everyone will know, soon enough."

"I'm sorry," Clara said.

"Well. I'm sorry about it too." He took the corner of the mattress cover she handed him, and they fitted it around the square edges of the new mattress.

When Paul stood up from stretching the last corner he cracked his head on the upper bunk, and yelped. He smacked his hand to the bump and ground it around, as if to smear the pain away.

"Ice?" Clara asked.

"Ow. No. Thank you. It's making my eyes water," he said, and he sat down on the edge of the bed.

She sat beside him. "How long were you married?"

"Twenty years next May. A long stretch," he said, thinking of an elastic band pulled all that time, getting thinner and thinner. How it would hurt when it snapped on the fingers.

An egg had bulged on his forehead. Instead of bustling off to fetch ice or rubbing alcohol as he would have expected, Clara sat still beside him.

"Are you heartbroken?" she asked.

He bent his head toward his knees. "I think I'm stomach-broken, more

92

than anything. I threw up after she left, and again after lunch. Do you think that's normal?"

"I felt terrible when my husband left me," Clara said. "Physically. I lay in bed for days. It was an ache in my chest. I thought I was dying."

Her gravity made him laugh. "I'm not dying. I think I'll calm down soon."

"We were only married for a year. I was being left when you were marrying your wife."

"And do you feel better now?"

"Oh, yes. A million times. Today, in fact, I'm happy as a lark. But I think that's the new bunk beds, and the crib, and the children."

"We didn't have children."

As of course she knew. As everyone knew. "That was hard, was it?"

"It would have been easier, better for us, perhaps, if we… I wanted to very much."

She looked at his face, what she could see of it, his head still bowed in his hands.

"You would have enjoyed having children," she said. "From the little I know of the whole business. I'm certainly enjoying it, in between the worry."

"I should have gone out and found some," he said.

Late at night Dolly and Trevor lay in their new beds. Trevor was sleeping, but Dolly kept herself awake. She could hear Clary walking down the hall to her room. Crooning to Pearce, telling him some story about how good he was, what a good boy. You start out good, and then you turn into Dad, or Gran. How does that happen? Or you start out good and you get sick— No talking about her mother. She quickly switched it to Paul. He must be good, he was the priest. He had a big bump on his forehead.

Darwin. Darwin is the best of our family, she thought. She could think about Darwin as she went to sleep, as long as she didn't think of him at the where-he-was. He would be sleeping on the pullout couch in the basement tomorrow, he would be there.

Clara's spine had grown used to the living-room chesterfield, and back in her bed she had a ragged sleep. About midnight Pearce woke, hot and cranky. She gave him a sponge bath by the kitchen sink, with only the stove light on in the dim night kitchen. Poor lamb. Was this mild fever from illness, or new teeth coming in? Or withdrawal from the Benadryl. He was good-natured about it, lying peacefully on the towel as she sluiced him with trickles of water. His legs slid open and relaxed, and he turned his melon head on his small neck to look at the dark gleaming window over the sink, and through the window, to the moon shining out there in the night.

"There is the world," Clara told him. "There is the moon."

He reached his finger out to it, and looked back at her, to make sure she saw too. *Beloved.* She dabbed him dry with a couple of tea-towels from the drawer, so the water could evaporate and cool him that way. She dried between his fingers and his beautiful toes while he stared and stared at her, at the amazing presence of another human being. Clara had never understood that a baby could be so physically, solidly satisfying. When she picked him up to take him back to the crib he put his arm around her neck in a tender way, a partner in this. Not only a baby but a person, too, already.

Pearce was still staring at the bears in his crib when Clara heard a noise from the children's room. It was Trevor, awake and crying.

"My mom," he said—she could hardly make it out. She lifted him down off the bunk, took him to her room and tucked him into her bed. His shuddering gradually calmed.

Dolly appeared at the door. One a.m. "What's wrong?" she asked, tears in her eyes too.

"They're fine, Dolly. Come and sit with Trevor for a minute, and we'll see if we can sing Pearce to sleep."

Clara went to their room, opened the window and left the curtains open, plumped up their pillows and added a fleece blanket over Trevor's duvet. Then she put them back to bed. She sat in the semi-cave of the lower bunk, smoothing Dolly's shin; Pearce lay curled on her lap, happy to be held.

"*Betty Pringle, she had a pig,*" Clara sang for Trevor, and he chimed in softly, almost with the tune. "*As on my way to Strawberry Fair,*" she sang, and "*Baby's boat is silver moon, sailing in the sky.*" She felt Dolly going limp as she patted her, and heard her breathing change. She stopped singing.

"That was wonderful," Trevor said from above her.

Clara sat on in the little cave, wondering if she would be able to recall this later, when she was an old woman alone in some nursing-home, if she would remember Trevor saying *wonderful,* and the sleeping weight of Pearce on her lap, and Dolly under her hand, and how she'd done that herself, put them at ease, even though they were not her own.

She counted to a hundred. Then she got up, slow and fluid. She glided Pearce down into his crib so that he didn't wake, and got herself back into bed. Out in the hall Mrs. Pell's door opened and closed, and the bathroom door. In a few minutes the toilet flushed, and Mrs. Pell stalked back down the hall to the kitchen, feet clomping on the tiles. Maybe her feet hurt. Some while later Mrs. Pell woke her again, shutting her bedroom door loudly, with who knows what in her hands, what mess. It didn't matter. Clara turned over and shifted her pillow and went back to sleep for the last four hours of the night.

11. Melancholy

*H*is car not being completely reliable, Paul took the bus to the Diocesan office in Regina to see the suffragan bishop. On the way down he read Stevie Smith (hardly a Christian poet, although presumably Anglican), her lines tramping through his head to the thrumming drone of the bus vibrating along the empty highway. *Can God, / Stone of man's thoughts, be good? / Say rather it is enough / That the stuffed / Stone of man's good, growing, / By man's called God.*

He had been leaving the church on Monday when the bishop's secretary called to ask him to come in on Tuesday. Short notice. *Away, Melancholy, away with it, let it go.*

The bus got in to Regina early, and Paul walked around the city aimlessly for an hour, dismayed as always by the number of street people, giving away all his change and two tens he happened to find in his pocket. When he arrived, on time, he still had to wait. The secretary gave him a plastic cone cup of coffee, the vessel he most despised. He fixed the cone more firmly in the holder and doled out cream powder, missing his own bad coffee. Bishop Vivian Porter, the first woman prelate in the diocese. Lisanne, suspicious, always waited to catch him in a compromising glance with Bishop Porter. He should have had the courage to scotch her stupid jealousy, for her own sake as well as his comfort.

When she appeared, the bishop was wearing a purple wool dress, a nod to her position, and suede shoes so velvety-looking that Paul had to suppress a sudden desire to stroke them.

"You're showing strain," the bishop said. She held his hand for a minute.

He forced himself not to give an airy laugh, not to sally.

"Come in," she said. "We'll be quiet in here."

Her office was a comfortable room. Much improved since her predecessor. ("*Much improved since her predecessor,*" he heard Clara repeat. He was stilted even in his thoughts.)

"What a good room," he said. "You've made it very handsome." (*Handsome?* Fine! He spoke as he spoke!)

Vivian Porter reached up and let her hand slide down the towering gold velvet drapes. "I love these, don't you? My daughter did them up for me. And they have a secret, subversive side—look—" She turned back the ecclesiastical velvet to reveal the lining: cherry stripes on a lime green ground.

"Perfect," he said. He sank into one of the leather chairs by her desk. His knees seemed too large together. He splayed them apart, but that looked clumsy. He put his jacket on his lap and tried to forget himself. No matter how kindly Vivian arranged things, this summons was a visit to the headmaster. There must be something very wrong.

She patted the drapes back, their sober sides out, and got down to it. "I received an awkward phone message yesterday from your warden. Rather than reply myself, I wanted to see if we could together come up with a response." She leaned forward to the machine on her desk, the gold chain weighing down her bodice. She was fiftyish, young for a bishop, and intelligent. He admired and respected her.

A click, then the tape beginning.

"This is Candy Vincent calling, the people's warden from St. Anne's. I'm sorry to bother you with something so—*hm*. But I didn't know whom to—to whom—to tell." Candy Vincent's familiar screechy voice filled the room, and filled the spaces inside his head. What was it going to be? His stomach was roiling. That *hm* of hers. The tape ran on, the voice ran on.

"Father Paul's wife—Lisanne Tippett—" Paul laughed, he couldn't help himself. He had heard her say *Xanthippe*, rather than Lisanne Tippett. It struck him, sharp as a smack: he had married Socrates' shrew of a wife. He had a moment of pure pleasure at the ludicrous joke of the world, and classical studies, and the joke of himself, his own ridiculous self.

Vivian Porter looked up at him, lines on her forehead as her eyebrows double-arched. He shook his head, which she took to be an answer of some kind.

Candy had gathered momentum. Paul could picture her holding one of the fundraising chocolates, at Tuesday's vestry meeting, talking while the chocolate melted in her solid fingers.

"She has never been *involved* in the parish, but there's no escaping the fact: she wrote an article on—" It would take her a moment to get that out, Paul thought. "On mastur*ba*tion."

There was a pause, a quiet space on the tape. Chocolate on her hands.

Vivian Porter's mouth had turned up at one corner. Possibly smiling, Paul thought. Difficult not to, at the word, at the word coming from Candy Vincent. "And other things—equipment."

The bishop pressed the stop button. "That's enough, I think."

Paul was mainly conscious of relief that it had been something to do with Lisanne rather than himself. They sat comfortably enough, knowing one another to that limited degree that let them expect the best of each other. The bishop would not be unreasonable, Paul would not be defensive, and what Lisanne wrote was not the diocese's business anyway.

"But it's awkward," Paul acknowledged. "Lisanne and I are—dissolving our—" He had sawdust, leafmould in his mouth. "She's left me. We will probably divorce. I only say *probably* because I still hope for a better resolution. Lisanne has no such hope." *Man, too, hurries, Eats, couples, buries, He is an animal also. With a hey ho melancholy, away with it, let it go...* "The article was written more than a year ago, a commission. It's hardly a sex magazine, it's *Women's Fitness*. The swimsuit issue is sought after, I understand, but the general tone of the magazine is clinical."

"How long have you been married?"

"I suppose a long time—nineteen years. We were married as students..."

"I'm sorry, Paul."

Nothing more for her to say, and nothing for him to confide. Except that Lisanne was making his life excruciating any way she could, exacting revenge for some sin he had not consciously committed—the sin of not caring enough that she was leaving him, perhaps.

"My wife may have drawn the article to Candy's attention herself," he told Vivian, suddenly filled with longing to tell her everything. She motioned with her hand, a closing gesture which he interpreted as distaste for tattling. Very well. He said no more. *Away with it, let it go.*

Everything ends. The motion of the bus and his lack of responsibility for that motion were equally soothing, crossing the empty inland sea of prairie.

They had not slept together—Paul corrected himself, they had relentlessly continued to share a bed—had not made love since she missed a period eight years ago. For the first few days, because they thought Lisanne was pregnant; then because she was in mourning; then for a few months because they hated each other, or at least she hated him; then for nothing. Because they didn't make love any more, that was not them.

> *Are not the trees green,*
> *The earth as green?*
> *Does not the wind blow,*
> *Fire leap and the rivers flow?*
> *Away melancholy.*

She had told her sister, in his hearing, that she wouldn't care if she never had sex again. Carol had bridled and whinnied, but Lisanne was set, something admirable in her unbreachable self-possession. *Admirable, implacable.* Words flittering in his head.

He had trapped her by agreeing with her, giving her no opportunity for rage. They had married too young, and he had not been careful enough to keep some dignity or authority or respect—which he could only have maintained by behaviour which he did not believe in: by coldness, or insistence on his own sovereignty. He had given over to her, and that was weak, and she hated him. Paul could not find it in his heart, not even in his brain, to blame her. But he deeply wanted not to be married to her any more. Maybe they had let it drag out so long, so painfully, in order for the pain of the actual event to be lessened. Telephone poles clicked past the bus window, tallying the distance, the wires swooping him on from point to point, back to his empty house. She had not been a good wife, even at the beginning. He knew of one affair and suspected others. She was selfish and base, and he was a fool, and between them that had been the best that they could do.

His head hurt where he had bumped it on the bunk bed. He leaned the lump against the cool bus window.

12. Comfortable, understandable

*B*ecause of the crowded schedule, Lorraine's chemo couldn't begin until Tuesday. Darwin wheeled her around the halls while they waited for her chemo training session. For an adventure they explored the fourth floor, the osteo ward: unfamiliar peach walls, and more art. This hospital was big on art.

"Can you believe the death pictures?" she asked. "Little plaques beside them: *in memory of Grampa, with thanks for the life of Myra…* They creep me out. There's one on my floor where the boy is fishing with a ghostly grandfather beside him, all whited-out, smiling at the boy like he's going to pat his head. Or maybe drink his blood."

"I saw that one," Darwin said. "It's just a print. Must be thousands of them, hung around hospital wards all over depressing the hell out of everybody."

They trundled past patients trying to walk, mostly old. A woman close to Lorraine's age kept her eyes weirdly still, her whole face turning as she used her walker. She gave them a beautiful smile. Lorraine knew that same beauty hung in her own smile now, in her eyes. Bad trouble makes you feel loving, she thought. Nine days ago she'd been crying in the Dart because she could not find Darwin.

Back in Lorraine's room, a crop-haired, athletic nurse popped her head in the door.

"You're here. Great. So! I'm going to go through what you can expect from chemotherapy," she said brightly. Her nametag said Nola. She fanned a set of pamphlets on the rolling table and pulled over a straight chair.

Lorraine shut her eyes for a minute. She couldn't stand to hear this. Darwin was listening, he would tell her about it later. Phrases fell through the air, names of chemicals, T-cell types, crashing around her like thin, thin glass, like the first film of ice on the puddles on a northern morning. Her boots crinkling through the delicate half-formed panes. Darwin was absolutely still beside her, the root of the world grown up through the floor.

The nurse was practical, not frightening. "Chemotherapy affects tissues with a high rate of cell division, like cancer cells: the lining of the mouth, the lining of the intestines, the skin, and the hair follicles. That's why hair falls out with some kinds of chemotherapy, and why it grows back again very nicely."

Lorraine felt her hair hanging heavy between her shoulder blades. She saw a quick flashing slide: Clayton turning her hair like a rope around his hand and wrist, on the porch in Trimalo, just before Trevor was born. She remembered the night sky, and her full belly pressing her down. Clayton's hand with his bitten nails twining and catching her hair.

"We've made some real improvements in treatment for nausea," the nurse said. "It's possible to go through chemo nowadays without the violent reactions you've seen in movies."

I bet, Lorraine thought. I bet it'll be a fucking picnic.

The other patient in her room came back—a furious young woman in a wheelchair, maybe twenty-five, and bitter. Her husband or boyfriend rolled her in. She stared at the nurse with scorching eyes, hardly blinking, burned down to a bright coal of rage. Try not to be like that, Lorraine told herself.

The woman snapped, "Get me out of here." The man dipped his head apologetically at the nurse and Lorraine as he swung the wheelchair around.

Maybe fury was a way of staying upright under this weight.

When they'd gone, the nurse said, "You don't want to get into the trap of blaming yourself for having brought this on by unhealthy thinking. But I've seen a lot of patients going through a lot of treatment, and here's one true thing about attitude: you can make the process easier on yourself. If you are angry or in despair you're going to have a harder time in the next few months. If you can manage to find some solace—whatever works, exercise or meditation or religion—and a sense of humour, the process will be easier. And we'll make it as comfortable and understandable as we can."

Comfortable and understandable. Lorraine's head was drumming. She went deaf, she receded from the room. She could hear blood pouring and pulsing through her veins. Darwin put his hand on her neck, cupping the nape of her neck in his warm hand, and she breathed more calmly.

The nurse looked at the paper for some length of time, then up into Lorraine's eyes. "Yours will be in-patient, twelve-hour drips, eight sessions."

She paused. *Nola, Nola,* her nametag flashed, because her chest was moving with her breath. "My father had non-Hodgkins lymphoma last year." She looked on the other side of the sheet, maybe needing the time to get her calm voice back. "It will be a long process."

Lorraine nodded. No need to go on, the pale father hovering in the air all around them. Nola nodded back.

"Good," she said.

She shoved her chair back and went off, no doubt to give the good news to others.

"That was good, what she said, making it easier on yourself," Lorraine said. Trying.

"Cheerful attitude won't change what they do to you," Darwin said. "You'll still have to do this."

He smiled at her though, because he loved her, and that was a help. In a shaky place, she could see that.

103

13. Doughnuts

*L*orraine was looking well, Clara thought.

"I'm a vampire," she said when she saw Clara at the door on Wednesday morning. She laughed, but there was a shadow of panic on her blooming face. "*Bride of Dracula.* Look at my skin! You can't buy creams for this, they ought to sell it. *Fresh blood, prices slashed!* They could pay for medicare. I keep thinking, what if we'd been in the States? We'd of been toast. There are charity hospitals though, like on *ER*—you don't see them turning people away at the sliding doors, do you? Maybe they get thrown out when they get taken upstairs, like my roommate. Like the red shirts on Star Trek, they're toast too. Rubber hospital toast."

She waggled the limp toast from her breakfast back and forth to show Clara.

Clara's first job was always to calm her down, lately. "I brought some buns from Mrs. Zenko. She tells me they're made of organic wheat, and she grinds her own flour."

"Oh goodie, I can hardly wait."

"She sent soup, too." Gleaming red and gold, Ukrainian Orthodox borsch with no meat in it. As Lorraine rotated the sealer jar in her long pale fingers, ruby cubes of beets shone and receded; dill splayed feathery against the glass, then floated off.

"Pretty kind of her for someone she's never met."

"She likes the children." And she's met Mrs. Pell, Clara didn't say.

Without warning Lorraine burst into difficult, tearing sobs. "The chemo is so hard, it's harder than I thought. My white cells were down so far they couldn't find any to count. And they had to give me blood. The nurses won't talk, and you know what that means, they want the doctor to do the dirty work."

She let her head fall back on the pillows and pulled the jar of soup to her chest. Clara made herself listen, not jump up to make it better. There was no better.

"I wish Clayton was here," Lorraine said, the first time she'd mentioned him to Clara. She continued to cry, the tears spilling vertically down her tilted cheeks and off onto the stiff sheets, almost making noise when they landed.

Clara sat still, a flurry of what she should have done fluttering in her ears, making her pulse race. She'd done the wrong thing, not talking about Clayton, not letting Lorraine know he was gone, so she could try to trace him. Now it would be too late.

Lorraine had stopped crying, it seemed. She might have fallen asleep. Clara leaned forward and took the jar of soup. No reaction.

Lorraine's eyes were closed, thin lids resting over those slightly-protruding eyes, her mouth slack. Clara felt so deeply sorry for her that for a moment she could not move, even to lean back. She was wracked with sharp pain in her abdomen and knew that it was for her mother's dreadful, clawing death, not very long before, at this same hospital. In the same yellow sheets, and as close as Lorraine was now. As far away.

Mrs. Zenko's empty house was not perfectly quiet. The fridge was making a whirring noise, and there was a radio on somewhere, playing swingy music.

Dolly stood on the back step, waiting to hear if Mrs. Zenko was not really out but busy somewhere inside, even though she had seen her walking off to the store with her yellow wheeled basket. Mrs. Zenko's car stayed in the garage unless she had to drive a long way like to her son's in Battleford. She liked to walk. It kept her going, she said.

Dolly already knew Mrs. Zenko's kitchen—her cleaning bucket, her cooking bowls, the plastic containers in their orderly drawers. But there was the desk in the living room, and the bedrooms. Everything was so clean, and almost empty over the polished floors. It was a nice airy house to roam around in. The desk drawer held pictures of her children and a letter from her husband who was dead now. Dolly read the first three lines and then she put it back because she liked Mrs. Zenko. Then she felt so holy and proud that she went zooming down the hall to Mrs. Zenko's bedroom and opened and closed all the drawers in there, checking. The tops of the dressers were stacked high with a thousand folded sweaters. Mrs. Zenko said her daughters gave her sweaters because she was always a little cold. The one Dolly liked best was white with big flap sleeves like wings that were meant to cross over, and a little tie belt. The small jewellery dresser on top of the clothes dresser had square sections of wood inside it, each holding one ring. She loved rings. Maybe when Mrs. Zenko died she would leave Dolly her rings in her will. She probably had to leave them to her daughters though. Dolly closed the drawers, leaving every ring exactly where it had been, because she would hate Mrs. Zenko to know that she had been snooping in her house. The thought made her stomach turn over, in fact, and without even looking in the bathroom Dolly headed for the back door.

But Mrs. Zenko came in the front.

"Hello, Dolly," she said, and laughed; Dolly did not know why. "Well, hello, Dolly," she said again, kind of singing.

"Hello," Dolly said back.

"Checking out my house, little mousekin?"

Dolly nodded.

"Find any surprises?"

Dolly shook her head. Mrs. Zenko left the yellow cart and put her arm around her. "You look through here any time," she said. "This is your place too, just like Clary's. Are you hungry?"

Dolly felt a big space opening at the back of her nose, and hoped that was not the beginning of crying. "I guess," she said. "Can Trevor have some too?"

Mrs. Zenko was already opening the fridge and pulling out a cookie box. "We'll run over and see how he and Pearce are doing, and have a picnic in the back yard."

It was all bad news. The doctor came in with Darwin while Clara was still there, and she stayed to listen. Mrs. Zenko would keep one eye on the children from next door. They were fine.

Lorraine was not. She sat very still while the doctor talked. He was casual, golf-shirted, a communicator, and he sat on the end of the bed with his hand on Lorraine's leg. Not that any amount of bedside empathy could really help. The counts were bad, he admitted, but they would be watching with interest as the chemo progressed. They were going to continue the blood transfusions every couple of days.

Lorraine looked straight at the doctor while he talked. She did not scowl or tremble, but Clara could hardly bear to look at her absorbed, serious face.

Darwin stood by the window, listening as calmly as Lorraine. They were good at sloughing off emotion when it wasn't needed, Clara thought. Everyone in this ward was like that, became like that. Clara's father's oncologist had said she loved working with cancer patients, because they and their families were all at their absolute best, in extremity.

The doctor gave Lorraine's leg a last kind squeeze, and left them.

"Well, that's scary," Lorraine said.

Darwin sat on the window ledge.

Clara wanted to list the reasons why it was nothing to worry about, but her whole head was enveloped in a white fog. She knew nothing, none of the experience she'd gained by going with her mother and father through illness had done any good.

Lorraine looked at Clara. "I feel pretty bad," she said.

"We'll be here. We'll be with you," Darwin said.

"I'm afraid to see the kids," Lorraine said. "I don't want to freak them out."

"It's not going to scare Pearce," Darwin said. "He'll just be happy."

Clara's heart swooped down. It wasn't the bringing Pearce in; he'd be ecstatic to see Lorraine. It was the taking him home afterwards, screaming with disappointment and frustration; and the smell of him in the room, and Lorraine's horrifying sadness.

"It'll be okay," Darwin said. "Bring them all."

Lorraine's eyes, shining dark in their big hollows, filled Clara's vision all the way home.

Trevor was silent when Clara told them they were going to visit his mom. He hadn't seen her for two weeks. Even Pearce went silent, as if by osmosis from Trevor and Dolly. Or else it was Clara passing along her own panic. She must not do that. Instead she made everything normal. She fed them, she insisted on brushed teeth and washed hands, and she laid out clean clothes for Trevor and Dolly before she went to change Pearce.

Her hands were shaking as she slid the diapers into the new diaper bag, which of course she would give to Lorraine, when Lorraine could take the children back—when they moved into some reasonable-rent apartment, here in Saskatoon, until they could find Clayton, wherever he'd gone off to, and until Clara could find Lorraine some work, and get Mrs. Pell on the old age pension, and give Lorraine back her life.

She had to stop for a moment to blow her nose and sit on the edge of her bed, all of her shaking, not just her hands. Pearce pulled himself up by the crib bars and stood watching her seriously. She stopped crying, and he gave her a giant smile and banged with his hand on the railing. Shouting *"Yah!"* at the top of his lungs.

Dolly came in, dressed in the clean pants and top. "Do I look okay?" she asked.

Clara turned to her drawer and found the bracelet with the beads from that first day. "This will make the outfit," she said. "I meant to give it to you before."

Dolly stared at her, and Clara worried that she'd made the visit more ominous.

"No big deal," she said quickly, turning away to lift Pearce out of the crib. "It's a little young for me, I think."

Mrs. Pell's door had been closed since lunch, and Clara didn't feel any need to tell her where they were going. She left a note on the kitchen table: *Back by supper-time.* It was good to have her own car back from the body shop, the car seat holder firmly attached to the tether-peg which they had installed while she waited that morning. Pearce stared out the window in what looked like ecstasy, patting Trevor's hand on the edge of the baby seat.

By the time they parked at the hospital Clara felt sick. She couldn't even guess how frightened the children were. She said to Dolly and Trevor, "It can be hard to visit someone you love in the hospital. You want them to come home and be with you, and you want to stay with them, and you're happy to see them, and sad about everything."

"One thing people do is, they bring people presents," Dolly said.

They spent ten minutes picking out flowers in the hospital store. On the way out, Trevor found a stuffed pterodactyl like his own, but much larger.

"This is the mother," he told Clara. She bought it.

There was no fighting over who would press the elevator button, no unruly jumping, no chatter. When they got to the fifth floor, Clara was the first one out of the elevator, and had to hold the door for them. In the hall they paused. Dolly put her hand carefully on the wooden hand-rail, and took Trevor's hand in her other one.

"Look," she said. "It's for people not to get lost when they're going back."

Darwin came to meet them, his big face peaceful, and Clara handed Pearce over to him. "You take them in," she said. "I'll run down and get some juice."

He gave her arm an oddly tender pat. "Got to be done," he said.

She nodded. Trevor and Dolly had already pressed up against Lorraine's bed, burrowing into her arms.

Down in the cafeteria Clara bought a paper and did the crossword. When her father was dying in this hospital she had brought it up for him every morning: the front section, business section and crossword, carefully folded, ready to work. The first order of each day.

Walking through the line for coffee, Paul Tippett saw Clara sitting all alone. She looked like a woman in a Hopper painting, he thought, like she hadn't slept since 1943. No wonder. Since he himself did not expect to be sleeping for a while, he felt enough kinship to sit down at her table without asking permission.

"How is Lorraine?"

"Oh—hello," Clara said, as if she couldn't dredge up his name. "I was in a daze, I'm sorry. The children are here. I don't know how they'll—" She stopped.

"Children's defences are strong," he said, to help her. "The world consoles them."

Those were not the words he'd meant to say, and not very useful.

"They like their bunk beds," Clara said, smiling.

What a soft cheek she had. The children must love her. He was very pleased that he had helped with those beds. As he went off to the second floor he felt happier than he had in days. Her deep blue sweater or jacket, whatever it was, he loved that indigo hue. He stayed an extra half hour with Joe Kane— his oldest and least likeable parishioner, and Candy Vincent's uncle.

Left alone, but less alone than she had been, Clara bought apples and cookies and went back up, glad to have given them some privacy. They weren't her family; she had shoved her oar in enough. But when she got upstairs they were all delighted to see her. Well, of course. She was always glad to see that Mrs. Zenko had a dish in her hands at the door. It was nothing to sneeze at, bringing the food.

Lorraine looked up from the magazine she was reading with Dolly. "*Celebrity Babes, Celebrity Babies*," she said, grinning with her slightly disarranged teeth, her very attractive smile. Dolly lay beside her; Trevor sat on Darwin's lap with his new shoes up on the bed, and Pearce was fast asleep at his mother's feet, bordered by two pillows and the bowed shape of her calves under the sheet. His mouth was open above his tilted chin, his arms raised above his head as if, at last, he could surrender to sleep.

"No celebrity baby is as nice as ours, eh, Dolly?"

Dolly's forehead rubbed against her mother's shoulder.

Clara could have cried, for how at home they all were, how much at ease, how everything she'd worked for had been useless. They would never be happy with her. Nothing but their own mother would do.

Lorraine said, "Pull up a chair, Clary. The kids said they would beg you to go get fried chicken for supper, but I said no, no, you're eating good now, I can see how healthy you are."

Trying to make her more comfortable, and that should not be her job.

"I notice you didn't bring Mom Pell," Lorraine said, making *Thank God* eyes at Clara.

"If she'd of come, we'd of been late," Dolly said.

Trevor said, "Waddle, waddle, waddle."

Nobody else laughed, so Clara didn't either. But she looked in Darwin's direction and saw that he had pulled his hat right down over his whole face, and was leaning back on the windowsill, in some silent spasm of laughter.

Lorraine's eyes were bright as black jet; but her skin was looking much paler than it had that morning. Clara sobered.

"The nurses reminded me that we shouldn't stay too long," she said, being the bad guy.

But Lorraine seemed glad she'd said it. "Yeah, you guys have to go get supper on your own, mine will be arriving soon and you'll eat it all if you're still here. And I need to keep my strength up."

Trevor and Dolly were easy to dislodge—they'd had a solid hour to lounge around. The room was almost boring again. Their mother was there, still there. They had been refreshed.

Darwin stood up, taller than she'd remembered. "Come on, you kids," he said, as if he was a stern man. "I'll walk you to the car."

Trevor and Dolly kissed Lorraine and went after Darwin to the door. "We'll take the stairs, get some exercise," he told Clara, giving her time to pry Pearce away. Giving Lorraine peace to be pried apart in.

After they were gone Lorraine shifted her feet under the sheet, her long legs. "Do you think you can take him without waking him?"

"No," Clara said. "Not a chance." She sat on the bed and began the long process of easing her hand under the sleeping boy.

"Thanks," Lorraine said, sitting up straighter. "I needed to see them, I should have asked for them before."

"It went very well. Nobody seemed to be upset."

"Nope. Except me."

"Is it bad?"

Lorraine stared at her, the bright eyes subdued. Black pearls, not jet, now.

"I have a feeling like a big hand," she said. "On a long arm, a hand coming from inside me, reaching around inside..."

Clara stayed listening.

Lorraine shook her head. "I can't say what it's like."

They sat silent.

"Well, the kids'll be down at the car by now. You'd better get going."

"I *can* go, because Darwin will be back up in a few minutes. You won't be alone."

"Yeah, isn't that the greatest?" Lorraine lit up again. "When we were little, we shared a room—I used to tell him stories at night. Now he tells me."

Clara slid her forearm under Pearce and picked him up, willing him to stay asleep. He did. She folded him up against her chest, and his fist came to rest on her neck.

"See you tomorrow. Do you want the children again tomorrow?"

Lorraine's face was dulled, quiet. "I'm sleepy," she said, not answering.

When Clara was almost out the door, Lorraine said, "Not tomorrow. But soon."

Darwin came home before the children went to bed, Lorraine asleep already. He had brought Timbits, assorted. The jelly ones, the tiny perfect jelly dough-nuts, made Clara cry. Because they were so perfect and Lorraine was dying. She had salt in her mouth and powdery, dissolving sweetness.

Dolly climbed on Darwin's lap, and then Trevor, and they both had a good time crying, but it would not last. Like the pleasure of doughnuts only lasts for a second. Icing sugar is like cocaine must be, Clara imagined. Lighter than air, filmier than dust, frail delight. Even if there were fifty she might keep eating them, she thought, weakly happy to see the children dusted with sugar, little puffs of strawberry jam spilling out, bright inside the cushion of sweet.

"My mother used to make doughnuts," she said to Darwin. She laughed to hear herself telling this, a sweet memory of her mother. "She made *orange* doughnuts, bubbles of dough with orange peel in them, and she iced them with orange icing!"

Remembering the orange doughnuts made her happy, and then of course sad, and the smell of the oil cooking in the kitchen, and how short a time the pleasure of the doughnuts lasts, but how long the oil smell lingers…

Clara shook her head as if she had been drinking, or was too tired to drive; she slapped her cheek to wake herself up. The children were staring at her. "What?" she asked. Darwin stared too, even Mrs. Pell. "There's nothing wrong! I'm just—"

She laid her head down on the kitchen table and sobbed. What a relief to cry out loud.

In the bedroom she could hear Pearce starting to cry. Now look what she'd done. She cried some more. Mrs. Pell lumbered up and went off to the bedroom.

Waddle, waddle, waddle, Clara thought, and a doughnut of laughter came bubbling up into her mouth and out, and she laughed at the children and Darwin still watching her. She leaned back in her chair, feeling much better. She was pretty sure that Mrs. Pell wasn't giving Pearce more Benadryl.

"I think I'm a little over-tired," she said. She couldn't keep a straight face, her mouth had to go up or down. "You never get a whole night's sleep, you know."

He nodded.

"You're listening even while you're asleep," she said, amazed that she could do it.

"Yeah, that's what it's like."

"How do *you* know?"

"I have a kid. A boy, he's sixteen now. Same birthday as Trev."

"I'm five." Trevor said from under the kitchen table. He had slid down to see if any doughnuts had fallen.

"Yeah, he's a little older."

"Phelan is his name," Dolly told Clara. "It means like a wolf."

"His mom picked it," Darwin said, grinning. "New Age, eh? They live out by Tofino, in a commune. No wolves there though."

Clary wondered, with half-drunk concentration, why she liked him, anyway. His ordinary, responsive face—too wide and smooth with healed scars. Laughing at her over there. His eyes were like Lorraine's. How transitory his life must be, that he could drop everything and come for her.

Coming back with Pearce, Mrs. Pell knocked the box of doughnuts off the table. Only a few rolled out, and Dolly picked the box up carefully so no more spilled. Mrs. Pell shrieked like a train when Trevor tried to eat one he dusted off from the floor.

"Why is it different now?" he asked her.

"It's different! That's enough for you to know!"

"I don't want it different, I want it the same." Trevor was almost going to cry again.

Clara would have liked to interrupt but his grandmother had a right to talk to him, more right than she did. She took the baby and checked his heavy bottom while Mrs. Pell ground on.

113

"*Everything* gets different, your whole life will be one thing and another to get used to. Nothing will ever be the same as it was two weeks ago."

"But that's the good thing," Darwin said. He pulled Trevor up on his lap again. "If it was all the same, it would just be boring. We would be begging for change."

"No begging," Trevor repeated. His eyes had gone slanted, in the way that Clara associated with dogs, when they were thinking like a pack. No begging for change.

14. Green door

*W*hen Clara woke up and couldn't remember what day of the week it was, she decided it was time to pull herself together. It was Thursday, 7:30. In the new life.

She had to go in to the office.

Pearce was still sleeping, head tilted back, mouth open. She hopped quietly out of bed—hoping the outward semblance of energy would create energy within, like goodness—showered in three minutes, then got Pearce up and fed him breakfast: mashed sweet potato for the first time. Mrs. Pell stayed in bed till noon these days, so she couldn't disapprove.

He loved the sweet potato; Clara fed him more. He put a grateful hand on her cheek and banged his spoon strongly in between mouthfuls. She loved his bowl in her hand, the rabbit bowl that had been her baby dish, and how well it fit in her capable palm.

Trevor and Dolly, tired after their visit to Lorraine, were content to sit shielding their eyes from the sunlight darting through the kitchen curtains. While they ate, Clara got herself properly dressed—usually, these days, she pulled on jeans the minute she got out of bed, in case Darwin might roam in from the hospital. Pearce stood joggling in his crib, seeming to like her in her

115

underwear. She found her good fawn suit and the Amalfi pumps, polished in their shoe-slot. Like old times. How many days since she'd worn lipstick? Lack of sleep was no excuse.

Dolly was tying Trevor's shoes in the doorway. Clara hoisted Pearce farther up on her shoulder, searched through the hall closet for her good briefcase, and found it. What an efficient morning. Pearce coughed against her shoulder.

She said, hearing with satisfaction her calm, motherly voice, "Don't fuss, sweetheart!"

But Dolly said, "Clary…"

Then she could feel how warm her shoulder was. She turned slightly to see it in the hall mirror, a fall of curdled sweet potato dripping down her back. Fury rose like a fountain in her chest, up, up—

Trevor began to cry.

Clara looked at the empty wall. It had been years since she'd felt her own temper.

"It's all right," she said to Trevor, when she was sure she wouldn't shout. "I can change."

At least Pearce had kept his own clothes clean, leaning over Clara. She buckled him into the car seat waiting by the door, and mopped first his mouth and then the floor. Dolly was crying too.

"You sit here with Pearce for a minute, okay, Trevor? " He squatted down obediently. "Dolly, come help me find something clean."

She tossed the jacket into the dry-cleaning bag. "I hate that suit, anyway," she told Dolly. "Makes me look like a prissy old lady. You find something better."

Through her tears Dolly picked out a yellowish Chanel knock-off. "And this," she said, dragging the violet shirt off its hanger, the one Clara always thought of as Easter Parade. But she had contracted for Dolly's opinion.

"Why are you crying?" Clara asked as she zipped the skirt.

Dolly thought Clary looked nice. "Pearce spitting up, that's what he did on my—when we were going to find Darwin, but we couldn't find him. But now we did."

"That's good, isn't it? Your mother is so happy to have him with her."

If they weren't down there by eleven, Clara knew, Barrett would be gone for lunch, which would mean all afternoon. She hustled the children out the door and into the car, and as she was getting in herself Darwin drove up in his pea-green beater. He looked exhausted.

She waited to speak to him. "A bad night?"

"Good to be there. She was dreaming, or maybe delirious, for a while."

"Did she ask for Clayton?"

"Don't worry, I told her. She'd figured it out anyway. She's grateful to you, what you're doing. She's working hard, right? No time for being mad."

Clara nodded.

"You off for an outing?"

"I've got to catch my boss to explain what's going on."

He laughed. "What are you going to say?"

Dolly got out of the car to give Darwin a leaping hug, and stayed leaning against him, twining one thin leg around his knees. Clara didn't think she should discuss it in front of her. Besides, she had not exactly worked it out.

"Something will come to me," she said, with a giddy, holiday feeling. "He's been kind to me, over the years. He'll be horrified."

"But you have the right on your side." Darwin said. "And you look good."

His easy assumption of friendship was obscurely flattering. It was good to have people around to like. She was not used to that. Her mother's social rigour had kept them mostly alone. "Have a good sleep," she said, pretending to be as comradely as he was, and left him to climb the steps.

She had to park far down the street from Gilman-Stott. They straggled back in the gritty breeze, colder than it had looked that morning. She wished she had a stroller to pop Pearce into. Catching the full glory of her yellow and purple outfit in the double glass doors she almost turned around. But she'd just have to bring them all back again.

Before hauling open the door, she said, "In an office, people are trying to concentrate—like a library, or a church. I need you to stay beside me, and please try to be quiet. Of course if you need to ask me something, do, but let's see how quiet we can be."

Sometimes when she spoke to the children she felt like an unimaginably old and inflexible librarian, all wrong for this job. They stared back at her with scared eyes, not even understanding that they should say, *Yes, we'll be good.* Oh well, she thought. It'll be interesting for them to see an office.

Mat was at her desk, her throne. Evie the office manager, always easy to deal with, would be in Hawaii by now. Too bad. Mat gave a lady-like squawk and shook her iron hair when she saw Clara.

"You're back!" Then she registered the children. "Now!" she said. "This would be?"

"First, Mat, has Barrett gone for lunch? I need to talk to him."

"You'll be lucky to catch him before he hares out the back."

Clara grabbed Dolly's hand, and hoisted Pearce higher. She seemed to have become a creature with four heads and extra legs. Trevor was dragging on her jacket.

"Come, children," she said, hearing her own voice sounding fake. She steered them along through the corridor of brown fabric half-walls to the real wall at the back, and Barrett's office.

He was putting on his affected green blazer, one arm halfway through a sleeve when he saw her. It seemed like he would speak, but nothing came out. He stared at the baby, face like a baby himself.

"Hello, Barrett," Clara said, carefully businesslike. "Could I have a minute?"

She bent down to Dolly and Trevor. "See the table with the magazines?" They nodded. "I need you to sit for five minutes while I talk to Mr. Gilman. I won't shut the door, you'll be able to see me. Okay?"

Dolly nodded, since she could see she had to. She pulled Trevor's arm to sit beside her. There were magazines, but they were all business stuff, nothing Dolly or Trevor could even glance at.

From her chair, Dolly could still see Clary. The fat guy sat down in the working chair behind the desk. He was old, with lots of grey hair and grey eyebrows like bug antennas growing towards each other. He waggled his finger at Pearce, not close enough for Pearce to bother to reach for it. She could see Clary leaning forward slightly, talking quietly, probably so that she and Trevor wouldn't hear. Clary's pretty feet looked nice in those toffee-coloured high heels. Maybe she didn't want the other people in the office to listen in.

The pink-eraser-mouth lady from by the door was standing at the filing cabinet by the guy's door, but she wasn't looking at the files.

Trevor started to hum, and Dolly jerked his hand again so he'd shut up.

"Absolutely impossible," the guy said in a louder voice. Then he quieted down.

Maybe they wouldn't let her go. The guy stood up. His face was all red. Clary spoke again, but still Dolly couldn't see her lips, which would have made it easier. Dolly didn't actually want to hear what Clary was saying, if she was saying things about Dolly's mother and how sick she was. But she needed to know, to have data. She walked slowly to stand beside the lady still listening by the file drawer, who stared at her for a minute with eyes like nails, and then ignored her.

Inside the office, Clara's heart was pounding. Once, at a Christmas party, Barrett had kissed her. This was almost worse.

"If a leave is impossible, I'll have to quit," she said. "But I'd rather not. I'll need to come back to work eventually, and this is where I'd like to be."

He sat down again, giving up, terribly disappointed by her irrationality.

"You know I value your advice," she said, picking her way. "But in this case, there's no room for advice. I don't have a choice."

"You didn't take leave when your own mother was dying!"

"She was surrounded by friends and a day nurse, and she had no small children." She had let frost into her voice, but it wouldn't help to alienate him. "Naturally I'm not asking for paid leave…"

"This is not your family, Clara, that's what troubles me. You don't owe these people anything."

These people. Pearce clutched her side, sliding on the blouse under her jacket, his little fist tightening to keep her with him. "It's my responsibility. Whether real or imagined doesn't matter."

"Another question, Clara, is your legal liability, which I believe enters into serious jeopardy when you take in these random strangers in as if you were *guilty* of something. Should you be exposing yourself to this kind of—" Overcome, Barrett choked, and started to cough, and the cough went on and on. He pawed at the desk for a Kleenex, and she pushed the box across.

"When I retire," he started, and of course he was going to talk about succession.

"It's not nearly time for that," she said, slipping into his sentence. "If you can't hold my job for me, fine. I just wanted you to know that it's not the work, or your management."

But it was, and she couldn't believe that she hadn't seen it before: the mind-numbing work, and his slack, self-satisfied management—it was to Gilman-Stott that she didn't owe anything. This felt like the recess bell suddenly ringing, like a green door opening in a brick wall.

Barrett leaned back in his fat executive leather chair, spent.

"I'll come in on Friday and sort through my files, and Mat has everything at her fingertips." (Mat would be listening at the door in her usual post—give her a plug.) "You might consider that woman from Biggar who came in last winter. She was looking for a move to Saskatoon." And she'd known how to deal with Barrett.

"Are you trying to ruin yourself?" Barrett seemed to be asking her from genuine worry, and she relented a little.

"I'm trying to mend myself," she said, without much hope that he'd believe her.

He pulled a face, like she'd said something socially inept.

"I'm being told what to do by the Holy Spirit, Barrett."

He stared at her, appalled.

She laughed out loud, as freely as she'd ever laughed in her life. "Not really! I'm just guessing."

Outside Barrett's door, Trevor said, "Clary?"

He sounded worried, it was time to go. She got up in a fluid rush, happy from her head to her feet, and turned to the door with Pearce twisting in her arms, searching for landmarks. She showed him Trevor huddled beside Dolly at the door. How the children threw the buff and brown into shadow—how their faces glowed in this drab hall!

Mat stood frozen at the filing cabinet.

"Come along," Clary said gently to the children. "Mat, you cope with him."

Mat nodded. One corner of her matte pink mouth lifted in her warmest smile. Clary tightened her grip on Pearce to carry him safely through the tangle of half-walls. Dolly and Trevor followed close behind like Hansel and Gretel, not wanting to be lost in this cloth and metal forest.

Outside, Clary realized what she'd done: she'd quit her job. Barrett would never take her back after she'd flouted his advice and laughed at him, the gasping fish. She should have quit years ago—her mother's money was sitting there, and the money from the store, what was she saving it for? She leaned against the car doing math, counting GICs, cashing in term deposits. She could certainly take a year off.

But everything was so expensive. They walked up the street to the shoe store and found baby shoes for Pearce, so he could walk around the house and practice. Another $30. Well, she'd cut back on her donation to the Anglican World Relief Fund. She would relieve the world right here.

15. Holy the fair

*T*hey weren't allowed to visit their mom these days because she was having too rough a time with the chemo. Dolly had a block in her chest, like a peachstone stuck halfway down, that stopped her from eating or drinking very much or from doing anything but thinking the same words repeated: *make her well, well, well.* Whenever anybody said *well, well,* her dad would always say *Deep thoughts.* But Dolly had blanked him out of her mind too, along with everything else.

Instead of thinking, she went out. She pretended to go to the basement, but really she'd slip out the back and away down the alley, looking for some sliding patio door open in the late summer heat. In one wide-open house she wandered around in bare feet while the lady was having a bath, singing away in the bathroom. It was a nice place, white and pink, more modern than most of these houses. But not what she was looking for, whatever that was exactly. Money, if it was safe. A house they could live in, maybe.

The apartments behind 8th Street, those would do. Poor apartments, Dolly could tell: ugly, three stories high, no balconies, looking out onto parking lots with old cars parked close up beside them in the alley, some of the windows covered with tinfoil—that meant people worked nights. The money in Mrs. Bunt's bear would be enough for sure. No point in taking it though until her mom was out of the hospital. If that would ever be.

She should think about it, about what they would do if their mom died. For a moment Dolly stood still in the alley, letting her mind roam down into the bottom of her brain where it lurked, her mom dying. It made tears leak out of her eyes even before she felt sad. Her heart fell down farther than usual into her stomach, to some root down there that she didn't want to touch. She gave up and walked on, but it was like she'd turned on a tap that wouldn't turn off. Tears kept trickling out. Her crotch hurt, because thinking about her mom—about it, about it—was too dangerous.

She'd go into a store, even though she didn't have any money. There was no way she was shoplifting, it was too easy to get caught, like Gran. She didn't want stuff, anyway, she wanted not to think, wandering down this dusty grey back-world of garbage bins. At the corner of the alley stood a used book store, Key's Books. She could dawdle through there for a while, you were allowed to browse in bookstores.

It was not a normal store, it was an old house half-turned into a store. The walls where the living room and dining room would have been were lined with teetering shelves of musty, crammed old books, red and brown and blue. The kitchen cupboards still hung, full to bursting, with books shoving open the doors. Everything was dusty, and there were no customers.

A huge old man sat at a grimy computer, almost hidden behind book-stacks teetering all over a kitchen table. Books piled under the table too. He waved a foot-sized hand toward the archway and said, "More back there. Kids' books upstairs."

Because of the shape of the rooms it was like sneaking into a house, but a dream house, a bookhouse. Rickety shelves climbed to the ceiling in every room and crowded down the middles. In the kids' books room Dolly sat on the floor under the dirty window, in what had once been the bathroom. You could still see where the bathtub had been ripped out. Before she looked up she had read half an old paperback called *The Children Who Lived in a Barn*, about a girl who looked after her brothers and sisters when their parents disappeared and they had no money.

But she had no money either. She had to go, supper would be ready and Clary would notice if she was late. She unfolded herself—one leg was asleep—and went down the creaking stairs on her sparkling foot, sad to leave that whole room of books. The old guy who owned the store looked at her like she was shoplifting. She only had a T-shirt on, no jacket. He could see she didn't have anywhere to put a book.

"Thank you," she said, like Clary said when they were leaving a store but they hadn't bought anything. "You have some very nice books here."

The old guy turned suddenly mean. He shouted, "Rich kids, no goddamn idea!"

He thought she was rich because Clary looked after them now. It made her laugh, secretly, and he saw that, and yelled at her some more: "You don't read! You haven't read a book in your life. Bookstores are going out of business all over—you think you can sit and watch TV and that's all it takes. You walk around in a bookstore and by osmosis, you've read something!"

What did he think she'd been doing up there for an hour, except reading?

"If you cleaned the place up and sorted your books maybe you'd sell some," Dolly said in a reasonable voice.

The old guy was not reasonable, though. "That's it. *That's it!*" he shouted. He got up, his head almost up to the ceiling.

Dolly looked at him and thought she might get hurt. She made for the door, and he followed, wide as a yardstick, faster than Trevor. Dolly got a good scare. She ran out the door and half-slid down the stairs to the sidewalk, hoping the little book shoved down the back of her pants didn't show. He filled the frame of the door, white hair crackling around his head, still threatening her. But she was just a little girl! He was crazy! It made her laugh, for a second, and before she could stop herself she stuck out her tongue and blew a fart noise at him.

"Oh, that's mature," he cried in triumph.

She ran around the corner, deked to the right through a different alley to hide her real direction in case he was following her, and then booted it all the way to Clary's.

Safe at home, she hid the *Barn* book under her mattress, and made herself wake up really early in the mornings to read it. It was the best book she had ever read. In the end their parents came back. They were not dead after all.

For the three weeks of chemo Darwin was at the hospital most of the time. Every day, Clary brought a jar of Mrs. Zenko's broth and watched the hospital staff dealing with Lorraine's fever and anemia, treating suspected infections, puzzling over bone marrow aspirations. Clary tried to erase it all from her mind when she went home, so the children would not see the pity she still carried. They were subdued and unhappy anyway, in need of distraction, and in a flash of good sense Clary phoned to ask her cousin Grace's daughter to visit.

Fern was back living with her parents out by Davina. Moreland drove her in and stayed for a quick coffee. As they came in, Mrs. Pell lurched up from the kitchen table and went out through the dining room archway, unobtrusively carting her sandwich along with her. Clary could not be impatient with her—an old woman, purple around the ankles, who had been hungry for a long time.

Fern brought her suitcase in from the truck, not letting Moreland do it for her. She was angry with her parents, blaming them for her life in Davina. Not that they had asked her to come back after university, but Fern had been disappointed in love in her last year, and she hadn't known where else to go with her wounded pride. Everyone in Davina knew all about it, but at least they hadn't seen his beautiful face, hadn't seen him walking out on her with that tender, long-lipped smile, that wide gazey way of lifting his eyebrows, to say *Where's the surprise? You knew what I was like.*

A couple of weeks' work would do her good, according to Grace. "Take her mind off her own drama," was how she'd put it, but Clary made automatic allowance for Grace's attempt to balance Fern's emotional excess with her own level-headedness. To Clary it seemed that Fern was still in pretty rough shape. Her thin skin looked raw, and she wouldn't make eye contact. Shame destroys us, Clary thought, and led her to the bathroom.

"No room at the inn," she said, opening the linen closet where she'd cleared a shelf. "Your things can go here. I'm afraid you're sleeping on the living-room sofa—I'm very grateful that you can help out."

"It's okay," Fern muttered, then added like a teenager, like she couldn't stop herself, "Whatever."

"Are you applying for pharmacy work this year?" Clary asked, and then wished she hadn't. "Or will you go back to cutting hair?" Even worse. Fern looked up and stared at her, as if politely not believing her ears that Clary could have asked such an insensitive question.

"Well, I must go and get—" Clary fled. Let Fern have a minute.

Dolly took one look at Fern and loved her. Her hair was the palest apricot colour. It glowed. And she looked so sad. Fern's back slanted in a long S, her pelvis tilted and swung, her legs were long and thin in her tight jeans, and she had a closed, secret shell all around her. Her face looked as if she washed it all the time. Dolly was struck silent, but Trevor had no trouble talking Fern's ear off when Clary took her out to the back garden where he and Pearce were playing in the empty wading pool. They filled the pool together, taking turns with the hose.

It seemed to Clary that Fern liked the children. That would help. The sight of Moreland walking Pearce across the grass by his two fists even made her smile at her father again.

Clary gave Fern a package of hot dogs and put her to work barbecuing them with Trevor. Trevor held the spray-bottle in case of flare-ups, and doused the hot dogs regularly. Moreland ate three watery piccalilli dogs before he went off to Early's Feed & Seed. And Clary left for the hospital, leaving Fern in charge with some relief.

Fern occupied Dolly's whole mind. She loved getting up in the morning to find Fern drowsy-eyed on the couch, and she loved the slow days they passed doing nothing more than walk to the park and back. Her beauty, her broken heart, how well she could cut hair—the best thing was that she treated Dolly like a person of the same age. They did their nails at the picnic table. Fern did Trevor's too, so he could see what it was like. They looked at fashion magazines, but no pages that Fern said were too old for kids. She cut Dolly's hair and blew it dry with product, so that it looked almost as silky as her own.

One amazing night, Fern took Dolly and Trevor to the Exhibition. She came on the rides with them, even the Zipper. Fern *loved* the Zipper. She said it was probably too rough for them, and they were going to get her in big trouble, and the whole time they were waiting in line she kept thinking better of it and almost leaving; but she made the guy put them all in the same capsule, Trevor in the middle, and she pulled their seatbelts tight, and they rode it. Trevor spent his whole ride trying not to pee because of the zig-zag feeling racing through his body. Dolly shrieked as loud as Fern the first time they spun upside down, but she got hold of herself and did not make one other sound. When Clary's money ran out, Fern spent her own money on more long coiling rolls of tickets, so they could go on the swings seven times and three times on the Ferris wheel. When the sun was a flattened orange, almost gone, but the sky still electric blue, they wandered down the sawdusty exhibition streets to the million-bulbed entrance and out of the daydream into the ordinary parking lot.

Darwin was there to pick them up instead of Clary. "I'm hungry," he said through his open window when they came toward his car, his old green slant-roofed Buick. "You guys have been eating cotton candy all day, I bet, so you won't want any, but I'm going to go get a cheeseburger."

They were so hungry! In the café booth Darwin made Fern laugh about being too light and floaty and needing to fatten up, until she said she would share a strawberry milkshake with Dolly. The hamburgers came with mountains of fries. Dolly automatically stopped Trevor from threading mustard strings all over his mound, but Darwin said, "It's okay, he can, they're his. Here come yours."

Dolly had forgotten. They hardly ever had to share things any more.

16. Selfishness

*A*t coffee hour after church a woman Clary hardly knew came up to her.

"You're overstepping," the woman said. "Christian action doesn't redound well when it's done in public."

Prickly from lack of sleep, Clary couldn't believe this. Redound?

"Does not *redound*?" she repeated, as cold as her mother in depressing this pretension.

"It's egotism!"

The woman was a lay reader in some other parish, and organized seminars and workshops. She had a huge chin—everybody in church these days seemed to have strange faces, tiny eyes or overhanging ears or out-of-proportion mouths. That must be over-tiredness.

"It's just practical," Clary said. "I'm helping, that's all. It's not public."

"Well, pardon me for saying so, but there are boundaries—and arm's length agencies—to remove the taint of appropriation. I think you're doing this for yourself."

The woman's eyes were desperate with effort, trying to convey some terrible conviction of wrong-doing. It would be simpler to hate her, but she was so painfully exposed that Clary could not.

She tried honesty. "Yes, I am. I like the children."

"And does that count, then? If it's pure selfishness?" The little eyes stared fiercely at her, demanding some defence. "What gives you the right to run these people's lives?"

"If I find I'm getting hairs on my chin like that," Clary said, "I pluck them."

She walked away and got a cup of coffee. That was the rudest, unkindest thing she had ever said. Her heartbeat galloped, but she didn't allow herself to leave. Of course, Mrs. Pell was waiting for her at home, to give her much the same talk, from the same overbearing chin.

Darwin was down in the basement with his measuring tape, a pencil between his teeth.

Dolly had seen this before. She started shivering. Partly happy, partly scared. Her dad wasn't even there, was Darwin going to do it all alone this time?

"You hold this end, Trev," he said, parking Trevor on one side of the freezer. Darwin pulled the tape down past the washer and dryer, as far as the back wall, sticking his hand in between the boxes piled up against the wall. The doorbell rang, and Dolly ran back up the stairs.

"Tell them to go round the back," Darwin called up after her.

Two guys carrying long toolboxes were on the front steps. Maybe they knew what they were doing, she thought. She showed them where the side walkway led around the garage to the back door. They took off their boots before they pounded down the stairs in big sock feet.

All afternoon Dolly and Trevor ran up and down stairs getting stuff from Darwin's car or the guys' truck, flattening back against the stair rail when people were bringing lumber down or carrying other stuff up. Darwin showed Dolly where the wall was going to go to close off the storage room, where the water heater was. Then there would be a big rec room from the bottom of the stairs around to windows in the back of the house, to have some light down there, and a little bedroom with a little window.

"Not too big," Darwin said. "It's good this way, dark and cool."

"Will the bedroom be for you?" Dolly asked him.

"For now," he said. "Until the wind changes…"

Did that mean that it would be a room for him till the wind changed, or that he would stay till the wind changed, like Mary Poppins told those kids she looked after?

"The spirit breathes where it wills, and you hear its sound, but you do not know where it comes from and where it goes," Darwin said.

Who ever knew what Darwin was talking about, Dolly wondered. He was kind of a freak. Pearce woke up and started to cry, surprising her. She'd gotten out of the habit of hearing him cry. He was standing in the playpen in the living room, shouting for attention, but he calmed down when Dolly gave him the bottle Clary had left ready in the fridge.

Mrs. Zenko rang the doorbell. She had the little stroller unfolded.

"Let's take Pearcey-baby for a walk," she said to Dolly and Trevor, who was moping around the kitchen looking for something to eat. "Is your grand-ma awake?"

It was no secret to Dolly and Trevor that Mrs. Zenko was not crazy about their Gran, so they said they thought she was asleep, and they got their shoes on quickly so that nobody lost the momentum of going for a walk. Dolly called down the stairs to Darwin that they were going and he said, "Good! Go play in traffic!"

He came up the stairs three at a time and said to Mrs. Zenko, "Surprise for Clary down here, you want to see the plan?"

He leaned the paper against the wall and Mrs. Zenko nodded her head, pointing with her finger at the good ideas, saying, "My husband would gladly have done it, but no matter how Clary argued and pleaded, her mother wouldn't have a thing changed from when George was alive. This is wonderful!"

That comforted Dolly and Trevor. If Mrs. Zenko thought it was okay, it would be okay. They went out and left the house to the clattering and hammering. Mrs. Zenko might walk them back past Dairy Queen. It had happened before.

"I've applied for the old age pension for Mrs. Pell," Clary told Lorraine, leaving out the four hours on the phone and three trips downtown, one with Mrs. Pell in tow to sign documents. "It'll take three or four weeks to kick in, but she'll be happier when it comes through."

Lorraine laughed.

"I mean, when she has a little independence…"

"Yeah, I got you. When she's got money coming to the mailbox. She's got the balls to be unhappy, does she?"

Clary let it go. No more talking about Mrs. Pell. She took out her notebook.

"Darwin's got something on," Lorraine said. "He was on the phone about five times last night, and he had that look."

Did that mean something crooked? Clary shook her head for even considering it, but she thought Darwin was probably wilder than she knew.

"A surprise for you?"

"Maybe," Lorraine said. "He likes to give presents."

"Is it your birthday?"

"Not till March. That can't be it." She got up, pulling the i.v. pole along the bed to gather the tubes in her hand. "They're coming to set up the chemo drip in a little while. Let me go to the bathroom before you ask any more questions."

"Have you seen the doctor today?"

"*Before* you ask any more."

Clary got up to help her, but Lorraine pushed her gently down and rolled the pole, clinking and squeaking, over to the bathroom.

The room was getting homey. Piles of magazines, extra blankets, dishes from Mrs. Zenko; she ought to take those back. Another woman had been put in the other bed and had gone, and then another, but Lorraine remained. Clary had a moment of painful dizziness, struck by the recurring awareness that if Lorraine was still here, she was in big trouble—too intimate a secret to know. She hadn't talked to Darwin out of the children's hearing for a few days. Maybe he had learned something from the doctor, and was sparing her. Strange to have to be *spared* anything about Lorraine, when she hardly knew her. But she knew her better than she'd known anyone since her mother died, because she had been paying attention to Lorraine.

Two nurses came in, a woman and a man. Both small and dark-haired. One rapped on the bathroom door while the other stripped the bed with quick, economical motions. Lorraine answered and the female nurse, satisfied, went to help with the bed-making. Clary got out of the way and stayed by the sink, leaning on the counter, to wait until they were through. Lorraine came out of the washroom and rolled her contraption slowly back to the fresh bed. She looked very tired.

The two nurses swarmed around her like tiny, intent shadows, the shiny i.v. pole between them. Lorraine let them have her arms, and what they needed of her, but her face turned to the window with an open calm which Clary had not seen before. The window showed the river and the peaceful city, and beyond the city the prairie stretching in all directions. It was like a painting: Lorraine still, translucent; the nurses, dark squiggles doing finicky tasks; and beyond them, the great expanse of the unmoved world—Lorraine connected to that, removed from the machines and the workers.

Clary was swept with a feeling of despair because she could not overcome her distance from Lorraine to talk to her, could not even listen to her. She was helping, the children and so on, but that was selfishness and didn't count. But there was Darwin. Clary remembered watching Darwin sitting beside Lorraine, slipping his hand through her hair over and over and over. Sitting on her bed, being with her, hers.

Opening the door, the children dodged back. Some kind of turmoil in the house—they couldn't see what was going on past the front hall. But they could certainly hear.

"Selfishness!" was the first word Dolly could make out, the snakey S's hissing out of the living room in Mrs. Pell's dank tenor. More roaring than words.

Darwin leaned over a pile of lumber and coiled wires to open the door wider for them, and his face broke into a huge smile at the sight of Mrs. Zenko's face behind the children. "She's headin' for the rhubarb," he said to Trevor and Dolly, nodding his head back toward Mrs. Pell.

"Oh boy," Dolly said.

More choked roaring, and a magazine flew out of the living room and crashed into the hall wall. Lucky there were no pictures right there, Dolly thought. Another magazine flew flapping and fluttering at the wall. The next one was heavier, so it stayed more solidly together, with a *whump* as it hit. Fern's *In Style*.

Darwin gave them one more crazy look, and dove into the living room. They could hear Mrs. Pell, gasping and wheezing, her hands smacking.

"Get your—let me go, you friggin'—slime-bucket—"

"He'll take care of her," Trevor said to Mrs. Zenko, who had put her arms around the children and was pulling them back out the front door.

"It's just a temper," Dolly said.

To her surprise, she saw that Mrs. Zenko had started to cry, a couple of sweet pear-shaped tears. "It's not that bad," she told her, to comfort her.

"It's not dishes this time," Trevor said.

"Oh, my dears," Mrs. Zenko said, as if this was awful. Really it wasn't *that* bad, a magazine wouldn't seriously hurt anybody even if it landed. Pearce in the stroller was craning his neck to see what all the interesting noise was, fat fists clenched around the bar to pull himself forward. Mrs. Zenko pulled him farther back against the porch railing.

Darwin came into sight again, with Mrs. Pell, hitching her along by walking close beside her, her arms pinned by her sides. He took her into her room and shut the door. Two more crashes. They could hear Darwin in a steady stream, talking her down.

Then it was quiet for a minute.

"She's probably done for now," Dolly said.

"We'll go to my house for supper, I think, my dears," Mrs. Zenko said. She was pressing her hand into her chest, just under the bone that goes across the shoulders, and that made Dolly worry about her. Her eyes were still damp and shocked.

"It's okay, really," Dolly said, and Trevor said too, "It's okay."

But they both loved eating at Mrs. Zenko's, so they shepherded her down the stairs, not wanting to calm her completely in case she changed her mind about supper.

"You don't have to call 911, Darwin will fix her. When she's mad, she goes straight up and turns left," Dolly said. It would have scared Fern too. She was already kind of weirded out by Gran. Good thing *she* hadn't seen this, or Clary!

Trevor shook his head, the straight, weightless hair floating away from his skull. "She got a crazy temper, boy—"

He was going to say some more, tell about that time when she chased him around the house with the wooden spoon, going way fast, but Dolly poked him. Maybe Mrs. Zenko would give them perogies. He loved those. But not with sour cream, no, not that.

Moreland had happened to have a few errands in Saskatoon, and he stopped by to say hello. Quite an amount of lumber clutter in the front hall, and the door was wide open, the screen not even shut to.

"Hello?" he called gently, stepping over the first pile. Acoustic tiles. Had Clary finally got somebody in to do the basement? Grace'd be glad to hear it.

Darwin stuck his head around from the bottom half of the basement stairs and said hi.

Moreland said hi back, and then Darwin came all the way up. "You a friend of Clary's?"

"Her cousin," Moreland said. "Cousin-in-law, I guess."

"She should be back already—but it's a good thing she's not."

Darwin was gathering metal braces, and Moreland automatically helped him.

"I've been telling her she ought to do the basement for a while now," Moreland said, making conversation as they took a load of lumber down the narrow stairs.

"Yeah, well, now's the time," Darwin said. "You want to help?"

Moreland was taken aback. What kind of contractor was this? Then he surveyed the surprising scope of the damage in the basement and understood that something else was going on. "I guess I better," he said. He took off his jacket.

Loitering by the café in the hospital lobby, in his usual post, Paul waited for an empty pot of coffee to be refilled. Avoiding visits. When Clara Purdy came out of the elevator and headed for the door, Paul found himself dodging in front of her, almost tackling her. "Sorry," he said, catching himself up. "I haven't seen you for—I wondered how Lorraine is holding up through this chemo, if I should visit her again?"

She looked distracted, but not unhappy to see him. "Some days she seems better," she said. "It was like this for my father, but she's younger, and stronger-willed, maybe."

"Whenever I think illness is all attitude, along comes someone who gripes and complains and whines and still gets better," Paul said. "Will you have a quick coffee? It must be ready now. Joe Kane, upstairs, is eighty-seven, still snarling and scratching."

"He was in hospital with my father, eighteen years ago," Clary said. "My mother called him *irascible*, and that's how I always think of him."

Paul handed her a cup of burnt, caramel-coloured coffee. "He demoralizes me. He's Candy Vincent's uncle. She's been—" He caught himself before mentioning her tale-bearing call to the bishop. "She's something of a force in the parish."

"You should have known her when she was Candy Kane, in Grade 8. She was a wild girl in those days, Elton John glasses and platform shoes. I thought she was amazing."

"But you can't have known her then?"

"We were in school together. I'm pretty old, you know."

He blushed. Clary was fascinated to see him redden from the base of his neck upwards, his ears included, while the polite expression on his face never altered.

"I'm forty-one," he said, meaning that he was old too.

"Forty-three," she said. "I guess that makes me the boss of you. Sad, really."

Then he laughed, the red receding. "*It is the blight man was born for*," he said. "*It is Margaret you mourn for.*"

"I can never remember poems," she said. "But I like when you quote Rilke in sermons."

He was grateful for that. What beautiful eyebrows she had.

"Joe Kane used to like to play chess," she told him. "He played my father in the sunroom at the old City Hospital years ago. See how irascible he'd be if you beat him."

135

"Kind of you to suggest I might be able to," he said. He took the cup she had finished, and she hurried away through the lobby, already gone from him, trying to remember where she had parked this time.

Clary walked in the front door and almost fell over a pile of metal struts. A man she'd never seen before was crouched down gathering the struts together, and he scrambled up to catch her; she caught herself, instead.

"Hello?" she said.

Darwin came running up from the basement. "Hey, Clary! Good!"

He edged past the large man and helped him manoeuvre his load past the woodwork. She could see no place to put her grocery bags that wasn't covered with hardware.

"Give them to me," he said. "You're pretty heavy-laden."

He side-stepped back through the kitchen doorway. Moreland was sitting at the kitchen table working something out on paper with a ruler and his trusty space pen.

"Moreland!" Clary said, surprised. "Is this your doing? You've met Darwin—Lorraine's brother?"

Moreland hadn't figured the exact relationship but had gathered something along those lines. He covered the paper with his arm, and then uncovered it, thinking maybe better she didn't go down to the basement. He didn't want her to see the big black lines he'd drawn on the wall downstairs, where they could put in a bigger window, if they dug four feet and lined the well…

"Where are the children?" Clary asked, refusing to ask about the rubble.

"That nice Mrs. Zenko of yours came over and said she had 'em," Moreland said. "Said she was feeding them supper and if we'd like to come along later she'd feed us, too."

Clary squeezed her eyes shut. She was putting too much strain on Mrs. Zenko, she had to find a better way of doing this. She could not bear to think what all this new chaos was about, the piles of stuff, Moreland roped in somehow here, and all these strange friends of Darwin's—what disreputable people did he hang around with, normally? Petty criminals, carnies, drug dealers.

But Moreland was here. And if they were making a better place for Darwin to sleep, that would be good.

Darwin said, "Mrs. Zenko is glad to have something worthwhile to do." That was true.

"She's getting all those perogies cleaned out of her freezer," he said.

"Perogies? That what's for supper?" Moreland asked.

"According to Trevor," Darwin said. "Might have been wishful thinking. Whatever she makes is good. Do you care what we do down in the basement?" he asked Clary. "Thought I could pay you back a bit, in kind."

"I don't care about anything," she said. What a pleasure to say that! Moth-eaten mink coats, old lamps, what was down there? An affliction of stuff in mouldy boxes. "It's all junk I haven't shovelled out. If you'll deal with it I'll be grateful. Oh, Grace wants the jam jars. But I don't need any of it."

Moreland gave her a wink. "Good to let go once in a while, eh?"

She laughed, and headed next door, where she could hear the children yodelling in the garden.

When Darwin stepped into the darkened room, Lorraine opened her eyes.

"You're late," she said, in a slow voice, stupid with drugs. He looked tired too. "Working too hard?"

"Hardly working," he said, and sat on the edge of the bed. He held her foot, forming its shape under the sheet. His hand felt safe.

"How's everything?" She meant at home, the children.

"Mrs. Zenko next door took them over for supper. Mom Pell blew a fuse."

"Oh, no."

"She's settled down now, off sulking somewhere. She's a crazy woman."

"What set her off?"

"I got some guys helping me do a few things down in Clary's basement, fix it up for her a bit. Mom Pell wants a room down there when it's done, but I told her no."

Lorraine wanted to think about Mrs. Pell's everlasting selfishness and about Clary's house turned upside down in the usual chaos of Darwin's projects, but she felt herself sliding backwards. A pleasant/unpleasant sensation, beginning to whirl. Like being drunk, only none of the giddy tickle. It was uncomfortably like dying. She could hear Darwin talking, she could feel his foot, no, his hand, on her foot... There was something... Darwin carried on telling her all about it, about Moreland coming and the little refinements they'd decided on, the new window Moreland was going to bring in the morning, so they'd have to dig the window well deeper; how the kids had comforted Mrs. Zenko when Mom Pell went round the bend.

Lorraine didn't have to talk. In between sentences he would hum, hum, one of Rose's tuneless, wordless songs from Avenue H, Rose sitting with them while they drifted off to sleep. Lorraine was unable to be afraid, half-listening. Freed from the long bead-string of things she had to finger over and over: money, the children, Clayton, the cancer, the bad feeling just there on the left side, hum, hum. Can't even remember the list, she thought.

At five in the morning, staring out the window while she waited for Pearce's bottle to warm, Clary saw Darwin roaming around in the garden. She went out onto the concrete patio to say hello. Pearce joggled along with her, wakeful but not grumpy this pale blue early morning, watching the sparkle on the grass where light was beginning to glance.

"Hey, Pearcey," Darwin said, looking back.

He had been staring at the back garage, Clary's father's workshop. Wide as a single car garage, but twice as long, opening onto the alley—it had become invisible to Clary, as familiar things do. Overgrown lilac bushes almost hid it from the house. She should trim those back.

"Mom Pell," Darwin said. "She's sleeping in a chair out there, an old recliner."

Clary hoped that the words would translate into English if she waited.

"She's mad at me," Darwin told her. Birds were singing their crazy morning alarms. "No need waking her up now. Wait till she comes out on her own, eh?"

"Okay," Clary said. Thinking, like Fern, *whatever...*

"You keep anything in there?"

"Oh, my father's old tools, and a table saw. It was his hideout. He was tidy, there's not much clutter. There's a furnace, he worked in there all year round. It's insulated, too—probably with asbestos."

Darwin smiled at her. A very personable, loopy smile, she thought. "Be a nice little house."

Pearce twisted around in her arms to stare at the windows of the shop, shining with reflected early sky. He pointed strongly toward it, meaning *Take me there!* but she said, "No, no, not now, Pearce," and turned to go into the house instead.

"Whatever," she said to Darwin. "Whatever you like."

Darwin just hummed. Clary left him to it. She went back to make Pearce's bottle, and maybe, with any luck, get a little more sleep.

17. Service

*T*ime to introduce the children to church, Clary thought, with the house a little more orderly and breakfast over by nine. Banging reverberated in the basement, and Dolly and Trevor kept slipping down to check on things and being sent back upstairs with urgent messages like *Tell Clary we need a three-pronged grommet by Thursday, go tell her right now.* Before Clary got the joke, she had started making a list on the fridge. *3-pronged– ?* it read. *Electric hat-saw w. grinder,* and *6 gross button-head hybrid bingo-nails(?).*

Church would get them out of Darwin's hair for a while. And that overbearing chin-wagging redound woman last week had made her determined to take them. She re-dressed Pearce and collared Dolly and Trevor to put on clean shorts the next time they came up to tell her what Darwin needed. (*A dark balance umbrella, if she's got one.*) She washed all their faces and combed their hair. They made a little crowd in the pale green bathroom, filling the big mirror when she glanced up. She brushed Dolly's bangs back from her face again and rummaged in the top drawer for a pretty bobby pin, the one with a butterfly on it.

Dolly stared at Trevor's fine hair flying up off the back of his head from static, at Pearce perched on Clary's hip. Clary's smooth head was bent in the

top half of the mirror, checking to see if they looked good enough for church. This was their life now: to be with Clary. Dolly stopped. No thinking about anybody else, white as a sheet on yellow hospital sheets.

In the porch of the church Clary thanked Frank Rich and took a second bulletin for Trevor to share with Dolly, since he could not yet read. But he looked heartbroken, so she gave hers to Dolly and smiled at Trevor.

"What was I thinking?" she said. "You need your own."

She led them through into the opening arches and pillars, the airy height. They were early, plenty of empty pews. Clary chose one near the front to give the children a better view. She tried balancing the baby-seat on the pew, but it slid off sideways, so she left it on the floor and took Pearce out to stand on her knee. He stared up at the stained glass windows arrowing high above, which Clary had not noticed for years.

Paul walked by in his black cassock, not yet robed for the service, going to check the readings. What a pure face, Clary thought. A medieval knight's face. He was thinner. In a month he would be reduced to eyes and a nose. Hard to advise the congregation on love and understanding and human relationships, when his own had failed.

Trevor watched Paul striding along up to the front. Wearing a long black dress! Nice buttons, and a long pleat in the back, swish, swish—with each long step the dress swung open and closed, swirling around the bottom like icing, or curtains. Paul went to a carved golden eagle with wings holding a big book. Up on the wall was the cross, bare. A big Jesus was right on it in the Catholic church their mom had cleaned in Espanola. Trevor could not look at him poked up on the cross like that: big nails through his feet, between the narrow bones, and a big drop of purply-red blood. Just plain wood was easier to take.

Dolly found church very irritating. The organ playing too quiet to hear was like something pressing on her. Behind the altar green velvet curtains hid the room of God, the inner secret part, she guessed, where only Paul would be allowed. He came back down the aisle, and Dolly thought he looked happy to see them, like they'd come over to his house by surprise. He leaned over and smiled at Dolly so his face made clean creases and he looked like an older angel. He must like us, Dolly thought.

"Good to see everybody here," Paul said to Clary.

141

Pleasure welled up in her at the achievement of getting them all here, all dressed and fed, all in a row.

Behind Clary a woman leaned forward to touch Pearce's cheek. "You have a lovely baby!" she said.

The music changed, and everyone was standing, so Clary didn't have time to explain. She helped Trevor and Dolly leaf through their hymn books, and sang softly to help with the tune. Pearce pulled her head down toward his face. He smelled good, he was all right. No more Benadryl. Clary prayed the first successful prayer she'd managed lately: *thank you, thank you that he was not hurt.*

Church was like a movie, Trevor thought, but you're in it. The words mostly washed over him, but when the bald guy from the audience walked up to read, he heard parts of that: *I was to them like those who lift infants to their cheeks, I bent down to them and fed them.* Like Clary's cheek. Everything tucking in so nicely there beneath her pointy little chin. When she lifted Pearce to her cheek Trevor always wished it was him. When she bent to kiss him at night, he saw the lines on her face, and breathed in her looping shiny hair and her neck. She smelled like soap. His own mother smelled like apples. He could feel the middle of his body empty, a dark cave running up and down through him, because his mother was sick. He decided he would kill Jesus, and be the new Jesus, and then he could get her better. Who cares that he would be the devil then.

Dolly prayed at first—since she had to be there—a short ferocious prayer that was no question but an order: *Get her well.* Her forehead pressing on the pew, staring into her clenched fists. When she stopped, exhausted, she watched Pearce's foot dangling beside her. His foot trembled like a bird's as he reached up to touch Clary, to be sure he was still being held. Poor Pearcey, Dolly thought, and tears began the long ride up into her eye. Then she remembered how *boring* stupid church was, and tears receded, and she yelled at God again in her head.

Clary was pleased by how peaceful the children were. This meditative time was good for them. Unfortunately the lesson was that difficult letter of St. Paul, *put to death fornication.* But maybe they had drifted off to whatever thoughts children drift to. Watching Pearce's intelligent gaze she wondered what he was thinking, with his white-paper mind; what images were being

142

painted on his brain. What indelible photographs were printed on Trevor's and Dolly's, already.

"*You must change your life,*" Paul said, and it was obviously the opening of the sermon, so she'd missed the Gospel. "Rilke says that—and I know I've quoted Rilke before,"—he glanced at Clary—"In the poem called *The Archaic Torso of Apollo...* St. Paul says it too, in the letter to the Colossians. He promises change in the new life in Christ, in which all are equal.

"Don't get distracted by the list, the fornicating and the unclean desires and so on. Go straight to the core: when we have clothed ourselves with the new self, there will no longer be any distinctions: Christ is all and in all." Paul stopped and shuffled his index cards, which he never referred to but seemed to use as a prop against nervousness. "It's a tempting list—to be on the lookout for nasty stuff, in ourselves and in other people, that dingy side of life. But the injunction continues: we must get rid of *all* the dross. Anger, wrath and malice, slander and abusive language— Of course I include myself in this. We must struggle against the temptation to malice, even when it's clothed in a self-righteous vestment of indignation against someone else's perceived sin."

His own indignant energy made his face look burnished. He needs to let himself be angry, Clary thought. Candy Vincent sat in the choir, her permanent can-do smile in place.

"One of the failings St. Paul warns against comes up again in today's Gospel—greed. Jesus warns us against a specific kind of greed in Luke 12: greed for the future. The rich man has had a miraculous harvest, too big for his barns. Instead of allowing the extra to flow into the hands of the poor he says to himself, 'I'll tear down these petty little barns and build big barns so I can keep all this for my Self, and eat and drink and be merry for a long time.' I'm paraphrasing, of course." Paul had an unassuming smile, acknowledging his own inadequacy but relying on your great mercy and kindness. "The rich man glorying in his harvest and thinking ahead to the party is going to die. He forgot that."

He looked down to Dolly and Clary, with one arm around Trevor and Pearce in her lap.

"We forget. It's hard to live with the constant understanding of death in the forefront of our minds. Scholars of old kept a skull on their writing desks

143

to help. The reminder of imminent death, *memento mori,* is one of the greatest spurs we have to right action.

"When I was a boy my mother fell gravely ill. I knew she was going to die, and that I would be left an orphan with my younger sister to look after. My mother knew it too, and our conversations during those months of her illness have been of use to me all my life. She was given radiation treatment and had a radical mastectomy—they were very radical in those days—and in fact she did not die. But the strength my sister and I received from her in those hard days stayed with us even when we returned to ordinary life and were able to go back to taking her for granted, which I still do, to this day, unless she phones to scold me for it…"

He allowed the congregation to laugh, to release some tension. He could not tell how Clary's children were taking this. They didn't seem to be listening, but of course appearances meant nothing, with children. With anyone.

"And there are other deaths. As you all must know by now, my wife Lisanne and I have separated."

He stopped, he remembered to breathe.

"A little death, the death of a marriage, is another one of those hard times when life becomes clearer. We thought we had stored up for the future, but we've had an early frost…"

His mouth turning down as if he disliked his own phrase, he shifted his cards again.

"God directs us to be joyful and free, unhindered by anxiety, and not to hang on to the stuff of this world, material goods or relationships, as our salvation. They cannot be. He tells us to have the courage to be open to one another, by compassionate understanding and by abiding, kind attention to our neighbours. To see God in those around us. If we are lucky, we see the God Hosea reminds us of, in those who *lift infants to their cheeks, bend down to them and feed them.*"

That time Paul looked directly at the children, and at Clary, and smiled at them all.

She bent quickly to rearrange the car seat, unable to bear his approval. She'd been the catalyst for this disaster, let's not forget, she thought. The least she could do was try to keep them safe for a while, before… She prayed one word, *Lorraine.*

Then the congregation were rising for the hymn, and automatically she rose too.

Dolly and Trevor stuck close to Clary at coffee hour. Weaving through the heedless crowd of congregation to the coffee table, Clary carried a glum consciousness that, like her own goodness, church was a fraud and a sham, and she should not be there herself, let alone dragging children along with her. But Paul was not a sham, and he seemed to be pretty stalwart in faith.

Trevor tugged her arm, wanting to get closer to the cake: the August birthday cake, made by April Anthony, who remembered the birthdays of the parish. She had listed the August people in icing down one side, and Trevor badly wanted a piece with writing.

"Two pieces, please," Clary told Mrs. Anthony. Did she make birthday cakes because she was named after a month, Clary wondered, or had she even noticed that? Was April's birthday in April? Clary's mother would have known. Mrs. Anthony handed her two pieces of cake, one with plain icing, and one with names.

Trevor snaked his hand up and grabbed the name piece, so rudely that Clary stared at him in surprise. He crammed part of the cake into his mouth and ducked down, disappearing under the table.

"Trevor!" Clary said, remembering that last table he went under. "Dolly, take this—" She bent and reached blindly under the table for his skinny arm, and pulled him out. "Trevor, it's okay, you're allowed to have cake. There's lots." She was speaking almost in a whisper, her face close to his. "Do you have to pee?"

Trevor shook his head. Then he nodded.

"Okay, come on, I'll show you where the bathrooms are."

Dolly had vanished in the crowd, but Pearce, thank God, was still slumped sleeping in the car seat, safe enough among the church women. Clary took Trevor to the washroom.

Dolly was looking for the way into that secret room back there, behind the green velvet curtains. Everybody had left the church part, it was all hushed. She climbed the chancel steps on quiet feet and dodged around the altar to where Paul had stood. It was weird back there. She stroked the green velvet drape along the wall, searching for a break where you could go through.

145

Nothing. Impatient, she reached over to the far edge and scooped the velvet up sideways.

Nothing! Just the wall. Well. That was a lesson all by itself.

"Dolly?" It was Paul. Her stomach swooped—what if she was trespassing?

"Hey, sweetheart," he called. "Your—Clary is looking for you. She's got Trevor and Pearce and they're ready to go home. Are you finding your way around up there?"

If the room behind wasn't even there, how holy was it anyway? Dolly skipped down the stairs and ran down the aisle, past Paul waiting at the back door. There might be seconds of cake.

Paul stood outside the church hall after they'd gone. The light blinding through the branches, a fluting bird's cascading whistle. A lost meadowlark, singing in the noonday sun, to the silent city around them. It wasn't so far for him to have flown from the river fields on a Sunday. *Quam deus in mundi delectus est*—God so delighted in the world… Paul lifted his face to feel the sun and thanked God, thanked God, as he did almost all the time. When he wasn't carping, carping for whatever ills he felt afflicted by at the moment. When light glanced around him and the bird poured light in his ears and the dust rose off the asphalt from the recently departed cars of his parishioners, he was convinced that he lived on God, that the earth itself was God itself, as self and selfless as—

He went inside, leaping up the stairs three at a time. This was a work-day, after all; there were doors to lock and service reports to sign, and then his hospital visits. And remembering his duty toward Joe Kane, he thought there might be a magnetic chess set in the Sunday school cupboard.

146

18. Clearwater

*W*hile they were eating lunch after church Moreland came back, with Grace in full overdrive, wearing knife-pressed aqua, her grey hair permed tight. Up since four herself with Pearce, Clary felt a little bedraggled.

"You need a break," Grace announced to the children. "Moreland's going to hang around here getting in the way, helping your uncle, and I'm taking you out to Clearwater."

Grace and Moreland had a cabin at Clearwater Lake, a large slough in the middle of the bald prairie, where a sandy beach waxed and waned depending on the water level. By this time in August it would be drying, but it had its own charm. Impossible, though.

"Grace, we can't go anywhere, I have to be at the hospital—"

"Nonsense, Lorraine can do without you for a couple of days."

"And I can't leave Darwin to do all this by himself."

"Not by himself, I just told you. Moreland's got a bee in his bonnet, he thinks they can get it done by Tuesday. He's got Henley for the wiring, and Henley's cousin has end-of-roll carpet from when they redid the golf course—

they've got it all figured out. We'll get the kids out of this rubble and dust, who knows what it's doing to the baby."

"But Mrs. Pell—"

"I'll take her too. She better not give me any grief, that's all."

Mrs. Pell stumped into the kitchen as Grace said that, but Grace was hard to faze. "Hey, there," she said immediately. "I was just telling Clary that I'm going to take them out to the lake for the weekend. You get yourself packed and you can come too."

Mrs. Pell wheeled around and headed to her room to pack.

"That was quick," Grace said. "Now can I have a coffee?"

Dolly wouldn't be allowed to see her mom anyway, so what did it matter where they went? She rode alone in the Pontiac with Grace, who blabbed on the whole time about Fern (interesting) and Davina (boring), so Dolly didn't have to worry about talking. At Rosetown, Grace got chicken for supper. Clary stopped too. Grace had told Dolly that Clary would see their car, but Dolly was still relieved. They sat at dingy picnic tables to eat, while trucks roared and blew fumes past them. It was a hot day.

South from Rosetown—stupid name for an ugly town, Dolly thought— another half hour, and another, and then Grace turned down on gravel and then bumped along a dirt road, and over a little rise they found the lake, shining pinky-silver in the evening sun. Around it the land was flat. On one side of the lake stood a row of cabins and a few old trailers parked forever, grey plywood skirts nailed in around their bottoms. They drove along the row of haphazard huts, Grace pointing out a round one made of concrete blocks, and one sparkling green and brown with broken beer bottles set into the plaster. At the end of the row Grace turned into a little parking place behind the last cabin, and turned off the car. She stared back along the road.

"Hope she remembers the turnoff," Grace said.

Dolly hoped so too. She was worn out from being alone with Grace.

"We'll take our things in anyway, and get the cooler set up. Take your shoes off on the porch there—we don't need any housework here."

Dolly was embarrassed not to have known to take her shoes off, even though this place was a tumbledown old shack. She left her new pink shoes side by side and hopped in the door. Inside, the cabin was painted pale green, like school bathrooms, and the walls were made out of flimsy pressed board.

"Moreland and I started building this place when we were in high school," Grace told her. "You go pick a bunk."

The other room was long, with three sets of bunks, curtains strung between to make fake bedrooms. A window looked out on the water. Dolly sat on the closest bunk. She thought she would wait there till Clary arrived. It all smelled funny.

"Hey," Grace said from the doorway. "I need some wood carried in from the back, and then you can run down to the store and get some pop."

Dolly stared at her, this woman who was not her mother, or her grandmother, not even Clary who was taking care of them. It was on the tip of her tongue to say no, but she didn't mind going out by herself. When they'd finished with the wood Grace gave her a twenty and told her two cartons: one cokes, the other any kind she liked. Twenty dollars. It looked big in her hand. She put it in her pocket and walked back out to the little road. Way down by the road was the orange-painted shed that was the store. She walked along the dirt track, hearing the pop, pop of grasshoppers exploding from the grass and sinking back down with a click of their legs, or their wings, she didn't know which. A coyote looked over the tall grass behind the fence, only twenty feet away, the same colours as the dry grass: half grey, half blonde. She walked closer, thinking she might tame it and then they'd have a dog, but it turned and loped away. Lope, that was the word for that kind of running. Lope, lope, she tried running that way herself, but it was too hot.

A pickup truck and another truck sat by the pumps in front of the store. A woman in the pickup putting on more lipstick. The closed-in truck was empty.

Dolly climbed the step onto the wooden slat porch and pulled open the door.

For a second she thought it was her dad standing at the counter. From the back his skinny legs reminded her, and the way his jean jacket hung over his butt. Her heart jumped and she took two quick steps forward, but the guy turned with a mean look to see who was there, and it was not him, of course it wasn't. Her dad was far gone. This guy went out past her, walking too close so she had to pull back against the rack of candy. He had sunglasses on. When he got to the door he looked back and saw her still staring at him. He stared back, then went out.

A round-cheeked girl with a bag of chips was next at the counter, must be the truck woman's daughter. "And $32 in gas," she said.

Dolly walked around the aisles looking for pop cans in cartons. There, at the back. They were going to get pretty heavy on the way back to the cabin. She lugged them up to the counter.

The pimply boy at the cash took her twenty and said, "$10.35."

Dolly said, "No way! They're $4.50 each. That's only nine dollars."

"Tax," the boy said. He was sure outgoing.

"Oh, right," she said, pretending she knew that.

The screen door spring snapped her in the arm when she went out. It was bright outside, compared to the store, and Dolly stood on the step, dazzled.

"You want a ride?"

It was the jean-jacket guy, over by his truck. Dolly shook her head.

"You come on with me, I'll take you for a ride into town."

What kind of stupid did he think she was? Dolly could feel the metal bar of the screen door across the middle of her back, and the saggy parts of the screen above and below. The truck with the women was gone, there was only the boy at the counter inside.

"I got some candy in the truck."

Dolly laughed. That made the guy mad. He took off his glasses. His eyes were big and pretty like a woman's. Bright blue, she could see, even so far away. He smiled at her like he knew her. How she was crafty, the same as him.

The pop was heavy. The sun flashed on the windshield of a car turning off the gravel. Dolly took off with a jump and ran across the dirt, straight at the guy, startling him. Then she swerved past him onto the dirt track. She flung the orange carton down with a rattling crash in the dirt as she stuck out her arm.

It was okay, it was them. Clary opened the window and called past Gran, "Hi! Sorry we're late, we stopped to get ice cream in Kyle."

"Hi," Dolly said.

"You got pop? So did I! Hop in, we can go as far as the cabin without your seatbelt on. You'll be safe out here."

Dolly picked up the pop she'd dropped and climbed in beside Pearce's baby seat. She leaned her head against Pearce's blanket and smelled how good he smelled. Trevor was sound asleep against the other window. What a nice boy he was.

Clary drove down the road, glad to have Dolly back with her. Grace was responsible and careful, of course, but she was no Mrs. Zenko. When Trevor opened his pop, ten minutes later, Grace's nice aqua outfit got totally soaked, orange everywhere.

On Sunday evening, without giving Paul any warning, Lisanne sent her sister Carol to get her things from the rectory. *Her things*—as if after twenty years there was any more such a thing as hers, or his. These things are all *ours,* he wanted to shout at Carol. Or sob. Which would come out, he wondered, if he pushed at that locked door? Instead he said, "Did you bring boxes, Carol, or shall I find some?"

Of course she had not brought boxes. She did have a list. And a van coming later on.

"Blake is coming to help, remember Blake?"

A paunch, and a small beard, Paul thought, finding it an exhausting effort to sort out Carol's sporadic boyfriends.

"We'd better have things ready for him, then," he said, amazed at his own civility.

She started up the stairs, getting right down to work. Lisanne had faithfully reported Carol's loathing of his "passive-aggressive fake humility"—he wondered if she'd actually said that, or if Lisanne had just wanted to say it herself.

He went to find boxes.

When Carol and Blake left they had nine boxes and three large suitcases. They took the mahogany armoire from the living room, originally Paul's grandmother's, which had been Lisanne's sewing cupboard for twenty years. The dining room chairs, all eight, but not the table, because Lisanne had put on the list definitely not to take it. It had a wow in the middle and she was sick of it. The brown velvet couch, the armchair, the sideboard, the carpet.

Paul was mildly glad that Lisanne had said he could keep the bed, symbolically, although he'd never much liked it. He tried to take some satisfaction from it standing in the almost-empty bedroom. The comforter slumped on the floor, she didn't want that either. (*Comforter, where, where is your comforting? Mary, mother of us, where is your relief?*) The dressers and night tables had gone. He wondered where she would store all this in Carol's house. The good dishes (he'd always hated them), the good cutlery, the good pots, the pepper grinder, and—moving back into the living room—the television and the cordless phone. He had not let them take the iron or the ironing board; he did need to iron his shirts. Carol said never mind. The ironing board was teetery and usually stuck halfway up, and it could have done with a new cover.

Blake had been unable to meet Paul's glance. Ashamed of himself for helping with this wholesale fleecing, or ashamed of Paul as a failed example of manhood, Paul wondered. Carol, though, stopped at the door and looked straight into his eyes, one of those long looks people rarely have the effrontery for. Her eyes were like Lisanne's, he realized—light, with black rings around bright pale irises veering toward blue. Lisanne's were darker blue.

"How are you doing with all this, Paul?"

He was surprised that she should ask. "I'm going to be all right, in the end," he said.

"Lisanne's *very* good. Better than I've ever seen her," Carol said. As if it wasn't him she was talking to, as if it didn't matter what she said to him. "Well, off we go! Have a good night!"

They had been gone for ten minutes when Paul found the remote, sitting on the bookcase. He clicked it a few times, imagining the television set in the back of the van flickering on and off, whispering to itself in the crowd of furniture.

Tuesday night Grace took Clary and the kids to the Clearwater drive-in. They'd been lots of times, outside Winnipeg, so it was not that big a deal. Both Trevor and Dolly were tired. They sat staring through the windshield, glad not to have to talk. It was almost ten o'clock, but the sky was not yet dark, so it was hard to see the screen. The first movie was *Dinosaur*, animated and pretty old, but they hadn't seen it yet. The second feature was *Dude,*

Where's My Car? but Clary had already said they would not be staying for that one. A man's voice kept breaking in over the movie lines on the radio, saying "Two cheeseburger, two fries, chocolate shake, Diet Coke," or "bacon double cheeseburger, onion rings." Then you couldn't hear the movie. The little dinosaur was getting separated from his family, which reminded Trevor of that other movie, and Littlefoot's mother dying, and that made his eyes tear up. Then a comet came screaming down through the atmosphere, and hit, SPLASH, and there was a huge explosion and a great big tidal wave of water came swooshing along the screen.

It was the comet that meant the extinction of the dinosaurs, everybody knew that.

"Boy, that was a short movie," Trevor said. Clary burst out laughing. Trevor was happy to make her laugh but did not get why that was so funny.

Dolly could see, because the movie was going to keep on, so the dinosaurs must not be getting wiped out right away, even though everybody knew they did. Trevor was so young. She leaned closer up against Clary's arm. Pearcey was slurp-slurping from a bottle again. He never stopped eating these days, Dolly thought. "Can we have a cheeseburger?" she asked Clary, tilting her head up, so she could already see Clary's mouth making a *No.*

But Grace stretched her arms up over her head and beat a drum tattoo on the car ceiling. "I think that's a great idea," she said. "Who wants to come with me?"

Trevor was watching the dinosaurs in their long line trying to get away from destruction, so Dolly went with Grace by herself. Grace had changed into lime green shorts, pretty bright even in the twilight. She told the boy at the counter hi, and ordered four cheeseburgers and two onion rings and two, no, make it three fries. Four chocolate shakes. Good thing Gran had stayed at the cabin. Before they went home to the city, Dolly thought, she would have to go through Gran's pockets and put back whatever stuff she'd scarfed. She remembered the change still in her own pocket and handed it to Grace, who was happily talking to the counter boy, both of them leaning their elbows on the counter while the fryer sizzled away.

This was more like what they were used to, Dolly thought to herself. Like up by Espanola, or Trimalo, except for the no trees. It wouldn't last forever, being out here. She should be paying more attention.

She looked out at the empty field, stretching right out to the sky, as far as you could tell. Rolling bare-bone land going away, away, away into a blue distance, and the huge screen standing up against the blue sky that was both dark and light at the same time. The faint sound of the movie through open car windows mixed with the whispery whistling of the wind, and the noise of bugs creaking and fiddling toward the darkness. And the smell of the burgers frying and the onion rings. Six or seven cars away she could see Clary's head bending down to Pearce. Except for what she would not think about, Dolly was happy. She could breathe this mixed summer air forever. Up above the movie screen the few visible stars sprinkled in the periwinkle blue—look! One slipped out of its place and shot silently down, arcing around the edge of the screen and down and gone.

That night Pearce cried and cried, to remind them that he was only a baby. The whole camp would be awake, Clary knew, a little village of people who already didn't sleep well, and now this. By one a.m. he was only gathering strength, stomach ache or gas giving him no rest either.

"A walk," she told him, finding her shoes in the darkness. "That's what you need. We'll go walk along the shore. The cool night air will do us good."

She could walk in her pyjamas, here at Clearwater. Maybe a sweater. She slipped out the front and cobbled Pearce into his stroller. But it wouldn't roll on the rocky sand; after a hundred yards she hoisted him out and abandoned the stroller. Pearce was comfortable on her hip, and happier outside in the night. Above them, filling the huge sky, the stars in their millions flickered and stood. Someone said there are only two thousand stars visible, but it must be more than that, Clary thought. A thousand times more. That person must have lived in a city.

It was a bit cooler than she'd bargained for, and she'd left the blanket in the stroller. Clary took off her sweater and wrapped it around Pearce, making a sling with the sleeves around her neck so they could keep walking and be comfortable. She had missed walking in the last few weeks. Too much to do, not enough time to walk anywhere. She strode along, stretching her legs out. Familiar with this path since childhood, when Grace and Moreland and their little cabin had been so romantic, when she had heard them whispering late at night, both twined into one bunk. The sound of them kissing and Grace laughing, saying *we can't*—and Moreland, the handsome boy he was then, murmuring *oh yes, oh yes.*

Trevor trotted along the path some way behind Clary. He didn't want her to hear him; he just wanted to be with her. The lake on one side, the wilderness on the other, in the dark night. Finally dark, even though the sun took so long to set that you thought it would never go to black. There was something in the grass beside him, he thought, and he went a little faster. So did the thing, scuttering along making noise only when he did, quieting if he stopped. He couldn't be afraid, it must be something small. The moon was small, too, not very bright, slung low in the sky. The grass was too scary, too close. He did not want to call out to tell Clary he was following in case she got mad. Trevor edged down to the water, thinking he might walk along in the mud, because an animal might not like to get its feet wet, if it was a cougar or a fox. A coyote might not care about water, or a pack of coyotes. They had been yipping along the black horizon earlier. Grace had shown him one silhouetted against the orangey-blue sky when they got home from the movie. She'd pointed with her finger where the other yippers were.

His feet were tough. The rocky sand and mud on the bottom of the lake did not bother them. Once in a while a sharp rock made his knee suddenly bend. He rolled his pyjama bottoms past his knees and walked a little farther out, where it was warm, muddy, squelching smoothness. A little farther. There was no wind at all. No waves, and the water was still except for the stirring his shins made.

Pearce was heavy, and Clary was tired. She sat down on a slight hummock above the lake. She should have brought him a bottle. She could hear motion, nighttime animals moving through the grasses. Fish in the lake coming up for sleeping bugs, an occasional tiny plop. A sound like something wading: a deer, or a fawn. Pearce pointed his finger up to the moon. He always pointed at the moon; he laughed when he saw it through the window at home. This time he was silent with attention. Wrapped in the soft darkness, Clary lay down on the grass and curled herself around Pearce. He was wide awake and not in pain any more. He stood against her hip and leaned forward over her body to get closer to the black sky over there, and the black fronds of grass.

Trevor had a bad moment, in water over his knees, not knowing which way to go back to the shore. The lake was not very deep in the daytime, not until you were way out there, he told himself. He was fine. He took a step one way, and thought maybe the bottom sloped down. He took a step back, and that was definitely sloping down. Any way he stepped, it got deeper.

He was frightened, but on the other hand, there he was in the middle of the lake, in the middle of the night, alone. No waves, no wind. He was in the world, himself completely, no part left out. The moon was in the sky. He stood still.

His flashlight carving a small oval of real world out of the darkness, Moreland walked down to the cabin from behind the store, where he'd parked the truck so as not to wake anyone up along the cabins. He was stiff from that marathon of work. Beautiful night, a far cry from the last few days of dust and paint. Grace didn't know he was coming out, wouldn't be waiting on him. There was time for the luxury of a walk around the lake.

His wobbling flashlight picked and pricked out to the lake, dancing on the mud as he walked—and what was that in the distance? It was a head shining over the water.

Hair flying upwards: Trevor. Fifty yards out, the nut. Moreland took his shoes off, since he hated cleaning shoes, and after thinking a minute, took off his pants too. His boxers were shorts, after all.

Trevor had crouched down to feel with his fingers which way the bottom sloped, and at first he didn't see the flashlight moving on the surface. Then he thought it was the moon. But it was a light coming bobbing from the land. So *that* was the direction! He would have walked the other way, he thought.

"Stay still, Trev," Moreland called gently over the water, not to alarm him. "I'll come out to you, and we'll have a wade together."

Clary felt a clutch on her waist, and heard Pearce answering Moreland, before she realized that she had heard Moreland. She had fallen asleep! Would she have woken if Pearce had crawled away down into the water? Her slow brain finally re-heard Moreland, saying *Trevor*, saying something—she sat up, grabbing Pearce, and stood to scan the darkness.

156

There on the lake, a moving light caught something—

"Trevor?" she cried, too afraid to keep her voice steady. The water's dimpling surface broke up the light—she had made Trevor fall backwards into the water.

"Oh!" she cried again, stumbling along the path with Pearce hanging awkwardly from her arm, the sweater swinging around her neck, no use now.

Then she saw Moreland, and heard him calling back to her to calm down, calm down, he had him. Moreland had him.

Grace made cocoa and found Trevor a soft old pair of Fern's shorts to wear to bed. He lay on the couch and listened to Grace scolding Moreland for coming out in the middle of the night and scaring them all, although if he had not, who knew what might have happened, and for letting Trevor have a midnight swim once he'd found him, which was just childish, and so on.

Clary was silent, sitting at the other end of the couch holding Trevor's feet in her hands, which were not warm themselves but seemed to make him warmer.

In the wicker rocking chair Moreland held Pearce, watching his drowsing baby face. "Good boy," he said. "I missed you, Grace, that's all. I'm allowed to miss you."

19. Tumbling blocks

*T*he house was still standing. No lumber or workmen around, no debris on the grass. It looked to Clary as if Moreland might have done some yardwork. The children were hungry, so she let Mrs. Pell stump off around the side of the house—mad again—and went straight to the kitchen, stepping lightly to let Darwin stay asleep in the basement. But Trevor and Dolly ran down the stairs before she thought to stop them: clatter, clatter, and then wild shouts.

Trevor galloped back up the stairs to grab her arm and pull her. She checked that she had fastened Pearce properly into the high chair, because everything was dangerous, and then let Trevor have her hand.

The stairwell seemed lighter. Fresh paint, she realized, as she was rushed down. At the bottom of the stairs, an empty field of bright green carpet was splotched with squares of light. A big window—Moreland must have helped with that, he was a great one for windows. They had scooped out a well to put it in, and lined it with ridged aluminum and pea gravel in the bottom, like one of Moreland's new buildings. The window was beautiful. The carpet was lurid, green as Astroturf.

"Look! See?" Trevor said, as the boy had in Clary's earliest school reader, showing Mother the new puppy. He flung open a pair of over-ornate louvred doors, and there were the washer and dryer.

Dolly found a separate room with the old basement window, looking small now, behind a gathered green panel. A single bed against the wall. She wanted it to be her room, she wanted it so bad—but that would mean that Darwin was gone, that the wind had changed. It would mean that her mom was dead and so Darwin was finished helping her. That thought caught Dolly up short. She'd been doing so well not thinking. She almost had to throw up, but she ran out into the big room and rolled around on the floor. She would go to the canning cupboard and break the jars into a million pieces. Trevor jumped on her and hurt her stomach but she didn't even mind. She grabbed him and hugged him as hard as iron, like a clamp.

Mrs. Zenko called down the stairs from the back door.

Clary said, "Come and see!" like the children. She wondered how much money she owed Moreland for all this, and if she could ever get used to this carpet. The furnace room was lined with boxes, more orderly and well-labelled than before; and the ancient rolled-up Persian carpet of her mother's. But she couldn't put that over the violent green, which would after all be a good playground for the children.

"My, my, my," Mrs. Zenko kept exclaiming, even as she was coming down, even before she saw the hidden laundry, and the secret door to the cold-room.

"They worked like bees down here the last few days. Your dad would have been so pleased," Mrs. Zenko said as they trooped back upstairs. That was true—although Clary's mother had resisted the tiniest change in the house after his death, in life her father had been a relentless fiddler and improver.

Clary felt strange, standing in the kitchen over top of that clear empty space down there. She felt like the graves of her parents had been hollowed out and aired, like their clinging spirits were lifting and drifting out of the house and up, beyond the garden into the tops of the trees. Not desecration, but opening. Out the kitchen window the tall birch tree was shaking its leaves in a light wind. Her mother would tangle in the gold lace leaves and her father would wind himself calmly around the trunk. Older in death, and more stable.

Darwin said he had a box of doughnuts.

"What kind?" Mrs. Pell asked him through the workshop door, not wasting breath on chat. Fine with her if he wanted to suck up.

"Maple glaze," he said.

She undid the lock, hooked the box out of his hand and shut the door again. She checked. He knew what she liked. She went back to the recliner, draped with an old quilt from the pile left out here for covering tomato plants. He was free with his money, give him his due. A dozen, and no *save some for the kids.* Trying to make up for manhandling her, the bugger. She crammed her mouth full of doughnut. The door scratched open, light streaming too bright for her eyes. He couldn't bully her. That Rose was a bootlegger or some such thing. She ran a still for a years, that's what Clayton had heard. Darwin upturned a garbage can and sat, making himself right at home.

"You don't want to live with Clary," he said. Like he was hypnotizing her.

"Maybe I do!" she said, quickly. Where else was she going to go, now that Millie Lyne had thrown her out for good? She was out here to make a point.

"You need a little privacy, a little independence," he said. "At your age."

Mrs. Pell agreed, it was not what she had coming. "I'll have the old age pension by the end of August. $450 a month. And she's looking into retroactive. I'll get what I'm owed."

"But you don't want to be at somebody else's beck and call. You need a place of your own, that's what I'm saying."

"You're the one with the fancy basement," she said, doughnut making her voice thick.

"You don't want to be climbing stairs all day long. Besides, you're not private in a basement. Them all walking around on top of you."

That was true. But she wasn't going to be parked in some seniors' poorhouse. Clayton had a duty, and if he wasn't here, then Lorraine had it—and she was getting everything done by Clary. Mrs. Pell's reasoning trailed along like a dog looking for the source of a meaty smell. They owed her. She bit another doughnut.

"I'm thinking this is a pretty good place, this shop out here," Darwin said.

She followed his eyes as he looked the place over: long room with windows along one wall. Blinds, so snoopers wouldn't see your every move. Sun coming in. Alley door down there. The long shape of it was like the cabin in Nanton where her sister Janet had lived when she first got married. The rag-pieced quilt was like what Janet used to make.

"You know this was here?" Darwin opened a door she hadn't bothered with. Washroom, with a sink and toilet. "Her dad was a plumber, first. Good carpenter, too. Built this place sound."

She'd peed in a cup the other night, thrown it on the gravel out the back alley. He had a grin on his face. Up to something. He wasn't pulling the wool over her eyes. They were trying to get rid of her. No way she was getting kicked out of Clary's.

"You set yourself up in here, nobody can tell you what to do. Your cheque comes to Clary's mailbox. Same address. I could find you a bed, some furniture. Give it a lick of paint."

Mrs. Pell got up and walked slowly, favouring her cramped hip, to check the little washroom. She flushed the toilet. That worked. She went back to the lounger. The quilt had been pieced properly, using up old clothes, not one of these fake quilts you got now. It was that one, Tumbling Blocks. Tiny stitches: the dotted line on a highway. Sweet itch under the fingers.

"I don't want to be stuck paying for power," she said. "And there's no TV!"

Darwin went out the open door. A minute later he came back, staggering a little, with the white TV in his arms. He waggled the TV side-to-side onto the counter, and pulled the remote out of his pocket.

"No cable," Mrs. Pell said.

He burst out laughing. "Hook into Clary's," he said. "I'll get my buddy at the cable company to run it out for you. All legal." Pleased with himself, big banana smile.

When the children were asleep, Clary knocked on Mrs. Zenko's door. Mrs. Zenko was quite likely to be choosing her numbers for the lottery at 10 p.m., or washing the kitchen floor. She was a nighthawk *and* a morning glory, she liked to say.

"Darwin says you lent him some furniture for Mrs. Pell," Clary said. She hugged Mrs. Zenko, reaching down because she was so compact.

"I was glad to find a use for that old couch," Mrs. Zenko said, blushing at the touch. She stepped outside and waved Clary to sit on the porch chairs. "And the bed's been in my garage since Nathalie went to England. I can't pretend to like that woman very much, but it's better for the children if she's less dissatisfied, isn't it? She washed that old pieced quilt your Dad's mother made—did a good job of it."

"She likes it," Clary said.

"Are you off to the hospital? I'll check on the children every little while, if you like."

"Darwin says she doesn't want me. They're pleased with the results, but she's not in good shape."

Mrs. Zenko's eyes filled. "I remember so well when your dad was ill," she said. "And John." She flicked away the tears and stood up to go in. "A lot of people have to go through this type of thing. It seems like the world is badly run, some days."

Clary drove over to do the banking on her computer in the office; easier when no one was around. The building was dark. She felt like a thief, though she'd come in to work in the evening countless times. Twenty years at the firm, but she shut the door quietly. The situation was a little grey. She hadn't heard from Barrett yet about her leave of absence, and wasn't sure whether she was still technically employed.

Her finances, once she got online, were a shock. At first she thought her salary must have already been stopped, but it had been deposited as usual. She had known that she'd need to transfer money, but she couldn't believe how much she had spent in the last few weeks. How could she have let this get so out of hand? And now Moreland to pay back for the renovations. Five thousand? If she was lucky.

She called Moreland in Davina.

"The basement is beautiful," she told him. "I thought Darwin was talking about a few sheets of dry-wall."

"Oh well, if you're going to do a thing at all," Moreland said. "Might as well do it up right. That Darwin, he's a good worker, he and Fern made short shrift of the painting, and she made that little curtain in the bedroom, did you notice it?"

"Of course I did," Clary said, seeing in her mind Fern's thin, tendril arms stretching up to set the panel in place. "Tell Fern it's the nicest curtain I've ever seen."

"Well, we're happy if you're happy," Moreland said.

Clary felt a weight of shame. Moreland had rescued Trevor while she slept. She wondered if he was worried about the children in her care. "Moreland," she started, then didn't know how to go on. "You obviously laid out a lot of money on the basement, and I'd like to reimburse you right away. I can mail you a cheque, or deposit it into your account, if you like."

A little silence, and then Moreland laughed.

"I mean it, Moreland," she said, jumping over his laughter. "I'd like to get this off my conscience right away."

"I'm just laughing because you're such a prickle-puss. Like your Mom."

Clary felt that pinch in her throat that she always got when anyone compared her to her mother. She was *not*, actually, anything like her mother.

"Okay, okay. I got the carpet for fifty bucks from Murray Frayne, end-of-roll from the golf course, as you might guess. Darwin's pals brought the lumber and the ceiling tiles, so you'll have to go to him about that, and the labour was all given. The window was a credit from Patterson's I never thought I'd get a chance to use, so you've done me a favour there, and Henley turned up with those godawful louvred doors because his wife hates them and he'd had to take them out of his own house; brand new, but she wants walnut. So—oh, I forgot one thing, you owe me a hundred dollars for the paint. It took four gallons, but I did get it on sale."

Clary was silent.

"And if you think you're the only person around here that can do the decent thing, you're sadly mistaken, Miss Clary. You get a grip on yourself and write me out a cheque for a hundred dollars, and I'd like to see it in the mail by Monday."

She didn't know how to allow him this.

"I had a good time, Clary, and I like that Darwin guy, and those kids. I got a kick out of doing this one little thing, and I've told you the honest truth about the costs."

She knew he hadn't, by him saying that. She knew him pretty well too.

"A hundred and fifty," she said.

"What?"

"You said you paid fifty for the carpet."

"Oh, right."

"Liar."

"Like I say, we lucked out there on the roll-ends."

She said, "Well, we're going to need more carpet—Darwin moved Mrs. Pell out to my dad's old workshop, and it's a concrete floor. Darwin's going to call Murray to see if he can find some more, but I want to pay for it properly."

Moreland laughed. "Good for Darwin," he said. "Get that old bat out of your hair."

The office was darker after she hung up the phone. The cold light from the computer screen didn't help. She still had to transfer money from her savings account, and without her salary for the next few months the best thing might be to cash in some GICs. She hadn't realized how much people eat, and the cost of clothes and diapers, let alone furniture. It was fine—she could have spent the same money on a Caribbean cruise. This was better. What was the worst that could happen? She remembered asking herself that as she went out the door to the grocery store, where Trevor had wet his pants and probably gained another emotional scar, and Mrs. Pell had robbed the place blind.

Clary reached into her desk drawer for ibuprofen, but her hand met nothing. The drawer was empty. She opened the file drawer below: empty hanging files, jingling faintly as they swung. In the bottom drawer, nothing. Barrett, hurt, must have ordered her desk cleaned out.

She found Mat's stash of blank CDs, opening her cabinet boldly in spite of a ridiculous impulse not to leave fingerprints. It took almost an hour to sort and burn her current work files, but she had them, she'd be covered. She erased anything personal and reset the password to ABC123, feeling both paranoid and sensible.

The evening cleaner came up behind her as she was locking the outer door of Gilman-Stott. She gave him a jaunty "Goodnight!" That would set Barrett's nerves jangling, when he heard that she'd been at the office. What did it matter, she thought. Time to check on the children.

Mrs. Pell turned in the new bed. Hadn't taken her long to get moved in over here, once the place was scrubbed down. Kids wanted to scurry all over the place, flushing the toilet and what-not. Getting them chased out took the longest. She turned again, then heaved off the covers and sat up, taking a long time over it, hand over hand. She could switch on the TV if she wanted to. Go to her own bathroom. Sock feet planted on the piece of green rug they'd given her, she laughed to herself.

Too bad her sister Janet couldn't see her now, she thought. Too bad Janet had died, screaming her head off with her breast. And now Lorraine. Even in the dark Mrs. Pell could feel the tumbling blocks diamonding down the quilt.

Once doughnut left in the box that she'd hidden under the bed when the kids came tearing over. With a grunt she slid off the bed onto her knees, and groped under the bed as far as she could reach with her swollen hands. Not so fresh anymore, but still. She hauled herself back up onto the bed and sat panting, taking a bite and breathing some more. She wasn't too well. She pushed that out of her head. A bite. Behind her eyelids a parade of people walked: Dougie Pell, Clayton when he was a teenager, her dad, Clayton's dad—that fucker. And herself, when she was six, sitting beside Janet, watching Janet's needle go in and out, in and out, little stitches.

20. Raspberry

*D*arwin wouldn't take any money either. In lieu of rent, he said, and nowhere near enough; he cut off any argument by telling her the hospital was talking about sending Lorraine home when she was released from this isolation period after chemo. Clary went in to find out the details.

The dire smell of the ward hit her in the face after a grace period away. She walked the familiar route down the hall—then farther, because Lorraine had been moved to an isolation room, with an ante-room for visitors to wash. The little ritual took time, and attention to the instructions printed over the sink, before she could move through to the room itself.

Lorraine was sleeping. Narrow drip-lines draped her in a spider's web.

A strange man sat in a chair against the wall; Clary saw he was there for the other patient in the room. He was staring at her: a young woman—a girl, lying flat down with no pillow, her closed eyes purple dents in her head. The man didn't move, or acknowledge Clary. He was not sleeping.

After hesitating a minute, Clary passed close by him to go to Lorraine's bedside. She put her hand on her own cheek first, to check its temperature in case she should be too cold, and then on Lorraine's cheek to wake her gently. Nothing.

Lorraine's chest rose and fell, her hair fell away from her brow and ears. She was as deep in sleep as Snow White, lying in this huge glass coffin. Clary turned from the bed and left.

Early in the evening, Paul knocked on the door. Clary was so surprised and glad to see his thin, sweet face that she almost leaned forward to kiss him, as if he were family, or Moreland.

She stopped herself in time, and opened the door wide.

To Paul's ears the house thrummed with life: Pearce singing at the top of his voice in the kitchen, Dolly and Trevor racing each other to be first to the door.

"We went to the lake, and I nearly drowned," Trevor said, beating Dolly to being interesting, at least. They crowded Paul with them into the kitchen, where ice cream was melting in their bowls. Pearce gave Paul a massive, tooth-splaying smile and shouted at him generally, waving a spoon. He had ice cream on the top of his head. Clary got a cloth from the drawer and ran warm water, adding to the wash of noise and light.

"You had dessert already!" Paul pulled a quart basket from the red-splotched bag he carried. "Look, I brought raspberries I picked myself."

"I thought that was blood," Trevor said.

"You probably can't have any raspberries now," Paul said sadly.

"No, no," Dolly said. "Raspberries are good for us, but they give Darwin blisters."

Clary washed Pearce's head and face while he spluttered. "You can put them on your ice cream. You dole them out, Paul. Where did they come from?"

"I had to go out to St. Peter's Abbey for a meeting, and the monks took me for a walk in the raspberry canes afterwards. Look, some are golden, not red—like beads of honey."

She turned her head to see, and he popped a raspberry into her mouth, warm and perfect, a bud of light. Everything smelled of raspberries. His nervous fingers were stained from picking, so she could see the whorls marked red on the smooth skin, the maze-marks that were only his. She laughed and opened her mouth for another one.

167

Pearce opened his mouth too, and Dolly and Trevor, birds in the nest demanding theirs, all the little mouths to feed. And Darwin came shooting up the stairs to demand ice cream before he went to the hospital, and raspberries too, allergy or no. He slapped Paul on the back and thanked him for the help.

"Help?" Clary asked.

"He came and painted, Monday," Darwin said, delicately sifting a huge fistful of raspberries past his lips, straight into his mouth. "You should see it now, man."

"I happened to be driving by," Paul said to Clary. "I stopped to see—"

The doorbell rang, one long buzz.

Clary sighed and unwound her hair from Pearce's fingers. "You stay here," she told him. "Sit with Paul, instead." She plopped him down on Paul's long, bony leg.

It was Barrett Gilman at the door.

She stepped back, wanting to shut the door on his rosy, self-flooded face.

"Clara!" he said, jocular and benevolent, which she knew from experience meant he had unpleasant news. She wasn't letting him in the house. Too bad Mrs. Pell had taken her dinner out to the shop and couldn't be rude to him.

"Well, Clara," he said, after a pause.

She stood waiting, door in hand, knowing that he was truly going to annoy her now, and said nothing.

"I've got some paperwork here, may I come in?"

"Sorry," she said, stooping for a sandal. "I'm on my way out. Can I have a look at it on the porch?" She called back over her shoulder, while easing Barrett backwards, "Darwin, Paul, I'm going down to the hospital, will you wait till I get back before you go?"

A shout of assent from the men and the children, and she could shut the door behind her, keeping the pollution of Barrett out of her house.

"It's awkward," he was saying.

"Oh, no, it'll be fine, here, on the bench." She swept toys aside, and let Barrett find his own space. "I assume the company wants me to resign," she said, before he could spin it out into endless blaming and condoling.

"Well. There were difficulties— I've got a form, and I'll explain the notations…"

He fumbled in the attaché case, the one his mother gave him for Christmas in 1992. She knew too much about this un-friend, and none of it good: his everlasting excuses for indolence; his pink satin tie, stained with a gravy-spot after the '97 awards lunch; the way he clung obsessively to the fountain pen he was now pulling out, to witness her signing away whatever rights she probably had.

"You know, I really don't have time. Just point where to sign," she said. She could hardly bear to be near him for another minute! But if she left now she'd have to see him again, to sign the damn forms.

"And here, and…" He gave her a Gilman-Stott ballpoint and pointed to the arrows where her signature was required. "This is really too bad," Barrett said, watching her sign and flip, sign and flip.

Sign, sign, sign—she grabbed her copies. Her vacation pay, her waiver of claim, and a standard confidentiality agreement; a cheque attached, paying her out for the last year and a half of accumulated holiday time and employee benefits and disengaging her permanently from the firm. Several thousand dollars. That would be helpful, in the short term. Her pension buyout: a letter delaying that for a few months, but it would mean a lump for investing somehow; time to worry about that later.

"You'll need my keys," she said, yanking them off her ring.

"I'm distressed about all this, Clara."

"So what?" she said, straightening up to look him in the eye. "You've made no effort at all to help me. After twenty years in your office, I deserved better."

His eyes boggled. He must not have expected rudeness from her. Or truth.

Well, there's a limit, she thought, skipping down the front steps and off away from his gravitational pull—a comet passing Jupiter and spinning away, free!

Lorraine was not completely coherent. She turned her head restlessly on the pillow, vaguely agitated, asking for Darwin.

"He's coming soon. I got to come first," Clary told her, damping a cloth in cool water to wash her face. A clump of stray hairs lay on her pillow. Clary gently brushed them off.

"That's good," Lorraine said. "That's good."

"I know. I was just washing Pearce's face, and his head—he had ice cream all over."

"Pearce."

"He's fine, he's with Darwin, they're all finishing their dessert while I run in to see you. Darwin says they're going to boot you out of here soon, that's wonderful."

"Yeah."

"Did he tell you about all the changes at the house? He's got Mrs. Pell moved into my dad's old shop, and she seems pretty tickled. As far as one could tell."

Lorraine smiled, her cheeks not moving. Clary washed Lorraine's hands, putting each in turn back on the green hospital coverlet, and they lay where she'd put them, limp and white under the brown remaining tan. There was great satisfaction in doing this small service for her.

"The children will be beside themselves with joy to have you home," Clary said.

Lorraine nodded. Without any change in her expression two tears slid easily from the corners of her eyes, and rolled down her cheeks. She made no move to wipe them off.

"You're too tired for chat," Clary said. "You've been going through all this so well. A couple more days, and you'll feel much better."

Lorraine nodded again, even more briefly than before, her chin dipping slightly. Clary leaned forward and kissed her ashy cheek. She was careful not to cry herself.

In the other bed, the young woman lay flat, abandoned.

Checking the mailbox when she got home, Clary found the phone bill. She opened it as Darwin was getting his keys and his hat. $439 in long distance— all billed to her phone card, which she hadn't used for months. There was some mistake. Darwin came through the hall and patted her shoulder as he went out, letting the screen door bang behind him. Calls to Spiritwood, to Onion Lake, Meadow Lake, Stanley Mission, Winnipeg, La Ronge—all within a couple of days last month. Fort McMurray. She knew it before her plodding brain caught up. Clayton, calling around to find Darwin, using the phone card she had not missed from her wallet.

The doorbell rang early in the morning, before the children had eaten breakfast. Barrett again, Clary thought, because of the angry insistence of the bell. She went reluctantly to the door, Pearce on her hip.

It was Bradley Brent from next door. Brent Bradley.

He burst into hissing speech, like a shaken beer bottle fizzing over. "What's next?" He glared at her, but didn't give her any time to respond. "What will it be? This is a respectable neighbourhood, where the bylaws still get taken seriously. The construction, the noise, the constant crying of that baby! And now some kind of ramshackle flophouse in the back yard."

"Our baby never cries," Clary cried, honestly indignant. "For a minute, maybe, once in a long while. He is a very good baby!"

"The baby has nothing to do with it. There is no bylaw—would that there were—against a crying baby. But there are rules and regulations about construction. I saw no permit posted, I saw no notice of intent to convert the house into a rooming house!"

Clary's heart was beating like a metronome, flap-flap-flap-flap, quick march time. Her mouth was open to rebut, but not being able to say *Mr. Brent!* or *Mr. Bradley!* with any kind of confidence seemed to be holding her back.

His little eyes looked crazy, and his lips pooched out when he talked. "I serve you notice, I intend to fight this thing to the limit of the law. You are lowering property values and introducing a very low-class element to the street."

Trevor and Dolly had crept up to watch. How dared he say low-class in front of them?

"The property inspector assures me that he will be paying you a little visit, very soon. And when he does—"

"Listen!" she said, arresting him in mid-rant. "You're disturbing us. If you don't wish me to call the police, kindly get off my porch."

He gaped, the whites of his eyes showing. "You *threaten* me?"

"Mr. Brent, stop! You're mistaken. There was no construction, just finishing drywall in the basement, and I'm certain that my cousin, the builder in charge, saw that regulations were meticulously followed. The existing structure in my garden has been a temporary habitation for thirty years. When the property inspector, who I believe is still my father's old friend Stan Granik, visits, I'll be happy to give him a cup of coffee and show him around. I know he'll be too considerate to arrive before the children have eaten their breakfast."

She shut the door. Her knees were shaking. Trevor squeezed her arm on one side, and Dolly patted her back on the other. She hoped that was true, that Moreland would have seen to permits. How badly she wanted to sit down! To be accused of lowering the tone of the neighbourhood—it was a joke. In a minute she would laugh.

But her house *was* ramshackle. Children's jumble crowded the living room: the rocking baby seat, the playpen, a huge box of Lego that Moreland had brought in from Davina (an extra half-hour of picking up at the end of the night), crayons, shoes, clothes. On the kitchen counters baby-food jars and cartoon plastic cups jostled appliances: the blender, the toaster, the sandwich-maker. She shouldn't give them grilled cheese sandwiches so often. The children's room was so much theirs now that Clary couldn't think what it had been before—the guest room, and before that, her own childhood room. She could hardly make her memory's eyes refocus. Her father's den had spun through the whole roulette wheel: first Clayton's tainted room, then Mrs. Pell's lair; now an empty shell waiting for Lorraine. At least that room was clean.

Clary called Paul.

"I'm going to pick Lorraine up from the hospital tomorrow," she told him. "I didn't want you to go looking for her and not find her."

But that was only an excuse. She wanted to talk to him, and had no other earthly reason but Lorraine.

"Thank you," he said. He sounded puzzled by her call, she could hear that.

He could too, and was quick to correct it. "I'm sorry—I just got off the phone with my wife's lawyer. Thank you, I would have been worried about Lorraine."

"They're letting her come home, she's officially in remission."

"That's wonderful!"

"No, it's not real. They know they can knock out 99 per cent of the lymphoma, but it will definitely come back. This is just the first part. They'll be waiting for her to recover for a couple of weeks and then she'll go through it all again." She felt an absurd hankering to cry. But it was not her who was in this terrible trouble.

"Clary," he said. "I'm sorry. I know that your mother's death must be refreshed every time you enter that hospital."

Oh, why would he say that? Why get her started?

"My father's, too," she said. "I thought I had forgotten it." She was not sure whether she was crying or only breathing too hard.

"It goes in waves, doesn't it, the long period of mourning?"

"His study is not his any more—my mother kept it bronzed! I'd always meant to do the basement but it's— And now I've moved Mrs. Pell into his workshop, and I don't even know where his tools are…"

"I don't think he needs a museum, Clary. I think if he is aware of your actions they must please him far more than keeping his tools in a vault."

If my mother is aware of my actions, Clary thought, the ether will be ringing with her wrath. And how she would hate Mrs. Pell!

21. Queen of Spades

A strange black van drove into the driveway. Dolly was at the window waiting for Darwin and Clary to come back from the hospital with her mom, who was coming home for a while, maybe a month. The van door slid aside and a woman's thin, stiff legs folded partly out, a strange crop-haired puppet sitting still, not getting out after all.

It was her mom, in new clothes. Dolly was supposed to run to the door and down the porch steps and into her arms, but not too fast, to hurt her or something. She stayed still.

Darwin's car drove up too and parked at the curb. He jumped out and yelled, "Dolly! Hey, Dolly! I need you!"

Then Dolly could move again, and go to the door, and pretend to see her mother for the first time. She did a good job of it, she knew her mother was fooled. She danced down the steps quickly, dabbing her feet like a dainty girl—when all the time, inside her body, her huge clumsy soul was a rhinoceros galloping full-horn at a big rock that would smash her to pieces.

"Dolly, Dolly," her mother kept repeating in some stranger's voice, still perched on the edge of the seat.

Trevor tore down the steps, and threw his arms around their mother's knees like he didn't even notice that she was like she was. Dolly stood beside them, not moving away, but it was hard. Her mother's arms moved like slow spider arms, patting Trevor's back and gesturing to Dolly.

Clary got out of the driver's door, struggling with a whole pile of papers and files and a white pharmacy bag. When she saw that their mom couldn't get up, she said, "Stay there a minute till I get this all inside, and—we'll take the children out to the country. We've got this big van for the week, so there'll be room for everybody! Trevor, shoes on. I'll get Pearce."

Dolly pushed by Gran, who'd come stumping out to get a look, and ran back in the house to grab her book. Her mom's hair! Cut off really short, and thin in strange places. She had known it was all going to fall out, but to see it patchy was weird.

She ran down not looking, and shoved into the van, into the back seat, by the window.

"Wait, Dolly," Clary said, leaning in with Pearce's car seat. "Maybe I'll put Pearce in the back, here, where the tether strap is…"

Dolly sat tight, listening to Clary clatter and chatter. Darwin's face came over Clary's shoulder, blocking out the whole doorway, his big huge face. He said, "You can do it, Doll."

They got sorted out, somehow, Dolly ending up beside her mother in the middle seat, Trevor on the other side. Her mother held their hands tight, one in each of hers. Every time the van turned a corner they would sway, and her mother would press on their hands more to keep upright.

The interior of the van was very dark grey, like a funeral car. Staring at her mother, Dolly looked particularly at the piece of skin from underneath the ear down to the chin. It was stretched over the bone under there, the jawbone, too tight. When her mother tried to answer Clary's questions the skin had to move over the bone, there wasn't enough room for it to relax. The collar of her blue sweater sagged away from her mother's chest and Dolly could see the skin too tight there too. The collarbone stood out like a kite stick. Dolly sat still as a stone, waiting for her mother to speak and the skin to move. She wished she could read her book.

Trevor sat on Lorraine's other side, breathing slowly through his pursed mouth to learn whistling. Holding on to her arm through the blue sweater. They went on along the river, beside the row of churches and gradually farther-apart houses and out into country. The roads out there were straight on the flat ground. Not like Trimalo, where roads ran up around hills or through trees, wherever was possible, not where the map would like it best.

"Isn't this nice, to be out," Lorraine said. Her voice sounded like half of herself, to Dolly.

Gran was up front with Clary. Clary told her to open the shopping bag at her feet, and she rustled around awkwardly for a while and then handed back a couple of wrapped parcels.

"For you," Lorraine said, handing one to Trevor and one to Dolly.

Dolly's was long and narrow. Inside was a Barbie doll, lying flat in the long box, eyes wide open. But she was almost ten! You don't play with Barbies when you are a preteen. It was wearing a nurse's uniform, not even a doctor's coat. Trevor had a baby-aged red plastic doctor's set. They'd seen both of those things on sale in the gift shop at the hospital.

Tight in his car seat, Pearce tilted his lower jaw up ferociously to grind at his gums, where more new teeth, coming in, were sending fountains of saliva drooling from his glistening mouth. Lorraine felt her breasts responding, after all these weeks, with the cascading tingle of milk letting down, even though there was none left to let. This had been taken from her too, as well as everything else. Looking past the children's heads out the dark-shaded van windows, Lorraine could see roads spread out around them. Possible routes. At the end of the horizon diagonals of light streamed down from the sky, like God marking the map—where they should strive for. But there was no heaven in those places, just more country. The children were quiet, she must have shocked them. Even Trevor, not one for noticing. She could hear Pearce telling Darwin some long list of interesting things, in his new babbling frog language. Her bones inside her felt too fragile for this trip. They should have stayed home.

Clary drove, looking ahead for some possible point of interest to distract the children with. Bad idea, a drive, and she knew it was because the van rental had seemed like too much money, and she'd needed to find a use for it right away—she was going to have to get a grip with the money thing. If she was left completely penniless after this, then what?

From the very back, Darwin sang out, "Hey, Clary! Turn right at this next gravel road, you can take us up to our cousin Rose's old farmhouse!"

So what, Clary thought, her spirits lifting. She would go back to work, that's all, and they'd be fine. She was hardly unemployable, just because she was unemployed. She turned and drove up a slight rise before the road slid down into a valley between two low folds of prairie. The gravel ran out, and then the dirt road curved around one end of the fold and they found a small abandoned farm, brown-grey outbuildings left to lean gradually back into the earth. The house had empty black windows and a bashed-in front door. Carragana bushes hugged one side.

"That's it," Darwin said, leaning forward, his breath warm on Lorraine's neck.

He put his hand on the back of her head and ruffled up the sparse strands of hair. She flinched a little, knowing that would make more fall out, and not wanting the children to see.

Clary had stopped the van and rolled down the windows. They could hear the sound of the prairie: a differentiation of tiny noises, and the wind. That almost-heard continuing hum was bees, an ominous, monotonous hubbub.

"Strange to think of her way out here with her sisters when she was young," Lorraine said. She could hear her own voice, cracked and strange. Keep quiet, she thought.

Darwin slid an arm past Trevor and opened the side door.

"Let's take a look around, man," he said. Trevor gladly hopped free and headed for the busted farmhouse door.

"Wait," Clary called after Trevor. "It won't be safe in there…" She ran after him.

Darwin kissed Lorraine on the cheek and climbed out with Pearce, and opened Mrs. Pell's door. "You come too," he said. "Do you good to trundle around out here."

It was like Hanna, Mrs. Pell had to admit. Not that she ever wanted to go back there. She creaked down from the high step and looked around for a place to pee.

Dolly and Lorraine were left in the car.

"How you doing?" Lorraine said, hardly above a whisper.

"I'm okay," Dolly said.

They sat silent again.

Dolly felt as if her whole life had come zooming down to this little pin-prick of time, in this empty place. Her eyes seemed to be able to see the bees roaming in and out of the bushes, even though they were too far away.

"I loved Rose," Lorraine said. Trevor came out of the front door, trot-ting along to the back, like Rose must have trotted when she was Trevor's age, Lorraine thought. "She had no temper, she thought everybody was great, she made you laugh. She was a great cook and she loved to keep things clean. I hope Clary is being like that for you guys."

Dolly kept staring fiercely out the open window.

It seemed to Lorraine that she didn't even know she wasn't answering. The pain of not being with the children for the last month pushed at her breast-bone, at her mouth. She held it in. Dolly did not need to see that. I guess I'm going to die of this, Lorraine thought. I guess my children will go on without me, the way I've gone on without Rose. She could see it painted on the walls of the broken-down house: death, abandonment. People do die, she thought. Everybody. And the bees come and hover through the bushes, even so.

She is their mother, Clary told herself a hundred times a day. Let her do it for them. But that was complicated by the weakness Lorraine was trying to hide. She needed help to lift Pearce to her knee to give him his bottle. She had to stand still in the hall for a while, after tucking Trevor and Dolly in, before she could carry on to her bedroom. Her energy peaked and troughed. During the day she moved from room to room restlessly, walking slowly but determined on exercise; she commented often on the freedom from i.v. lines. She tried to eat with the children, but halfway through lunch she would get up and make her way back to bed, fragile eyelids shut, lying on her side with the afghan over her, one hand out into the air of the room, in case the children wanted to sit beside her. Sometimes Trevor did. He would sit on the floor, very still, his back up against the bed, his hand lifted up and resting on his knee to be able to keep holding his mother's hand.

On Thursday night Pearce cried and cried, his gums hurting, and Lor-raine was too exhausted to do anything about it. At 2 a.m. Clary stood in the doorway, the hall night light shining behind her nightgown, and Lorraine was glad to see her.

"You take him in with you tonight," she said.

Clary laid Pearce back in his crib, which made him yell in frustration until she gave him a fresh icy soother, and manoeuvred the crib on its little wheels down the hall to her room. She shut the door on his subdued disgruntled grunts and sucking, and went back to help Lorraine into bed.

Lorraine was crying, jagged tears streaking both sides of her face, leaning forward on the bed to ease her abdomen.

"Are you hurting?" Clary asked her.

Lorraine shook her head. "Just sick," she said. "I'm hot, I don't feel right."

Her temperature stayed high through the night, no matter what Clary did. She put her in a cool bath finally, hoping to keep it from rising any farther, and phoned the cancer ward. There was a brief wait while the nursing station got hold of Lorraine's medical oncologist, and at 5 a.m. the resident called back to say they were sending an ambulance for her. Her temperature was 104 on the old Fahrenheit thermometer, and Clary was glad not to have to torment her by folding her into the van.

Clary woke Darwin, then phoned Mrs. Zenko and asked her to come over to be with the children. They were all awake by now, huddled on the floor beside Lorraine's bed with frightened faces. Clary wished she could send Mrs. Zenko to the hospital and stay home with the children herself. She shook off cowardice and shoved her wallet in her pocket, and backed the van out to follow after Lorraine.

Once the ambulance had gone, the children sat with Mrs. Zenko, watching *Cinderella* for the fortieth time, Trevor still snivelling gently. Dolly was afraid Mrs. Zenko would try to hug her or hold her, but she did not, she just let Trevor tuck his cold hands under her sweater elbow where it was warm. Pearce slept and slept, as though he had had enough life for a while.

From the hospital, Clary called Grace and Moreland and asked them to help, just for a few days.

"I can't manage on my own," she said, and it was a relief to admit it.

Grace came up trumps, of course. They drove in straight away, and while Fern settled the children, Grace got a fridge-full of groceries and ran a mop around the place.

When Clary dragged herself home at midnight the three of them were sitting in the clean kitchen playing Hearts, and Grace immediately put a mug of tea and a shot glass of brandy in front of her.

Clary hated brandy but she took a gulp. "She's okay," she told them. "She's hooked up to every line in the universe, again, and that giggling student nurse hurt her hand again putting in the i.v. line, so they had to go back to the wrist, but she looks better already. Darwin's staying the night, and I told him I'd go back early in the morning. It's bad timing, because school starts next week and we were going in to register the children…"

She paused to drink the tea. And the brandy was good. She finished it.

"Care to play a hand?" Moreland asked. He was a demon at Hearts, he never lost.

"I would," she said, and prepared to receive the Queen of Spades.

22. Jesus, Mary and Joseph

*T*he next night was bad too—Friday night. Darwin was in the orange chair when Clary left at midnight; closing the door she saw his eyes open, and he nodded, never really sleeping. Hours and visits blurred, but by Saturday's evening visit antibiotics had brought some light back into Lorraine's grey skin. While Darwin played euchre with her, letting her choose cards with a bent straw, Clary went back to help Fern put the children to bed, and to get some sleep herself.

Leaving the hospital after a hard visit with Joe Kane, Paul saw that it was raining and stopped to put on his windbreaker, hoping vaguely that he himself would be more willing to let go, at eighty-seven. The zipper wouldn't do up—he should break down and buy a new jacket.

He was conscious of added weight in the building, Lorraine back on the fifth floor again. In a room alone this time, never a good sign. Paul said a quick silent prayer for her, pushing away death. (*Binnie is dead, dead—how can it be true?* ran the constant subtitle under all his thoughts.)

He was afraid to go up, that was the bare truth. Coward. At least he could stand in the hall and say hello. He turned and caught the elevator as the doors were closing, and was raised up in one smooth swoop.

Darwin was standing in the door of Lorraine's new room.

"Hey, man," Darwin said. "Lorraine'll be glad to see you. I'll go down the hall for a while, since you're here for a visit."

He was not, he did not want to be. He had visited enough death today. He nodded, and clasped Darwin's hand, and went in.

Lorraine was restless in the bed, her legs moving constantly beneath the sheets, but she held out her hand to him.

"Hey," she said. "You didn't come round Clary's while I was home, I was expecting to see you."

He said he was happy to have been expected, and sorry not to have come.

"Darwin's gone to get more ice," she said. "I like it."

Paul nodded. He could see, now, that she was feverish and off-kilter.

"He's good to me," she said. "He's better than Clayton. Poor Clay."

He should be soothing her, comforting her, but she was going full tilt. "Clayton would be here if he knew but nobody knows where he is, you know." Her eyes were bright but slightly unfocused. "Jesus, Mary and Joseph," she said. Her legs switched—one side, other side of the bed. "He knew he couldn't take it, there's no shame in knowing you can't handle something, you know yourself the best, nobody can know for you. Clary thinks he stinks but I still love him, I shove him, I glove him."

Paul kept her hand in his, gripping back when she gripped his, releasing a little when she released. He said nothing, but gave her all his attention.

"I have to watch him," she whispered, urgent to tell. "He will—he tried—he shook Pearcey when he was—I stopped him, I stopped him in time, but it was rough. But it's only from time to time, when things get him going, I can manage it."

She stared deep into Paul's eyes, needing something from him that he tried to give. Not absolution, he didn't think it was that.

"They're his. They're *mine*. They're not hers."

"No," he said. "They are your children. They know that very well."

Maybe that was it. She lay back, and her legs ceased their constant restless movement. She kept his hand, but then Darwin came in, and she turned to him instead.

"I know what I have to do," she said. "I know how to do it."

Darwin sat on the bed beside her and let his hand rest on her abdomen, spread wide, very still.

"I know now," she said, more calmly.

"She's been straying this last couple of days," Darwin told Paul, without taking his eyes away from Lorraine. "A bad night last night."

Paul nodded. "I thought—"

Darwin looked up and caught his eyes. "The nurse will be in pretty soon with some more serious stuff, it'll calm her down again."

Lorraine tried to sit up. "I've got to go—"

"No, sweetheart, you got to stay for a while," Darwin said. He pressed her shoulders down, sliding her pillow into better comfort as he made her lie back.

"I don't have to go," she said obediently. "Not right now."

"Not now," he said, agreeable.

Paul thought he would get a coffee before tracking back up to see Lorraine again. But while he was still waiting in line, Darwin came down.

"She's out, she'll be out for a while," he said. "I could give you a ride."

Since Paul had walked, he agreed. But Darwin turned right from the hospital grounds, and drove across the bridge over the shining black water, the lights reflected in arch after arch of shadow-bridge. His big slow car slid down the streets to 21st and parked in front of the Senator Hotel.

"I'm going to get some off-sale—Clary doesn't have anything but her mom's old sherry in the house, and I could use a beer," he said.

"I could too," Paul said.

"Let's go in, then. You play any pool?"

The hotel was crowded and hot on a Saturday night, the music loud, a grey veil of smoke hanging four feet down from the blue Styrofoam-tile ceiling. Darwin got them a table by the wall, working his way through the jostling bodies, saying *Hi, Sheldon! Hey, Chris,* as if this was his regular bar. Paul felt a strange mixture of exhilaration and panic. He had not been in this kind of bar since university, and he must look like a—a priest, he said to himself. He took off his jacket and rolled his sleeves up. Maybe he could look like an off-duty accountant, if he tried.

The girl leaned down to Darwin, but Paul couldn't hear what he said. In a few minutes she was back with a full tray, placing glass after glass on the table. Six glasses of draft beer, and two shot glasses overflowing with whiskey of some kind. Paul could feel a murmur of protest working its way into voice, and he stifled it. A couple of beers weren't going to kill him. His sermon was already finished, for once. The shot was Irish whiskey. It caught at the back of his throat and filled the whole upper half of his chest with a warm transfusion of relief.

"She's delirious," Darwin shouted over the racket.

"I thought, yes," Paul said, nodding his head many times, in case Darwin couldn't hear him either.

"It's some kind of a reaction to her medication, they're not surprised."

Paul was surprised that he could hear what Darwin was saying. The whiskey was helping. He drained one of the beers.

Two older men leaned down, palms on the table, talking to Darwin. Frowzy fellows. They were surprised and pleased to see him, it had been quite a while, and so on. They ignored Paul, after a short nod, so he was free to stare around the room, or what he could see of it in the haze. The noise seemed to be affecting his eyesight. At least a third of these people had to be older than himself. Women with caked, gluey make-up and outfits revealing leathery bosoms and bony shoulders; men with softened faces, noses fallen off their original line, red-blotched skin; those sets sat together in silence or argued, their talk spiked with jeering wheezy laughs. Philosophizing tables of freshly returned university kids too young to be out were sprinkled here and there, as hardened as Pearce, some with goatees or strange sideburns. Eloquent hockey fans leaned toward each other across a large long table, faces all broken and patched-together, little girls with sharp eyes and soft mouths sitting between them.

More beer. These were small glasses, but the draft, although watery, was surprisingly delicious. "*I liked the taste of beer, its live white lather, its brass-bright depth, the sudden world through the wet brown walls of the glass, the tilted rush to the lips and the slow swallowing down to the lapping belly, the salt on the tongue, the foam at the corners.*"

"What?" Darwin yelled, through the arms of the old guys.

"Sorry, nothing—it was Dylan Thomas talking about beer, I'm sorry."

Paul waited to become furious with himself for quoting out loud, but shame did not arrive. Instead, he felt quite happy to have remembered all that, and he began cudgelling his memory for more. Those famous last words, of course: "'*I've had eighteen straight whiskies,*' he said. '*I think that's the record.*'" He was on a roll.

Darwin's eye shifted to him again, even though the larger of the two men was telling him a long, convoluted story about a trailer and two dogs.

"HE SAID," Paul shouted, leaning forward, "He drank to reconcile the disorder outside and the order within himself."

"Me too," Darwin said.

"I drink to forget," Paul said.

"Me too," Darwin said.

"Lisanne."

"Before we die of thirst," Darwin begged the waitress as she sailed by, empty tray skied above helium fingertips.

She gave him a huge heartfelt smile, as women must always do for Darwin, Paul thought. She vanished, but only to serve them the faster.

"I wish Clary was here," Paul said, suddenly.

Darwin drained his glass to the bottom before he nodded and put it down again.

"Someone has to stay home with the babies," Paul said. Then he worried that Darwin might not realize he was joking. But the beautiful waitress came back with that three-cornered, bountiful smile, and Darwin gave her a fat tip—but it wasn't Darwin's turn to tip her, it was Paul's turn, so he tipped her too. There were beers and a couple more shots of Irish on the tray for them, and this time they clinked before knocking them back, and the Irish hit Paul in the places in his throat that had been missing alcohol for too long. He needed a beer to go chasing after it, which is why they call it a chaser, like the hair of the dog who chases.

"I don't normally drink in the evening," he told Darwin, and Darwin nodded and agreed and they were swept up in a group of people Darwin knew who were going on to the Pat, and wanted them to come too, so they drank up the beer and wandered in a straggling strand, a skein of loose knitting, unravelling up the street to the Pat. Good thing they didn't have to drive, Paul was going to say to Darwin, because they should probably not have driven, but

Darwin was far ahead talking to some people who were laughing, and the two drunk university boys beside Paul wanted him to settle a question for them: how do we know that we exist? Are our senses evidence enough? If we can touch a table, then do we know that it is there? What is *there*?

Paul laughed to be in such a conversation, and bent his mind to explicating how we know what we know, in a spume of eloquence that gave him enormous pleasure, riffing on the constantly-shifting boundaries between tacit knowledge and focal knowledge, and how this boundary shift in itself is a tacit skill and is used to blend new information with old, and even to create new, extrapolated knowledge.

"We categorize the world in order to make sense of it," he told the boys, at least the closer boy, the one with the nose rings. "And that gives us unconscious shortcuts. Knowledge is rooted in the tacit. Look, look, this sign,"— staring up at the *ABJ All Makes Pawn Shop* sign, gappy neon fizzing in the quieting night—"is made up of small characters, originally from the Phoenician. But are we ever aware of the alphabet? You don't have to think—you see the words and know what they mean. How do you know English? You don't put conscious thought into how to speak—phrases come already-strung to the tongue. How do you know how to sing? You just sing!"

The smaller boy had the bar door held open by the big brass handle, and it looked too heavy for him. Paul hurried the other nose-ring boy inside.

"But this is epistemology—I am on steadier ground with ethics."

He stopped himself before he told the boys that he was an Anglican priest, because he suddenly found that he was no longer certain whether he was pretending to be slightly drunk to humour them or whether he had slipped ahead of them and was truly drunk. It was like Kelly whatsisname from *At Swim Two Birds*, listening to the little man discoursing on Rousseau: "*Kelly then made a low noise and opened his mouth and covered the small man from shoulder to knee with a coating of unpleasant buff-coloured puke. Many other things happened on that night now imperfectly recorded in my memory, but that incident is still very clear to me in my mind.*"

Where he had been when reading that was still very clear in Paul's mind, sitting on the windowsill at Trinity, perhaps the year before he met Lisanne, perhaps the same year; but before, before. When buff-coloured puke and

JESUS, MARY AND JOSEPH

Rousseau and an addiction to language had seemed all part of one package that he would be untying all his life.

Naturally a wife changes you. As I changed her, Paul thought. He could feel tears coming like blisters, like cold sores ready to sport. He opened his eyes wider and forged his way through the crowd to Darwin, to bid him good night before setting off on the long walk home.

But Darwin reached out a long arm and clawed Paul in beside him to listen to what this guy was saying, and there was another conversation just as fascinating as the tacit knowledge one, this one about some kind of spiritual awakening the guy had had while out all night on a skidoo trip, lost in the wilderness, the moon a pumpkin to save him.

"You never know who's going to tell you the good story," Darwin said. "Wherever you go, there's your teacher."

Paul was thunderstruck by the wisdom of that.

The music was louder than before, it was—someone was playing "Rock Lobster." How long had he gone without hearing "Rock Lobster"? It must be either too long or not long enough. The halls of Trinity came back again. He was old, and maudlin, washed in nostalgia, showing off for the boys.

Paul sank into another trance, watching crazy people gyrating and flailing on the tiny dance floor. Darwin nudged him to go dance, but he was only plastered, not insane. He leaned against the pillar behind him and watched the dancers' shifting, sharding colours. It seemed they were all waving scarves, but those were just their arms.

23. Lonely, lonely

Paul was not in church. Clary didn't like the replacement priest, a sneakered athletic type. He had an air compounded of insecurity and complacency. Absurd even to be noticing Paul's absence. It would have been strange for him to let her know. They had no connection beyond his pastoral duties. She felt abandoned.

The replacement priest's mouth was screwed up into a sugary ecstasy as he opened his sermon with some sanctimonious claptrap: "God flows through you—and because of that *so many beautiful things* have come your way!"

Her heart was littered with hate. Everyone irritated her—even the children. Lorraine had never taken them to church, and that was a perfectly legitimate choice. Clary could not say, *You must believe!* You must be good. You can be good without approaching church. If she had not come to church this morning she would have been much more good.

Trevor slid back into the pew after Sunday school. He opened her hand and pressed something into it: a folded paper bird. He said urgently, "I have to make nine hundred and ninety-eight more of those. Dolly's going to give me hers."

Bile came springing up in Clary's mouth, that some cruel chance would make cancer the story this week—a thousand cranes to save that little Hiroshima leukemia girl. There was no saving her either, and anyway, this was the end of August; they should have been talking about nuclear disasters on the 6th and 9th, if they had to talk about them at all. She was furious. And there was no Paul. Where was he?

Darwin brought Paul a plate of scrambled eggs. Paul shook his head, but his head was filled with exploding drums of used motor oil. He stopped moving so the bed would lie still.

"There's pills there. You should drink all the water. You'll feel better faster, if you eat," Darwin said. It sounded like experienced advice.

Paul ate the eggs. Darwin watched Paul eat, then vanished into the bathroom; no singing in the shower. Paul sat with his plate in his lap, remembering his phone call to Candy Vincent at 6 a.m., telling her that he had a serious case of the flu. She'd been very kind. He had never missed a Sunday service before. He wondered, in a detached way, if they had found anyone to replace him. The sun was high and white—*a flame-white disc in silken mists above shining trees,* like William Carlos Williams's sun. Waving his shirt around his head, wasn't he? Like the people on the dance floor last night.

"*I am lonely, lonely,*" Paul sang softly to himself, from the poem, padding downstairs with his plate. Nobody to hear him, Darwin still in the shower.

"*I was born to be lonely, I am best so!*" His bare feet made a strange noise walking around on the bare living room floor. He kind of liked the new pared-down look.

Dolly's head was jittering with Hiroshima and radiation, but she had read her *Barn* book too many times, it was not working any more. When they got home from church she slid it out from under the mattress and dawdled around the house till Clary told her to take lunch out to Gran. She went out the back, and ran all the way down the long side alleys to Key's Books.

But it was closed, because it was Sunday. Dolly felt like crying. Maybe she could get in somehow. She peered in the window, her hands making a dark frame. There was the old guy, sitting at his desk. He was crazy. Maybe he never went home.

He looked up, his old Bible head turning like an eagle, and saw her staring.

She pulled back from the window as he lumbered over to the door and opened it.

"Looking for something?"

She nodded.

"Come in, then. Kids' books upstairs."

Like he didn't remember chasing her that other time. She slipped past his big arm holding the door, careful to keep her back away from him, where the *Barn* book was hidden. It meant an awkward turn, trying to keep his eyes on her eyes all the time. She put her hand on the middle book table to keep her balance, and pretended to be interested in those books while he went back to his computer.

Mistress Masham's Repose, she saw under her hand. Mistresses were dirty. But the picture on the front was a girl holding a little barrel with a tiny man in it. She opened it—a map inside the cover, the kind of map she loved. This was a kids' book, even though it was down in the old books. She read the first line: *Maria was ten years old…* and looked at the ink pictures of the big-shoed girl and the tiny people and their sheep. She went back to the beginning and read down to *Unfortunately she was an orphan, which made her difficulties more complicated than they were with other people.*

Dolly wanted the book so badly she never thought of stealing it. She wanted to keep it forever, not to borrow it. She left it on the table and went up the teetering stairs, and slid the *Barn* book back onto its place in the shelves, so she was even with the giant. Then she went back down.

"How much is this?" she asked him.

He blinked away from his screen and glared at her, and held out his hand for the book.

"$4.25," he said. "An even five, with the tax."

"Will you save it for me while I go home for some money?"

His eyes were scary, but she kept looking into them. That's how wild beasts could be tamed.

"Take it," he said. "Bring the money later."

Clary was surprised when Dolly grabbed her arm, and surprised by the pinch of her grip.

"Please can I have five dollars?"

Automatic questions occurred to Clary, but she saw Dolly's desperate face and turned instead to get her wallet. Stupid Sunday school teachers. "Do you need a drive somewhere? We're out of coffee anyway."

Dolly shook her head and shot out the back door.

Clary watched her running through the back gate. If it was candy she wanted, fine. Whatever helped.

Coffee. The route took Clary past Paul's house, standing on its corner looking bereft. The grass was long, the vines reddening and drooping off the roof of the porch. The porch light was on in the daytime, sad—he must have turned it on from habit, waiting for his wife to come home. She drove on, forgetting the coffee she'd gone for until she was at her driveway. She made an exasperated sound which Pearce, along for the ride, picked up. He *tsh*ed all the way back to the store, laughing every time she laughed at him. Good to have a baby to make fun of you.

Paul came round the corner of the house, dragging the lawn-mower, in time to see Clary driving away. He looked on the porch to see if she might have left something. Parishioners did, these days, but he would not have lumped Clary in with the set of women likely to drop off a casserole. He'd forgotten to turn off the porch light.

Was that her driving by again? Perhaps he was seeing her where she wasn't. *Heart of silver, white heart-flame of polished silver, burning beneath the blue steeples of the larkspur.* Madonna of the Garden, that was. *Te Deums of Canterbury bells.* Foolish stuff, not even memorable. *More lovely and more temperate,* that was better.

24. Stone school

*L*ife had to continue anyway. Whatever happened to Lorraine, the children had to go to school. Iris Haywood, the principal of Brundstone School, two blocks south and one block west of Clary's house, was married to the parish treasurer from St. Anne's. She had seen Clary with the children on Sundays and had gathered the whole story from mysterious parish sources. She welcomed the children to the school with grave formality, and then sent them to wait in the hall.

"The mother is not expected to recover, I understand," she said.

Clary's heart seemed to stop entirely. She stared into Mrs. Haywood's face, wishing she could jump toward *Yes! She is!* But unable to do so.

"Sometimes the doctors are wrong," Mrs. Haywood said. "We'll have to hope for that."

How far away were the children? Would they have heard? Clary's heart beat again, painfully, and she said, "We're going from day to day."

"Well, you're very good." Iris Haywood was a tall, imposing woman, blonde and almost graceful in a suit and little heels. She made it to the door before Clary, and opened it. "Now this is lucky, it's kindergarten orientation today. Let's take Trevor down to Mrs. Ashby's room and introduce him."

192

They went down long corridors past empty, tidy, gaily decorated rooms waiting for the invasion. Dolly lagged behind Trevor, trying to memorize the school. Old stone on the outside, fresh paint everywhere inside. The big gym in the centre. Every door on the right opened into it. The classrooms were along the left side of the hall. Maybe the big woman was going to put her back because this was a new province. Opposite the last door into the gym, the second kindergarten room, a nice skinny young woman with sparkly glasses and curly black hair sat on a desk. She smiled at Trevor and put her red-sweatered arm round his shoulders while she crouched beside him. He'd be fine, Dolly thought. Her feet were damp in her new school shoes. Grade 4 teachers were not all sparkles like Mrs. Ashby.

On September 10th Clary woke up early and stared through the crib bars at Pearce, lying flat on his back, arms and legs flung out, head tilted skyward as if his closed eyes could see. He was one year old today.

She didn't say anything to the children, and Mrs. Pell was oblivious to everything but her third piece of French toast. When Clary had walked the children to school she decided, blown by some needling zephyr, to take Pearce over to the hospital.

In the parking lot she was fine. Pearce gabbled his strange language to her and then, leaning strongly over her shoulder, to the man they passed walking down the hall. But halfway up in the elevator Clary lost momentum. She hit L again and stood still while the doors opened and closed on 5, even though Pearce strained around to see where they ought to be going, then rode down to the gift shop for a present. Pearce insisted on getting down on the floor to look at the books. Clary could not pry his fingers away from *Spot the Puppy*. He didn't complain or cry, he just wouldn't let go of the book. She stared around the store while the volunteer was ringing it up, searching for something for Lorraine. Give me one of those little doodads, she would say, *that* will console a woman who has lost her family and this beautiful one-year-old boy, that's just the ticket. She went back to the flower fridge and got out a cream velvet rosebud with a pink centre. And a huge blood-red rose, fully opened. She carried them unwrapped, thorns biting into the soft part of her palm, and went upstairs before she found more reason to delay.

Lorraine was awake, no nurses or doctors around her, no breakfast tray in front of her. She sat propped up, empty hands on the tidy sheet, one cupped in the other.

"I thought Pearce needed to see you today," Clary said, sitting on the end of the bed.

Pearce dropped the book and listed forward off her lap toward his mother, Clary holding him around his sturdy waist, his hands reaching out for Lorraine.

"It's his birthday today," Lorraine told her. She held Pearce's hands, and between them he walked across the bed, silent with effort, over the green rolling country of the coverlet.

"Well, that would explain it," Clary said.

"This has been a long year."

Clary nodded.

"Darwin said he'd get a cake, and a candle, one of those Number One candles," Lorraine said. "He's going to Dairy Queen, the kids like those ice-cream cakes."

"That'll be good," Clary said. "We'll make birthday cards after school."

They sat silent, watching Pearce, who had found the hollow nest his mother's bent legs made, and was tamping it down with his feet, his fists holding her fingers. No talking about how his birth had been, what a day that was, or Clayton, how happy. Lorraine looked up and caught Clary's eye, then looked away, to her hand lying over the bed's footboard. "Flowers?"

"Oh, yes! White for Pearce, red for you," Clary said. "You hang on to him, and I'll get a vase." She made herself get up and walk out of the room, not looking back to see if Pearce would fall, if Lorraine would be too weak to hold him.

Mrs. Kernaghan, Dolly's Grade 4 teacher, was famous as the one who used to strap her kids when they were still allowed to—that's how old she was. Dolly had forgotten school's weird, stretching time. It seemed like forever every day until she could go home and read *Mistress Masham*. From her seat Dolly could see Trevor going out for recess, or lining up at the drinking fountain with the other little kids. That helped, for the first few weeks. The girl be-side her, called Ann Hayter, was new too. Todd Bunchley said "Love her or Hayter," and then they called her Lover, or Lover Ann, or made smooching sounds when they saw her coming in the playground. Sometimes they said Sucker Ann or Lezzie Ann. Dolly was desperate not to be treated like that. Nobody had teased her yet. Maybe they would be too busy with Lover Ann. If Ann had told Mrs. Kernaghan, Todd would have got in trouble. But Ann didn't talk, except to say yes or no when Mrs. Kernaghan spoke right to her. She had stick-straight hair, more green than blonde under the school lights. Her clothes were ugly: a sweatshirt with a Mickey appliqué, a pink one with glitter rubbing off. Pink pants, grey around the bottom edges. Filthy socks. Dolly's socks had been dirty in the old days and she was not shocked, but she could imagine Ann's life because of it.

Clary brought Lorraine a small white box.

"Mrs. Zenko thought you could make some use of this."

Lorraine looked blank. She took the box, turning it in her thin fingers. Her wrists were thinner too, but her face puffed. And her poor bald head. What a disaster. But she was back in an ordinary double room, and the de-lirium had not reappeared.

She opened the case, shifting her i.v. lines carefully to avoid the cold rush of drugs that sudden movement brought. Twelve cough drops of colour, a neat steel paintbrush. She looked up and caught Clary's sad gaze, and laughed. "Okay," she said. "I need something to do."

"There's a waterproof pen too, and cards to paint on, and extra brush-es," Clary said. "Dolly told us you're a good artist."

"I used to paint on stones for them," Lorraine said. She cranked the head of the bed up and pulled the rolling table closer. "Hand me a glass of water, will you?"

Clary filled two paper cups at the sink, one to wet and one to rinse, and left her to it.

Mrs. Zenko was so good, Clary thought, standing by the elevators. Use-ful and peaceful, she'd gone through the torrent and sailed on into calm.

195

Clary remembered her wild teenagers. Strait-laced Mr. Zenko tore his hair out over the youngest daughter, Nathalie—an artist in London now. That was her watercolour box.

Paul came down the hall. He spoke immediately, as if he had been looking for her.

"Joe Kane died this morning," he said. "I won't be haunting this place quite so much."

"Oh, I'm sorry," she said.

The elevator pinged. He held the door to let her go in. "He was very old, and didn't have much pain. I never did beat him at chess. Are you going home?"

"Yes, I have to run—I thought I'd be twiddling my thumbs by now, but the children come home for lunch, and Trevor only has half days, and it's busy."

Paul watched a nerve trembling under her eye. Her skin was not as flowery as usual. "You look tired," he said, in case she wished to talk, in the little confessional of the elevator.

"No. Well, I'm always tired these days. Pearce is so good-natured, but he wakes up early, and school is an adjustment for the others."

"Do you need some help at home? Should I ask the parish?"

She laughed. "Millions of women look after three children—I'm not even working!"

"You've been swept into it, though, no gradual acclimatization. You're doing very well."

"We're always in a scramble. I need to make a push to reorganize."

"I give myself a false deadline—I say that I have to have the sermon done before I can have supper on Saturday. Otherwise I'm still writing at 2 a.m."

"My mother used to invite the bishop for dinner," Clary said.

Paul laughed, knowing some bishops. He held the door open to the lobby.

"It worked very well," she said, remembering the whirlwind her mother liked to spin up. "Since we don't know any bishops, will you have dinner with us on Saturday? Then you'd have to make your deadline, too. Darwin would be happy to see you."

He paused, not sure how to answer.

She immediately gave ground. "Or—you're already booked—I'm sure you must be always going to parishioners' houses."

"Well, you're a parishioner," he said. "I'd be very happy to come."

He waved goodbye as she went out the door. He hoped he would remember to phone Iris Haywood and get out of the fellowship dinner on Saturday night.

Lorraine liked the picture, once she had done with it. In her experience you usually did like your picture, until you had to show it to someone. She set the postcard-sized paper flat on the bedside table to dry. She had to twist awkwardly to clear a space big enough for it—too many things on this table. She was learning what she needed, here: less than she'd thought before, less than she'd had in the Dart. Not clothes or cutlery or a box of treasures. Not Clayton, turns out, she thought. The kids. Someone to talk to from time to time, Darwin or Clary. Maybe a stone to paint on.

25. All that may be known

After a good supper on Saturday night Paul and Dolly stood washing dishes, looking out at the back garden: Trevor and Mrs. Zenko tossing the ball to bounce between them, bonk, bonk; Mrs. Pell in the rocker. The low-angled sun caught on fractured surfaces of yellow leaves and glass and droplets of water, the sun like God walking in the garden, touching everything.

"This is my favourite line of Paul's," Paul said to Dolly. She thought he meant of his own. He handed her a wet plate. "St. Paul. My namesake, or rather I am his. *For all that may be known of God by man lies plain before their eyes, God himself has disclosed it to them.*"

Dolly watched his mouth while he spoke, as if that might make it clearer. She loved the way he talked, and his beige mouth, that hardly had any lips until he smiled.

"*His everlasting power and deity have been visible ever since the world began, to the eye of reason, in the things that he has made.* To the eye of reason— to someone who thinks about what she observes, like you do." He smiled at her, his nose stretching down. That's right about me, Dolly thought. I think about what I see. The plate was polished, so she added it to the stack on the table behind them.

Clary went through with Pearce under one arm, on the way to changing him, and lifted the clean plates up into the cupboard as she went. She was getting muscles from doing two things at once. She hefted Pearce higher and went on to the bedroom, where a neat pile of diapers and all the proper changing things pleased her as much as the muscles. It was orderly, and she had ordered it this way. Pearce stared up at the ceiling, at the glints of sun making arrows of burning gold. His mouth curved into an awed gasp that made Clary's heart swoop with almost-painful love. Showing his teeth, five little white spades. Trevor's new teeth stood like Chiclets in his mouth, she had to take him to the dentist. Dolly too, and Mrs. Pell—Clary fell into grim contemplation of whether Mrs. Pell's teeth were her responsibility too. Was there was some kind of seniors' welfare program for dentistry? "There must be something," she told Pearce, taping him up snugly.

His feet beat at her abdomen, his fists hurled lightning bolts at the sky, or at least the gold-charged ceiling, and when she picked him up he twisted his head to a horrifying angle so he could still stare upwards, until she had to see the flooding light that he was seeing. All the things she wouldn't notice without the children to point at them like hunting dogs.

She called out the window to Trevor, who had started up the big birch tree. They hadn't had dessert. "Trev! Tre-ev!" she called, singing out to get his attention. "Ice cream?"

He slithered down the tree, leaving a green mark where his heavy new runners skidded, which Mrs. Pell crabbed across the grass to fuss over. Ice cream would lure her out of the garden too, Clary knew. One day last week Mrs. Pell had eaten six ice cream bars. Clary could imagine her huddled near the basement freezer, poor Gollum hugging his ring to his chest, ice cream hard for those old precarious teeth. *Oh Mrs. Pell, you are too hard for me,* Clary sang inside her head.

She was cheerful, because Paul was here, and she thought she had not been wrong about those raspberries. Darwin was going to take the children for a walk before bed. She would hold on to Pearce, he could take the others.

They were happy to go, they came leaping into the front hall, hearing

199

Darwin ready at the door. Trevor pushed his hands against the door frame and dashed back again and down the basement stairs to get the new bag of ice cream bars; he even knew in which corner of the freezer they lay waiting. He grabbed their jackets from the landing halfway up the stairs because Clary would say they needed them. Dolly wanted Paul to go for the walk with them, but Darwin said, "No, he has to finish the dishes, and then he has to make Clary stay in the garden and do nothing. It's a big responsibility but I believe he is up to the task."

He handed Paul a six-pack of beer in bottles, which made Paul laugh for some reason, and then they slid out the front door into the long evening sunshine. Trevor and Dolly ate their ice cream as they walked. Darwin would pounce on one or the other bar to take a wolfish bite, but they would pull the bars away just in time and he never got any. He doesn't mind anyway, Trevor told himself, although he felt a bit bad that Darwin didn't get one. There were fewer in the bag than Clary had thought there were, so she didn't get one either. Or Paul, neither. Either. Only the kids did. Fair enough.

26. Downhill

*T*here was a girl in Grade 3 whose mother was dead. People's mothers die. Dolly could not even stand to look at her. In assembly when they talked about about car accidents or crossing safety everybody would stare at her, because her mother had been killed by a drunk driver, and then the girl, whose name was Janine (but Dolly did not want to know it, did not want to see her face), would stare back at everybody, her eye twitching, which made Dolly want to throw up. She crossed the hall to avoid Janine, held back in line never to be next to her, as if she might catch it. That was stupid but she could not stand near her. Janine's mother was dead, already dead.

Dolly put her head down and read. She stuck her book inside her language arts book, and she whipped through her math so she could read, the book under the desk and the textbook on top. She read *Mistress Masham's Repose* as hard as she could. She did not mind reading about Maria whose mother was dead too, because it was in a book, and it was away from here. And it was pretend.

When she opened the front door, coming in with the groceries on Thursday, the house smelled bad. Clary was shocked. Everything had gone to hell in a handcart again. Maybe she'd skimped, aiming for the false bishop's deadline. Maybe it was harder than she'd allowed for, to keep three children and an old woman fed and clothed and reasonably clean.

The living room had not been picked up since the morning rush; toys and pyjamas were scattered over every surface. Useless to expect Mrs. Pell ever to lift a finger. Clary had the baby seat in one hand and six bags of groceries in the other, and Trevor trailing behind, tired and whiney. Dolly was due home any minute, and then it would be time for supper, and then homework—she put a video in and propped Pearce in front of it while she tidied up.

Trevor kept playing with Pearce's hand, tapping on it no matter where he moved it, until Pearce was screaming with annoyance. Then she saw Trevor lean over and deliberately poke a finger in Pearce's eye, and lost her temper in one furious shout: "*Trevor!*"

He flicked his eyes toward her and hid his hand under the cushion. Pearce wailed and collapsed, gibbering like a tragic old man, rubbing at his eye. When Clary bent to pick him out of the seat he swatted her away, curling more ferociously into his seat. She picked him up anyway, a squalling fiddle-head, and realized that he had a filthy diaper.

"You must not hurt Pearce. I'll be back to talk to you in a minute," she said to Trevor in a weighty voice which made him start crying loudly.

When Dolly came home, late, she banged the front door loudly enough to wake Pearce from a grouchy sleep. Trevor was still sobbing as he watched *Dumbo*, and Clary had reached a pitch of extreme annoyance as she circled the living room picking up what seemed to be every single article of clothing the children had. Dolly dumped her muddy knapsack on the living room carpet and announced that she had to have $15 for the field trip by tomorrow, or she would be the only person in school who didn't get to go, and that Mrs. Kernaghan had kept her in and given her an X in organization. She headed for the basement in her dirty shoes, giving Trevor an idle swat as she went by.

Crossing the living room in a flash, Clary grabbed Dolly's arm, snatched the shoes off her feet and threw them to the doormat.

"No hitting in this house!" she said, much more loudly than she'd intended.

She marched Dolly into the children's room and stood outside the closed door to listen for any weeping or swearing she might give vent to. When nothing came, Clary went back to deal with Trevor and Pearce, hating herself, her own mean old voice and bad temper, as much as these horrible children.

Things went downhill from there.

The one comfort was that Darwin wasn't home; he had started working odd days for one of Moreland's pals, and must have gone straight from the hospital to work. Mrs. Zenko was visiting her daughter in Winnipeg, so there was no witness to Clary's complete failure as even a surrogate mother.

She stood by the stove, stirring cheese sauce into whole-wheat macaroni, listening to Trevor and Dolly bicker over which cartoon they should watch. The noise was unbearable. She snapped the set off.

"Enough," she said, staring into their frightened eyes. She was a monster.

She whipped the macaroni off the stove and peeled carrots briskly into the sink, a monster of cold efficiency, at least. When she put supper in front of them they ate quietly. Even Pearce was listless and subdued. Mrs. Pell had been pretending to be sick for a few days, so Clary took a supper tray out to her. The walk across the garden cooled her spirit enough that she could knock civilly and wait for Mrs. Pell to grunt "What?" before she opened the door.

A terrible mess out here too, visible even in the dim light. All Clary's bad temper swept back like a wave going over her head. She put the tray down and left, wanting to shriek. This would be intolerable in serious winter, catering to that lazy old boot out here, shovelling a path back and forth, snow boots and parkas all over the house, plugging in the car—lugging the car seat in and out at forty below, dealing with cantankerous cabin-bound awful children. Everything was too much for her.

She could not do this any more.

Her head hurt with the effort of not thinking how stupid she had been to take all these people on, how bad she had proven to be at all this. But there was no way to get out of it.

That night Pearce couldn't settle. At midnight Clary sat up in a frustrated rush, picked him up out of the crib and took him into bed with her. He rolled sideways between the pillows and squirmed himself into a comfortable position, leaving her not quite enough room on the edge of the bed. She sighed and turned off the light again.

She must have fallen asleep, but Pearce's fever woke her, heat coming off him in rolling clouds. She crawled out of bed, sore and stiff, got the infant Tylenol, and managed to get some of it to stay in his unwilling mouth until he had to swallow. The sheets would be sticky, but she could change them tomorrow. The medicine seemed to work, he was cooler quickly.

They drowsed off again, Pearce curled into the curve of Clary's arm. But there was a noise—Clary sat up, and was down the hall in an instant.

Trevor had thrown up from the top bunk. Whole-wheat macaroni, Clary thought. What is the harm in plain white macaroni, for God's sake? I should have known they were ill when they were behaving so badly. Trevor was sitting upright, gasping, and Clary put her hand on his ankle to keep him calm.

"Here, Trevor, I'm here. I'll get you down in a minute, let me get a towel."

In the bottom bunk, Dolly was hot and damp, but fast asleep. Clary came back quickly with towels and paper towels, mopped up what she could and stripped the bunk, and then helped Trevor down and took him to the bathroom, wrapped up safe. She rolled his pyjama top so she could pull it over his head without getting any more mess on him. Nothing in his hair, thank goodness. She washed his face and dried him gently.

"Stand still, sweetheart," she said, "Till I get you clean jammies."

All the while Clary re-dressed him Trevor wept, saying, "I miss my mom," which he had not allowed himself to say before. He said he missed his dad, too, and Clary had not heard him mention Clayton until then. But by the time he was cleaned up Trevor was happy enough to chew a Tylenol and crawl into Clary's bed. He fit himself snugly against Pearce and fell asleep almost right away, and Clary got in too, in the space left on the other side of Pearce.

Five minutes later Dolly came in.

"Our room smells," she said. There was room beside Trevor, if Dolly lay on her side. That was the most comfortable way. She was asleep again before Clary could get pills, and when she touched Dolly's forehead it seemed a little less hot.

Clary lay in the dark deciding not to cry. She reached out and turned the alarm off. Nobody would be going to school. It was all school's fault, the germs the children got there.

At 8 a.m. Mrs. Pell stuck her old turkey head through the bedroom door, looking for breakfast. By then Clary had a raging headache and a fever herself. She waved a hand toward the kitchen and let Mrs. Pell go off and make whatever mess she liked. The bedroom was dim and cool, and the children were sound asleep.

Clary managed another hour's sleep before Darwin came knocking at the door with a cardboard cup of coffee.

"Pretty cozy in here," he said.

Clary could only keep one eye open at a time, but there were still three children with her, and they were all breathing. Nobody had thrown up in the bed. All you could ask for.

Mrs. Pell checked the mailbox while the whole boiling of them were still sleeping. Finally! Miss Bossy Clara might have made her pay rent out of it. $446. It was a start.

She put on her shoes and set off down the street, turtle-pace on cramped feet, lists curling in her mind: mint chocolate cookies, teabags, smoked oysters. Cheque every month! One thing she needed: a little wire cart with wheels, or plastic like that Mrs. Zenko had. And these shoes were killing her. That doctor hadn't even looked at her feet, and damned if she was going to say anything. She dawdled along the windows of the bargain store. Why not? A barette with a rainbow on it for Dolly. A Maple Leafs baseball cap for Trevor; her brothers had liked the Leafs on the radio. Nothing for Pearce, Clara was spoiling him already. In a tangled basket Mrs. Pell found a locket that opened up double to make four places for pictures. $1.99, you couldn't beat that. A bent book of household cleaning tips in the bargain bin. That'd do for Clara. She stumped home.

27. Wellwater

*W*hen Clary took the locket to Lorraine that evening, she brought the household tips too, to give her a good laugh. "I was worried at first," Clary said, and then tangled herself up trying not to mention shoplifting. "But she's got the receipt if you don't like the locket." That was the best she could do, to let Lorraine know that it was safe, not stolen.

The roses had blown open on the nightstand, the red one showing its whole heart of gold, the cream with a tiny bud still withheld in its centre. Lorraine put out a finger to touch the blown one, and the bud, and their perfume swung through the room.

Clary walked downstairs instead of waiting for the elevator.

At the turn of the last flight, Paul had his foot on the bottom step, coming up, looking tired. He backed down, and she backed up, neither of them wanting to cross on the stairs.

"Your mother said that too?" he asked, laughing up at her.

She came down, happy that he was there. "You're always here!" she said, and then worried that that might seem like a complaint.

"What a good dinner that was," he said. "I meant to write you a proper note—"

"Oh please, no note! My mother would never invite anyone back who didn't write one!"

"I'm only teasing you," he said. "You have a happy household. You've made it their home."

Clary knew she was smiling too strongly, mouth splitting hoyden-wide, like her mother always mentioned. She stopped herself, put her fingers to her mouth, said nothing.

"I was happy to be there, thank you for inviting me. How is Lorraine?"

Clary made a face. "Holding steady, I guess. Her hair is coming in. She looks badly shorn, like a French collaborator."

Paul felt a movement in his chest, a physical stirring of the deep unhappiness that Binnie had left behind her. Her poor plucked head, her sorry eyes sunk into steroid-round cheeks, her pain. Her bravery, he told himself quickly. Laughing in her hospital bed, asking him to take her picture, so she could have it for later.

"My younger sister died," he said. He could tell Clary. "Two years ago. Her name was Binnie. Robina. Bald as an egg, a lemon on two sticks, nothing left of her but pain."

"Yes, I'm so sorry," she said. She took his hand. She was kind.

Late in the evening, Paul looked in the door of Lorraine's room. No Darwin. He had hoped to see him for some restorative conversation, or even a beer. His hat was hung on the top of the i.v. stand, though, so he would be back. In the meanwhile, Lorraine was sleeping.

Paul sat down to wait for a few minutes, and let his mind go blank. A little later, he saw that Lorraine was gradually opening her eyes.

"Hey," she said slowly.

"Hello," he said.

A fresh jug of ice water dewed, pearled, on the rolling table. The water-women must have been around.

"May I have a drink of your water?" Paul asked.

"How can you, a priest, ask me, a Samaritan woman, for a drink?"

"Are you a Samaritan woman?" Paul was surprised at Lorraine's phrasing. Was she quoting from the well at Sychar?

Lorraine smiled at him with her wolfish teeth. "Go ahead," she said. "Everyone who drinks this water will be thirsty again, though."

Paul poured himself a glass of water, but he did not drink. It was late, and perhaps he was more tired than he had realized.

"I have no husband," she said.

"No," he agreed. "But no, I—I think you do, don't you? Clayton? He's not gone for good, is he?"

"Oh, I think so," Lorraine said, shaking her head. Flutters of black hair fell off in all directions, outwards in a spray. The bed was littered with strands and locks of hair.

"I have no wife," he said, able to say it out loud.

"No, the woman you have been living with is not your wife," she said, seriously.

"I could not rule her, I wouldn't do it. My choosing not to—I was not what she needed."

"You need some of the living water."

She leaned forward, she leaned perilously over the edge of the bed which had run far away into the distance, she reached back and she was Binnie, reaching, or no longer reaching—Binnie turning her head away and floating off along the current of the living water, turning again one last time to say, "Goodbye!"

When Paul woke up he felt a tear running into his ear. Lorraine was sound asleep, her mouth delicately open. Not looking like Binnie at all, Paul was glad to see.

Darwin was sitting on the orange chair, watching him. "Need a ride home, man?"

"Thanks," Paul said. "I'm okay, really. I'm well." He had not dreamed of Binnie since she died.

Darwin put his heavy hand on Paul's knee. Then he stood up to his always-surprising height, and helped Paul stand too.

28. White box, yellow box, gold box

*T*he white box of watercolours was the hospital in a box: compact, functional, the steel brush like a scalpel, the hi-tech waterproof pen. The rolling table's drawer had become her glove compartment, Lorraine thought, missing the Dart. In the stretches of time where nobody wanted blood or came to change an i.v. bag, she drew, like she had done for the kids. It was calm.

During one of those solitary drawing times a woman came to her room, carrying a big bosom on her slight frame. Her shoulders hunched a little—permanently embarrassed, Lorraine thought. The woman came to the end of the bed and introduced herself as being from Social Services. Her white plastic nametag said *Bertrice.*

"We were notified by the hospital that you might need a visit," she said. She had a deeper voice than fit her build; her mouth twisted slightly when she spoke. Nice enough, but Lorraine felt a cold clench in her gut from government, intervention, interference. She found her toque on the bed and covered her bald bird head, to be less vulnerable.

"My kids are with my mother-in-law," she said. "They're looked after just fine."

Bertrice was quick to reassure her. "You're lucky to have her."

"I am," Lorraine said stiffly, substituting Clary for *her* in her mind.

"But I'm here for financial assistance for you."

"Welfare?"

"The hospital reported that you might be in need of… since you can't work right now…" Bertrice pinked up, stumbling over herself not to cause offence.

She should get a thicker skin, in this job, Lorraine thought.

"Do you have any savings, any assets?"

Lorraine did the math in her head, $366 minus the $189 from the bank, that Clayton must have spent by now: $177 minus $23 at the gift shop for the kids' toys.

"I have a couple hundred dollars in cash, but that's all I've got." Why up it? Why not just say exactly how much—trying to impress the welfare lady? Lorraine was surprised to feel pride still springing up. But she did need to get some money, here.

"Our car was totalled. We might get paid out for it, but it will take months, they said. We were going to Fort McMurray for work, but we were stretched pretty thin. We're from Manitoba, can I even qualify here?"

Bertrice nodded. "We'll be able to get you some assistance, at least enough to help your mother-in-law with the kids."

Like Mom Pell would ever see a penny, Lorraine thought. Her with her secret bank account. But Clary could use it, that would be good. Only no mentioning Clary, in case Family Services took the kids away from her and put them in foster care. Even thinking the words made Lorraine's body race, more stress-acid flooding through her veins.

Bertrice sat in the blue chair and fit a big aluminum clipboard on her small lap. "You carry on with your art, and I'll take some notes and see how we can work it out. I can talk to Manitoba. Your husband—will he be in to sign too?" Receiving no answer, Bertrice went smoothly on to last address, social insurance number. Not bad at this after all, Lorraine saw.

Dolly was bringing Ann Hayter home with her after school. Clary had phoned Ann's mother, and had said they would drive Ann home after supper because they were too disorganized for sleepovers yet. So Ann sulked all afternoon, until Dolly wanted to say *Fine, don't come.* When the bell finally rang, Dolly found her at the coat-hooks, with Todd Bunchley making some drooling kissy noises at her. Dolly gave him a shove, plucked Ann's jacket off the shelf and stood in front of her while Ann got it on, moving slowly like she did whenever Todd went at her. Trevor wandered up and Dolly decided to take them all out the front door, closer to where Clary always waited for them. It was raining and cold, but Clary would bring the umbrella.

Going through the front hall they ran smack into Mrs. Haywood, who ruled like iron in the school, nice as she might be at church. Her heels made a hole-punch noise on the linoleum. Dolly made herself keep going even though there was a rule that kids were not allowed to go out the front door ever.

"Good afternoon, Dolly, Trevor," Mrs. Haywood said. "Ann."

Ann jumped. What a basket case, Dolly thought. Why do I have to be friends with her? She knew why: she couldn't be friends with anyone real, only with an equal outcast.

Mrs. Haywood opened the front door for them. Clary was holding the umbrella over the stroller, looking to the side door. Trevor ran for the umbrella. Mrs. Haywood followed the girls down the walk. Clary hugged Trevor and gave Dolly the umbrella. She said, "You walk ahead a little—don't get too far, I'll run after." Not wanting to let them hear whatever Mrs. Haywood would say, Dolly could tell. It didn't take long, whatever it was. Dolly looked back after fifty metres and saw Mrs. Haywood already back at the school door, Clary pushing the stroller fast, loping towards them through the rain like that coyote at Clearwater Lake.

"Oh, children, I should have brought the car! Let's run for it!" She took the umbrella back from Dolly, and they all belted along as fast as they could, Ann hanging onto Dolly, shrieking faint complaints all the way until Dolly shook off her hand and ran.

The house was warm after the rain. Clary gave them banana bread and a plate of cut-up oranges, proud of the wholesome snack, and sent them to the basement to play. She didn't like the look of Ann Hayter, didn't trust her, for Dolly's sake. She looked too weak to be an easy friend, and her voice was without inflection, almost stifled. Clary thought she should sit on the stairs and listen. But Pearce needed changing, and Trevor's reading work had to be done before supper or he fell into tears over it. She let them go.

211

Dolly had nothing Ann wanted to play with, only one Barbie and no computer games. For a while they did a movie Ann had seen about some woman who danced really sexy and some guy wanting to kiss her but Dolly did not want to pretend all that and would have had to be the guy, and she was bored with it. Ann let it drop quickly, knowing her place. After a while of doing semi-cartwheels and other gymnastic tricks, they just sat there.

"Your mom gives good snacks. I mean your—*whatever*," Ann said, being mean because Dolly wouldn't play the kissing movie.

"She's my aunt." Nobody could hear her. Nobody knew at school exactly what Clary was, except for Mrs. Haywood, but she didn't talk to any kids.

"She's not married. If she's not married, she can't have kids. It's illegal, they won't let you stay here."

"She is so married. She's *married*. She just doesn't have a husband anymore."

Ann shook her head. "Liar," she said, all smug here in the safe basement. She wouldn't be talking like that at school.

"I'll prove it," Dolly said. She stood up slowly from the carpet. "But we have to be quiet."

The room was cold and the light had gone, the sun moving behind clouds. She'd noticed it happening before, everything getting dark because here was Dolly, in trouble. She led the way up the stairs, wishing Ann had not come, wishing she was lying in the cave of her bunk, reading. Clary was making supper, with Pearce in his high chair. She would be busy a long time.

"We're going to play in my room," Dolly said. She shut her bedroom door loudly, not letting Ann's chicken-skin arm out of her fingers' grasp; then she shoved her into Clary's bedroom and shut that door too, as silent as a bank vault. Her hands were shaky, because Clary was right there in the house. She dropped Ann's arm and pulled the armchair over to the closet. "What are you doing? What is it?" Ann kept asking. What a whiner, and a bad spy too.

Leaving Pearce behind in the playpen while she ran to get a diaper, Clary had only barely opened the door to her room when she heard Dolly say, "See?"

She stopped, wondering what Dolly was showing Ann in her closet. Evening dresses?

"Here is the proof," Dolly was saying in a dramatic, unfamiliar tone. Clary did not want to embarrass Dolly by catching her showing off. She stood still, smiling to herself.

"She is so married. Clara Purdy and Dominic Raskin, June 19, 1982."

It felt foolish to be still smiling, but nervous horror would not let her stop. She put her fingers to her mouth, hidden by the turn of the wall.

Ann Hayter said, "Let me see it."

"You don't have to hold it to see it. I have to put it back. I told you she was married."

"Where is he then?" Ann's flat little voice demanding more fodder, more gossip.

"Fern says he was very handsome—but there's not even one picture left after the fire."

Fern? Fern told Dolly what? Fire?

"I have to put it back. It makes her go crazy if she sees it."

Clary could hear Dolly standing up and rustling in the closet. God, she didn't want them to see her, or know she had been listening. She turned silently and slipped into the bathroom.

She sat on the edge of the tub and ground the heels of her hands into her eyes, trying to work out whether, morally, she had to interrupt Dolly, punish her for snooping, and expose those bald-faced lies.

What was in that yellow box? Whatever she hadn't wanted her mother to leaf through; her mother did not like to climb. Photos and pathetic mementos from her few sterile romances, maybe a letter or two. None from Dominic. Fingering his name in her mind made her cheeks hot with interior shame. *Handsome!* For an instant the bridge of his nose came into her mind's eye, and a faint twinge of the aching love she had felt, which had been murdered by his belligerent, determined, multiple and humiliating adulteries. Of which Fern knew nothing. But of course Fern might not have said anything of the kind—of course she hadn't, Dolly had made that up—and the fire!

She couldn't even blame Dolly, remembering that childhood need to seem informed and intimate, and to protect any small stability. It was such a relief to be past that, to be an adult. The last time she'd felt like that she had been married to Dominic. All that—detritus—should have been thrown out years ago, especially the marriage certificate, years ago. The divorce papers were in the safe deposit box at the bank, and that was all she needed. She had spent too long despising herself for being stupid, hating her mother for being accidentally right about him, despairing of regaining her father's respect. What a dreary little past to have.

Clary scraped at her eyes again and got up off the bathtub rim. No one was in the hall. She told herself not to be short with Dolly. Supper. She should get Trevor to read to her while she cooked.

But before she had hauled him away from the TV, Mrs. Zenko came through the back way with a box of angel cookies. At the sight of her bright little face Clary forgot shame and pride, and remembered her proper worry.

"Iris Haywood says they think Clayton might have been at the school today," she said, before Mrs. Zenko could even put the cookies down on the counter.

"Oh, my dear," Mrs. Zenko said. "That will worry you."

"It's him skulking around that makes it sinister. He could come here any time," Clary said, hearing the false note in her voice. "They're his children, he doesn't have to be—"

"He may feel a little sheepish," Mrs. Zenko said.

The word made Clary laugh, and made her see Clayton differently. Sheep, not wolf. Maybe. That night when she leaned down into the cave of the lower bunk to check on Dolly, Clary remembered to be kind, and on an impulse, kissed the top of her head.

Dolly said, "*Give me a kiss, please, Miss, I like your nose.*"

Clary said, "What?"

Then Dolly was stuck. She wished she hadn't said anything.

"It's from my book, the one I bought with my five dollars that you gave me."

Clary laughed. "Say it again?"

"*Give me a kiss, please, Miss, I like your nose.* It's a poem, in their language. I do like your nose," Dolly said. Then she shut her eyes to prevent any further talk.

They always had to be careful about Clary, to keep the balance between them and someone who was not their mother, who they couldn't be too nice to; but they couldn't make her mad either, or be mean to her, because she might give up on them, or because it wouldn't be fair. They had to be good, and then they got to expect things from her, but there was a set of invisible rules about how much they could be hers. There was almost math in it: pluses and minuses, even brackets like they were learning (Trevor + Pearce + herself), but it all had to come out with an equal sign in the end, you had to get the equation right. Like in *Mistress Masham*: Maria found those poor little people and took care of them and bought them candies, but then she started bossing the death out of them, and then one of them almost did die, and they told her to back off! So she did, but her heart was broken. But there was more book, maybe they could somehow be able to be friends with her again. She had learned her lesson.

Lorraine lay curled behind her curtains, which the nurse had pulled to get a new patient into the next bed. The curtains and the glazed light made a kind of sanctuary. Noise beyond them turned into waves, like the ambient machine at Clary's. This was one of the crests of the waves she was becoming accustomed to.

The BMT test had come back. Darwin was a good match, they said, so they would go ahead with a stem cell transfer as soon as they could get her healthy enough. The pretty doctor said, Dr. Cormarie. Dr. Lester with her. Dr. Tatarin, Dr. McCluskey, Dr. Starr. In the creamy twilight Lorraine told over the doctors' names like rosary beads, but the big bead at the bottom must be Darwin. Because it seemed, they said, that he was her full brother. Which gave her a lot to think about. Her mother, pregnant with her before her father died, before her mother married Dennis Hand: if they were full siblings then it seemed like something had been hidden. Maybe back then there was plenty of reason for hiding, when to have a baby without a husband was disgrace. Somehow there must have been some time in there after Don Berry died, before she could get married to Dennis Hand—Lorraine gave up. Some things you could never find out, because the people were all dead. Whatever her mother had had to do to survive as long as she had done... Not long. Every current flowed to that flat shore of death. Driftwood.

Clayton wouldn't like it, though, he'd always been glad to say *half*-brother about Darwin. What made them brush together so badly Lorraine could not say. Clayton was always expecting to be judged, waiting to be put

215

down, not that Darwin ever did. One thing she was sure of, no matter how she rocked upon the waves: she'd been better for her children than Clay's mom, or than her own. She and Darwin had had Rose. Clayton had nobody, except her. She wondered, before sleeping, where he was.

On Sunday Pearce threw a complete shrieking fit because she would not let him bang the kneeler on the floor, and Clary had to carry him out of church. He writhed under her arm and pounded on her stomach with his hands, so furious that it made her laugh and clench him tight. She sped down the side aisle, sliding out the rear door before he had time to explode.

Lisanne Tippett was in the vestibule. Pearce stopped yowling to examine her. Clary found it hard to look at her smug, sly-minx face. She's probably pretending so no one will know how sad she is, Clary told herself, and nodded a greeting, but Lisanne was staring off into some private distance, so that was wasted. She must be waiting to talk to Paul.

The final hymn came swelling through the doors, "...*that soul, though all hell should endeavour to shake, I'll never—no, never—no, never forsake...*"

Paul was there, on the church side of the closed doors, turning back to give the congregation the blessing. Clary found it uncomfortable to be near Lisanne, and she moved aside, using Pearce as her excuse, joggling him peaceably and talking to him in a whisper.

At last Paul opened the doors and came through. Seeing Lisanne, his shining face went dull. He smiled, being civilized, but with a feeble mouth that made Clary sad.

Then people were filing out, and his hand was demanded, and he could turn away. Lisanne stood in the brilliance of the outer doors, staring out as light streamed in. She did not move out of the light or give ground for the leaving congregation, so the ebb-tide had to part around her.

Pearce on her hip, Clary went round the line and took her turn too. She shook Paul's hand and held it for a minute. He must be shrinking from all these eyes. "Sorry," she said. "Never mind." As if those two things would help.

She should not be sorry. With his other hand Paul touched a bright spike of sunlight on Pearce's round cheek, a happy boy again after his tantrum. He felt Lisanne's gaze behind him, scorning his surplice, the mask of office. Like that year in Dunnett, when she'd stopped going to church: 1989. The Sunday she'd shouted at him in the sacristy that she was leaving. Her turn had come round that morning to play the organ for the service, but nobody had told her of some change—Crimond for the hymn instead of Dunfermline, or some new Alleluia the choir was singing while she played the wrong tune. She was through! When he walked home after the second service, the car was packed (the K-car from Bishop Perry's mother that they had bought for $2,000), her suitcases and books and the good duvet stacked in the back seat: regimental columns, crimson and black, on the border, and the classical gold box of its burning centre.

But she had not gone. Another dozen parishioners filed through the door; he smiled, he greeted them by name, he asked pertinent questions, but all the time his pinhead brain was asking him, why had she not gone then?

Old Mrs. Chapman next in line, her sparkling, squashed-pansy face turned up to him wearing all her eighty-six years, reminded him. Lisanne had stayed because they had gone upstairs and made love, and it had been a startling time, wide open, in flames, because he was as angry as she was. He remembered her beside, beneath, above him, her white thigh under his cheek; and the holy tent, the covenant-box of the gold duvet over and around them. Mrs. Chapman's accepting expression—like Lisanne's, when she did not go.

She was gone now. The tide of parishioners ebbed, all of them in a seemly hurry to let Paul and Lisanne be alone. The big doors shut them into sudden twilight; the ACW ladies headed back up to the nave to tend to the flowers and the linen. His heart pounded, painful in his chest.

Then the left door creaked open again, a glare of sun peeling in with a two-headed shadow, Clary and Pearce. "Forgot the car seat," Clary said, apologizing. "You'd think I would remember by now."

Lisanne laughed, a sharp bark, suddenly attending to Clary. "*You* had a baby?" she asked, her eyebrows arcing on defined ridges of muscle.

Was the incredulity for her age, or her old-maidishness, Clary wondered. She shifted Pearce to the other hip, smooth in practice, and shook her head. "Not mine," was all she said.

Lisanne laughed again. "Well, I didn't think! But you never know, these days. Anyone can have a baby now. That sixty-year-old in Italy."

Paul's temper ran out, like water flooding out of a broken glass. As

217

much because Clary could not explain, as from Lisanne's scorn. "Clary has taken on the care of three small children while their mother is in hospital," he said, his voice neutral. Neutered.

Clary ducked through into the church and left them to it.

Paul looked at Lisanne's face, her mixed attitude of defiance and regret, but did not pity it this time. If she flailed less she would have less to regret. Nothing he did would change her.

In the church, Clary took her time finding the car seat and unwedging it from the pew. With any luck they would go off to the church office to have their talk. Pearce saw the seat and pointed fiercely, cawing out something, almost *car*. In her pride she forgot to dawdle, and had pushed the door to the porch open before she saw Lisanne still there. Alone—waiting for Paul? Clary gave a nod, her mouth jerky with nervousness.

"Sorry," Lisanne said. "I was rude."

Now Clary was stuck.

"I'm bad-tempered these days, at least around here."

"No, no," Clary began, and then didn't know how to carry on.

"I'm remarrying," Lisanne said. Out of the blue, like most of her remarks.

It caught Clary by surprise. "Oh good!" she said, and then felt her face heating up like a stove element. "I mean, I'm happy for you. Everyone in the parish wishes you well."

"Yeah," Lisanne said, looking up with her narrow jealous eyes. "They love me." She had perfectly cut dark hair, almost black, falling in sleek threads around her head. What a nice child she and Paul would have had, her vivid colouring with Paul's bones.

"Well, I guess it's a loss for the whole parish, in a way. That you and Paul have split."

"My heart breaks for them. It's all about the parish." She ignored the rules of polite conversation. Clary was bored by her, suddenly, which was a relief.

"Goodbye, then," Clary said, and took Pearce and the car seat out into the fresh cold morning, to the children waiting at the bottom of the steps.

Paul was spotting Trevor as he high-wired along the concrete curb.

"I came looking for you," Paul said. "I have to go to Toronto, they've made me the Diocesan rep on the Faith and Worship committee. It's supposed to be an honour. I'm gone for ten days—but I'll go to see Lorraine as soon as I get back. And I'll call you."

"All right," she said. She was tempted to add something light about seeing him in church, anyway—to make him think it was not important to her that he was going away, or that he would come back, that he would telephone. But she stopped. He was going to call her because they had become friends. And he liked the children. She smiled properly, and held out her hand to say goodbye. What a lovely hand he had to hold.

She let go quickly, and scooped up Dolly and Trevor with her to the car. It was good to have company through all this: Mrs. Zenko, Darwin, Fern and Grace and Moreland, all of them. But Paul was her friend.

29. Test

*Most transplant patients who survive the procedure and who
do not relapse (experience a return of their disease) lead active and productive
lives.* Lorraine read that sentence over. It was fully loaded—that little twitch
in the middle about the relapsing, and the helpful definition because you
would probably be too stupid to understand a big word like *relapse.*

*Some patients, however, develop chronic (long-lasting) or delayed complica-
tions. These complications have many causes, including the transplant itself, pre-
transplant radiation and/or chemotherapy, and...* Her eyes wouldn't read any
more. There was no point, because knowing would not help her. Ignorance
might help her to be oblivious, and strong, and placid.

November was cruel, Paul thought, not April. *No warmth, no cheerfulness,
no healthful ease.* Toronto at least had charcoal smoke and chestnut vendors.
Back here in the west it was full winter. Seven parishioners in hospital, and
Lorraine.

He pulled into the parking lot and checked in the visor mirror that he
did not have blood on his mouth from that morning's shave. He remembered

Binnie's mouth in hospital, the dear pearly teeth and her lips all cracked and painful with thrush. The little spaces between Binnie's teeth had kept her face always young. Well, she was young. He could not do any more of this. He could not go upstairs.

He went up. But he took the stairs to give himself a little more time, winding up the echoing, wheeling metal flights.

When he got to the door and Lorraine looked so happy to see him, he was sorry not to have taken the elevator. She was tired but talkative—couldn't seem to stop talking, in fact.

"You know what I want? People I used to know, to know how their stories are turning out. How many kids they've got, and what they do now, and where they live, and who they married."

He said, "We can find out some of that, if you want."

"I don't want to actually call anybody, or look people up on the Internet or whatever. I'm just thinking about them. Like there was one set of brothers, one called Dog and the other called Pickle. Darwin remembers them too."

Paul said he had people like that in his own memory.

"Or the girl who lived over the Chinese restaurant, Rosalind. Or that girl who took me to the revival meeting where the woman spoke in tongues—I want to tell them I liked them, or something." She was silent for a while. "It's obviously got to do with thinking I might not be able to, later."

"Yes," he said.

"Only thing is, I don't want to tell anyone. I can't stand talking about all this." She put down the brush. This one was not working out. "I didn't think I'd be ashamed."

"I don't think it's shame. People are devastated when they find out, not just for you but for all the people they've known before, and you have to lift their spirits for them, you have to make them think you're not dying."

"Yes."

They sat quietly.

Dolly went for a walk after school, not telling Clary she was going, not telling Trevor even. She was sick and tired of this place. Her math test came back marked 4 out of 12 and Clary had to sign it, and she was going to be all concerned. Dolly wanted her mother to sign it, but her mother's bones were being sucked out and tested and if the bones got 4 out of 12 she would die.

Dolly said *crap* when she stepped on her left foot and *shit* on her right foot, walking down 8th Street in the grey snow and traffic-scum. Way up ahead she saw Key's Books and realized that was why she was walking down here. She needed a new book. The fat librarian at school made you sign up on lists for books, and anyway she was sick of ordinary books, she wanted something good, like *Mistress Masham*. She had no money again but maybe she could talk the old guy into letting her work for him, dust the books for cash. He bought books, too—maybe she could find some of Clary's old books to bring in. Or Mr. Bunt's.

The door was wide open this time. A metal ramp sloped up the stairs, covered with moving rugs laid in a path to a big truck.

Dolly jumped up on the ramp and sidled quickly through the door before a man in grey coveralls came out with a huge box blinding him. He blundered down the ramp too close to the edge, but saved himself and stomped up into the truck.

The store was dark inside. Dolly couldn't see anything but movement: grey men going around with boxes. They were emptying the shelves, throwing the books into boxes like they were leaves or wood chips. The old guy was sitting by his computer but it was not turned on.

"We're closed!" he yelled. A man packing books almost dropped his box.

"Why?" Dolly asked.

"Retirement."

She knew he was lying. He looked drunk. She should have come in before and dusted his books for him. What a mess this place was, as usual. Even worse with the people trampling around. There were books splayed open on the floor. The men with boxes were just walking on them. She picked one up: *Bleak House.*

"Take it and go!" the old giant shouted. There was a loud crash from upstairs.

"How much?" Dolly asked.

He leaned forward in his chair and reached his arm out for the book, flipping the inside cover page with huge clumsy fingers. "$95. Nice early edition." He closed his eyes. Dolly looked at the dark eyelids under his flaring white eyebrows.

"Well, I don't have that much," she said, speaking only to him in the crowd of workmen.

The old guy got up from his kitchen chair—taller than the busy grey men. He bent to grab his stick, and walked around the store picking books off shelves, looking at them, dropping them on the floor.

"Always orphans, eh? You'll like this better, for now," he said, hanging on to one. He held it out to her. "*Vanity Fair,* she's an orphan. Good tips in there, how to cope."

She took it. It was a very old red book, the pages still creamy inside, with little pictures at the front of every chapter. She smelled it, it smelled like church.

He grabbed it back and smelled it too. "Nothing wrong with that," he said.

"No," she said. "I like it."

Suddenly moving fast, he grabbed the one he'd dropped, *Bleak House,* and then more, pulling from the shelves—*The Secret Garden* was on top, she couldn't see the others.

"Jane Eyre. Oliver Twist. Mary What's-her-name—orphans galore," he said. He shoved the stack into her arms, and pushed her toward the door.

"How much?"

He waved his stick around at the destruction of his store.

"Forty thousand dollars," he said. "You can owe me."

Darwin said he'd seen Paul walking away down the hall. "Did he tell you that his sister died of cancer a couple of years ago?"

"What kind?"

"Leukemia."

Lorraine let her eyes drift off, away from Darwin. He didn't blame her for being sick.

"He's still cut up about it—maybe he didn't want to cry in front of a girl."

Lorraine laughed. "A bald girl." She pushed the rolling table aside. Her scalp-fuzz had promptly fallen out again; her head was as smooth as a pear. The daily blood transfusions buoyed her up physically, although it made her feel trembly in her spirit to think of all those arms, all those Red Cross cots at all those donor clinics that had poured blood into her.

She was grateful to this round of chemo, which had given her back lucidity and seemed to be calming her down almost the way Darwin did, and gave her a window of time to talk to him. It made her want to talk to the kids too, but it was too hard a burden to place on them. When Clary suggested bringing Dolly for a visit, Lorraine did not want to say no. "Wait, okay?" she said. Clary said yes, of course, and they left it.

The full team of doctors trooped in to announce it: Lorraine was in remission, and ready for transplant; Darwin had had all his tests and passed them. He said he felt like a matchbook career-college graduate: *be a donor, or just look like one!* Only Dr. Cormarie and Dr. Lester smiled. They were the kind ones. They conditioned Lorraine's marrow—ridiculous euphemism, Clary thought: they killed it by sticking her in a room and giving her total body irradiation, four days in a row. Clary and Darwin sat down the hall on turquoise vinyl seats waiting for the small Hiroshima to pass over her. Clary found it strange to think of that bone-blood, that pale, innocuous, powerful fluid, made sterile. It made her own bones feel hollow and frail.

The buzzer went and the door was opened, and Lorraine was rolled out. No outward sign of the destruction showed, but she was sleepy. Clary held her hand all the long way back to the ward, keeping her face mildly positive, as always at the hospital. And then all it was was a blood transfusion. Just her regular old i.v. blood-bag. A little disappointing, after all the waiting.

Then there was was longer to wait.

30. Headlights

*I*n spite of herself, in spite of all this tragedy and waiting, Dolly could not help sopping up knowledge in huge violent spasms of brain-expansion in school; she read all the time, at lunch and at home. *Vanity Fair* was like everything, like her life only clearer. She loved it from the very first moment when Becky gets a dictionary after all, and then she throws it back. She was as good a liar as Dolly.

After *Vanity Fair* she had more books, like insurance: the whole stack left to go. It was as if all books had suddenly unlocked, and now she understood everything. Trevor would never catch up to her. Poor Pearce could not even talk. He made truck noises, *brrrmm-brrrm* around the carpet with the yellow truck. Dolly would teach him her name, since their mother was not there. *There*, lurking in the black water under her top thoughts, was the always-there absence of her mother, while everybody waited to see what would happen, or would she die, with all her bones empty.

Dolly glared out the window, not yet able to read because she was supposed to be finishing her math. Dirty snow everywhere. Teachers' cars plugged in had blue wires dangling like skinny tongues from their hoods. Down that street and down the next, another few blocks, turn right—that way was the hospital. In order not to think of it, Dolly craned her neck around to look back down the grey street past the playground.

There was a car with its lights on, and a man beside the car, leaning on it, staring through the chain links at the school. That was not allowed, there would be a lockdown practice, when the PA system said *Alert One, Secure Your Doors* in that creepy quiet voice and the teachers scuttled through the halls back to where they should be to shut the doors and lock them and make the kids practice heads-down on their desks, and if you were in the bathroom, too bad for you.

Dolly's head hurt suddenly, an arrow through her forehead. It was her dad, at the car. He turned his head and she knew him. He did look like that weird guy out in Clearwater Lake. Like a grown-up kid who had to be old. She looked away.

She was not, actually, an orphan. Dolly tried to think of herself hanging around with her father and his friends after her mother was dead, but that was not too likely. The only friend of her dad's she could think of was that scary Garvin guy from Winnipeg.

The bell rang for recess. Dolly did not stand up. If she stood up she would have to look out the window again and see her dad. But if she didn't, Trevor might see him and go running over and then he'd get into trouble and maybe the police would come and arrest him. She bolted for the door to find Trevor.

Giving the children a bedtime snack Clary looked at them at the table in their pyjamas, listless and tired and itchy: an ordinary Thursday night. One more school day to struggle through. Nobody talked. Mrs. Pell had come in for a cup of tea but she wasn't staying long, she said. Figure skating was on her TV back at her place. Clary set cut-up apples on the table in front of Dolly.

As she was leaning over she saw something—what?—something *moved* on Dolly's head.

Her hands clamped onto both sides of Dolly's head, holding her still as Dolly squeaked with surprise. A bug crawled across the part. A brown, hair-coloured thing. A louse.

Deep shame blossomed painfully in Clary, in the bottom of her groin.

She had never seen lice but there was no doubt in her mind at all. A notice had been sent from the school, Clary back-remembered. A cold pink sheet, *Headlice Bulletin*. What could lice have to do with her?

"Oh, Dolly," Clary said out loud, not meaning to. "Lice!" She was sunk, sunk.

Mrs. Pell's beetle eyes squinted, and she backed her chair away from Dolly's.

Trevor said, "There's kids in *my* class who have lice, they aren't allowed in school for three days, that's what happens to you."

"If she's got 'em, you've got 'em," Mrs. Pell wheezed, almost laughing.

"I can't miss three days!" Dolly cried. "I left my book at school!"

"I'm sorry, Dolly," Clary was saying.

But Mrs. Pell interrupted them all, pushing her bulk up out of her chair, making the loudest noise possible scraping it back. "I had four kids," she announced. "And we never had lice. Not once."

She picked up her teacup and stalked out the back door.

Clary could hear herself shouting after her, "*Fuck you, Mrs. Pell!*" But thank God she found that she had not actually done it. Her head was itchy.

Trevor and Dolly sat very quiet. Even Pearce was still.

"Well," Clary said. "I guess we've got a problem."

Oh my God, she thought. All of them. And me? She turned suddenly to Pearce, unable to bear it if his head was—*infested*—that was the word for it. And Darwin—and the hospital! Had they been sending lice over to Lorraine?

Clary sat down on the kitchen floor. Dolly and Trevor stared at her from their chairs. Pearce leaned down, over the arm of his high chair, stretching to touch her with his applesauce spoon.

"I don't know what to do about this," Clary said. "I have no idea, I'll have to look it up."

But she couldn't look it up, because her computer was at work, and it was no longer her computer, or her work. She had nothing left of her original life. Only lice. Her mother would have been so appalled! Clary could hear her—standing beside Mrs. Pell, in fact, saying "*We* never had lice..." That made her laugh, but only for a second.

Driving down the dark length of 8th Street to the drugstore, she could feel self-pitying tears seeping behind her eyes, but she dismissed them for now.

Later on, she promised herself, in bed. After she had done whatever you had to do—washed their hair with toxic chemicals and combed them with those sharp tiny-toothed combs until everyone was ready to scream with tiredness and frustration. *Then* she would cry. She hated them all, even Pearce; she hated lice, and the whole dirty business of being human. The shame of having to tell Iris Haywood that they had lice almost made the tears spring forth. And *Paul.* He had visited, had sat on the chesterfield—the squalor of it felt like a weight pressing on her head.

The headlights were not working properly. When she parked at the drugstore she saw the car reflected in the glass front: her left headlight was burnt out. The complication of getting the headlight replaced was so overwhelming that she had to lean against the car door for a moment before she could get the children out to come trooping in with her, parkas over their pyjamas. What a relief it would have been to leave them in the car. But a woman last winter had left her car running at the store and come out to find it gone, and her baby with it. If they were her own children she could weigh the likelihood and decide; but they were Lorraine's. She only had them in trust. Trust her to let them get lice.

Darwin didn't have lice—Clary phoned the hospital and the nurses checked—and neither did Lorraine. Trevor and Dolly did. None on Mrs. Pell, that Clary could find. None on Pearce: no live ones and no eggs, no matter how painstakingly Clary searched his round, sweet head.

She took the advice of the kindly pharmacist and washed everybody's hair with tea-tree oil instead of the poisonous stuff, and put her energy into hair-combing to get rid of the eggs, rather than obsessive cleaning. But she stripped, vacuumed and remade the beds (trusting that sheets which had lain unused twenty years in her mother's linen closet were safe), and put every stuffed toy and pillow in garbage bags outside to freeze for a few days. Finally, at midnight, she got the de-loused, subdued children into their lavender-smelling beds.

She let them watch videos all day on Friday and cleaned around them, pausing only to make meals. She even vacuumed the car, hauling her mother's old Electrolux out to the driveway in the bitter cold. Mrs. Zenko saw her and came out to help, and when Clary told her what was going on she laughed till she had to hold on to the side mirror.

"It's combing that does the trick," she said, echoing the pharmacist. "I've got a very good metal fine-tooth comb myself, left over from my girls' school days—I'll come over when you're through out here and give you a good going-over," she promised. "What a thing! But it's all a matter of luck and whose coat hangs next to whose."

When Mrs. Zenko went through Clary's head she found no bugs at all. Darwin came back from the hospital and took over the children's hair, combing through strand by strand gently, patiently, checking each hair and pulling away the tiny, sticky eggs and telling them long-winded jokes.

Clary blew through the house once more with the overworked vacuum until it seemed to her to be possible to live there. But Mrs. Pell might be carrying some eggs that she'd missed in her first panicky check. She took a cup of coffee out to the workshop.

"Hi," she said, when Mrs. Pell answered the door. "I've brought the rat-tail comb. I'll check your hair for you."

Mrs. Pell stared at her, without any observable social response.

"It won't take long," Clary said. She sighed. "Can you hold the coffee?"

Mrs. Pell took it and creaked aside to let her into the workshop. Clary transferred the comb and oil from under her arm. She looked around, trying to be neither furtive nor obvious.

"Satisfied?" Mrs. Pell said, her voice catching like a rusted saw in green wood.

"Of course!" Clary said quickly. "It's your home, you keep it as you wish."

But she seemed to want to keep it fairly orderly. There was a smell, but that might be old-woman smell, rather than poor housekeeping. Cozy warm out here, with the furnace going. The bed was made, the tumbling-blocks quilt neatly spread over the blankets.

"I should wash your bedding again."

Mrs. Pell grunted. "Don't be so hasty. Shouldn't run old things through the wash just because you think they're lousy."

Understanding her, Clary said, "I meant to tell you, I want to give you that quilt for your own. When Lorraine—wherever you are. It's yours."

Mrs. Pell moved her bottom lip up toward her top lip, nothing that could be called a smile. Then she said, "Don't just tickle me with your eyes. You going to check my head? Take that chair out into the light, can't see well enough in here."

Clary took the old kitchen chair out into the snow. Mrs. Pell stumped after her, sausage feet in snow boots. They shifted the chair till the light was right, and then Mrs. Pell sat, arms folded, braced against the rat-tail and the fine-tooth comb. Clary worked through her old grey scalp, section by thin section, burying her fingers in the grey horse-hair skeins, pulling through, checking, looking down in the brilliant sunshine. No need to talk, and nothing to say anyway. Mrs. Pell's old neck strings stood out strong on the back of her head, depending on how her skull twisted inside its papery bag of skin.

"Would you like a haircut?" Clary asked, testing the water.

"Hmmpm," Mrs. Pell said, which Clary took to mean possible acceptance.

"My aunt Bet, Grace's mother, used to go to the beauty school every few weeks, and they'd give her a cut and set. Sometimes a perm, even. They had a seniors' day discount."

Mrs. Pell tilted her head on its bony stalk to catch Clary's eye. "They do a good job?"

"Not bad," Clary said. "You could try it out."

She pulled the rat-tail down another line of scalp and divided off another strand of hair. Another, and another. No lice to be found. The sun shone on them, as warm as you could expect, that late in the year.

31. Potlatch

*P*aul was having a party. Urgent papers all over his desk: the sermon, the call to giving. But every Christmas since his ordination, against Lisanne's yearly protest, he had held a parish party at his house on December 6th, early enough that no other party conflicted. The Feast of St. Nicholas. He had a fondness for that narrow, looming, eaves-dropping, purse-tossing, pickle-barrel bishop. Old Nick, the devil's name. Saints and demons, rewards and punishments… He could not drift off into consideration of devils and their place in the pantheon, because he was tied down to earth, to the calendar, December 6. He flung his hands up in the air, smacked them down on the strewn papers, and went home.

On the kitchen table, surrounded by cookbooks—Lisanne had forgotten those—he made a list. *Chili?* the heading said, and underneath, things that matched, for a good, frugal party. Then he drew a thick zig-zag through it. Nobody likes chili. Tourtière, for Christmas. Cinnamon sticks, eggnog, spruce boughs. His mother had always made white fruitcake, at the last minute. The battered scrapbook of recipes fell open as it always did to the splattered card in Binnie's handwriting, *Current Biscuits,* with her squiggly drawing of herself: a long-haired girl waving at him, electric eyebrows surprised. He would make biscuits too.

Clary would come, with the children and Darwin. Unless he was at the hospital. These days Lorraine was fluttering through the engraftment period like a pale moth, waiting for Darwin's stem cells to be accepted by her body and begin to proliferate, cells riffling through her in cascading, exponential, astronomical multiplication. They'd said several weeks, but nobody had told Paul how many several was. Maybe they did not know. Lorraine was under restricted access until it had settled, so he had not visited her lately. Even when the engraftment was successful (he phrased it that way carefully in his head), the onset of graft-versus-host disease would be the dangerous time. He had e-mailed the doctor he'd become friends with during Binnie's illness, to find out what to expect, and Julian had replied quickly:

> GVHD can kill patients from overwhelming multisystem organ failure. The balance is to have engraftment with a little GVHD (which is difficult to control). Other scenario is horrible, which is no engraftment, leaving patient with no marrow function. Usually a terminal situation…

How much of all this did the children know, or Clary? He hated having that knowledge, the long unwinding tapestry of Binnie's life, and illness, and death. Doctors must find some way of carrying that contagious experience.

Darwin did all right with it, most of the time, but one night he had come banging on Paul's door at 2 a.m., drunk and miserable. That was the benefit of being single again: he could pull Darwin in and drink with him, listen to him rage against illness and death, and put him to bed in the spare room without having to consult or appease Lisanne.

Lisanne's lawyer had served the papers. Before vestry meeting on Tuesday night Paul had been climbing the steps of the church when a young man came up to him, looking like he might need a handout, and then slapped a sheaf of papers at Paul, crying "You're served!" on a reedy note of triumph. *You're It!*

No amount of delay would change any of it. He would remortgage the house, give her half, halve the RRSPs… The division of spoils was not complicated. Lisanne had bought a bright red car. She was marrying an editor. He had to assume that she had been sleeping with him for some time. You couldn't change horses in mid-gallop unless the other was saddled and ready, *tlot-tlotting* along beside you like the highwayman's horse, ready for Bess the landlord's daughter, *the landlord's black-haired daughter*, to jump over, Red Rover. Her black hair flying, a sudden laugh cracking open her face, reaching toward the other, with joy.

He would make fruitcake. Curried shrimp. Yule logs. Lark's tongues.

The kitchen was empty and cold, December clawing in under the back door. Paul put on his coat and went to shop for plates and candles, and a draft-excluder. Christmas crackers. A new cover for the duvet.

Darwin lay on Lorraine's bed, curled over her feet, almost fetal. She had been out for a long time this time; coming back to the surface was weirdly difficult. Like swimming up to the starry glittering border between out and in. If she let herself, she would slip back down and be lost in blueness, wavering down to black. Darwin's arm across her ankles was anchoring her here. Or she might be dreaming him. Dreaming the bed.

She had got used to this. In the morning they were going to start giving her something different—she had forgotten. They were so careful to tell her what was happening, and so distinct, removed from her. That border lay between her and them—they were in, she was out still, still out in the blue, not well. Dying, it was possible, possible. She had to rally because she was not yet allowed to go, she had three children. She could breathe, still, she could keep breathing slowly and calm down, not be afraid, most of the time she could.

The afternoon slant of the light had not changed for hours, but it must have, it must have. This must be some other afternoon. Darwin was asleep in the chair. Look at that, he never was asleep when she was awake. He was the chain back up from her to the kids and he would not let go. She drifted to Clayton, wondering without any effort where he was, what he was doing, why he was not her anchor and never had been, but she was his. So long since she had thought of him, of what he had found to do. How he was surviving, without her or the kids to hold him steady. *Clayton?* she called to him through the water. *Are you okay?*

He would hear her, he would dream of her, or think about her while he did whatever he was doing. She could see him walking down the street, a sad body going along, slanting back while going forward, because he never wanted to be doing whatever he was doing, poor Clayton. Some square of her heart was perpetually sorry for him—it was distracting her from curing this. She had to stop that.

She fell through the ocean for a while, not knowing the word for deep. Darwin's hand moved and pulled the sheet taut over her feet and made her shift under the sheet, he was pulling her back in, reeling her in again, up again into the air. It was easier to stay down but Darwin was right, she had to come up and open her eyes—the lights were on. It was darker, finally, some time must have gone by, some part of the day or evening. She had gone through another day and could float. Clayton's boat *Irresolute*, drifting somewhere in the fog and ice.

Paul shut the lid on a trunkful of booze, an elephant snootful. Bill Haywood had been at the liquor store at the same time, buying a specially selected case of superior red wines. Paul felt poor and young—when would he ever buy a case of wine? Two 24s of beer, two bottles of white, two red, a vodka and a Scotch, and he was out of money. This divorce business was expensive. He shrugged that off. He had room on his credit card. He would spend it all on the party if he wanted to. After decades of dry frugality, Paul felt a growing desire for profusion or purge, the need to blow everything, fill the hollow space with pleasure and vengeful excess. Before the lawyers divided their assets, he would have some use of all the years of penny-pinching. He told himself that this was a common expression of sorrow, a reasonable part of the grieving process for the marriage. *Whatever,* his squalling monkey-mind shot back. *More!*

He put twenty dollars into a panhandler's cup. He was an idiot, a broken man, attempting to stave off soul-hunger and beat back the intimidation of solitude with the consolation of philanthropy.

At the butcher shop—he'd never been in there before, far too expensive—he bought a huge sirloin tip. They told him how to roast it so he could serve it cold. A ham, too; then he spent two hundred dollars in the grocery store on olives and chips—every fancy treat he'd ever fancied. He could see the festive sideboard filling, and it fed an appetite he'd never had before: an overwhelming need for potlatch. Everybody was dying, or already dead, or leaving other people, and the year was dying into winter, and the only thing to do was make some noise.

Dolly was allowed to go to Ann's after school. Ann's mother had finally called back. She was a strange, dim woman, like a flashlight with the batteries almost run down. But she had said she'd pick the girls up from school, and Clary had agreed. It was an adventure, to be going to someone's house. Ann had told Dolly stories about her family, mostly made up. But if she made weird stuff up then there was other, real stuff going on. Dolly knew that Clary had meant to look Mrs. Hayter over before she let her go there, but Pearce was sneezing and crying with a little cold, so Clary was not as picky as she might have been. Mrs. Hayter looked okay, anyway, in a plain navy coat with her grey van, a special-edition one with swirly paint on the sides.

Clary told Mrs. Hayter she would pick Dolly up at suppertime, and they went off in different directions, Dolly and Ann driving away in the leather-seated van with the sunroof and the television in the back seat. The leather was really dirty, and the TV didn't work any more, Ann said. It was missing the on/off knob and there was something crusted on one side of the screen. Ann's mother didn't pick up Ann's brothers, they came home on the bus from the high school, but they weren't home yet. Dolly was a little scared of the idea of them, plus Ann did not talk about them much, which made Dolly think they were probably trouble. Ann's mother went right to her room when they got home, without saying anything.

Ann took Dolly into the kitchen and went through the disorganized pantry closet looking for a snack, but all she found was broken crackers. She said, "Want to look at my Barbies?"

But Dolly didn't want to bother with Barbies, they were childish and boring. Instead, with a kind of pride, Ann led her to her father's den in the basement, to a big black chest of drawers. In those drawers were flat arrays of dirty pictures. Dolly had seen Playboys before at houses where her mom cleaned, but these creeped her out totally, yucky black and white things with naked people fighting and other stuff, with masks on their faces—Dolly almost gagged.

She said, "This is lame," in a scornful voice that she knew would make Ann stop showing them to her. Ann was easy to boss. It was cold for playing outside, but they got their boots and coats on again and wandered around in the pink playhouse in the back yard, but it was dirty too and sharp with the stale winter smell of plastic. Dolly had nothing to say to Ann after looking at those pictures. They opened and closed the shutters for a while, and then Ann said they should go back inside. There wasn't anything to do out in the yard, anyway. Ann had her hand on the back doorknob when they heard a crash in the front hall, and two big boys yelling at each other.

Ann dropped her hand but stayed staring at the door.

Dolly said, "I know!"

"What?" Ann's eyes never moved, even though she was listening to Dolly.

"Let's take the bus downtown and look at the Christmas decorations."

"On the bus? By ourselves?"

Ann looked at Dolly then, a narrow blankness in her eyes like she was adding things up in her head. She looked in the window at the kitchen clock. "Yeah, okay," she said.

"Only we don't have any money," Dolly said. "We'd have to walk."

"I hid five dollars in the playhouse," Ann said. "We can get down and back on that."

She dug underneath the plastic window edging, and came away with the five dollars in her hand. They went out through the snowy back yard into the alley, down the alley to the street, and around the corner to Cumberland. It was only a block to the bus stop, and the bus came along pretty quickly. The driver didn't question them, but sighed when he gave Ann change.

It was the first time Dolly had ever been on a bus. The bus swung left at University and went piling along through the snow-slushed street, and all along the way Dolly knew the hospital was coming and looked, or didn't look; but no matter where her eyes went it was still there. She could get off and go in. They'd only stayed five minutes when Clary took her the last time, and she hadn't been allowed to hug her mother, only to wave at her from the doorway with scrubbed hands. She hadn't even dared to blow her a kiss in case germs went with it.

Ann started to cry. What did she have to cry about?

"What?" Dolly said. "Are you scared?"

"My mom is going to kill me," Ann said.

"Don't be stupid. We'll be home before she knows we're gone." Dolly hoped that was true, because Clary was coming to pick her up at 5:30 and if she wasn't there, Clary would freak. But if they did get into trouble, she could phone and Clary would come get them, right away, no matter what was happening. She could say to people, I live with Clara Purdy. She was stronger in the world than Ann, not just from her ordinary brain but now also from Clary's place in the city.

They got off the bus downtown and zig-zagged on foot for blocks and blocks, trying to find decorations to look at other than the wreath-lights on the lampposts, but the only colour was neon until they found themselves at the decorated skating rink between the pine trees at the Bessborough Hotel.

Ann trailed behind Dolly, as if she'd never had an adventure in her life and never wanted one either. The skaters went around and around and Dolly let her eyes focus and unfocus on the swirl of black pants and bright jackets, like twirling on the little merry-go-round in the park by Clary's. A tall old man skated by, a moving castle, his legs big scissors, long and dark and straight. His skates seemed to go slow while they cut long skirls of ice.

Dolly was happy to stand and watch the skating, but Ann kept whining about the cold. Then an older teenage boy came over to talk to them. He was not skating, just hanging around the little cabin where the fire was. His nose was round and fleshy, and he stared too hard.

"Want some gum?" he asked, talking to Ann, not Dolly. He had thick lips like that bad John Reed guy in *Jane Eyre*.

Dolly couldn't believe it when Ann took a piece. Didn't she know anything?

"Want to go in the hotel?" he asked, still to Ann. "I got a friend who works in the kitchen, we can get a snack."

"Forget it," Dolly said. She pulled Ann's arm, but Ann pulled back, like she wanted to stay talking to the guy. Not getting it at all. The boy turned his weird stare onto Dolly.

"You're ugly," he said. "But you can blow my friend." He grabbed his crotch.

Dolly was scared, partly because he was wearing a lot of black eyeliner. She pulled Ann away onto the ice, thinking they could cross the rink to get to the road.

They flew inside the whirling circle of skaters, Christmas lights blinking between bodies and shadows like slides. Ann was heavy to pull, and Dolly's boots slid, useless on the ice. The weird boy's high Doc Martens had better traction. He was dodging between skaters to catch them. But the tall old man glided toward Dolly, long legs, long skateblades crossing, and swirled around her and crashed into the boy, who went down yelling on the ice. The old man was stooping to help the boy up, or to get in his way.

She ran, yanking Ann, off the ice on the other side and onto the hard-packed snow. It was getting dark. It would be a long way to run to the bus mall, now—but there was the church. They would take care of you, there was a word for it. She ignored Ann's whining to slow down, and half-dragged her across Spadina Avenue to the big red church, around the brick corner of it and up the main steps. The door to the church was locked. But the boy wouldn't know that. He probably wouldn't follow them here. She hauled Ann past the big steps and made her crouch down behind them. Safe for a minute.

Dolly was tempted to go into the church office. The lights were on. She could ask them to call Paul, they would know him, and he'd come and get them. But he'd have to tell Clary, they'd better not.

"Can you run now?"

Ann shook her head. Her nose was running.

"Well, we'll have to walk fast. That guy isn't going to follow us any more. He'll be scared by the church. Hey, spit out that gum! Don't you know they can stick stuff in drinks? They could do it in gum too."

"My mom is going to kill me, if she wakes up," Ann said.

"Maybe you'll be dead already from the gum. It's five o'clock," Dolly said, hearing the church bells begin. They were in so much trouble. She stood up like a gopher checking out of its hole. No guy.

In the distance, there was the bus barrelling toward them.

"Quick! We can make the bus!" They ran like racers, even Ann. They reached the stop just before the bus, and it cranked to a halt, and they climbed on—and Ann had lost the change.

Dolly said, playing it with everything she had, "We are in so much trouble, we've got to get home, and we lost our money. Please, can we pay twice next time?" Well calculated, she thought, for the prim-looking bus driver. Already heading down Spadina, he checked their clothes—Dolly's clothes, at least; Ann was sliding behind her—and Dolly's face.

"Sit down, girls," he said. "You can owe me."

It was because she didn't look like the kind of person who would cheat the bus system. Clary looked after her now, and she looked rich. But she could have done it before, anyway, even living in the Dart—made him believe that she was trustworthy.

Dolly sat back on the red vinyl seat, not touching any part of herself to Ann who was such a stupid idiot, and decided that she was pretty lucky. They would make it back before Clary came to get her. She wondered how she had gotten to be such a good liar, but when she went back over what she'd said, she hadn't told any lies at all that time.

32. Twelve layers laying

On the morning of the party Trevor helped Clary make a twelve-layer chocolate torte to take with them. They drew circles on skinny stiff paper and Trevor spread the dough inside the circles with the back of his spoon, his tongue sticking out at the corner of his mouth to get them perfect. Into the oven—out of the oven! Stack them on the racks. Another, another, another, six sets of twos. Six plus six was twelve. He was way ahead in math.

The fancy plate was in the top cupboard. Clary had to climb on a stepladder, not just a chair, to get it. Her smooth arm when she strained for the top shelf, the way her head had to turn away so she could stretch farther, her foot on the ladder: Trevor could not say even to himself how beautiful she was. He was so lucky. She had tied her hair with a black ribbon and one of the tails of the ribbon sat on her shoulder, curling towards her ear.

Clary found the pedestal plate, her mother's wedding present from an Irish cousin. There was an envelope taped onto the plate—she flipped through it. Seven hundred pounds! Old sterling, from the 70s. A nest egg of her mother's for a trip to England, maybe. Worth far less now, too bad. But it would be useful. She turned awkwardly to get down without breaking anything, and saw Trevor staring at her. "Are you all right?" she asked him.

"Yes," he said. She was not his mother and you could not be saying you loved Clary. Instead he loved the carvey glass plate with one leg. They whipped a mountain of whipped cream and Clary let him fold the chocolate into it, slow and light, piling it on the spatula and turning it carefully. When it was all emptied out on the cake, he would get the bowl and Dolly would get the spatula. Even while he folded, Trevor's mind stumbled blindly off, his tongue buds leading him down to that dreamy future, twelve layers, six plus six was twelve. *Twelve layers dancing,* like in the song for the school concert. *Twelve lays a-laying.*

The torte assembled into a towering improbability of cinnamon-smelling dark and light stripes, pastry flake held together by chocolate air. Clary was pleased with it. She showed Dolly how to make the chocolate curls, pulling steadily to peel chocolate pencils off the marble slab. This was an occasion, Paul's party. He must be still bruised from Lisanne's leaving. Time for a party. In a post-lice fit of celebration she had bought the children Christmas clothes, the same red as her red silk. They would be a fine crowd.

Pearce clamoured for some taste, something to be doing, so Clary put a dollop of cream on his nose and watched his eyes cross to find it, his tongue reaching, reaching for whatever treasure it might be. It took him a long time to use his fingers to find it. He seemed to be convinced his tongue would have a lizard's length, if he could only work it right.

Six p.m., and people would be coming at seven. Paul looked around his empty house. They might suppose that he'd taken the dining room chairs away on purpose to make buffet-style simpler. But the hollow shell of the living room had to be addressed. He'd put pine boughs along the mantel and up the stair rail, magazine-style, but even with borrowed church-hall chairs there were not enough seats for the older people. A new carpet sat blankly in the middle of the floor, like the raft of the *Medusa.*

In a flash of inspiration, using the folding luggage trolley, he brought his grandmother's loveseat in from the garden shed, where it had sat for years. Dusted off and covered with a navy sheet it looked all right, he thought. Loveseat, the seat of love. *Tell me, Where is fancy bred? Or in the heart, or in the head?* The cheap carpet smelled strongly of chemicals, even though he had left the windows open all day. He brought the spice bottle from the kitchen and sprinkled cinnamon all over it. Nobody would notice, brown on brown. Cloves would be even stronger. He sprinted back to the kitchen.

The doorbell rang while he was still dressing the carpet with cloves. Bill and Iris Haywood, their children behind them carrying trays of fruit and cheese and sausage. Bill said he would set up the bar, and Iris went straight to the kitchen, children like tugboats afore and aft her.

Paul let them go and ran up the stairs two at a time to change his shirt and put on his red tie.

Then there were more people at the door, Frank Rich the people's warden and his family, with their famous fruitcake, all wearing identical Santa hats. Not St. Nicholas's mitre, but never mind.

Candy Vincent was at the door, giving Paul a hug—a wash of perfume and a painful scrape of sequins from her glittering sweater. "The place looks so empty!" she cried. "We're going to have to drum up some furniture for you, Paul! I'll see what I can find in Uncle Joe's things. Can't have our priest living like a monk, what would the Lutherans think of us?"

He took her coat and hung it up, turning away with that vacant smile on his face that he struggled against. A Christmas party was no arena for strict honesty. Iris Haywood handed Candy a tray of hot hors d'oeuvres and asked her to find a place for it in the living room, so he was rescued. But quick, coats, because the door was filling again, old Mrs. Varney, Sally King and saintly Mary Tolliver, all carrying Tupperware, the whole parish tramping onto the porch. Still no Clary, no Darwin. Kerry Porter and her two monstrous little boys. The Carvers behind them, and the Newtons: benefactors of the church hall, but people he genuinely liked, and he turned to greet them with some non-building-fund gratitude.

Mrs. Pell wanted to go too. She had stumped herself over to Mira-Cal beauty school that morning for Seniors' Day, and they had curled her hair, for heaven's sake. She was wearing a purple outfit from the Goodwill store, and looked strangely presentable. There was no reason why she should not go, except that she was as unpredictable as a chimpanzee.

Clary shut her eyes to the purple suit and managed to be glad that Mrs. Pell could hold the chocolate torte in the car. They got her seatbelt fastened (she complained, so there was some predictability in her) and Clary ran back for the torte. She almost tripped coming down the porch steps in unaccustomed heels, but she recovered, and showed Mrs. Pell where not to put her thumbs, and they were off.

Paul's house! A party! Clary had a vibrating beat of excitement under her breath, under her thoughts. People would be there, would they see that she and Paul were friends? She tried to erase that, but it kept popping back under her thoughts like an Internet ad screen.

The street was full of cars. Clary parked in the next-door driveway. Her father's old friend Melvin John lived there; he spent every winter in Arizona, but of course he had a boy come and shovel the driveway anyway, in case thieves should see that no one was home and make off with the Zenith clock radio or the ten-year-old sixteen-inch colour television set. On this wintry Advent night, streetlights shining on floating snowflakes, household anxiety—any anxiety—seemed foolish. The Holy Spirit hung over the world, hidden or revealed, watching them all.

The torte! Mrs. Pell was struggling to get unbuckled, and the strap would behead it. Clary caught her arm in time, and said, "Wait—I'll come around and help."

Dolly helped too, taking the torte from Clary and standing in her new black shoes, their little heels making every step older and new. The world was so quiet in the snow that you could hear the noise of the party even over here, even with Granny grunting out of the car. Dolly did not know what to expect. Fancy food, probably, and people from Sunday school would be there, the Haywood girls who were snooty because their mom was the principal even though they went to the other school so she wouldn't have to give them detention. Her Sunday school teacher would be there, Miss Tolliver, who had said that there were two Moseses in the Bible, when Dolly asked if the baby Moses and the old man Moses were the same guy. Clary had told Dolly later that there was only one, that the baby had grown up to free the Israelites and take them into the wilderness, but Clary had promised not to mention it to Paul because Dolly didn't want Miss Tolliver to get in trouble.

Mrs. Pell was on her feet and steady enough, Pearce's seat came out without the handle jamming, and Dolly could carry the bottle of wine—wait. Clary reassigned all the duties, gave Trevor the diaper bag and asked him to help his grandmother on the icy sidewalk, and then took the torte and the car seat herself, one arm for each, with the wine tucked in beside Pearce. Then Dolly had to close all the car doors, and then they were off, down the driveway and up Paul's walk.

The house was lit up, music spilling out and the porch light glowing with a wreath of berries around it. Clary had a moment of panic as they all went up the steps, stamping to loosen the snow, but she told herself it was only excitement. Trevor rang the bell, and there was Paul opening the door in high spirits, to welcome them. Surprised to see Mrs. Pell but turning it into happiness. The torte! How beautiful. Clary handed the torte off to Iris Haywood (who was suitably impressed and carried it off to the dining room respectfully). Bill Haywood shepherded Mrs. Pell into the living room and sat her beside Candy Vincent in the loveseat.

Naturally Pearce had filled his diaper in the car. The smell became obvious when they'd taken their coats off in the warm house. She swung him up the stairs ahead of her, Paul pointing to the bathroom at the back of the landing.

"Or the bedroom, or my study, whatever works," he called up the stairs. He took Trevor and Dolly to the kitchen to give them punch glasses. He had rented those, proud of himself for remembering that such a thing was possible. Anyone could give a party.

Upstairs one door stood open, all white tiles. The bathroom was plain and spare, like the rest of the place, and dazzlingly clean. It took Clary a moment to realize that it looked so white and open because there was no shower curtain. Did he not need one?

Pearce was still almost asleep from the car, but he moved his head toward the noise of men laughing, filtered up the stairs. Clary could remember hearing that noise from her bedroom, almost forty years ago. Wild parties for a while in the 60s, the house smelling of cigars and rye, her mother nervous and angry in the afternoon. What a strange changeable time that must have been, society heaving into a new world. Her mother had urged her father to invite important people, so-and-so's husband because he was head of the Chamber of Commerce. Trying to advance him to some level of prestige; not accepting for years that he did not want to be advanced. The store was the manageable world. He was president of the Chamber one year, but it meant too many meetings and he bowed out; her mother subsided from ambition and turned to ferocious bridge and organizing the life out of the Ladies' Auxiliary. How had they filled their days? How had she filled hers, till the children came? She could have grown old like Mary Tolliver, good and mild and empty.

Pearce's golden bottom was perfectly clean, a false alarm. He was not smelly at all. He regarded her with steady thoughtful eyes while she refastened his diaper efficiently. "Clah," he said, staring at her.

He was saying her name! She stared at him for a minute, then said, "Clary."

"Clah," he said again. He beamed and smacked his hands together. She almost wept but she didn't want to spoil her make-up—ridiculous to be crying just because Pearce, now fifteen months old, was finally saying her name.

She said, "Yes, Clary, that's right! Good boy!" and she popped him on her hip and took him downstairs to show him off.

As she arrived at the bottom of the stairs there was another peal of the doorbell—Darwin, taking up most of the doorway. Paul came through from the kitchen too, as happy to see him as she was.

"Darwin!" Clary cried. "Listen! Pearce, say Clary, say Clary."

"Clah," Pearce said, no bones about it.

"A *genius*," Darwin said, taking Pearce and swinging him up in the air. At the top of the arc Pearce's hand clutched for the mistletoe hanging from the hall light, and both Paul and Clary reached to keep it safe, their fingers touching.

"Mistletoe?" Darwin said, laughing. "You're stuck now," he said. They pulled their fingers away.

Mrs. Pell's voice was loud in the living room, telling Candy Vincent, "That's my brother-in-law, Darwin Hand."

Clary was confused and embarrassed, and did not have Pearce to hold; she couldn't sort out exactly what Mrs. Pell should be saying, what relationship Darwin really was to her. Amazing how carrying that thick old voice was in all this throng of people and music.

Dolly saw Darwin there—Trevor headed for the hall, but she ran the other way, to the dining room to get the torte, to show Darwin the incredible, unbelievable dessert that they had made.

A straight passage had opened in the crowd, from Mrs. Pell's purple jacket out to the hall, so they could all see Dolly coming through from the dining room with the torte towering on its pedestal plate. She was holding it like a candlestick to make an entrance, maybe thinking of the crucifer carrying the big cross in church on Sunday, and Clary could see that it was going, it was already sliding. Dolly's face was bright and excited and Clary could hardly bear to say *No,* but it was going—

The inch-high heel of Dolly's new black shoe caught the edge of the new carpet in the living room, and the pedestal wobbled, and the twelve layers of chocolate torte and whipping cream went smearing, veering off in a long slide of damp puffing beauty, everyone in the room transfixed, watching the layers flying outward like owls' wings that make no sound, until there was finally a series of little whumps as the pieces of torte landed, one after another, three or four of them on Candy Vincent's legs and the rest segueing out over the whole carpet.

Dolly held on to the plate.

Mrs. Pell had tucked her own legs away, in an almost-elegant gesture, and she leaned back against the cushions of the loveseat and laughed out loud, her mouth wide open and all her awful teeth showing, helpless with heaving gulps of laughter. She patted Candy Vincent, who was staring at her heavy, suede-panted legs, and laughed all over again.

Tears splashed down Dolly's poor face, and Paul put an arm around her and said idiotic comforting things: "Never mind, never mind, there are a hundred desserts here, you can make us another one, it's only fluff, never mind."

"Sorry, sorry, sorry," Dolly kept saying, trying not to make any sobbing noise.

Clary was grateful that Dolly had not dropped the Waterford cake plate. Because then her mother would have appeared in a cloud of lightning to open the gates of Hell for Clary and the whole rag-tag set of clumsy gypsies who had invaded and pillaged her lovely house, leaving nothing undamaged. But the Waterford plate was safe, and her mother was safely dead.

Darwin still had Pearce, so Clary could catch her breath and put her arms around Dolly, making a sandwich of her with Paul. "It's all right, really, it's all right," she said, kissing the top of her head. Trevor was scooping pieces of torte off the floor and cramming them into his mouth. The youngest New-ton child had brought a spoon from the dining room for a salvage feast.

The boys were interrupted by Candy Vincent, moving through the wreckage mopping at her suede pants with a cocktail napkin.

Clary said, "I'm terribly sorry, Candy," and Candy turned her bulk to-wards them, her pale eyes finding Dolly. Clary felt sick, knowing she would have to defend Dolly, but for Paul's sake not wanting any kind of a scene.

"You've done me a favour," Candy told Dolly, not smiling, but calm. "These pants were killing me, and now I've got an excuse to run home and change."

"Of course we'll pay for the dry-cleaning," Clary said, suddenly re-membering Candy in Grade 7, going home in tears with a bloodstain on her skirt.

"Nope," Candy said. "I've never liked them, and I'm going to throw them out. Good excuse to shop, Karl!"

Across the room her heavy husband laughed and rolled his eyes. "Go for it, Candy," he called back. He was wearing a too-tight blue knit suit cut along rodeo lines, with pearl buttons. But Karl Vincent was kind. He was one reason to like Candy.

"Thank you," Clary said quietly. "She was a little over-excited."

Candy waved her hand and leaned closer to speak in Clary's ear. "That grandmother is something, though." She looked meaningfully at Clary. "Quite the tales she's been telling."

Mrs. Pell was still whooping away on the little couch. Who knew what wild lies she'd been confiding. She had Trevor snugged in beside her eating a slab of torte, ignoring the chocolate oozing onto her jacket. Clary would clean it for her anyway, of course, why should she worry?

Paul decided that the carpet was not cleanable, at least not in the middle of the party, and he asked Dolly to help him roll it up and take it to the base-ment. They let people step over them as they rolled, like a game of Twister. It was so light because it was such a cheap carpet, Paul explained.

"In fact," he said, when they opened the basement door, "Let's just con-sign it to the netherworld." He tugged the whole thing out of Dolly's grasp and slid it down the stairs. It was still so new that it didn't even unfurl.

More people arrived even before the torte mess was cleared up. More food was pulled out of the oven and people's incoming arms, and replenished on the table and the rented plates. Everyone found people to talk to and other people they also wanted to talk to, and nobody had any axes to grind; or their axes were tucked away for the evening. Paul found himself introducing Mrs. Pell to everyone in the parish. She had never yet been to church and although he hoped professionally that she would receive the astonishing gift of the Holy Spirit, he could not help hoping she would experience the spirit in her own way at her own time, perhaps in the Temple that was the Great Outdoors. He thought he might have drunk a little too much of his adult punch, which had turned out very well. Darwin seemed to be enjoying himself too, whenever Paul caught a glimpse of him: listening to Frank Rich on the donor campaign, or getting Miss Tolliver to boast about her nephew the magician.

Clary, too, found herself enjoying the party. She and Iris Haywood ended up in the kitchen managing the endless stream of hot dishes people brought, and the equal torrent of things Paul had made. From time to time he remembered something and would dash back to find the champagne grapes at the back of the fridge, or the five fancy mustards for the ham. Then he would be ear-pinned away to the living room again by some other parishioner. Clary thought he looked happier than she'd ever seen him—he enjoyed entertaining. She liked his new shirt, and the nice red tie. She liked him so much.

Iris Haywood's eldest daughter Ivy took Pearce in hand, walking him from room to room, keeping him happy. Bringing scalloped potatoes into the dining room Clary thought it was time for another diaper, but she gave Pearce a quick sniff, and he was fine. She hoped it was not Mrs. Pell who smelled. Something certainly did.

To atone for her disaster, Dolly gave herself the job of finding and stacking the dirty plates: Cinderella enough that she cheered right up. When Candy Vincent came back wearing a blue dress, carrying a bag of ice ("You're psychic!" Iris Haywood said), Dolly felt able to slide off with the second-oldest Haywood girl, Francine, to sit on the stairs and talk about youth group, which they would be going to when they turned ten. Francine told her she had gone to a sleepover once and made the toilet overflow in the middle of the night, which was even worse than dropping the torte—the parents had to get up and all the other girls woke up too, it was so humiliating. It was a holy pleasure for Dolly to talk to such an established, clever, uncrippled girl. At this party she was like that too. Francine wouldn't let some weird guy grab his crotch at her. Although she would never go and die, Dolly thought she looked like Jane Eyre's friend Helen. Her fair hair rippled over her shoulder and she sat sideways on the stairs with her shins neatly together, flowered tights under her black velvet dress: Dolly's friend this evening. As perfect as Ann Hayter was pitiful, so that Dolly felt a stab of guilt.

Underneath them, close enough that Dolly could have reached through the banisters and touched the top of his gleaming bald head, Frank Rich— his Santa hat now on Mary Tolliver—told Paul that he had a lot to be thankful for.

"I know this must be a sad time for you what with the whole divorce thing," Frank said, "But you have a lot of friends in this parish, and most of us are happy to see the backside of her."

Paul found himself mesmerized by Frank's bright, protruding, blood-shot eyes. Had he had too much to drink?

"Not that she was ever anything but polite to me, Reverend."

How could Frank, a pillar of the church, forty years of service to the parish and the diocese, still not be able to grasp that Reverend was an honorific, not a name? Maybe no one had ever told him before.

"You know, Frank," Paul said, and he could hear the rest of it already curdling in his mouth: "*I am not Reverend. Reverend is not a synonym for priest. Call me Paul, or Mr. Tippett, or Father Tippett if you like it High, or The Reverend Paul Tippett—*"

A strange, unsteady name, Tippett. Like himself. He smiled at Frank. "You know, I'm grateful for your sympathy, but I'm doing pretty well."

He probably needed a drink himself, Paul realized. He felt a hand patting his head, and he reached up and touched it. Squeezed in beside Dolly on the stairs, Trevor smiled down at him.

"Want a ride?" he asked Trevor. Trevor climbed over the stair railing and onto Paul's shoulders, and they stomped off to scare the ladies in the kitchen.

The Principal wasn't scared. She handed Paul a glass of eggnog and gave Trevor children's punch in a plastic cup, way up there in the air. Clary went to lift him down but Paul said "No, no," and hung on to Trevor's ankles. "He's keeping my neck warm in this wintry weather."

Trevor made his legs tight to hold on better and Paul pretended to gag, and then Clary did lift him down, but they didn't spill one drop of the punch. Trevor slid back into the crowded room. The party was a forest of people, all burly bodies in rich clothes, pressed together at the top but thinner down below. If you were short enough you could get through the mass by crouching slightly. As he wandered by, Mrs. Pell told Trevor to fetch her a glass of the white wine. Darwin caught him carrying it back, holding it like the holy grail so he didn't do a Dolly. Darwin filled it with ginger ale instead and let him carry it again.

Mrs. Pell glared at Darwin. Busybody. But she wasn't too mad. Edith Varney was from Medstead, it turned out, and she knew people who had known Mrs. Pell's sister Janet's husband from Medstead, or at least his brothers.

More punch—when the girls wandered into the kitchen Clary set Dolly stirring the still-frozen orange juice while she searched for ginger ale. None left in the fridge. But Paul, coming in on a waft of music with a plate to refill, pointed Clary to the back porch for more pop in cartons, and then went with her through into the little passage between the kitchen and the back porch, where two doors stood closed, one to the porch and one to the basement.

In the suddenly darker quiet of the passage Clary leaned against the basement door so he could pass, and Paul could not pass by her. He looked into her face and leaned to see her better, to see her eyes, and then to kiss her.

His lips were cool and smoother than she'd thought and her chest contracted at the smell of his mouth, and then the taste of it, immaculate, and her arm fell around his shoulders and neck like Pearce's arm around her neck. He pressed her against the door, their bodies intruding on each other. A rush of heat flooded up her body—although her mind was clear and surprised and calm, her body was ecstatic. The bones of his face were close beneath his skin. His hand touched her cheek. She felt that melding encroaching on her like dizziness, and tried to pull away. He stood back instantly.

"I'm sorry," he said.

"Oh no," she said.

She tried to straighten up, and swayed, and he braced her waist. The molecules there too seemed to be merging, hand and body more than touching.

"Clary," he said, as if he was satisfied with her name.

She smiled at him, half-smile splitting open, her whole self visible. She

250

must be blushing. She stretched her arms above her head and pulled at her hair and reached out to kiss him again, but the Haywood girl came rushing through, joyful, oblivious, running to get something from the back porch—some urgent unimportant rush that blew between them and brightened the hall from velvet darkness.

So Paul went out to the porch and got the ginger ale, and Clary went to find Pearce. He was sitting safely wedged on a church-hall chair between Sally King and Mrs. Rich, blathering gossip to each in turn.

"What a wonderful job you're doing with this little fellow," Mrs. Rich said when Clary swooped down on him. The parish must not have heard about the lice.

"He's no work at all," Clary said, and Sally King and Mrs. Rich both smiled at her like they knew *all* about it. Since they were both over sixty, Clary thought they had probably forgotten it, or most of it. She doubted that they'd missed a night's sleep or a peaceful meal for many years. But she smiled back at them because after all, she was in their club, the club of women who have been with children. She stood breathing in the smell of Pearce's neck. Did he need changing again? Nope. There was a definite smell, but not from Pearce. Maybe it *was* Mrs. Pell. But that was a new dress, new to her; Goodwill would have cleaned it.

She shifted Pearce, and he hid his head on her shoulder, face away from the ladies. Too much excitement. Children were overflowing through the party like a forgotten bathtub, the sugar in the punch beginning to tell. Cynthia Newton started rounding hers up and couldn't find Kevin, so there was a general hunt upstairs and down. Dolly got the prize, finding him sound asleep behind a dining room curtain, propped against the window, sticky spoon in one hand and chocolate all over his chin.

Someone put John Coltrane on the stereo, *Giant Steps*, as people went out the door.

"When do you put up your tree, Reverend?" Frank Rich asked Paul on his way out the door. "I've got a couple extra marked out this year, when I bring in the tree for the hall, coupla weeks, I could drop one off for you too, if you'd like?"

Paul thanked him and wondered where the Christmas decorations were. In the rafters of the garage? Lisanne might have overlooked them. She and the editor were going to the Mayan Riviera for Christmas. He advanced the CD a jab, to "Spiral." She'd never give the box another moment's thought, all those ornaments collected over all those years. One minute he was leaning into Clary in the back hall, and the next washed into sadness by a box of tinsel baubles that might not even be in the garage. Schrödinger's Christmas cat.

Clary wandered through the rooms with Pearce on her hip, searching for Dolly, who was in the back porch with Francine. That would be nice, if that worked out. Better than that listless Ann Hayter, whose mother was too odd for comfort. When Clary had picked Dolly up last week Mrs. Hayter hadn't seemed to remember that she was there. See how my charity only extends to the ones I care about, she thought. I don't care at all about Ann Hayter, even if she's in trouble, even if that household has something clearly wrong in it. "Time, Dolly," she said. "We've got to get Pearcey home."

Dolly did not complain, thank goodness—probably because Francine got up right away. The Haywoods kept strict discipline. Dolly and Francine said good night with some formality, respecting their long evening's conversation.

"She's going to ask her mom if I can come for lunch on Sunday," Dolly told Clary, who was busy keeping her heartbeats from going crazy, and hardly heard. Paul had kissed her, right there.

"I think she'll let me, don't you?"

"Oh yes, probably," Clary said, wondering what she was agreeing with, pressing her free hand to her chest to stop that quaver in the breath.

Out in the kitchen a posse of women were cleaning up, leaving the place spick and span. If Lisanne had still been there the women wouldn't have done it, Clary thought, with a moment's temporary sympathy for her. But of course she would have bristled if anyone but Paul had tried to help, and scoffed at him. Impossible. Possible. Her cheeks went hot again. This was annoying. She went through the kitchen arch, stalking Mrs. Pell. There she was, all alone in purple splendour on the dark loveseat. Looking old and a little the worse for wear, but she had been comparatively unexceptional all evening. As she struggled to her feet, Mrs. Pell said, "That settle's comfortable enough but there's something dirty inside it. You'd think a minister would have a cleaner house."

Coats were dealt out into the proper hands, those who had boots had found them, the music softened and slowed. Trevor was sitting on the bottom stair by the time Clary and Pearce and Mrs. Pell and Dolly worked their way through. Getting them all dressed was easy enough. The hard thing was Paul. Clary put her arms back obediently for him to help her with her coat, but she found it hard to turn around. His hands fitted the coat onto her shoulders and stayed there for a moment—not long enough for anyone else to see.

She might not have been able to look at him at all, but she suddenly remembered and turned to say, "I hate to tell you this, but there's a bad smell in the living room. I think it's the loveseat."

"Oh, good Lord, I just brought it in from the garage."

"Something died inside there, man," Darwin said. "I thought it'd better wait till after the party. I'll help you take it back outside."

"I can't—Candy Vincent sat there half the night!"

"Everything else was perfect," Clary said.

"Everything else?"

She bent her head. "Oh, yes," she said. She fastened Pearce back into his seat and took his comforting weight in her hand. "Children, we'd better—" She held out her hand to shake Paul's. Their hands fit together. After a moment, because she had to, Clary let go.

They trooped out into the cold air.

Sparks of stars flew above the rooftops and northern lights were flaring, slashing, bright yellow and green and red flowing into each other. All the people who had left the party were still standing on the sidewalk, looking up, sighing as the curtains swayed.

33. Rose window

*P*aul stopped at the house on his way to do his hospital visits on Saturday morning. "In case I don't see you there," he said, when Clary answered the door. "I thought if I didn't—I thought I'd stop to see you, just in case. In case you—"

She laughed and asked him to come in, but he could see children in various stages of pyjamas running back and forth, and he said he wouldn't, "Only I hoped—"

He started again. "I wanted to ask if you could come for dinner tonight, to my house." He was already halfway down the steps, as if to give her room to refuse.

"Of course," she said. "Yes!"

He was off. "Six-thirty?" he called back. "Seven?"

"Six-thirty, please," she said, wondering what she would do about the children.

At six p.m. Mrs. Zenko knocked on the door and stepped inside, calling for Clary.

"Darwin and Fern and I are taking the little ones to the lobster place," she told Clary. "It's Seniors' Saturday and I've got a coupon, so we'll have a party too."

Clary found their jackets and tied two pairs of shoes and kissed Pearce, and then she went to do her hair and change her own clothes. She tried on the grey wool dress—too severe, cloisterish. She tightened the belt. Took it off. She put on the brown skirt. Without the sash it was plain enough. It was only dinner.

Leaning in the doorway of her room, Darwin said, "He's a seriously good guy. You know that. Why are you confusing yourself? Get over there."

She tried a necklace, then took it off. She shouted, "Oh!" and Darwin laughed at her. Nothing, unadorned. That was her. Darwin found her keys.

Paul was watching through the window when Clary got out of her car. Her chestnut-hull jacket, hair in a low braid twisting over the collar. Autumn beech leaves, with a little plain white peeping through the neck. Always a pleasure to look at her. How familiar she was, her legs moving the way he knew, her back straight, her straight gait, and her heavy skirt moving easily through brown and gold. Dressed up for this, but still herself. He opened the door. They stood looking at each other.

"What's for dinner?" Clary asked.

"Well. I thought—carbonara—I have some good pancetta."

Paul backed into the living room, giving her the room, empty as it was. No pungent sofa, at least; the church-hall chairs returned and the floor bare wood, this time, Murphy-soaped. His mother's Jacobean crewel-work curtains vacuumed to banish the lonely settled dust. Clary's clothes looked beautiful in there. Clary did.

She was carrying a bottle of wine. He had bought wine glasses and some pretty good wine himself. He was competent. It was only spaghetti, he told himself. Even if it curdled, it would taste good. He talked about Italy while they grated cheese and broke eggs. He had not known that she'd lived in England, with her mother's cousins. They compared notes on the plummy voices, the quaintness of the packaging, the beauty. He had done graduate work at Cambridge after U of T, cold and hungry all the time. His mother still lived in Toronto. His sister Binnie had died, she knew that. No other family to rush to his side.

"My mother would, gladly. But it would only make everything harder. She and Lisanne never—could not—" He stopped. No need for this fumbling.

"My mother hated Dominic," Clary said. "That made it easier, because I didn't have to justify anything to her—being left. She never sullied our ears with his name again."

Paul hated to hear the flat note in her voice when she spoke of her once-husband. He consciously brightened his own voice, saying, "What we look for first is someone as unlike our parents as possible—we did a good job on that, both of us. Congratulations!"

He lifted his glass, but caught its base somehow on the wooden salad forks and spilled red wine into the greens waiting in the bowl.

"Never mind," Clary said, dabbing at them with a paper towel. "It'll be a vintner's salad. Take the edge off the vinegar."

As she did. Paul turned away to light the stove, quickly, in case he might touch her. *While up from my heart's root / So great a sweetness flows I shake from head to foot.*

The carbonara was the best he'd ever made. He was flushed with achievement, or with wine, didn't matter. Able to talk freely, to hold forth to someone who didn't look puzzled by his train of thought or ask what some word meant, who laughed when he made a mild joke. She might even have laughed at his marrying-Xanthippe epiphany, he thought. *Xanthippany.*

He steered his thoughts away from Lisanne, but too late. She was present enough at the table, sneering at his attempts to be engaging.

He fell silent. Clary, too, seemed to run out of talk, or the need to talk. She smiled at him. He understood that her kindness would not let her be stiff or seem uncomfortable. Her perfect courtesy, her upbringing. Or maybe, he told himself, she was not uncomfortable. Not conscious, as he was.

There was a pint of fancy ice cream, frozen impermeable. He left it on the kitchen counter to soften, and found the old coffee grinder which Lisanne's sister had scorned.

While Paul made coffee, Clary went upstairs to find the bathroom.

She had drunk a lot of wine, not too much. A little too much. The bathroom, straight ahead. Where she had changed Pearce, at the party, and he had said *Clah!* Perfect boy. She looked into the other doors, stepping lightly on the bare floors so Paul would not hear her snooping. A shelf-lined study, the desk not as untidy as his office desk; a little room with a daybed and a bookcase; then his bedroom, which had been his and Lisanne's. A big pine bed, a dresser, nothing else. No night tables, so the bed stood bare against the wall. An ironing board set up in one corner for him to iron his clerical shirts. She must be drunk, she was getting sad.

Back to the bathroom, that white empty shell. No shower curtain— Lisanne must have taken it, of course. It felt strange to be alone in Paul's house with him, as if his house was an extension of his body. She was so bad at this! What was this, even?

She splashed water on her face, then remembered that she had worn mascara. She carefully tissued off the raccoon eyes, and was left clean but no longer sultry. As she should not be. Ridiculous to try to be attractive, she was too old and he was too broken, never mind his sweet mouth and the pale, strained skin at his temples.

No time for this, much as they might want it. Far too early for him, and unfortunately too late for her, as she could see in the mirror in that all-white bathroom. With any luck she had not made a complete fool of herself, and could gracefully say good night and go home to the children. She drank a palmful of water, then buried her face in the full white towel. At least his towels were new and rich-feeling, so he had one kindly, soft thing in his life. Her face was old, no matter how she turned her chin to look. She switched off the harsh light and opened the door.

Paul was standing in the hall. "I came to find you," he said.

"Here I am," she said. His face was so bare, it took up her whole field of vision. Open. Looking at her completely—who else saw her?

She was old. She was who she was.

"Your face is beautiful," he said, needing to tell her that, at least. The light of hidden flowers. Her head was bent, looking down at her feet beneath the edge of the brown skirt. Where it curved, there it was golden, and then dark brown in the shadows.

"This is impossible, isn't it," he said. To let her leave.

Neruda, that was: *I love you as the plant that never blooms, but carries in itself the light of hidden flowers.* But that was between a husband and wife, together for twenty-five years. Why would he think that of Clary, whom he

257

hardly knew, had known hardly any time at all? Who he knew as if she was himself, who seemed to fit and match him everywhere. Clary looked into his eyes, and walked through the doorway, three steps, and was in his room.

"I bought a new bed."

"I'm glad it's new," she said, and they sat down together on the edge of it, in the pale, empty room. After a minute he knelt down and took her shoes off.

As they made love Clary thought of lines she had not believed, of images in art. She saw a rose window, and understood, in some translation of spirit, why cathedrals had them—that arching, redoubling, million-faceted rose-wide opening, that springing, flooding light. The reason of the rose, in the first place.

They lay silent, Paul's arm bent around her shoulder and collar-bone, his other arm beneath her. No need to move yet.

He said, "*Where I does not exist, nor you, so close that your hand on my chest is my hand, so close that your eyes close as I fall asleep.*"

But she could not fall asleep, because there were children at home. After what seemed like a long time, she got up and dressed in the darkness. She knelt beside the bed and folded her hand over his. His fingers twitched, lightly.

She went home. Past midnight, but Mrs. Zenko waved a gay hand from the couch, saying, "Darwin took Fern off to some party, some old friend she wanted to see, you just missed them. Well, my sweet, I'll say good night. You look like you had a lovely evening."

Mrs. Zenko gathered up her jacket and her purse. She squeezed Clary's arm as she went out, and kissed her on the cheek. "Sleep well."

Clary dreamed that Lorraine came to her room and sat on her bed and asked for a report on the children. She began obediently with Pearce: gaining weight nicely, walking all the time, frustrated now if he was left in his playpen. She did not say that Pearce knew her name. Trevor: happy enough, a few friends he talked about, seemed to be doing well as long as they kept at the homework; she vowed to do better with printing practice, she promised faithfully.

Dolly? Lorraine asked, her shadowy shape bending slightly.

I have no idea, Clary had to say. I have no idea how she is doing. I have been too busy with my own affairs. Tears tracked down Lorraine's ghost cheek, shining in the beam of the streetlight outside.

Clary climbed up out of sleep and checked on Pearce; then she went down the hall to the children's room. Trevor was breathing loudly in the top bunk. He muttered and then sighed, still in his dream. Dolly's duvet had slipped off, and Clary straightened it, looking at the tangle of thin arms and legs, the wild hair straying on the pillow. She could not be in love, she had children to look after.

At five in the morning Paul came down and found chocolate ice cream melted all over the kitchen counter. He whistled while he cleaned it up, even though it was before breakfast.

34. Blood, bile

*F*ern called Clary at 6 a.m., too scared to wait longer. She and Darwin had run into a little mayhem at the party, a fight had erupted; it was unclear. He had a broken nose, they thought, and concussion; he was still unconscious and they weren't sure how bad it was. Darwin had not been fighting, Fern said, he'd been *in* the fight, but not—it was hard to understand her. Clary went to Emergency right away.

Fern could not stop crying. "It was all pushing, coats and fists, and then he fell! There was ice—"

But where had they been? When Clary asked, Fern just shook her head and wept some more. "It's all my fault, I shouldn't have taken him there—everybody was wasted and—my friend—was mad and he wanted a fight, he was being an asshole. Darwin wouldn't fight with him, he said he was too drunk to fight with, but he was swinging anyway, and the others, and then Darwin turned away and got dropped, his fist caught his nose, crack! And he went down backwards. It was all ice out there, they'd thrown Jack out, I was worried that he might get hurt because he was with these… They were all so drunk, and then the police came…"

Clary could not untangle the hes and hims but gathered, mostly from

Fern's woe, that Darwin was blameless and unlucky. Fern seemed not to be drunk, but having a hard time getting herself back under control. Clary stood with an arm around her while she got it all out.

"He sat up and his nose was bleeding and smashed, and I said, I think you've broken your nose, and he said, It's all right, it's been broken before—and then he passed out."

Fern was too old to be this young, Clary thought. She must have seen fights out in Davina. And Darwin was an idiot to have milled in there.

He looked stricken, flat in the narrow bed, the energy that usually zinged around him gone dead. A huge scrape on the side of his cheek was cleaned, but still oozing blood. His nose was a swollen mess packed with gauze. In a while she'd go up and tell Lorraine, when they knew what was happening.

They had not used any birth control—why think of that now? She had lost the knack of all this: how long of nobody, nothing, only the crumbs from under thy table.

Clary got home at noon to find Moreland parking outside. Tears sprang into her eyes at the sight of his competent bulk. "Not enough sleep last night," she said, hugging him. Remembering why she hadn't slept enough, she turned her face so Moreland wouldn't see that joy sparking through her. He'd think she was hiding tears for Darwin, but that was not dishonest.

"Is he bad?"

"He looks terrible! But he's awake, and they've packed his nose."

"Well, I'm on a mission to calm Fern down. I forgot, Grace sent—" He opened the passenger door and slid out a large cardboard box. "Plug in the slow cooker right away for the barbecue beef, five hours, she said, and there's three dozen buns for the freezer and two squares and that other pot is beans, and beet pickles and a bunch of new tea-towels."

Moreland hopped into his truck. Clary took the box—Grace in cardboard—and struggled with it up to the porch. Mrs. Zenko opened the screen and helped her manoeuvre it through the door. "No trouble here, I just popped over, busybody that I am," Mrs. Zenko said. Mrs. Pell was snoring on the chesterfield, but the children were still watching TV in what seemed to be a contented stupor.

While she was plugging in Grace's slow cooker, Paul walked up the front steps. Clary could hear his feet stamping off the night's dusting of snow, and knew it was him. He must be on his way home after church—she could tell him about Darwin. He opened the door without knocking, which made her happy, and came straight into the kitchen. She turned to look at him, now in some way her own.

He walked across the shining tiles with his boots still on and put his arms around her. He said, "I forgot to say, but you must know: I love you."

Maybe it only seemed unreal because she was not used to it. Trevor had to tell Paul about the movie they'd been watching. He slid his chair against Paul's, and Dolly came to find out what she was missing. Pearce in his high chair growled comments. Paul was enjoying them all.

Clary had a dizzy sensation of artificiality. *True/False*. We are a little family. That was not a thought that was allowed. It is true, she insisted. But her other mind yelled *False*, and that was true too.

She was not hungry. She put soup in front of Dolly, and some for Trevor; ladling, turning, but seeing Lorraine with the delicate oxygen tubes trailing over her ears and into her nose, and Darwin caught in the hospital's web too, and Clayton, all of them, disappearing.

The verdict was simply a bad concussion from the fall, the impact of the sidewalk on the back of Darwin's head. Paul sat on the end of his bed, like Darwin sat on the end of Lorraine's, and disliked it. He did not want to be Darwin for Darwin. I'm not up to it, he thought. Who did he care for like Darwin cared for Lorraine? Binnie, he told himself, but that was only partly true; he'd gone when he thought he could, for two weeks here and there. He had allowed his job and his marriage to rule his time, as if either one mattered. Darwin had simply left whatever his real life was and come.

"I'll sit with Lorraine tonight," he told Darwin, who shut his eyes. Paul warmed Darwin's ankle through the sheet, as he had seen Darwin doing a thousand times to Lorraine's, and was rewarded with a creeping smile.

"You're a model patient," Paul said. "Patience on a monument." It took him a moment to remember where that was from: Viola promising endless devotion to her secret love, wasn't it? A flash of elation darted through him at the thought of the loved one, the electric linkage of *love—loved one—Clary*, all complete and coursing with current. He put on his coat, and with it, her smell. He took it off again, and put it on—there it was. She was in his coat, his hands, in his skin.

Closing the coat around him, Paul went down two floors to sit with Lorraine.

The change in her was frightening. She was horribly thin. Her colour was strange, and the nurse said that as engraftment took hold she slept most of the time, but fitfully, waking prone to panic. Understandably. Paul settled himself in the blue chair to wait for her to waken.

"I slept with Clary last night," he imagined telling her, the one safe person he could tell. He was grateful to be so rationally smitten with Clary, not to have to consider any possibility that this was revenge on Lisanne.

Clary, the most beautiful—the broad map of her brow—who would have thought he could fall so Victorianly in love with a forehead? He loved her lovely face, her small strong hands; he loved the gentle decrease of her ribs, cello-shape on her side in his new bed. He remembered—he could see— the new map of blue veins on her breasts, the unfamiliar clasp of her body around him. His mind's eye turned backwards to look at Lisanne's sharp, angry body, and back farther, to when she could lie quietly beside him, their legs twined together, yielding to each other's spirit. He found that tears were pouring out of his eyes as he thought of her.

In all this time, his whole life, he had only made love with Lisanne, and against all his wishes he could hardly bear that Clary had not been her last night. That she was going to the Mayan Riviera to be entered, entered, and everything that was holy was profane.

He constrained himself before he broke into sobs. This was not even real, and it was ungrateful. Clary was infinitely worth loving, infinitely kind, entirely herself. He pushed back on the turquoise leatherette to recline, determined to meditate, and fell asleep beside Lorraine.

Self-righteous about their need to know, Mrs. Pell had told the children that Darwin was hurt. Now they would have to be taken for a visit after supper. It would probably do them good to see Lorraine, too, even in her present state.

But in fact, Clary wanted to leave the children safe with Mrs. Zenko and drive to Paul's house, and never go to that charnelhouse hospital again. Her mother's had been an awful, staggering death, everything about her ravaged and ruined, all her beauty gone. Her father, eighteen years earlier, had died more beautiful than before, pared to bone and sinew, made clearer, his soul visible. Her mother had drained away in despair until only the husk was left and the poor husk suffered longer. Which would Lorraine be?

She could wonder that in comfort, while at the same time the smell of Paul rose from her hands, her clothes, clouded around her and made her beautiful. For a bitter moment she hated her own health and luck, and everything else that made her different from Lorraine.

Dolly could not eat her supper. Too bad, because she loved Grace's beans. She was afraid to see Darwin if he looked bad too. She wanted to cry or hit Trevor but she tried to distract herself from that, since it would only lead to more badness. But he was stupid, and Pearce was gross, smearing beans on his face. They should not let him eat by himself if he was too young for it. Disgusting.

She pushed her chair back from the table quickly and ran down the hall to the bathroom because she was going to throw up. She shut the door tight so nobody would come in there, and leaned over the toilet. There was spit coming up in her mouth. She spit, but she didn't let herself throw up. She wiped her mouth and looked at herself in the big clean wall of mirror: eyes sloped-down at the corners, flat brown hair, crooked teeth hidden because she was keeping her mouth shut. She looked sad. The hospital made her neck feel tight, but you could not tell anybody you did not want to see your poor skinny mother. Dolly grabbed the big towel off the rack and buried her face in it and screamed as loudly as she could. It made no noise at all. Then she went to get *Vanity Fair,* to have something to read if her mom was sleeping.

Down the hospital halls Trevor tapped his knuckles on Pearce's car seat over and over in a certain rhythm until Clary asked him not to because Pearce was sleeping. So he touched his thumb to the wall, then his baby finger, then his thumb, then his baby finger, in exactly the right order. But what about Darwin? As he walked he did his toes for Darwin, left big toe, right little toe, right big toe, left little toe.

When they got there, Darwin was fast asleep and Fern said the nurses wouldn't let them into the room. She promised he was okay and Trevor had to believe her. But he kept on ticking while they all went upstairs and into the special washroom to wash and mask, to see his mom. He got to be first this time.

Dolly couldn't stand to stick around and wait for her turn. Too many bodies in this little washroom. She slid backwards without anyone noticing. Maybe she'd go back to the third floor and check on Darwin again; she could sneak past that nurse. She took the right turns, and it wasn't like she didn't know the hospital, but she found herself in a dark dead end anyway. This was wrong. Through a passage by the staff elevators she could see lit rooms.

She ran on quiet feet, turned sharply left, and almost bumped into a stretcher lying against the wall. Or into the feet stretching off it, wrapped with a sheet. At first she thought it was a dead person but when she got to the head it was not covered, so he must be still alive. It was her Keys Books man. Just left there in the hall like a piece of machinery.

His nose pointed up to the ceiling. His closed eyes were sunken in around the eyeballs but the bony parts stood out, and his flaring white eyebrows like antennae. Except that he was so long, everything else about him had shrunk down flat.

Nurses were far away, busy. It was almost the end of visiting, and the night things were happening in the rooms: people's friends being hustled out, their medicine bags being changed.

Dolly stood by the Keys Books man for a minute. She wanted to touch his eyelids, smooth them the way her dad liked her to do, but she was scared he would wake up and bite her fingers off.

"I'm almost through my book the second time," she said. She showed it to his closed eyes. "*Vanity Fair.* You gave it to me."

He didn't even have a room to be in. He was probably dying, that's why.

They all were. Her mom, and the old guy, and now Darwin. And she herself was dying, shrivelling in her own body, already. Everybody, everybody, every body dies.

So it's not so bad, it's not unfair. She left him and went away down the hall to see if she could find Darwin's room before she'd have to go back and wash up for her mom.

Trevor saw that Paul was in their mom's room—sound asleep in the blue leaner chair. Their mom was asleep too, it was quiet and shadowy in there. Clary went and put her hand on Paul's cheek to wake him up, the way she woke Trevor in the mornings. Paul opened his eyes and saw where he was, and looked up at Clary and smiled, his stiff face creasing. He was okay. Trevor had thought maybe Paul was sick too. Paul put his hand up and touched Clary's cheek that same way, and then he looked across and waved at Trevor and Fern. The pink nurse grumbled and swished her tight pants right by Trevor's nose, going to check the bag on the big pole. Flick, flick, her finger jigged the lines, and then she leaned over and said, "Lorraine! Lorraine! You've got some visitors here." Her voice sounded crisp and slightly mean, but she was busy. Trevor didn't hate her, the way he did the short-haired one.

His mother dragged her eyes open and saw him, before anybody else. She held out her arms and he went in close, squeezed between the i.v. pole and the bed. It hurt a bit but not too much, and his mother's soft thin face was close. He could not remember the last time he'd been able to talk to her all by herself. He could not think of anything to say.

"Hey, Trevor," she said, taking the worry away from him. "I'm so happy it's you. I miss you so much! Is Clary taking good care of you?" He nodded. "Are you okay?"

The others were outside the door, they couldn't hear.

"I'm just tired," she said. "I love you, baby."

He stared at her face.

"After you're gone from sight, and can't be seen, or be with us, will you still love me?" Trying to get at the idea of dead without saying the word of dead.

"Oh yes," Lorraine said. "I'll love you forever."

"So will I," Trevor said.

Paul came in and leaned down over the bed, saying quietly, "I'm going to see Darwin, but I'll be back to keep you company. May I say a prayer with you?"

Lorraine looked up, surprised into a laugh. "Sure," she said. "Fill your boots."

Everybody stood still. Paul said, "Dear God, comforter and healer of the sick, we commend Lorraine to your care through this long—"

He stopped, because Lorraine was suddenly gagging. Paul grabbed the kidney basin from the rolling table and handed it to her, and she filled it, all in one expelling, with watery, bile-coloured vomit. Clary traded him a towel for the basin, and emptied it in the sink. It was all smoothly done, and when Lorraine looked up and grinned at him, Paul went on.

"Speed her recovery, and Darwin's, and give her, and all of us, courage. Dear Lord, give them your peace, tonight and always. Amen."

Everyone said *Amen.*

"Well, that was nice," Lorraine said. "I never know what a prayer is going to be like, but that was good. Thank you."

Paul considered himself dismissed.

He went out past the ante-room into the darkened evening hall, lingering a moment to see if Clary would follow him. She did.

She held the room door almost shut, and leaned against the outer wall, and Paul pulled away his mask.

"Do you love me?" he asked her.

"I love you," she said.

"And I you," he said.

Everything else aside—everything included—that was true.

35. Swingline

*L*orraine had passed the point of bravery and acceptance of whatever they did to her; she was truly afraid now. They had explained the kind of death rejection would mean, if her counts did not improve. Quick, she told herself, meaning to console, but it set her heart racing, pounding, painfully staggering after an unreachable goal: the old life.

Dr. Lester had talked about the possibilities of graft-versus-host disease, like for example that it sometimes made people shed their skins. Lorraine had a strong mental picture of that, but she shut the eyes of her mind, the lids behind her lids. She shut her brain from accepting that as a possibility. She lay there thinking, *I have children, I have children, I have children.* Wrong thing to think—she was wracked with loud weeping. It was night, but Darwin was not there, and crying hurt but she could not stop for a long time.

When Clary arrived in the morning Lorraine begged her straight off.

"I need to see Clayton," Lorraine said. She could feel belligerent weight behind her words and tried to tone it back, but her sense of time passing was too painful.

Clary stopped taking off her gloves.

"I need to talk to him, I'm too scared now. Darwin heard he's in the city somewhere, but he can't find him while he's stuck in here, so I have to ask you."

Clary nodded.

"You go find him, okay? Bring him as soon as you can. Will you?"

To Clary's eyes, Lorraine seemed to be slightly on fire. The fever breaking out in actual licks of flame. "No?" Lorraine demanded, her voice crackling.

"Oh! Yes—of course I will. I was trying to think where to look for him."

"Darwin heard he's got a job upholstering, look there."

In Darwin's room Clary sat on his bed, since all the chairs had been dragged over to the other half by family members of the bedraggled old man in the next bed. Down-at-heel, up-at-heart, lots of laughing, the old guy snuffling and wheezing happily while they told each other one story after another. Some of them were the fattest people Clary had ever seen, some were tenderly skinny, with flake-white skin, and they were all semi-drunk, even on Saturday morning. Darwin was leaning back against his headboard, himself again, but with a taped and swollen nose.

"Swingline Upholstery, Avenue D south, little grey building. He calls in the morning and if they need him he comes in. A pipe burst or something at the last place he was staying, he had to leave. You're going to have to ask around. Try the Silver Tap, or this morning maybe ask at Chevy's Café, if you ask one of the girls."

Clary had her notebook out and was writing, *Swingline, Ave D, Silver Tap, Chevy.*

"It might take a while. Remember what he looks like?"

"Oh yes," she said. His face thrust forward, eyes bulging at her, shouting *My kids! You could have killed us!* "I know him. He knows me, too."

"Yeah, but I don't think he'll avoid you. He knows you're doing good for the kids, better than he could do now." The reassurance was unreassuring.

A big burst of laughter from the window side of the room, the older woman rocking back and forth in her chair wiping tears from her eyes, hooing and hawing. Darwin laughed too, and Clary, too—she couldn't help it. They were having such a riot.

"When are you—" Clary asked Darwin, not even knowing how to finish the question.

"They'll let me out soon. It's not like I feel bad."

Clary nodded. They all made a fiction of everything, it seemed to her. There was the story of what was happening to Lorraine, to Darwin, to the children, and then there was the happier story they told each other, pointing out the funny parts, riding the surface over the bad. She was the worst, letting the children believe this was just ordinary treatment. When the fire was bright around Lorraine's bed, and Darwin was kindling.

Avenue D South: *Swingline Upholstery* in flowing 50s writing. Modern, from the time when everything was getting better and better in the space age, illness and death being beaten back. The storefront was baked white by the sun, dazzling on this cold bright day. Inside the small front office, Clary touched the bell on the deserted counter. It made no noise. She knocked on the door to the workshop, then pushed it open. Brighter back there, a big open space crammed full of couches and chairs in various stages of recovery. Some were peeled down to bare wood and canvas straps, others were being pulled together, their backs buttoned snug. A middle-aged man was leaning into a spring, forcing down to fasten it with wire pliers.

"Excuse me," Clary said. "I'm looking for Clayton Gage."

The man turned his head, but left his shoulders and arms to control the spring.

"Well, if you find him, tell him to come pick up his cheque," the man said.

Clary's heart sank.

The pliers twisted twice, three times; the man straightened up. "Hasn't been in for a week, or called. The deal *was,* he would call every morning. Six rush orders. If I can't deliver I'm out big-time."

"I'm sorry," she said. "His wife is in hospital. She needs to see him."

"Guess he doesn't want to see her."

"She's undergoing—difficult treatment. She needs him."

The man came around the low platform he'd been working on, and steered her back out to the front room. "We'll look on my phone," he said.

He hauled the phone up from under the counter, and hit the buttons, peering at the little screen. "Best invention in the last fifty years. You can see who's calling you, but you pay for it." Tap, tap, tap, tap—he worked his way back through the phone's memory.

"Here," he said, pointing at the numbers. "That's where he called from, that's last Friday week, you could start from there."

10:30 a.m., Friday, the number and a name: Perry Paddock. He shoved the phone towards her, and she dialed, and waited. No answer. Too much to hope. Clary wrote the number down and thanked the upholsterer.

"Davis," he said, sticking his hand out for her to shake. "You tell Clayton to get back here when he can. I got lots of work for him, I just need steady. My wife thinks he's a good bet."

She found a phone booth with the book torn out, so she called Fern, told her what was happening, and asked her to look up Perry Paddock—it was an address on Avenue R.

"Any emergencies?"

"Not yet," Fern said, in her gentle, half-breath voice. "But three big diapers so far."

"Oh my God. He had broccoli yesterday, it may not be agreeing with him."

"I'd say not. Dolly helped me with the last one, didn't you, Doll?"

Clary could hear Dolly laughing in the kitchen, making retching noises.

"Can you give them lunch?"

"As long as it's not broccoli. My mom and dad called and said they were coming in to shop and they'd bring burgers, and I'll give Pearce some banana."

Clary wanted to race home and have a hamburger with Grace and Moreland. Instead, she drove farther down into the alphabet streets, to R, a warren of shoddy brick apartments built in the 60s. Moving up through the decades, she told herself. Half the windows in the front were covered with tinfoil, many broken. One or two were boarded up entirely with plywood. Mail boxes and buzzers inside the foyer were labeled haphazardly, but there was Paddock. Clary pushed the button, still pearly white in all the grime. Nothing. She buzzed again. Coming in the front door, an old woman with frizzled hair said, "That's the one that burned out. They're gone."

"Paddock?"

"Gone." She went up the stairs, not pausing or giving Clary another glance.

The Chevy Café, car parts incorporated into the sign, was a dingy little dive with an interior reek of old grease and sour milk. Clary waited while the skinny waitress took a pan of plates and cutlery out through the swinging door and then came back.

"I'm looking for—" She had a moment of hopelessness, but went on, anyway. "For Clayton Gage, who comes in here sometimes, or maybe a Perry Paddock? Clayton Gage was staying at his place. His wife is sick, and she wants to talk to him."

The waitress looked at Clary as if she couldn't connect her with Perry Paddock. It was her fault, her too-fancy clothes. She looked like she could only be chasing Clayton for a bad reason.

"Darwin told me to ask here," she said. "Darwin Hand, do you know him?"

The waitress smiled then, gums showing wetly pink. "Oh, yeah, I know Darwin all right. Perry went back to La Ronge, but Clayton couldn't leave, so he's gone to Portia House on 26th. Not much of a place, but I guess he was desperate. Always room there."

"Thanks," Clary said. She wished she could tip her.

Portia House was a beige clapboard building, an ugly rectangle with tiny windows. It might have been a hotel in the 30s, or earlier. *Rooms*, it said above the door. The front door was propped open with an old running shoe, even in this cold weather. The air inside was dank, and either the bulb was out or the electricity had been cut off. Buzzers in three lines to the left of the door, fifteen of them, but under the buzzers the name tags were mostly unreadable. No Gages. But there was nowhere else to look.

On the first floor, she got no answer at the first door, marked *H. K.* in black marker on the wall. She knocked on the second door, then the others. Nothing. She climbed the creaking stairs to the second floor, trying not to look at the grey splattered carpet while she avoided the torn patches. It was very cold. She pulled her gloves up, to give herself some comfort.

The hall was even narrower up there, and there were more doors, closer together. One was wide open. Inside, a grizzle-whiskered old man lay on a single bed under a small window. The room was all white, a messy white-washy job, plenty of paint splashed on the window panes. An opened can sat on a sheet of newspaper on the table, and a burnt mess in a saucepan. The floor was littered with dark junk, an undifferentiated mass of rags and paper. The man wore a torn undershirt and a pair of filthy trousers. He was lying on his side, staring at the door, and transferred his stare to Clary's face when he saw her.

"I'm sorry," she said, apologizing for something. *That there is such a place in the world, and that you've ended up in it; that by my agency, my fault, my own most grievous prosperity, you are condemned to this shithole.*

"I'm sorry, I'm searching for Clayton Gage. I need to find him because his wife is ill."

The man said nothing, but his mouth moved, the whiskers twisting together and rotating. She realized he was pulling his teeth back into place. "Who?" he said, finally.

"Clayton Gage. His wife wanted me to—she needs to talk to him."

"Younger fella, nose, smooth hair?" The old man struggled to sit up, and Clary, watching him, steeled herself to step into his room. He had managed to get up on one elbow, and she held the other sharp elbow to give him some leverage. His skin had a grey tinge, probably grime more than illness. Finally he swung his legs around and was upright.

"I seen him," the old man said. "Next door but one. Eleven, I think it is."

Clary didn't know how to let go of him. Would he fall over?

"Don't get many visitors here," he said. "Except the NDP canvassers last month. Gave me a ride over to vote." His bone-fingered hand patted her sleeve.

"Are you warm enough?" she asked him.

"Been through worse winter than this," he said. "What's your name?"

She was reluctant to give it to him; but it held no magical protection, after all. "Clara Purdy," she said. "Maybe you knew my father, George Purdy?"

"George Purdy? Plumbing and hardware store by Stepney's?"

"Yes, that was him," she said.

"I sure knew of him," the old man said. "You're his daughter."

"Yes."

273

"I heard he died, though."

"He did, nearly twenty years ago."

"Not such a bad thing to go early," the old man said, grinning, his whis-kery whiskey mouth hanging open. Three teeth showing. Clary laughed too, but felt a nasty clutch of grave-stink from him.

"Well, I should look for Clayton," she said. She disengaged his arm, waiting to see if he would collapse.

"You tell your dad, Harry Benjamin said hello," he said, winking at her.

She could not tell if it was a joke or if he had forgotten that her father was dead, so she smiled and nodded and went out.

"Don't close the door!" he yelled. "That's my TV, that doorway."

The next door down was 10, and the one after that, 11. Clary raised her hand to knock but had to force it to make a sound. Knock-knock-knock— she made her knuckles obey her. No noise from inside. She knocked louder this time. The old man—Harry Benjamin—had said he was there.

"Clayton?" she called. Still no answer. She didn't know what to do. Leave a note?

She moved toward the light coming through the small front window, which looked out onto the snowy street. Her car was safe, nobody stealing the battery, which happened often each year in the first few weeks of real cold.

A man came walking along, talking to himself, arms gesturing jaggedly in the air, angry about something. It was Clayton.

She flinched back from the window. In a minute he would be coming upstairs. She couldn't— Clary ran silently up the last flight of stairs, pulled her coat around her and sat hidden on the top step. His boots clumped up the stairs. He was muttering to himself, she couldn't hear.

Harry Benjamin said *Hey!* but Clayton ignored him, key fumbling in the lock, and the door opened and shut behind him.

She sat huddled on the top step. It was darker; no window onto the street up there. The building creaked and cracked in the cold. Somewhere, someone flushed a toilet. As her eyes grew used to the inner twilight she saw a magazine on the floor, and the vague image became clear, an enormous pair of breasts bursting out of some leather contraption. Instead of jumping up and running away, she sat still. To keep her mind quiet she prayed, for Harry Benjamin in his

274

dirt, for the waitress, for the upholsterer. For Lorraine, almost out of habit. As usual, her prayers seemed to be swallowed by clouds, by the earth's gravity.

She got up and went down the stairs. This time she knocked on the door of number 11.

When he saw her, Clayton made as if to shut the door, but stopped.

"They all right?" He was thinking of the children, of course.

"They're fine," she said quickly. "They miss you."

That was the right thing to say. The muscles of his face unknotted.

"It's Lorraine," she said. "They've done the transplant, it's just the waiting now—but she needs you, needs to talk to you."

He stepped back into the room. Unlike Harry Benjamin's, his was orderly. The small table was clear, the narrow bed's blankets had been smoothed.

She stepped over the threshold and waited for him to speak.

He moved to get his papers and can of tobacco and stayed by the table, rolling a cigarette, lighting it, blowing the smoke out the window gap. His body was strung up tight. Beneath the tension, he looked like he'd been doing some hard physical work.

She almost said something about Swingline Upholstery, but stopped herself. She kept her hands folded in front of her and her eyes lowered, like an old maid, or a Salvation Army poster.

"What does she want me to do?"

It was a complaint, not a question, but Clary tried to answer it. "You're her husband, maybe you can give her some support that she can't get anywhere else."

"I can't handle it. Cancer."

"She's thinner, but you won't be too shocked. I know it's hard."

"How would you know?"

"My father died of cancer, and my mother just two years ago. I know a wife is— But there's a chance she might get better now, after the transplant."

He turned and glared at her, daring her to keep on. "She's going to die, you know it."

"Well, we have to bet against that." But she did know it, deep in her heart, and it was hard to hold that knowledge away from him. "Darwin is betting that she'll make it."

From the blank look he gave her, she knew not to harp on Darwin's virtue.

"Lorraine misses you," she said. "Please come."

He stood silent.

"Please," she said. A hundred thoughts ran through her head—offer him money, say *Come back and stay in my house*—threaten him with the police for his earlier thefts. She did none of these. She pretended she was Darwin, who was so good at not talking.

"What's her room number?" he asked, his voice rusty and effortful.

"536." She turned and left.

Harry Benjamin waved to her as she went down the stairs, stepping carefully because her knees were shaky after the great exertion of talking to Clayton.

Grace and Moreland were still there when she got back, even though she'd stopped for groceries. They were always out of milk, and it had sounded like diapers might be a good idea.

Grace had already saved that day, with a huge multi-pack from the bulk warehouse store. She'd made shepherd's pie for supper, and was sliding it into the oven when Clary came in. Clary crossed the kitchen and hugged her, a rare thing between them.

"What's with you?" Grace asked, suspicious.

"I met a guy who used to know my dad," she said. "I miss him, don't you, Grace?"

"I do. You need a coffee and a bite of cake," Grace said. The remedy for any spiritual distress.

Clary sat down and drank her coffee, listening to Moreland playing Lego with the children in the living room. Fern was folding laundry on the dining room table, talking away to Pearce, who was talking back to her, *la la la*. How could anyone have children without a family around them to help? What on earth had Lorraine done with nobody? Clary put her head down on her arms for a minute, wondering how Darwin was, and Lorraine, and whether Clayton would actually go in. But mostly just resting.

When Grace brought her a piece of cake she ruffled up Clary's hair and said, "Moreland and me are at Auntie Ann's, and we'll stay a week or so, till all this excitement is done."

Clary lifted her head to say thank you, but Grace was already off to the living room to nag at Moreland about the mess. In a peaceful way.

36. Leaning on the sky

*I*t was a relief to pile Dolly and Trevor into the car and head off down the street with no other adults to alter the balance. Moreland and Grace had gone Christmas shopping, taking Pearce, and Fern was spending the afternoon at the dentist with Mrs. Pell. Lucky Fern, Clary thought, gliding along down snowy Cumberland Avenue to pick up Darwin, being released at noon.

In the back seat Trevor began to sing in a high, thoughtful drone, at first wordless, then adding a chorus to it. "*I can fly, like an eagle,*" he sang, staring out the window. Driving felt like that to Clary, a release, an eagle in air, a good skater on big ice.

"*I can fly high...*" he sang. "*I'm dreaming of the sky, I'm leaning on the sky.*"

They loved their mother. Seeing her often was better for them, Clary thought. And who could count how many more visits there would be? When she got very bad they would not be able to go. She could not bear to think of Trevor and Dolly watching their mother die as she had watched her own. Not so soon. She prayed, *please, God, make her better—please.* Every muscle straining to ask it, to beg it. Trevor's reedy song sharpened her desire, her will.

Please. The prayer went out of her and drifted away, like a message had been successfully sent.

The children clattered along the hall, not spooked this time, first to Darwin's party room where the old guy was holding court with four cronies, wheezing and laughing. Darwin had clothes on! Dolly felt her heart skip, up in the air—he was not going to die! She clutched him until he squawked, "Hey! Watch the nose! I'm delicate!" Trevor piled on too, but Darwin said, "Wait, you don't want to get infected— I've got lice! Get back!"

Clary said, "Oh, stop, don't even—" and couldn't stop herself from scratching her head.

Dolly loved it when Clary was funny. Her stomach felt so good! She was not worried in this room, and when Darwin said they should wander down and see her mom, she could stand it.

Her mother was sitting up awake, looking see-through, but not actually dead. She smiled that little apologetic smile that Dolly was so sorry for. Why were *they* all being sorry? *God* should be sorry.

Lorraine told Clary they'd said that the engraftment was looking good, good counts. Her voice was mostly air, but her mind was with them, as it hadn't always been lately. She looked at Clary steadily and her gaze was painful to bear; and the children: Trevor leaning over the bed so he could rest his cheek on her leg, Dolly's hand motionless on the pillow.

Please God, please, Clary said again. *Please.* She went into the bathroom and leaned back against the door and cried, buckets of tears washing out of her eyes and mouth and nose, making no sound. She washed her face in cold water and went back out.

Paul turned up at the house that evening with three big white bags of take-out food. *Yes, sir, yes, sir, three bags full,* Clary sang to herself. *One for my master, one for my dame.* The bags were balanced on an old cardboard box marked *Xmas.*

"You weren't coming to me, so I thought I'd better—" he said, quickly, as if he was shy with her. "I don't know if you like Vietnamese, but I thought the children would, it's plain and fresh-tasting. And Frank Rich brought me two trees, so I have one outside, and a few decorations…"

Clary helped him put the bags on the kitchen table, and put her hands on either side of his face and kissed him. He was foolishly happy to have done the right thing. Pearce staggered in and Paul caught him around the chest and whirled him into the air.

The children unpacked the white boxes and tubs. They loved the little rolls, the fried ones and the rice-paper plastic-glove ones. Dolly gave Trevor the shrimps out of hers. Vietnamese was Fern's favourite, it turned out. Grace sat by Pearce and kept a weather eye out for choking while he had a great time sucking rice noodles, draping his head with a select few.

Moreland went down to the basement to get the decorations, and rummaged out a few beers from the cold room he had carefully retained during the renovations. When the children had eaten they drifted off into the living room, tired but peaceful. The adults sat on at the table, talking about complications and other horrors. They could hear Trevor singing around the corner:

I'm dreaming of the sky,
I'm dreaming of the sky,
I'm leaning on the sky,
I'm dreaming of the sky...

Dolly sang it with him, and when Trevor trailed out she added a chorus, *boola boola boola boola BOOLA.* Pearce ran into the living room where there was room to really dance. They loved their mother.

After they'd put the tree up, Clary went down to get more beer. In the cold room she found her mother's Persian carpet, rolled tight as always, but stood on end during the renovation. That would do it no good. She took the beer up, and since Paul and Moreland were deep in a theological discussion, borrowed Fern to help her carry the heavy carpet upstairs.

"To replace the one we ruined with the torte," Clary told Paul. "Please, please take it, it's crowding up the basement and has been for thirty years."

"It's too good a carpet," he protested, but only formally. He wanted part of her in his house. She had peeled back a corner to show him the jewel colours, the golden antelope and leaves curling around a dark blue ground.

Moreland offered to put it in the truck, but Grace, coming after him into the hall, said, "Don't be silly, Moreland. Clary can run it over there with her back windows open."

Grace usually assigned all the delivering to him, but Moreland shut his mouth.

"Paul will need a little help rearranging things, I'm sure," Grace said, putting Clary's coat on her.

Shunted, Clary and Paul walked out into the night at either end of the carpet, their boots creaking on the snow.

"Is this all right with you?" Clary asked. Paul slid back down the length of the carpet to kiss her, the sudden heat of his mouth and face reviving her in the cold air.

Unwrapped and unrolled, the carpet changed Paul's living room completely, transporting the barren chapel to a Persian garden. He had never seen one with that arch-shape—inside the night-blue arch a golden tree, and above the tree, within the arch, birds cavorting in air.

"But this is—this is valuable," he said. It almost filled the bare wood floor.

"It's been rolled up all my life. Better to be used."

"*A garden inclosed is my sister, my spouse,*" he said. "I think it's silk."

"Is it?" She was slipping the buttons of her blouse through their loops.

"It's probably 19th century."

"Probably."

He turned off the light, rather than draw the heavy Jacobean curtains and shut out the moon. She unbuttoned his shirt. All the buttons in the world still lay between them, too many things to pull off, to shrug out of. The beloved should come into his garden. She leaned into him, pulled him down.

"Do you think we need to talk about what we are doing?" he asked her. She put her mouth and her hands on him. He said, "We are talking."

Finally then their skins were the only barrier, and they knelt on the Turkey carpet. The silk pile caught the skin on her knees like tiny knives, and stray moon or street light flayed the skin on his shoulders, his chest, his stomach.

"It's never been this valuable before," she said.

37. Whale eye

*C*lary looked out her bedroom window and there was Clayton, turning up too early on a cold Saturday. She yanked the sweater over her head and ran to look out the front door. He had parked over toward the Brents, as if he might keep going, and was still sitting in the car, looking mulish. Had he been in to see Lorraine yet?

Bradley Brent came bustling down his walkway and headed over to the car. Oh, no! She wondered if Clayton had a weapon of some kind, and tried to dismiss that thought as she stuffed her feet into boots. It must be forty below. The insides of her nose stuck together as she ran down the steps.

Mr. Brent was in full spate by the time she got to the sidewalk, puffs of white air coming out of his red mouth in the cold. Clayton had opened the car door and was standing up slowly. Her mother's car! How nice to see it, but she really should have sold it long ago, she thought, with the one extraneous piece of her mind that was not shrieking *Alarm! Alarm!* Maybe Clayton had a knife—he was so touchy and short-fused. Not that she cared about either Mr. Brent or Clayton, but she did not want the children to see anything violent.

"There is an allotment of curb space in this city!" Mr. Brent was shouting. "Parking regulations are strictly enforced. I could get a bylaw officer over here in ten minutes and you would be towed, sir!"

Clary went around to Clayton's side and took his arm. "Come in and get warm and have a coffee, Clayton," she said. "Mr. Brent, Clayton is a guest of mine. You are overreacting."

"His nose is six inches past where it should be!"

"Your nose is going to be six inches past your ass," Clayton said, ruffling up his coxcomb head.

"That was a threat!"

Clary gave Clayton a friendly shove towards the house. "The children are excited," she told him, seeing Dolly's pinched face in the doorway. "Go on in."

As Clayton went up the walk, she turned to Mr. Brent, glacial as her mother.

"Mr. Brent, it's early on a Saturday morning. Are you expecting any company? I wasn't, but I can tell you that my guest won't be staying long, because his wife is in the hospital dying of cancer. Say hello to Mrs. Brent for me."

He eyed her. She knew he was hating her and her company. But that cancer card trumps everything, Clary thought.

"It's Bunt," he said. "B-U-N-T."

"Oh!" she laughed, she couldn't help it. "I'm sorry. Mr. Bunt. Bradley Brunt, isn't it? Badley Bent, I mean." She clamped her hand over her mouth to stop more laughter.

He stalked off toward his house. Mrs. Bunt was leaning on the glass door, hair in curlers, watching the whole thing. She gave Clary a silly little wave.

The awkwardness of Clayton's reunion with the children and Mrs. Pell (who didn't seem to have the time of day for him) was interrupted by Darwin, calling to say that Lorraine was in ICU. She had developed sepsis, one of the million hazards of graft-versus-host disease.

Her youngest doctor, Joan Lester, was waiting in the hall. She had a kind, lined face with very dark eyes. "Sepsis is—um, a challenge to treat because toxins in the bloodstream will trigger a whole cascade of problems," she said. "We have a new clinical trial going on, we could add Lorraine—if you?

I am, we are—the trials are going pretty well, you know, and I think—" she stopped.

Clary thought perhaps she had remembered that she was not supposed to offer too-concrete encouragement. Her own spirits had sunk terribly, and looking at Clayton's white knife-edged face she was sorry she'd dragged him into this.

"This one is worth trying," Dr. Lester said, finally. She lifted her shoulders even higher.

Lorraine lay in a corner of the ICU, her bed hung like a Christmas tree with tubing and wires and blinking machines. Hearing them all talking in the hall, she wanted Clary to come in first, to brush her hair and wash her face, but couldn't muster the energy to call. It was hopeless anyway, she would still look like death warmed up.

Clayton took one look in and stepped back, but Darwin set his hand on his back.

"It's okay, man," she could hear Darwin saying. "Looks worse than it is. Say hello."

She'd long since stopped looking in the bathroom mirror, but Clayton's eyes would be worse than the mirror. She was sorry-looking, she knew. He turned into the doorway. Now he could see her. His face was as revealing as a child's, eyebrows going up in the middle. The sight of her threw him, she saw that, but he stood it.

She held out her hand, the un-needled one, and he came forward and took it.

"Sorry," she said.

"*I'm* sorry," he said.

"Don't," she said.

"I was here, I was working, I've got about enough saved for a place and a deposit," he said, blurting it all out, everything he'd probably been trying to bottle up to tell her later. Or not tell. He was such an open book to her! She had almost forgotten that.

"Well, that's good," she said.

"I saw the kids this morning, I went over to Clara's. They look good."

"Clary's been looking after them good. They're happy there. They've been okay."

"I guess."

"You see what Darwin did to her place?"

"He's a good worker, give him that."

"So, he's been there with them too."

Like she had to apologize, for how the kids had been looked after when he'd been gone. Lorraine shut her eyes. No point in getting mad, no point getting him mad either. Better if he hung around for a while, particularly now. When who knew what was happening.

There was something she had meant to tell him about the kids, about how to be with them when she was gone, but the need to prepare had been stilled by whatever they'd given her today, whatever miracle combo was pouring into her through the i.v. tubes. She kept her eyes shut when Clayton bent down to kiss her, but then she changed her mind, and opened them, his familiar eye so close to her own that it was like a whale eye. Hazel, dark-lashed, ashamed. Child's eyes—they were why she loved him, anyway. She kissed him back and then shut her eyes after all.

38. Shook foil

From morning to night, Christmas Eve was taken up with running and wrapping. Lorraine was supposed to have come home for two days, until the sepsis scotched that. But they'd manage. Clary was keeping her balance. Today, then tomorrow; then it would be Boxing Day and she could lie down. Grace was bringing Christmas breakfast, and Mrs. Zenko was putting their turkey into the oven at her house at 7 a.m., before she left to spend Christmas at her son's house in North Battleford. They'd been taking food to Lorraine for months—Christmas dinner was only slightly more complicated. Picnic baskets, covered casseroles; it was exhilarating, coping with everything.

Clary was glad to see, when she stopped in on Christmas Eve morning, that Lorraine was clearly getting some relief from the sepsis. Hollow and white, though, and painfully thin. Bald again. A prehistoric chick, abandoned in a cold steel nest.

"I need," she said slowly. "You to get."

"I'm on my way to shop," Clary said. "What'll it be?"

"Darwin's…"

"Darwin's present?"

"Darwin's getting some stuff."

Clary slowed herself and waited.

"A watch, for Clayton," Lorraine finally finished. "Got Darwin's." She fished weakly around under her pillow, and pulled out a plain old watch, a man's watch with a leather strap. "Rose's," Lorraine said. "Her dad's. Wrap it?"

"Of course," Clary said. "What kind of watch for Clayton?"

"Cheap," Lorraine said. Almost laughing. She had her wallet under the pillow too, and fumbled through it for a couple of twenties, her ashy fingers long and slow. "Army, you know. Iron thing."

"With a stop watch and so on?"

"Yeah. All the stops."

"Something athletic. Got it. Anything else?"

"Darwin has it covered."

Clary adjusted the orange pillow and Lorraine let her head fall back. Poor face, poor swollen cheeks. Clary kissed her. "Thanks," she said, with her eyes closed.

The shops were crowded, of course, but Clary found a good watch on sale, only twenty more than Lorraine had given her. She splashed out on wrapping paper and tags, bright ribbon and sprigs of real holly.

Christmas was always like this for most people, she supposed—complicated, urgent, full of events. For the last few years Clary had driven down to Davina early on Christmas morning. Gliding over the snowy prairie, on the one day in the year when nobody went anywhere, all alone under the sun-dogged sun.

Paul watched them troop into the midnight service: Clary carrying Pearce, Mrs. Zenko next, then Grace and Moreland holding Dolly's hands and Darwin shambling up behind. Fern must be at home with Trevor. So many people to be connected to: last Christmas he'd never heard of most of them. Clary, with her red silk on. (Without it, the pale silk of her flank.)

He wandered through the last Mass of the old life, the first of the new. He lit the candles, sang where it was required, and listened to the readings as Frank Rich intoned them, his sad basset-hound voice trying to trumpet: *Fear not!* When it was time for the homily, Paul stood and spoke to the congregation, but of course he was speaking to Darwin, to Clary, to the children, and Lorraine. "Angels, we're told, have intense, painful, beauty. Shining with the grandeur of God—the invisible world made visible. Terrifying, for those ordinary people they spoke to. The first thing the angel told Zachariah was *Do not be afraid!* And to Mary, before telling her she would have a child who would be the son of God: *Do not be afraid!* On Christmas night, with the heavenly host, the angel says to the shepherds on their hillside, *Do not be afraid! I bring you good news of great joy, which will be to all people...*

"Fear is always with us: that we are not good enough or strong enough, and so will fail; that we will be hurt. Fear that what we love will be taken from us. Fear of dying, even fear of God, or of no God. But God surprises us by giving us strength to bear what we must; by giving us joy when we think nothing but sadness is possible. God became human to experience the power that death had over us. Do not be afraid—God is aware of us in the world, aware of the world we live in, striving for the great good of all people. The light shines in the darkness, and the darkness has not overcome it. *The world is charged with the grandeur of God, it will flame out like shining from shook foil.*"

He sat down. ·

Shook foil made Dolly think of Mrs. Zenko's house, where she smoothed out the tinfoil and used it again. She had a special drawer for keeping it. If Mrs. Zenko shook people, she would smooth them out again and save them for later.

Clary, tired and abstracted, felt a cold doubt about the Gerard Manley Hopkins she had wrapped for Paul. He must have it already—but this one was beautiful: heavy paper, all the poems. She could have got a pair of gloves for him, he needed gloves. But meeting his eyes as he sat in his chair to allow a moment of quiet, she thought, it's all right. *It will flame out...*

The hymn began, "Silent Night." Dolly loved that one. Trevor could not keep awake this late, poor Trevor, but it was all right because Fern was with him. Grace said she had pyjamas to give her later, because in her and Moreland's family everyone always has new pyjamas on Christmas Eve. Fern's new ones had a little ragged silky frill around the bottom of the pants, maybe hers would be like that. Dolly leaned against Clary's warm arm in her soft wool coat, that colour called taupe, with the black velvet collar. Dolly wished her mom had a coat like that. But she leaped backwards from the brink of that. *Do not be afraid,* Paul said. *Dear God,* Dolly thought, but did not know what to put next. *My mom.* The organ was playing and Paul was coming down the aisle again and now past them and out, but he had smiled at them more than at anyone. Because he loved Clary, but also the rest of them. Maybe that would count for something.

At the church door Darwin said he would see them in the morning. "I like that surprise thing," he said to Paul, and headed off for the hospital through the snow-floating night.

Clary held out her hand and was surprised herself when Paul put his arms around her tightly, in full view of all the parish, at least the late-night parish.

"I missed you today," he said. He had snowflakes in his hair, and on his red satin stole. He looked strong and happy. She loved him.

"Will you come for breakfast?"

"I will," he said.

"And for presents, and for dinner? We need you to carry turkey."

"Mrs. Zenko told me how to make cranberry sauce, and I'm doing it before I go to sleep."

The street was quiet, even with the departing congregation and their cheerful voices. Moreland fit Pearce's seat into the holder while Grace got the sleepy Dolly in, and wedged herself in beside her.

"Home, James," Grace said to Clary. "And don't spare the horses."

Paul watched them go. *The dearest freshness,* he thought. The night had a glow to it, streetlights refracted in the falling snow, the city lights staining upwards in a peachy aureole into the night sky. *Because the Holy Ghost over the bent World broods with warm breast and with ah! bright wings.*

Cranberry sauce. No time to waste.

39. Christmas present

*A*t 8 a.m. on Christmas morning Moreland opened the door to Paul and Clayton, standing together on the porch with their arms full of presents. Odd pair, Moreland thought, but Christmas makes strange bedfellows, probably on purpose. He gave them coffee and kept them out of Grace's way while she got breakfast going.

Dolly felt mysteriously irritable, like she'd eaten too much candy. She unwrapped each present carefully, peeling the tape so slowly that Trevor begged to be allowed to open another one while they were waiting. Pearce beat on the drum Darwin had given him until Darwin said he'd changed his mind and put it away up high.

Dolly's present from Clary was boots, red suede with rubber soles so you could run, embroidery up the sides, and sheepskin lining. They were so nice that she leaped up and hugged Clary with one boot in each hand, and the boots swung around and whacked Clary by accident, but she didn't get mad. Fern gave her magnetic earrings, and Grace and Moreland gave her a fleece hoodie, and Gran gave both her and Trevor a lifesaver book. Then there were only Darwin's present and her dad's left to open. She was scared that she would like Darwin's present better, and that would make her dad mad. The grown-ups were opening too, so she could delay things by folding the wrapping paper, rolling up the ribbon around her hand, tidying her pile of presents so far. Darwin and her dad liked their sweaters from her and Trevor; they put them on right away. They were twins, except her dad looked uncomfortable, sitting cross-legged on the floor, but he always did.

Clary opened a present from Paul, a book of poems, and she laughed, and handed him one to open from her. "You're joking," he said—and when he unwrapped his, it was the exact same book by the same guy. That was funny.

"Great minds think alike," Grace and Moreland said at the same time.

Dolly picked up the one from her dad. Whatever it was, she would make sure that she didn't like Darwin's better. It was bulky but not too heavy. She pulled the tape off. Purple, soft, what was it? She tore the paper. A big—a velvet pillow, with a round velvet button in the centre, frayed-out fringe all around it in different layers of purple and blue. The velvet was the softest thing she had ever touched. It went one way, and when you brushed your hand over it the other way it changed to a darker, sweeter colour.

She lifted her eyes and saw her dad looking at her. "I made it," he said. "For you. For when I—"

"I love it," she said.

He looked so happy.

Lorraine pulled herself up out of empty sleep and looked at the rectangular whiteness of the window. Christmas. The freckly nurse was on, she was a kind one. She found the new lipstick and blush from Clary, and propped up the mirror. Lorraine wiped off most of the lipstick because it looked so weird over the bled-out whiteness of her lips, but what was left probably cheered up her face.

The nurse looked at her critically, then flicked the blush again. "My mom always used to put a dab of rouge on her chin," she said. "*Instant pretty,* she called it."

Lorraine looked again. "Okay," she said. She smiled, to test it. "Less sick, at least."

291

"You're doing well," the nurse said seriously. Sherry was her name, like the drink, and her freckles were that colour. "You're doing a good job."

"Will you get the bag in the closet?" Lorraine asked. "Presents."

If she lay on her side there was room for them on the bed, except for the tricycle Darwin had spirited up last night, with a huge bow on the handle-bars. That could stay in the closet for Pearce to find.

She could hear them coming: Trevor's voice piping closer, wanting to be the one to give her their present. The room filled up, the children all crowding up to the bed. She hugged them over the bright pile.

"Don't wait," she said, when Clary tried to stem the tide. "Open every-thing!"

Paper on the bed, on the floor, everywhere, ribbon wrapping around them. Darwin helped Pearce open the closet door. He stared at the trike for a while, touching the white handgrip, then the saddle, then the wheel; he let them help him onto it and sat while they put his feet on the pedals. Trevor offered to show him how to ride.

Where was Clayton? She pulled Darwin's present out from under the pillow, and watched him open Rose's dad's watch. He put it up to his ear, to hear it ticking, with his eyes closed.

Six strange white orchids on a bending stalk from Paul; they found a good spot for it on the window ledge. A cream-coloured shawl from Clary, soft wool, very pretty. Flowers and a shroud, Lorraine thought, but she put it around her shoulders and thanked Clary nicely.

In a momentary silence they could hear footsteps coming down the hall. Dinner already? Dolly went to the door to see.

Her dad. He was carrying a chair, a big chair with legs that clumped on the floor every few steps, sounding like several people. He put the chair down at the door—then had to back it up awkwardly to get in himself. Finally he and the chair were both in the room.

"For you," he said to Lorraine. "For our place."

Lorraine pulled the covers away and Darwin helped her to sit up. Clary said, "Oh—" but stopped herself, even before Paul touched her arm. Dolly swivelled the rolling i.v. pole to let her mother walk across the floor slowly to reach the chair and sit, the arms holding her, the chintz pillow sinking under her back. "That's *down*," Clayton said, and she smiled at him in her old way.

Everyone exclaimed at the beautiful chair, the workmanship, the cord edgings. Trevor sat on one arm, Dolly leaned on the other, and Clayton showed how he had put wheels on the legs, so it could be rolled around to vacuum under it.

Grace and Moreland and Fern arrived in the middle of all that, and admired it too. The wheels were good enough to go down the hall, Clayton said, sure they were. After a little trouble getting the chair back out through the door, they rolled Lorraine down to the lounge where the movable feast was laid out on coffee tables. Lorraine asked Sherry the nurse to eat with them, and Clary was grateful when she sat chatting away to Mrs. Pell while still keeping one eye on Lorraine.

The food was hot, even the gravy; none of the good plates got broken; and even if only Clary and Grace knew how complicated the transport had been, everyone enjoyed the dinner better than any Christmas dinner they had ever eaten, so there was a considerable feeling of Dickens in the room, but nobody, not even Paul, said *God bless us, every one.*

In the evening Clary heard Mrs. Zenko at the front door.

"Now tell me there's a bite of pudding left, and some of your mother's hard sauce," she said, slipping out of her short boots. "That's a long drive back from Battleford in the dark."

"We saved some for you," Clary said, taking the packages from her arms.

"One more present to open," Mrs. Zenko said. "All mitts, I'm afraid, no originality at all. Well, slippers for Mrs. Pell," she confided. "It's bound to be cold on that floor out there."

Clary found the package with her own name on it, and opened it. Not mitts: an elegant pair of black leather gloves. She kissed Mrs. Zenko and reached for the top of the hall shelf where she had left the tiny velvet box with her mother's pink tourmaline chrysanthemum ring.

Two dew-drop tears came spilling out of Mrs. Zenko's eyes when she saw the ring.

"I should have given it to you long ago," Clary said.

Trevor brought Mrs. Zenko the knock-down birdie toy. "Do you want to hear China?"

"Yes."

Trevor shook it. Little bells sounded inside. China.

Too much activity, too much company, left Lorraine shaky and sleepless for a long time. Finally, when all the lights were dimmed and the nurse (not Sherry now but the oldest one, Debbie) had given her a back rub, Lorraine fell asleep. She had a terrible dream of Dolly dying by falling into Christmas ornaments. She fell straight into the tree in the apartment in Trimalo, and all the glass ornaments shattered, and she was cut to shreds. Lorraine woke up with her heart pounding. It was not true. It was not true.

At home in his empty house, in his empty bed, Paul had a complicated dream, that Dolly had asked him to drive her out to a big field full of stones. They walked across the dry yellow grass to Lorraine's grave, and Paul drifted off along yellow paths where every tilting old stone said *Robina Tippett, 1968–1998*. All the other stones were stones, with bones lying near them, but under that one was Binnie, still brightly alive. It didn't matter that he'd seen her dead, and knew her to be gone. That parcel of bones and skin that had been shown to him was not her, anyway, it was a puppet of Binnie. The real one was down there under the dead grass. He looked back. Dolly was crouched low over the middle of Lorraine's grave, right about where her mother's stomach would be. Poor child, she was looking down at the yellow grass between her hands, flat on the slight round of the grave. "You left us all alone," she shouted through the funnel of her hands into the earth, but the wind sucked her voice away. It was a wild wind. Dolly pounded on the turf with her fists and shrieked into the twisting roots of the grass, as loud as a train coming screaming around the track. Paul helped her up. Crying with dry, wide-open eyes, she kicked at the gravestone as he led her past it, and turned back to kick it again, hard. He almost woke, almost broke through the dream's surface, but he dove back down and took Dolly for an ice cream cone. Then he could wake up.

Clary dreamed that she took Dolly to the graveyard by mistake instead of school, and she lay down on the cold grass on her mother's grave. She cried and whispered *how good a mother, how good.* Whose grave was that? Was it Dolly's mother or her own? What girl was lying on the grave? It was Clary herself. Paul lay on his sister's grave nearby, whispering *good, good.* No response from them, the quick or the dead.

Waking, breathless, Clary knew that Lorraine would die soon.

Pearce was asleep beside her. It would be all right, she would look after him. She would take care of all of them. Even Clayton, only a lost sheep, not evil, making that good chair, which would actually look fine in the living room. The children would like that, to remind them of Lorraine.

She slid back to sleep, telling herself that this was the best thing she had ever done in her life. She loved how brave Lorraine was, how valiantly she struggled against this terrible illness. She even loved herself—how she had made a safe, orderly life for the children, had learned to do this hard good thing. Paul would come and live here too. They would come home in the evening, after a dinner party with the Haywoods, and carry the sleeping children in from the car. And although they would make love, she would have one ear open for Pearce, and for the children, who would be so sad when Lorraine was dead.

Dolly dreamed that she fell in love with a bald man, and he took her on a rollercoaster ride that lasted for hours.

40. Cut-out hearts

*B*ut Lorraine did not die.

Graft-versus-host disease swept over her in three ugly weeks of sores and thrush and cramps—and then it swept away again, because she told her body to smarten up. It was Darwin's marrow, there was no reason to panic. She did the ten breaths of Zen over and over, the way Darwin had read to her. In the almost-darkness of the hospital night, Darwin's big shape in the cot against the wall, she wandered through her body with her mind's eye, allowing his marrow into her own bones, her self, becoming partly him.

Almost secretly, she turned off from that long sloping downward hallway.

After a few weeks she was measurably better. She was walking around. She was healed.

One thing Lorraine was not prepared for: the shame of recovering. When the chief doctor came in one morning to tell her officially that all her results were good, very good, she didn't know who to tell. Darwin was driving out to Davina to talk to Fern most days. Clayton was working all the time. She hoped the woman who had been moved into the bed beside her had not heard the pleasure and relief in the doctor's voice, how glad he was to be able to say, "Well! This is good! Very good!"

They said she could go home on Monday, if the weekend went well. Something for them to plan for.

Clary was the one to call. But Lorraine was ashamed to talk to her, for everything she had been doing, the huge unpaid, unpayable debt, and afraid of what that obligation would mean now.

There was also the shame of not being completely, freely, happy. How could she not be happy? Especially compared to the woman in the next bed, not so lucky, who was having exploratory surgery in the evening and sobbed to her daughter on the phone about the black options they had outlined for her.

The desperate clench in Lorraine's stomach might take a while to relax, she thought. She was not ungrateful, just slow to realize change. Having to pick up life and cope again. She didn't want to tell anyone yet.

On Monday, they said Tuesday.

Every time Clary went in Lorraine looked better. Wasn't it wonderful.

Things were improving, that was obvious, but everything was so busy, and it was February already—almost Valentine's Day. The children had to have a valentine for every child in their classes, twenty-seven for Dolly, twenty-nine for Trevor. Clary had run over to the scrapbooking store for card and pink tissue and paper lace doilies, and more manly trim for Trevor, and there were cut-out hearts all over the dining room table. Trevor's hand ached from printing names. When Clayton came to take Trevor out to a hockey game Clary had to say no, he couldn't go till the printing work was all done. She tried to broach the subject of some extra help for him, or maybe testing for dyslexia, but Clayton clearly didn't want to hear it.

"There's nothing wrong with my kid," he said, staring at her aggressively. His hands were dirty.

She left it for later. She could just arrange it without consulting them, after all—the times Clayton came by were few and far between. He was no help at all.

Fern had been back and forth, but after Grace and Moreland left for Hawaii on their long-planned anniversary trip, Fern told Clary she was going to Vancouver. Clary wanted to ask why, but it would seem like she was spying for Grace. She said the children would miss her, and tried to pay her for all her help. Fern wouldn't take anything. The last few months would have been impossible without her, so Clary was impatient with her, having budgeted for fair pay; and impatient with herself for resenting Fern's desertion.

She was more disturbed when Darwin said he was driving out to the coast with Fern.

"I'll go out to Tofino, see Phelan," he said. "And I'll help Fern out, like she's been helping us."

His son Phelan, she remembered with some difficulty. Who seemed to have been getting along fine without him till now. And how would Lorraine manage without him there, how would the nights be? She did not ask, but he answered.

"Clayton's going to stay late Fridays and Saturdays, but she'll be okay without me now. The nurses know her, and she's not so scared."

Besides, Clayton did not like Darwin, so maybe it was time for him to go. They packed their bags to the rafters in Fern's old car, and headed off. Trevor chased the car down the street, crying, but really the children were all right. They knew he was coming back, they were fine.

Lorraine did not need her any more, either; especially now she was getting stronger. Clary hardly ever visited the hospital these days, since Clayton was around again and clearly didn't want her there. She was busy with planning and managing; it was even hard to fit Paul in.

And she suddenly couldn't stand it at the hospital.

Instead, she let all her energy go into the children and the new school term. Things were busier than ever, with school and dentist and field trips, and getting some order back into the house after the Christmas chaos. There was a lot to arrange: the children should be taking lessons, the piano was just sitting there; and Trevor really needed to start at Kumon if he was going to keep up, but Clayton was so resistant that she hadn't brought that up again, she'd wait for a while. There was Dolly's museum trip to help plan, too, and Clayton never showed any initiative; even when she asked his opinion, whether the children should take piano lessons or join the church choir, he seemed peevishly content to let her see to everything—and pay for everything too. His surly whipped-dog arrogance was beginning to irritate her.

And if Lorraine was getting better, there were arrangements to work out at the house.

Clary was working out what would be best for them: they could have the basement bedroom now that Darwin had gone west, but she'd have to find a double bed. Maybe it would be better to put them in the TV room upstairs, closer to the bathroom. That would be better. Only there wouldn't be room for Pearce's crib in there, he'd have to stay in her room.

She'd think about it later, when all those Valentines were done. The days seemed to be speeded up—time was moving like electricity, the meter-hands whirring around, ticking away money and energy and life.

On Tuesday, Clary went to the hospital in the afternoon, because Lorraine had left a message asking to see her. She left the children at home with Mrs. Pell in case Lorraine needed help with anything complicated.

She thought she had the wrong room. Lorraine was not there, and the bed was stripped. But—they were saying that she was doing well—she could not be—

Not dead, no. She was in the washroom, the door slightly open, brushing her teeth. Wearing clothes.

"Lorraine?" Clary said, her voice sounding weirdly ordinary. "Are you all right?"

Lorraine spat into the sink and rinsed, and stood up. She dried her toothbrush with a white hospital washcloth and put it in her toilet bag.

"I'm good," she said. "I'm really good."

Clary stood in the middle of the room. The other bed was empty too— what had happened to that poor woman?

Lorraine said, "They say I can go home."

Clary did not speak, for a second. Then she shook her head, and smiled, and shrugged her shoulders.

"Wonderful!" she said.

"Yes, so I'm going."

"Well, of course!"

"Clayton's got us a place, we'll go over there this afternoon."

That did not make sense. Clary's chest was tight.

Lorraine went to the closet and added her toilet bag to the already-packed suitcase.

"Seems pretty amazing to be getting out of here," she said. She moved a pile of magazines from the closet to the bed.

"But, Lorraine," Clary said. Then she didn't know how to continue. All her bones moved downwards, as if in deeper gravity.

"He's gone to get Dolly from school, and he'll get them packed up, but I wanted to tell you about it alone," Lorraine said.

She was carefully meeting Clary's eyes, every step of the way, every word she said. Not shying away from it, even though it would be bad. Clary looked like she'd been punched, but hadn't figured out what had happened yet. Lorraine thought her own face must have looked like that, her first day in here.

"Does Darwin—?" Clary was speaking too slowly.

"He phoned last night from Vancouver, I told him they would be letting me go home."

"Did he say—"

"He said, to give you a kiss from him."

Lorraine did not move, but Clary flinched anyway.

"So, Clary, I have to say thanks for everything," Lorraine said. "There isn't any way to thank you for looking after my kids all this time. But I know I owe you big time."

Inside the hollow globe of her head Clary was unable to figure this all out. She fought the pressure in her chest. She stood up straight, making more room for air.

"You're—Clayton has a *place*? Not the room?"

"It's okay, he says. An older building but they're renovating, and our suite is already done. He'll be the part-time super, there's a little money in it. Looks like a good deal."

"Where?"

Lorraine stopped talking.

Clary asked again, "Where is the apartment?"

Lorraine looked at her without smiling. "They are our kids."

"Well, I realize that." Her legs were shaking. "I realize that. But if you are planning to move them out of the school district, they would have to transfer, and which school would they be—"

"It's in City Park," Lorraine said. "It's not a bad place. It's an older building, a little run down, but it's what we can afford. The kids will be fine."

"You're not ready, though! This is impossible. You can't—you can't look after children in this state. And Clayton! You think *he* can manage them?"

But that was enough, for Lorraine.

"You can't stop thinking of us as low-class, you can't stop!" she said. "You keep thinking you're better than me, even though you try not to. It's built into your whole life. But we're the same as you, we're just the same."

Clary felt hot tears welling up, like tears of blood. To be accused of prejudice, when she had worked so hard—how could Lorraine think so? She would, she *would* think so, with her trailer-park ignorance. Shocked, Clary smacked the thought away, but it was there. Less worthy. Less human.

Lorraine said, "Here's the difference between us: you got taken to the dentist more, and your mother filled your head with stuck-up shit about how great you are, and you got to live in the same house all your life. That's most of it. You went to school for longer, and you worked in a clean office instead of cleaning the office. You have a better-looking face and better-looking clothes, and that gives you some feeling that you're better than me."

"I don't, I don't. You're mistaken."

"I'm trying to tell you how it is for me," Lorraine said. "Here it is: it's the *same* as it is for you."

Her eyes were hard to look at.

"When you're hurting because you have to lose Pearce, that means you know exactly how I hurt to lose him. I don't have less feelings because I don't know the words to say them, I don't have less to say to my kids because it's not always—" She shook her head sharply. "It's not just grammar. You think I'm not as good for them as you are."

"You're right," Clary said, sadly. The tears had receded, and the hot blood behind them. It was too important, it was the children. She could not be silent or polite, there was only now to say it. "It's not you, it's Clayton. I think it will be—hard for him to look after you all well enough." Still polite after all.

"Well, he gets to give it a try," Lorraine said, not angry any more. She gathered her paintbrushes from the water-cup and set things in place in the paintbox. "He was doing okay until you crashed into us."

That was the first time she had mentioned the accident since it happened. She had not blamed Clary for it then.

"But what will happen to you if things get hard—if you run out of money? You can't work, you have to be careful. You can't leave the hospital behind, or head for Fort McMurray—and the children, they need stability, and their ordinary life, not to be shunted around the country living from hand to mouth."

"*We* are their ordinary life, not you," Lorraine said. She stopped, the cup still in her hand, and looked straight at Clary, piercing her with the stern arrows of her eyes. "The kids don't give a rat's ass whether they have money or a nice house, they just want me and Clayton with them. They love *us*. Him too, not just me. Don't kid yourself. You are a babysitter, to them. They'll be glad to leave you."

Clary didn't speak. She was having trouble with her ribs, like a stitch. They didn't seem to want to expand properly to let her breathe.

"It's not your fault that you don't get it," Lorraine said, red smears of rouge bright on her cheeks. "You never had kids of your own, and you weren't very well brought up."

That was it.

Clary turned and left the room.

She drove out of the parking lot crying, tears splashing on the steering wheel, on her skirt, running down her face and into her collar, wetting her chest—which still wouldn't open to let her catch her breath. Her feet were clumsy on the clutch and the brake.

Without meaning to go there, she found herself at Paul's house. She stood on his porch trembling, pressing the doorbell. He was not going to answer, he would not be there.

He opened the door. He saw her distress and took her hand, her arm, and pulled her inside. "What? What is it?" he asked.

She could not answer, she could barely breathe.

"Clary, tell me. Is it Lorraine?"

She sobbed, nodding, not intelligible, *yes*, she sobbed, *yes, yes, it is all Lorraine*.

"Is she—what—has she died?"

"No! She has *not*! She—" It was too hard to say, to have to hear it out loud.

302

Paul sat her on a kitchen chair and pulled the other chair close enough to sit right beside her. He held her shoulders and arms, enclosed her. "She wants the children back?"

It was not really a question. She had known he would know, he would help her.

"Yes, she is, she is coming out today, and she will take them somewhere, Clayton has a place—she can't take them there! I can't—" Clary shuddered away from what she might have to do, reporting Lorraine to Family Services.

She couldn't do that. She had to find some way to stop it without betraying them—but only because if she did report them, betray them, they would take them away, and she would not be able to see the children any more. The yawning space inside her chest spread larger, it was going to be impossible soon, no way to breathe at all.

"How can I stop them? You must know, who I should talk to, how I can get custody, just temporarily, to keep them safe."

"No," he said. "You can't do that."

"But you know they can't go live with Clayton—I told you what kind of—"

"I know," he said, not letting her go on. "But they're his children, Clary. And they're Lorraine's, and they have a right to raise them, however much you want to help."

"No! You don't—you aren't listening! She's taking them today, to some place Clayton's found, as if it's going to be all right. It will be some filthy place on Avenue X, they'll be surrounded by drug dealers and prostitutes. The carpets—you haven't seen—"

"I have," he said. "I've seen bad. But Clary, they're *theirs*. We've been praying for Lorraine's recovery, but it was always going to lead to this, to the reunion of their family, whether we like to see them go or not. They need their independence again."

How could he be arguing in favour of this lunacy? Was there no help? Mrs. Zenko could not do anything, Moreland. Darwin. She could not bear it. She couldn't breathe.

"I have to—let me—"

She slid off the chair and lay down, curled in a half-moon on the carpet, but couldn't rest there—nowhere. She rocked back and forth, trying to sit up, her mouth wide open in a square gape of pain.

"Breathe slowly," Paul said.

He crouched on the floor beside her and looked into her face, and then got up. He ran to the linen closet for pillows and Binnie's mohair blanket, with lavender tucked in its folds—he shook the blanket loose, sprays of dead petals patterning the floor. He filled a glass with cold water and one with brandy. He lifted Clary slightly to let her blow her nose with a fresh Kleenex he found (a miracle) in his pocket, then made her drink, first brandy and then the water. He gave her a pillow and put the other one beside her, and let the blanket cloud over them, that soft purple Binnie had loved. He curved his knees close behind Clary's on the carpet she had given him and held her, one arm carefully around her waist, one arm fitted under her neck. Gradually her sobbing ceased. From time to time her body twitched, but her breath smoothed down again. He lay with her while she slept.

The afternoon was darkening down, time to think about supper. That might have been what woke her. His arm was too hard a bar under her neck, now that she had calmed down.

She had to go home. The children were alone with Mrs. Pell, if Clayton had not turned up, or if he had gone to get Lorraine. She was covered in shame, that Darwin had heard that she was losing the children—it was all confused. Why would that shame her? It was nothing to do with her, it was Lorraine's decision, it was a joy to them all that she was not dead, recovering, every possible good sign. She could weep again with shame.

Everything she had tried to do had been for nothing. Paul said he would drive her, but she would not let him. She was ashamed in front of him, too, and it made her brisk and cool, hurrying into her jacket and boots, not able to stay another minute, and not able to bear any longer his goodness and his *fucking understanding.*

41. Gone

They were not there. None of them. Clayton had already taken them. Empty house. Drawers empty, closets. Beds not made, but already cold and empty.

She packed the clothes they had missed, the few things that had been in the laundry, in a cardboard box. Everything fit in one box. They must have worked hard. The valentines had all been cleared off the dining room table. That would have been Dolly.

Pearce's special bowl was sitting on the draining board. Like a dog's dish. Like they'd come to get their dog, their lost puppy that she had been looking after all this time, but they'd left his new dish behind, because they had their own special dish for him.

She cleaned the kitchen. She put oven cleaner in and let it sit searing away while she took all the pots and pans out of all the cupboards and drawers, stacked them on the kitchen table, and cleaned out the cupboards and drawers with the vacuum cleaner and hot, soapy, bleachy water. As if her mother was watching.

Paul came to the door at midnight and knocked until she let him in.

She had nothing to say, and neither did he. She put the kettle on to make tea. He put his arms around her but she couldn't do that, be comforted, and she excused herself to get the milk, to get cups. The kitchen smelled sterile. She thought she might ask him to help her dismantle the bunk beds, because she wanted to send them to the Gages, wherever they were. Would they even call to let her know where they were?

She didn't mention the beds. She couldn't say any of this to Paul, not now. He had said they were *their children*, as if she didn't know that. She could barely be polite to him, and yet when it seemed like he would leave, when he was turning to the front door, she said, "Please, stay."

"I will," he said, surprised. "I left my shaving kit in the car. I came to stay."

But she did not want him to stay, either. She did not *want* anything, except Pearce back, and Dolly, and Trevor; except the life she had left this afternoon to run over to help Lorraine—to help her again!

She was afraid she would start shouting. Instead, she said she thought she'd have a shower; that might make her feel a bit better. When she came back to her bedroom Paul was there, still standing. Looking at the books on her bedside table. He was kind, he was trying to help her. She could not bear to be helped. Even his vulnerability grated, but the shower had calmed her, and she could touch his arm and speak.

"Thank you for coming," she said.

Which put him in his place, Paul thought. A parish visitor. He lay down beside her and held her again, while she wept in silence and he could not console her.

In the morning her mother's car was outside the house.

Paul had left a cup of tea on her bedside table, with the saucer on top of it to keep it warm. He had kissed her, smelling of shaving cream, and said he would come back in the afternoon. She kept her eyes closed until he was gone, and by accident fell heavily asleep again. It was after nine when she woke and pulled herself out of bed, only because lying there meant thinking.

She opened the curtain and there was the car. How could even Clayton bring it back without saying anything? She dressed herself and drank the cold tea.

The keys were on the front seat, and there was a note on the dashboard: *Thanks. We'll be in touch. Lorraine.* It was spotlessly clean.

Clary went back into the house and rifled through her purse, her coat pockets—where else? Her own car—she ran back outside and found it, tucked into the notepad in her glove compartment. The social services woman's card. Bertrice Morgan.

Bertrice's voice was low-pitched and a little tight. "Family and Community Services, Bertrice speaking," she said.

"I am calling—this is Clara Purdy," Clary said. "I'm calling about Lorraine Gage."

"Oh yes?"

"Lorraine's children were staying with me while she was in hospital, and I—"

"You're her mother-in-law?"

"What?"

"The kids were with her mother-in-law."

"No, I had— Yes, they were. They were all with me. Staying in my house. Or at least—while she was in treatment."

"So what can I do for you, Ms. Purdy?"

"They've gone, they've moved out." What could she say? She sounded insane. She adjusted, tried not to let uneven breath crack her voice. "I have— some of the baby's things here, and some schoolwork for the children, but I've misplaced the address of their new place."

Bertrice did not answer right away.

"I wanted to send them on, you see, to give the children—I need to be able to get these things to them."

"You sound a little upset," Bertrice said.

"Clayton brought back my car," Clary said, and then stopped talking. There was a long pause.

"I'm worried," Clary said.

"I can hear that."

"I'm afraid of what will happen to them," Clary began, but she could not bring herself to say anything more. Partly because it was not fair, and she knew it. More, at this moment, because if she said anything hulking sobs would come up into her throat and drown her. She was a lunatic, she should not be doing this. She wanted—

"Ms. Purdy?"

Bertrice must get a lot of calls from lunatics.

"How about you give me your number, Ms. Purdy, and then if Lorraine needs to get in touch with you, I can give it to her."

Clary was afraid she was going to scream. Her hand was shaking on the receiver. She let it fall down in its cradle.

The hospital knew her. The oldest nurse, Debbie, was on duty, and that was a stroke of luck.

"She did, she—where did we stick that?" Debbie flipped taped papers and stickies up and down behind the nursing station counter. "She left a number for Darwin, because he was going to call, and I think he did, but did we—hmmm. That's the question."

Clary leaned as far as she could, to help look.

"There! I knew nobody would have torn it down. It's always me who cleans this place out. Huh! I thought it was a phone number, but it's just this."

Debbie handed her a yellow sticky, with Darwin's name and an address on 38th Street.

"Thank you," Clary said. "You have all been so kind, all the way through this."

"Well, look who's talking. I don't think she'd have done it without you and that brother of hers pulling her through. You take care," Debbie said. She put her warm, plump hand on Clary's arm, and Clary felt like she'd been branded. She accepted the mark.

"Oh, and we found these, too," Debbie said, handing her a manila envelope.

Clary's shoes made a loud noise on the floor, walking away. The elevator was too slow; she ran clack-clack down the stairs. Backing out of her parking stall she nearly hit an elderly man, and she braked sharply, heart clanking, trying to calm down. The bridge poured her over the river, the streets led her north like iron filings, and there was 37th, and there was their street.

But she could not turn down it. She drove down 39th instead. Post-war houses, horrible apartments; that block must be it. Maybe their windows looked back this way, and they would see her, spying on them.

Across the freeway she could see the cemetery. She wound her way over there, and walked along the lanes close to her mother's grave, and her father's. No flowers, nothing to leave. It didn't matter, anyway. Her mother was not there. Just an old dress and a pair of black shoes. Shoes for a corpse, what stupidity. We really should put our dead in trees and let them blow away, she thought. Her father: something of him was still there. Probably because she had visited this place so often with her mother. Iron filings, iron filings. She bent down and kissed the gravestones, one after the other. George Purdy, Elizabeth Purdy, *United in Death*.

Back in the car, the sun was coming through the car window, warm for February. The manila envelope was lying on the seat. She tore it open: a bunch of sketches and a half-finished watercolour of Pearce, done by the rules from the portraits book, with a penciled cross through his eyes and forehead, abandoned. Lorraine must not have liked it. But it was pretty close.

Clary stared at her boy, at his eyes, his mouth. What could she do? She could try to do better.

The truth was she did not need her house any more. She should have moved when her mother died. She needed to get shucked of it, and now, with all the empty rooms rattling around her, it only made sense that they have it.

Paul would let her stay at his house, while she found something small. She booked a truck, rented a storage unit, and spent a couple of days packing the china and crystal as carefully as their value required, clearing out sideboards and doing the sorting she had been putting off for years. Her mother's treasures would need appraisal before selling; about time to get rid of this burden of glittering pride.

Thinking of burdens, she put a *For Sale* sign in the window of her mother's car, with her phone number and the price. An hour later Mrs. Bunt knocked on the door and offered to buy it for cash. Nice for her to have some independence from Mr. Bunt, Clary thought, and gave her the key. Mrs. Bunt started the car and drove it forward twenty feet. It looked right at home.

Once everything breakable was packed, and the place ready, she washed her hair and dressed in jeans and drove over to 38th Street. The apartment complex was as bad from the front as from the back. Tattered curtains in some of the windows, tinfoil creased onto others. Dirty snow drifted the courtyard, baring odd patches of dirty grass. There was a bell for *Super*, with no name plate. Clary pushed that one. The linoleum tiles in the foyer were lifting and broken. The glass between the mailbox area and the inner lobby had been cleaned, though, so Clary could see when a door opened down the hall and someone came out.

Lorraine. Her step checked, seeing Clary. But she pressed the lever to open the door.

"Hi," she said. No questions.

"Hi," Clary said. She didn't know how to start, now, seeing Lorraine. A kerchief on her head to cover the cropped hair; navy pants and a blue blouse. Too big for her shoulders, but her poor abdomen was still rounded from the steroids. Maybe she had more colour in her skin; it was hard to tell in the bad light of the lobby. Her eyebrows were drawn on. Clary remembered kissing her cheek.

"Come in," Lorraine said, holding the door wider.

"I don't—I didn't come for a visit, really." The children wouldn't be home, but Pearce would. She stopped in the doorway, and took over holding the heavy glass.

Lorraine turned her head back to see the apartment door, still open a few inches.

"What's up, then?"

"I have a proposition," Clary began, as she had decided to. "You need— naturally, you need your own place. But I have been thinking of—"

Lorraine interrupted her. "He already called. This place isn't great, you were right. Clay hasn't had much luck talking to the management, either. We were going to find something better, but then we lucked into the duplex, and we're very— It will work out good. It was really kind of him. I probably have you to thank about that too."

Clary tried to understand all that.

"I know he's giving us a break on the rent, but he won't have to for long. And we'll take good care of it, so you don't have to be worried about him and Grace losing out."

Moreland's duplexes. Clary leaned against the steel door frame. From the open apartment door she could hear Pearce, his grizzling complaint-cry.

Her chest hurt. She was going to have to see somebody about this. She could not bear so much physical pain.

"Darwin said Fern called her dad to ask if he had any ideas, and it was so lucky because those tenants were leaving this week, so we don't even have to wait. Moreland arranged it all over the phone. It's the blue set on Palmer, the right-hand one. The kids are going to like it way better over there, and the other thing is, it's just inside the Brundstone School area—you'll be glad to hear that. They'll have to bus, but it'll work out good." Lorraine smiled, almost a laugh. Wasn't she going to see what was wrong with Pearce?

"So what did you—?"

"Oh. I was at the hospital, and they gave me this envelope for you," Clary said. She handed it to Lorraine.

"Huh!" Lorraine shuffled the papers out of the envelope. "These were just garbage."

The picture of Pearce was not there. Clary had left it on the kitchen table. Because she had known, all along, that this would not work.

"Well," she said. "I wanted to say that I would send over the bunk beds, for the kids." She never used the word *kids*, it felt strange in her mouth.

"That would be great, if you can't use them."

What for, would she use them? She looked at Lorraine, and Lorraine looked back at her, matching her weight for weight.

"Bertrice told me you called," Lorraine said. "She wondered who you were."

Clary said nothing. Nothing to say.

"I said you were our friend, who had helped out. What was your plan there?"

311

Salt taste licked at the back of Clary's throat. They were both very angry, the small lobby was full of heat.

"I'll tell them you said hi," Lorraine said, taking back the glass door to let Clary go.

Clary just nodded, because she had a dragon inside her mouth, and it would come out in fire if she opened her lips and let it.

42. *So various, so beautiful, so new*

*S*o she did not need to ask Paul if she could stay at his house. And now she had to stay in hers.

She left a message on his machine at the church, saying that she was going to Davina for a few days. He would not know that she could not drive out to Davina, as she might if she was in trouble, because nobody was there—and because of the amazing betrayal of Moreland giving them the duplex. She put the painting of Pearce in the kitchen junk drawer, turned the ringer off on her phone, and didn't answer the door. When Moreland and Grace called from Hawaii she did not answer; she did not listen to her messages. She lay in bed, not knowing how to get up, and gradually slept herself out of the worst of it.

Mrs. Zenko called twice from London. The only time Clary answered the phone was when it was a Vancouver number, 604.

"How you doing?" Darwin asked her. The line was crackly, a cell phone, it sounded like.

"Not too good," she said.

"It's hard," he said, then silence; was that the whole sentence?

"How could you do it? How could you let Fern?" It was a bad connection, she couldn't tell if he wasn't speaking, or if the phone was cutting out. "Are you there?"

Silence, then a phrase, "…you always…" Always what?

He faded in again: "…Moreland to have a turn…" Then empty air. "Darwin?"

After a minute she tried again. "How could you leave?"

She didn't even know if he could hear her, if he would answer. She babbled into the phone, "I miss them too much, I can't remember how to function without anybody. I couldn't say goodbye or tell them what was happening, they didn't let me! The house is empty—I can't eat, or sleep—it's too hard, missing them."

She stopped. Was he hearing? There was no answer.

"I thought she was my *friend!*" What a babyish thing to say, how exposed, and how exactly honest. There was half of the hurt, right there.

Nothing but air replied. Then after a moment, faintly, "…miss you…"

"Oh, I miss you too, and Fern, and—" She couldn't say the rest of them.

"…back," he said. He seemed to say.

When the truck she had forgotten to cancel came, she had the movers take the packed boxes to the storage space anyway. They'd be out of the way until she arranged for the appraisal, when she was ready to work her way out of the financial hole she'd dug, this wasted year.

She got the movers to dismantle the bunk beds and deliver them to the right-hand blue duplex, 1008 or 1006, she couldn't remember which. One of Moreland's nice duplexes, spacious enough, two bedrooms on the main and a couple of extra rooms finished in the basement. Clary knew them well, she had often helped Grace clean them before new tenants. Blindly she bundled up the bedding, and at the last moment added the curtains from the children's room.

After the men had left she realized that she had forgotten Pearce's crib, in her bedroom. She took it apart herself and put the pieces in the children's room closet, and shut their door.

Once the box mess was out of the living room, and nobody could know what a fool she had been, trying to give away her house, she called Paul. She did not want to, because his presence brought their absence too near, but it was not Paul's fault that they were gone and she could not punish him for it, now that she had regained her balance. He came over immediately, out of loneliness or out of duty, she could not tell.

He had been to see the Gages, had arrived as they were moving into their new place.

"They should not have shut you out," he said. "I can't understand why they would find it necessary to cut the children off from you, from your help."

From him, too, Clary saw, because he was associated with her, even though he could pretend to be on a parish visit.

"The man from Swingline was there, helping with the move. And his wife, she seemed very involved. She told me they're very fond of Clayton." Paul's tone had an edge to it, the first time Clary had heard him like that; as if he thought the wife was a bit too fond of Clayton. It satisfied her in an ugly way, to think of the wife being foolish, and to imagine Lorraine seeing it too. She had a bad taste in her mouth, but of course she did. How long since she had eaten anything but toast?

They went out for dinner, but it was an unhappy evening. Paul took her back to her house. They'd been apart for more than a week, and found themselves making love without consciously deciding to, and continued because it was better than talking, better than thinking.

Lying beside Clary in the dark, Paul said, "...*the world, which seems To lie before us like a land of dreams, So various, so beautiful, so new, Hath really neither joy, nor love, nor light, Nor certitude, nor peace, nor help for pain...*"

Clary turned her head and looked at his barely visible profile.

"Everything you say to me is a poem. You never speak to me yourself."

"I—"

"I— You—" She waited.

"I say what I can."

"Not enough."

He said nothing.

I am alone, she thought. No point in saying that out loud.

"God talks to you in poems, does he?" she finally asked him.

That was true, he thought. But God also talked to him in the world. Maybe he should talk to Clary in the world. He was too tired to think. But he was remembering poetry, poor Ted Hughes, or poor Sylvia Plath: *In their entwined sleep they exchanged arms and legs, In their dreams their brains took each other hostage, In the morning they wore each other's face.*

On Saturday night they went to a movie, because they had to do something. Afterwards they went to Paul's house, since it was clear that Clary did not want to return to hers. But Paul's house was empty too. Luckily it had been a late movie; it was late enough to go to bed. Paul turned off lights, opening the fridge for a last drink of milk. "Nothing," Clary said. They climbed the stairs in single file and went into the bedroom, and took off their clothes without any haste or disorder.

Clary hung up her skirt in the almost-empty closet. Leaning in to shake out its folds, she caught a scent—Lisanne. She carefully smoothed her hands down the material, not breathing. She could fold it on the chair instead. She left it.

"Do you miss her?" she asked Paul. He was setting the alarm.

"Yes," he said.

They made love anyway, and it was as it was. They knew what they were doing by now, it was almost ordinary. They were tired. He came, shuddering, sighing as he came, and kissed her, and slept; she lay with dry eyes open for a long time. They were too alike: hesitant, lacking in ordinary gumption, disconnected from other people and the world, taking refuge in elevated language. It was all a waste anyway.

Paul could not button the last four buttons on his cassock. He sat for a moment to recruit himself. March 3rd, First Sunday in Lent: "We must not embrace the deprivation and humiliation of Lent without remembering God's unconditional love." A way of making even the penitential season equalized and mediocre, now that he thought about it. After the long time of Lent, it would be Easter, and then all those Pentecosts, twenty-four of them this year, until it could come around to Advent again.

He could not find the strength to call on God. Was it the Baal Shem Tov who kissed his wife and children farewell every morning before he went off to the temple, because what if he called on God and was killed before he could ask for His mercy? That was not him, though. He was weaker, stupider, less faithful. He could not find the energy or willingness to carry God into the church for all those people, or the emptiness to become the vessel. He heard Frank Rich tolling the bell and felt nothing but a faint annoyance that it should be expected of him. He must be getting the flu. He ran the stole through his hands, skin catching rough on the Lenten purple satin.

Inside the church Clary sat at the back. When Paul came in she caught herself despising the way he stood, his defeated posture; she insisted to herself that she respect him. He was tired. But his self-effacement—she could shake him! How arrogant he had been in his moral stance when she wanted to get the children back.

She considered herself, her position in the church. She came for Paul now, for her mother before, bracketing that brief period when she was there for the children. Now there was no pleasure, no help, only hypocrisy. She had no business being there.

After the service Clary drove to Paul's house. She was waiting on the porch for him when he arrived home from coffee hour.

"We should stop this," she told him, the moment his foot hit the top step. If she waited any longer she might lose her determination, and the whole sad business would drag on. He stared at her as if surprised, but she knew he could not be. He sagged under the weight of her disappointment, her selfish inability to get over this. She could see it in his body and his face.

"We—I—created a false idea," she said. "A lie. I knew it was too soon for you, after Lisanne. I was fooling myself that we could make a kind of family."

He looked at her still. He could stop looking at her, she thought.

She looked away herself, since he would not. "I don't want to do it any longer," she said. "I'm sorry that I led you into it in the first place."

Paul's hand went automatically to the door, as if to let her in.

"No, thank you," she said. "I think I'll go home, instead."

Although it was easier this way, she was perversely hurt that he did not speak, say something about it being good while it lasted, or having enjoyed her company—she shook her head violently, hurting her neck. She did not want him to say any of those stupid things. Silence was better.

317

She did not look back to see if he was still standing there. She drove down the street, talking to herself furiously. *I loved them too much. God is punishing me for loving people the way I should love God.* Something was wrong there, too, that God would punish her, but she could not be bothered to think it through, because she was tired of God. Demand, demand, demand, and never any good to come of it except loneliness and despair, it was all—

Enough. She'd had enough of all this. She would have revenge. She would go to movies by herself again, and go out for dinner wherever she wanted, and she would have a tidy house and a little job.

She had to have groceries. In the grocery store on Thursday she ran into Mat from Gilman-Stott, who asked how her family was doing. She said they'd moved on, the mother had recovered, wonderful. She could say it lightly, by then, without wanting to lie on the tiles of the grocery store and weep.

The next morning Barrett phoned. He was desperate, the Biggar woman had not worked out, would she come back? Had she come to her senses?

By then she could laugh, although she hated the sound, throaty and phony. "Good sense has been forced upon me," she said. "Won't this make the paperwork difficult?"

Nothing could be simpler. Nothing would make head office happier. Barrett was effusive.

To occupy the weekend, Clary cleaned the garage. Finding the stack of sanctimonious soul-searching self-betterment books she'd stuck out there when they first came, she took pleasure in tossing them in the trash, Thich Nhat Hanh and all. She tackled her closet after seven months of neglect; it was a shambles, and she hated everything in it. She weeded half the business clothes, even with the prospect of going back to work.

On the top shelves, her eye lit on the document box where Dolly had found her marriage certificate and shown it to that sad little Ann Hayter. *That* could go. The box was full of old photos and papers from her few other attachments: three letters from Harvey Reimer, the last one with a picture of the new baby, the one that had saved his marriage, who must be nearly nine by now. A snapshot of Gary, with a sleeve of photos from that shoddy place in Cancun. Everything else in the box was school stuff, report cards and photos.

SO VARIOUS, SO BEAUTIFUL, SO NEW

Her BA graduation picture, holding the sheaf of red roses they had handed to each girl in turn.

What a waste of a life. Not even a letter from Paul, or photos of the children. She carried the box to the back yard, took the grill off the hibachi, and piled the letters and photos in the coal-ash. She lit one corner of the marriage certificate with the long-handled lighter. It burned up into a little triangular flame, then caught properly, brown curling to black, backwards toward her fingers until she had to drop it into the other papers. Smoke rose up, the photos rusted and lost definition—they were gone. She put the grill back in place and left everything tidy there too. Then she went to the movies by herself. Two in a row. From time to time, like windshield wipers, she passed her hand over her face to clear her eyes.

In the morning she got up at seven, showered and dressed, made herself a poached egg, and left the house perfectly neat behind her. Her keys were exactly where she'd put them. Nobody else's boots were tangled on the mat in the hall closet. She did not look back, because no one was waving to her, pulling the living room curtains too far along the track, getting hand-marks on the window.

Mat said, "You're back in your same desk."

Evie said, "You're back! In your same desk!"

Barrett was not in. His sciatica was acting up again—that was the only thing that made the day bearable. For three days Clary sat at her desk or in the staff room at Gilman-Stott, chit-chatting. Wondering how could she have borne to wear stockings every day, to bring her shoes with her in a little draw-string bag; how she could have led this empty life, examining disasters but Olympian above them, clean of any smudge of reality. She wanted a lightning strike, an Act of God.

On Thursday Barrett came back, using a cane, very courtly. He ushered her into his office in the afternoon, pulled the chair out for her, and said in her ear, leaning down, "It should really be you and me, you know."

She reared her head back from his.

"Oh, come, Clara," he said, his boiled-onion eye still too close. "Don't be coy. You know we have always had a special rapport."

So she quit again.

319

43. Drunk

March 16th was Lorraine's birthday. Thirty-six, but they didn't make a big deal of it—she didn't even mention it to the kids. It was a Friday, and Clayton had to work late that night, because Davis's wife wanted him to get her guest-room headboard finished before her sister arrived. When he was done he was bringing home a bottle of white rum, Lorraine's favourite, and they'd get drunk. After no alcohol for months and months, it was a night to look forward to.

She put the kids to bed, just as glad he was late, because she didn't like them to smell it on her breath. Clayton would not want to share with Mom Pell, so Lorraine took a night snack down to the basement bedroom and listened to more complaints about there being no TV down there. Then she hauled herself back up the stairs and got the kids settled. They were all tired; even Pearce didn't put up much fuss, although he was hard to get along with these days. He wanted Clary, or whatever she fed him. He would push against Lorraine's chest sometimes, push himself away from her while she held him, and stare at her face with a frown. That was something Clary had done. The cancer had done.

In the dark bedrooms she gathered up dirty clothes, but she was too tired to go downstairs again. She gave up and left them spilling over the big chair Clayton had given her. Nobody ever sat in it, it was always piled with stuff. In the morning she'd have enough energy to pack them down the basement stairs. The dryer was making a weird noise, but she didn't want to bug Moreland. Trevor had grown out of his pants.

She felt lousy. She had to pull herself together. No way she could work, like this. Good thing Bertrice had put the family allowance stuff through, so she had grocery money, and there'd be disability allowance for a while, when that came through. Good thing for Swingline, too. She was still worried about cash, but there was more coming in than they'd had for a long time.

And the duplex was so much better than the apartment. They were lucky.

When he finally got home, around eleven, Clayton brought her a plant from Davis and his wife, but she knew it was really Davis alone, since Mrs. didn't have the time of day for the sickly wife who was actually supposed to have died. They drank the rum with cans of no-name cola Clayton had also brought.

"Thought of everything," he bragged, almost in a good mood.

It was kind of fun. They sat on the couch drinking side by side, watching some teenage horror movie, pretty funny. No cable yet, but the reception was okay here in the duplex. In one of the commercials, Clayton said Davis was getting a big order in after Easter from some church redoing their kneeler cushions, meaning lots of overtime. Lorraine could feel some knots untying at the thought of more money.

"Maybe Paul's church?" she asked. "I wonder how he's doing. I guess we should go some Sunday, pay him back for helping us move."

"You're not too good company as a drinker. I wish Darwin was here," Clayton said, sticking on the *shh* in *wish*. "I never thought I'd say that."

"He'll be back."

"Yeah, next time, whenever." He stuck his legs up over her knees and lay back farther.

"I don't need him now, I've got you." She still had to work to make him feel better. Anyway, he was here, like she said. She was feeling dizzy—rum or leftover stress.

"You got me," he said. "You got my number."

He had worked his way halfway down the forty-pounder. Beer would have been better. She pushed back into the corner of the couch and adjusted his legs in her lap, her left hand cupping his warm neat feet in their clean socks. Look at him: drunk already, head leaning stupidly, eyes mostly closed. With her right hand she held his rounded knee.

What a birthday party. He put his hand on her hand.

"You left me," she said, staring at his face, the bones in it. Knowing he wouldn't answer her. "How am I supposed to trust you?"

But she knew, both what she could expect from him and what would be beyond him. It was a big deal that he had not left Saskatoon when she was in hospital—that he was still working for Davis. And Davis's wife was not the attraction there. She knew him very well. She did not want to have sex with him, couldn't even imagine ever wanting to again, but the teaching nurse had said that would happen for a while, after all the treatments. She hadn't told him. Didn't really matter anyway, he would not bug her.

He patted her hand, eyes still closed. Moved his knees against her legs, as if he was hugging her from the hips down. She tried to remember being in bed together, how it was—they were always better at that than at talking. But she couldn't. Her memory was bad, and it was late. The rum was not doing her any good. The bad memory was good for one thing, it was easy to veer away from all the cancer stuff. Not to be that woman any more. Soon she would be able to go forward, pretty soon. She was not dead. This would not be her whole life, looking after Mom Pell, working when she could again. Saskatoon was better than Winnipeg, for one thing, and probably better than Fort McMurray. The kids were happy, they were worth it.

She got up and let him slide lower on the couch. She covered him with a blanket, then gathered all the laundry off the big chair, took the stairs very carefully with blind feet, and started a load of whites. She went back upstairs again, slowly, and lay beside Dolly in the bottom bunk in the kids' room the way she often did, snuggling along the back of her now that she was sleeping and couldn't smell the rum-breath.

Dolly was still hers, even if Pearce was not.

In the morning Dolly climbed out from behind Lorraine early and woke up Trevor, and they went to watch TV. Lorraine heard them go, but she did not really wake up till Pearce started to scream, alone in the other bedroom waiting for someone to get him out of the high steel crib they had found at the Goodwill. That would be great, when he figured out how to climb out of it—how to fall out, Lorraine thought. Nine a.m. already. Her head was killing her.

She got coats on the kids and walked them over to the mall to get a few groceries. It wasn't till they'd been back a while, a good hour, that she missed Trevor. Dolly helped look, Lorraine grabbed Pearce and they went up and down the alley and the street, but he was nowhere in the neighbourhood. They ran back to the mall—nowhere.

She felt sicker than she ever had with the cancer. Slicing waves of fear-pain ran down her arms. She was so tired and hungover she couldn't think straight, and her head was drumming. There was nothing to do but call the police, so she did it, she called 911. She could imagine every dark grove of pines, every closet from here to downtown. Where Trevor was being tied up against a metal pole, in her mind's eye—she shut that eye and lay down until the police came to the door.

She could not remember what he had been wearing, when they asked her. He only had one jacket, the blue parka, so that was a start. But was he still wearing the red sweat pants he'd slept in? What year was he born? She couldn't make her mind give up the year. 1995? The headache was confusing her.

Dolly stood beside her in the doorway, pale and scared, and wouldn't say a word, even when the policeman asked her where she thought her brother might be. They asked if they could come in, and there was Clayton still out cold on the couch, the rum bottle and glasses on the floor beside him. One of the police officers shook him by the shoulder. Clayton moved his arm vaguely, but didn't rouse, thank God.

Pearce was yelling again from the kids' room, and she squeezed Dolly's hand to go get him, when Pearce appeared on his own.

"Rev!" he yelled. "Revvvv!" Drool coming down his chin. The woman police officer laughed. Pearce was wearing Dolly's pink runners, on the wrong feet. He waved at Lorraine and pointed down the hall. "Rev!" he said again.

She finally got it. "Trevor?" She ran down the hall and up onto the ladder to look on the top bunk where she could have sworn she had already looked, and there he was, not just the blankets rolled against the wall, but Trevor under them, waking up.

She was up the ladder in a flash and holding him in her arms, more lightning jolts of acid up and down her arms and legs, saying "Oh, Trevor, oh Trev, I was so worried," like a crazy woman. It scared him and he started to cry. Dolly was already crying, but the police were very happy that he was found. They turned pleasant. Clayton stayed asleep through the whole thing.

Darwin had not called Clary again. She had no claim on him. She wasn't sick, she wasn't his sister. He was back to his own life. But she began to worry that Fern and Darwin were—it had not seemed to her, when they were staying with her, that they were sleeping together, but what did she know? Fern was pretty and kind; that old boyfriend of hers had been an idiot. But Darwin and Fern did not make sense, and that depressed her.

As everything did. The clean, empty house, the silence, the meted length of a day. Everything that had kept her frantic in the last months was gone: no children, no Mrs. Pell, no running back and forth to the hospital. Her ordinary life was gone too; no church—she could not go back there now— no work. She had to find a job, but had not yet made herself even work up a resumé or call insurance acquaintances from other firms.

In the middle of March Iris Haywood phoned, out of the blue.

"I hear from Paul that your friend has done wonderfully well," she said.

Clary murmured yes, oh yes.

"And Dolly tells me that the children are with their parents again. That's very good."

Even to hear Dolly's name was a spike of pain.

"But this must leave you with a bit of time on your hands, if you've finished your good work there."

Clary said yes.

"So it occurred to me, when I was talking with the district superintendent yesterday, that you might possibly be interested in some work with the school board, a short-term contract—unless of course you're planning to look for insurance work immediately."

Iris Haywood was very well-informed. Did she know that Clary had quit Gilman-Stott?

"What kind of contract, Iris?"

"Three of our schools have lost librarians to maternity—a rash of Great Expectations! We won't start their replacements this late in the year, but each school has a backlog of books to be catalogued. I have twelve boxes already here at Brundstone, and if we leave this till next September it will be a mess, so I've got permission to hire someone to go round all three schools and get this tidied up. I know it's not up to your calibre, but it's a pleasant, manageable task and I can pay you substitute-teacher wage. Would you like some time to consider it?"

"I don't have to consider," Clary said. "I'll take it."

Trevor could not believe his eyes when he saw Clary in the hall. He thought he was imagining her. She did not see him, in the press of kids heading out to recess. He felt his stomach go crazy. He ran to the bathroom and locked the door of the stall in case she came in. What should he do? Was she here to take him away? His eyes were smarting. How could she not have come to see them all this time? Did Dolly know she was here? He stayed in there the whole of recess, and he went to the toilet twice, all diarrhea. Once right in the middle of pooping he thought he had to throw up, it was awful. His dad was going to kill him if he talked to Clary. His mom! Trevor had never felt so bad, even when his mom was sick.

Dolly didn't get surprised, because Trevor told her at lunch recess. He was still shaky and shivering even in the warm sun.

"What are you freaking out about?" she asked him.

"Because if she wants to take me to her house!" he said. How could she not get it?

"Well, so? You don't have to go. Don't worry, she won't ask you anyway, she's mad at us because we left without saying goodbye."

That was exactly it. They had run out on her, and she would be so mad. Trevor gave up on Dolly, she just did not get it. He skulked around the school, shadowy against the walls, following behind other kids so nobody could see him. When they had library on Friday he tried to go to the bathroom but Mrs. Ashby said no, she held his hand. But Clary was not there. Then he was miserable, because he wanted to see her.

Dolly was surprised at how homesick Clary's face made her feel. She stuffed that down—it didn't matter, she told herself. But she kept thinking about going to the library and happening to run into Clary. She was wearing the grey wool dress. Dolly could smell it. She knew where it hung under the yellow boxes, and then around the corner into the clean bathroom with green towels. Clary's house. Moreland's house was okay but it was a mess. Her mom got even more tired now because that lady from her dad's work had found some people who wanted cleaning, a couple days a week. She took Pearce with her.

When Dolly went home the day she saw Clary she was planning to clean up, but there was a mountain of clean laundry on the big chair, and she was no good at folding; there were dishes in slimy cold water in the sink, papers and beer cans and socks all over the living room. Gran in her housecoat and bare old blue feet, watching the soaps, doing nothing. Then her mom came home all crabby because she was so tired.

She stood Pearce, crying, in his crib, and told Dolly to watch him for a while so she could get supper. But she said it in a sharp voice, and when Dolly said "Forget it," her mom slapped her.

Dolly slapped her right back. Then she burst into tears.

Lorraine grabbed her and held her and they dropped onto the bed, falling back tangled together. Lorraine's kerchief slid off, showing her hair, short straw that she knew scared the kids. She tried to smear it back into place, then gave up and pushed it over her eyes for a blindfold.

"You don't know how scary it is!" Dolly cried, tear-water everywhere on both their faces. "I have to go to school all the time—everybody knows you almost died, you know. They all say, *She's the girl whose mother got cancer you know, blah blah blah,* like it was something I could do a single thing about! They hate me because I'm weird, and it's all because of you. You're mean, you're mean," she tried to say, but it ran into all one loud screaming *eeeee* sound, because she was so furious, and there was nothing to be done.

"I know, I know, I'm sorry," Lorraine said over and over until the scream faded out. It was almost a relief to be able to lie back and cry, but she knew it would give her a headache, so she stopped. She stroked Dolly's hair and face, and kissed her, and got them both calmed down. She had made $80 at that day's house, and the woman had tipped her twenty bucks. It was worth it, but it was hard.

"I can't," she said, muffled in Dolly's hair, but the words dissolved into salt. She just had to calm down, and be good for the kids.

44. Sore

*I*ris Haywood had invited Clary over for dinner. "I'm sorry Paul was not able to come," she said when she was taking Clary's coat. "I hear it can be very painful!"

What can be painful? Clary did not feel that she could ask. Iris might not know that she and Paul were not—whatever they had been—any longer. Or maybe she'd engineered the dinner to bring them back together, and Paul was choosing to stay away. She went in to the Haywoods' living room to meet the others. She had a lump of coal in her chest all the time now anyway, a cold charcoal briquette. But she would eat politely.

Paul could not go to dinner because he had shingles. He stayed at home instead, lying carefully on the bed, trying to read Milton. Might as well, while suffering anyway. From time to time boredom and pain would connive to make him get up, and he would range down to the kitchen for water, avoiding the living room where Clary's carpet lay, or up to his study to stab at the keyboard until the pain in his side was too bad.

He was in a worse temper than he ever remembered being, and he had lost, it seemed, the ability to pray for himself. Because he was carrying too much bile, he was too angry. He felt that this—everything—was Lisanne's fault, but knew that it was not, it was the combination of all the various stresses he had been under over the last year or so, made manifest on his body. His hair had begun to fall out in clumps.

Hopkins was better than Milton: *I am gall, I am heartburn. God's most deep decree Bitter would have me taste: my taste was me.*

He pulled his shirt up to look: thin lines of blisters, like cold sores, running down the right side of his chest. Hideous. Metaphorical. He had not allowed himself to long for Clary. Instead, these scabbing sores, external evidence of his interior pain. The pain was crazy. He'd been to see Hughes and dutifully accepted painkillers, not intending to use them, but he had twice doubled the dose, last night and again early this morning. They sent him sinking back down into sleep, and that was better than lying awake, frozen in place to prevent another of the jarring, searing stabs that accompanied every movement. He tried to breathe slowly. The tingling on his neck was troublesome because he thought that might mean more of them. He had heard of a woman, a parishioner's mother, who had developed shingles *behind her eyes.* The thought of that almost made him weep, he had to pull himself back from the brimming brink. It was possible, the doctor had said, that he would be among the half of those who develop shingles in whom the pain persists for months, for years. Turning his shirt-less torso in front of the mirror to search for another line of small fluid-filled blisters, he begged his body not to be like that. Before he could stop himself he said, *Please, Binnie,* although he did not believe that she listened to his petitions—a private saint, his own, sitting on a white kitchen chair at the curling edge of some cloud. He could see her, elbow leaning on the cloudbank, cheek cupped in her hand, watching him. No, he could not see her. She was nowhere to be seen, but had returned to God to be subsumed into the divine and would not be waiting for him when he died himself; that was a feverish dream to dwell on, Binnie sailing up in a boat to help him over that black river. Helping Lorraine, too, probably, who had come so close to drowning in it.

Back in bed, awake, he lay carefully on his other side, trying not to think about Binnie any more because it did no good, as it did no good to think about Lisanne. He could think about Clary, a little. Her eyes, the sweetness of her eyelids. But a too-deep breath was too much pain. He lay still, and willed himself not to think at all.

Clary saw the children every time she was at Brundstone: Wednesdays and Thursdays. It was like probing a sore tooth with her tongue, almost pleasurable. She had not even said hello—she thought they might be worried about whether they should speak to her, so she was careful not to run into them. They looked tired and unhappy, but she might be imagining that. They were still themselves. They took the bus now, so she never saw Lorraine or Clayton. Thinking about Lorraine still gave her a sharp shiver of antagonism, but she tried to work on that too.

The library at Brundstone had long windows onto the concrete courtyard, and the weather at the end of March was warm enough to leave them open while she worked: one box of uncatalogued books emptying, one box of catalogued books filling, the library silent. School librarian seemed like the perfect job, from that peaceful part-time seat. The other schools were easy too, but Brundstone was home.

From time to time she saw Ann Hayter, and wondered if Ann recognized her. She guessed not, from Ann's dull animal stare. One day she passed by as Ann was bending to the water fountain, and saw that there were marks on her neck. Dirt? Bruises. She stopped and turned to talk to her, but Ann slid away back to her classroom. Finger marks? If they were bruises, she should do something, help Ann, even if she couldn't help the others. But she couldn't. Ann was not hers. Dolly and Trevor were. And Pearce.

She could be wrong, and then there would be all kinds of trouble; she didn't know Ann's parents, except the mother was so odd, or unhappy. It would be better to leave it.

Iris Haywood stopped by the library the next day, Thursday, to talk to her.

"I want to tell you how glad I am that you've been able to help us out here," she said, in her stooping, graceful, authoritative way. "It's hard to com-pliment people, but I think you are *good*, and I wanted to tell you."

Then she moved on, a full-bodied clipper ship navigating the hall.

Clary blinked. She was not good. She got what she wanted by ma-nipulation and sweetness and good grooming. There was no good in her. She wanted Pearce back. She had selfishly wanted him the whole time, and then Trevor, and finally even Dolly, and what had she done? Tried to run their lives, and then sulked when they said no. That *redound* woman had been right—she had done nothing for them that was not self-serving, and then she'd had the nerve to be angry with Lorraine.

Disgusted with herself, Clary went home at the end of the day and dug out the Family Services woman's card. Bertrice.

"I'm sorry to bother you," she said, calm this time. "I think there's some-thing wrong with a child at the school where I work, but I'm not a teacher, and I don't know the proper protocol, or who I should talk to. Should I go to the principal?"

Bertrice told her no, to call emergency social services, and gave her the number. "You do have an obligation," she said. "If you become aware of a problem. But it's kept confidential, don't worry. They won't know it was you who called."

That wasn't the point, but it made Clary feel like a prying busybody. But she kept seeing Ann's neck, bent over the water fountain, and the long reddish-brown marks, so she called and spent an awful fifteen minutes giving names and details and her suspicion. It seemed thin. Then she hung up and walked around the empty living room, unhappy about everything. Sun sliced through the dining room's western window. The world was hopeless.

Out the front window she watched Mr. Bunt crashing into the driveway with his Hemi truck and Mrs. Bunt, a moment later, parking Clary's mother's car in its new home in front of their house. Poor frazzled Mrs. Bunt struggled back and forth with bags of groceries while Mr. Bunt vanished inside the house. Everybody's life was miserable.

A noise at the back pulled her away from contemplation of the Bunts: Mrs. Zenko, back from London, coming through the garden way with Jaffa cakes and Branston pickle in her hands. Clary's mother's standing order.

Clary sat down on the back steps, took the pickle jar in her lap and said, "I missed you so much. But you're too late, everybody's gone—what will I do?"

Mrs. Zenko sat beside her and said, "Never mind. You come to enjoy being alone. I was quite glad to leave my daughter's place, when the time arrived."

Clary leaned her head against the stair railing. She was not ready to be Mrs. Zenko yet, she thought.

45. Fool

*N*obody was around. Early enough on Sunday morning. Mrs. Pell went up the back alley and paused behind the workshop. Not for long, in case that meddler, Mrs. Zenko, was out hanging laundry on the line. That'd be like her, nose into everything. Couldn't just use the dryer like everybody else.

Mrs. Pell unlatched the gate and lifted it up awkwardly on one bent arm, to stop the metal from grating on the cement sidewalk at the bottom, and went along, hugging the side of the shop close to the bushes. It wouldn't be locked, she hadn't locked it when Clayton hustled her out of there, and she did not think Clary would have. Open—in—shut. Enough light through the blinds to see. The TV was still there, but no sheets on the bed. She stumbled along to the back of the building, to unbar the alley door. There, she'd be set in case she needed to get in the back way another time.

She sat on the bed picking her teeth—a popcorn hull from last night. She had to go to the toilet in a minute. Those kids, always nagging to get into the bathroom. An old woman ought to be able to count on a bathroom to herself. It might be a question of rent. After spending money on the kids all those months like it was going out of style, Clary might welcome a little income. Say $100, or $75. Light and water included.

Mrs. Pell sat on in the morning twilight of the workshop, nobody bugging her. She'd sneak in and out, sneaky-snake back and forth. Nobody needed to know where she was.

Dolly was awake, lying in the bottom bunk. If she closed her eyes, she could still think she was at Clary's house. There was no going back there, she knew that. She couldn't even go to the library at school now. She wished Keys Books was not closed, and hoped the guy was not dead yet, but he probably was. She shouldn't need books now anyway because everything was better: her mom was back, they were safe in Moreland's house, they didn't need first and last month's rent any more. That money could stay in the bear's butt at Mrs. Bunt's house. No need for any of the things she knew from people's houses, all their secrets. That made her think of Ann, and she turned over in bed. No goodbye, nothing, moved away on a Thursday night. Ann could have come here, Ann's mother didn't care where she went. Those two girls in the other duplex were mean; one of them had hit Trevor. She could hear his poor stuffy nose snoring on the bunk above her. These sheets still smelled almost like Clary's house.

Her mother came softly in and sat on the edge of the bed. It was so early in the morning that Dolly thought her mom might have been awake all night.

"Hey, have you seen Trevor? I can't find him anywhere," her mom said.

"What?" Dolly sprang up in bed.

"April Fool!" she said. "He's asleep, don't worry."

Dolly laughed. It had fooled her, even though she'd just heard him breathing over her head. She couldn't think of anything to joke back with, though. She stared at her mother's face, the same as before if you didn't count the baldy hair. She remembered the day they went to the hospital the first time, after the accident. She shuffled her legs over to make more room, and reached for her mother's cold hand.

"What're you thinking about?"

"School," Dolly said. "Stuff."

"Are you sad these days? Everything's pretty different now, from Clary's."

Dolly sat up and leaned on her mother's chest. "It's better now," she said. Liar.

Later, when her mom walked down to the bulk store with Trevor and Pearce, Dolly decided that she should go visit Mrs. Zenko, who was old. Nobody would be mad at that. She had her bus pass. Maybe Clary would come over while she was there.

She swung onto the 1:12 bus and up the steps, flashing her card at the driver but mostly ignoring him; you didn't have to be friendly when you had a pass. She sat by the back door, in a sideways seat, and passed the time reading the ads. There was a boy in one of them, leaning back on a rock laughing. He looked like her dad when he was a kid, if he'd had a different life. Along 8th Street, the place Keys Books used to be was open again already, a cell phone store. She should get that money out of Mrs. Bunt's bear after all, and go find the Keys Books guy and give it to him. Except he might be dead.

The bus stopped at the corner by the school. She could see Clary's house from there.

But she was shy to go there, now that she could see it. She climbed down the stairs and off the bus, since she'd pulled the cord, but she couldn't make herself walk down the street once the bus wheezed away.

She was an April fool to come. After a minute she crossed the street to the other bus stop, hoping it would not be the same driver when the bus came back. Then down the block a dumpy figure inched out of the alley— Gran, her feet bad, it looked like. Dolly walked over to meet her and gave her an arm.

"Huh!" her gran said. "What are *you* doing here?"

"What are *you* doing?"

Neither of them answered. Three-legged-race, they made their way back to the bus stop. They didn't have long to wait. On the way back down 8th Street, Dolly looked out the window and saw her mom and dad walking along from the bulk store with the boys. Her dad was carrying Pearce on his shoulders, and Trevor had a cinnamon bun.

"You got to watch him," her gran said. "He lies, you know. And he steals. He's stolen money from me."

335

"I know," she said. Gran always talked about her dad like that. "I'll be careful."

There was that same laughing boy ad on this bus too. People were so screwed up.

Paul drove to the superstore. He was having some difficulty remembering to feed himself. After communion, while he was finishing the Host (torn pita bread, not papery wafers, in this historically careful time), he had thought, that's what I need. Good bread.

As he drove down 8th Street Paul saw Clayton and Lorraine walking along in the persistent sludge of old snow, finally melting now. Clayton had Pearce perched on his shoulders. Lorraine held Trevor by the hand. Maybe there was something wrong with their car. Strange to see them, and not be able to wave or stop and talk—strange ever to have known them in the first place, he supposed.

Stopped at a red light a few blocks farther on, he looked up and saw Clary Purdy walking west. Maybe there was something wrong with *her* car. He had not seen her for weeks. He really had to give her back the carpet—he remembered the strength of the tendon tensed in her inner thigh. She was wearing the taupe wool coat with the black velvet collar, long black boots: she looked like a Canada goose, a helpless, honking goose. He felt a painful contraction in his throat. Over-dressed, over-precise—he could see her getting old, alone.

In three minutes she would walk straight into the Gage family. He did a wildly illegal U-turn and stopped ahead of her.

He leaped out and leaned on the car. "Can I give you a ride?" he called. "Please?"

She stood still, bewildered.

"I—needed to ask you—I had a question," he said.

She remained serious, but she came over to the car, contained and careful. No goose. He held the door and kept her attention in time for the Gages to pass by, oblivious.

"Do you think," he began, pulling away from the curb with no idea what the rest of the sentence would be—anything— "That I could take Mrs.

336

Zenko out for dinner? When she's back from London?" Ludicrous thing to ask. *Fool.*

"Well, I guess so," Clary said. "She is back. I walked over to church with her this morning." He watched the flush climb her face. "The Ukrainian Orthodox," she added.

Because she could not go to his church anymore.

"You sound awful," he said, to relieve her discomfort.

"I have a cold," she told him.

She was not looking at him. His elbow was too close to hers. He pulled himself in. "I didn't mean awful, just sick. You sound hoarse."

"Are you sick? Iris Haywood said you were in pain, but I was too shy to ask why."

"Oh, it was shingles," he said. "Nothing, really. They're almost gone."

They had arrived at her house. She thanked him, still without meeting his eyes, and got out of the car. He watched her go up the walk and into her empty, echoing house. He was an idiot.

That was horrible, Clary thought. She took off her coat in the silent house, pulling off her protective outer skin. She would not let herself even begin to think about Paul's face and his fingers on the steering wheel, the spiking thorn of not being with him, and all that being wrecked. The only thing harder would have been running into Lorraine, her most constant dread. She felt tired, and as foolishly heartsick as a velvet clown.

His eyes were set deeper in their hollows; even his hair was patchy. Everything was so hard on him. She went to fill the kettle at the kitchen sink and looked out absently on the garden.

There were footprints in the clean old snow all over the back yard. From the back alley gate around the workshop; in meandering arcs around the garden and up to the windows of her house. Like a large, curious rabbit had come sniff-sniffing around her house, to see who was there, what was happening. April Fool.

46. Eye

Sitting at the kitchen table late at night, Lorraine wrote Clary a letter. Her handwriting was not good, and she was self-conscious about it. But she could make a rough copy. It was hard to start.

Dear Clara,

She thought Clara was better, because this should be more formal.

I have to write to thank you for everything you've done for us in the last year.

Yesterday I had my first checkup at the cancer centre. They took more blood and did X-rays and I sat in the waiting room for a long time. It made me think about how kind you were all through all that long time. It probably saved my life that you were there looking after the kids and coming in all the time, and I wanted to fix things up between us.

Also because I am not sure how things will go from now on, and I know the kids miss you very much, and I think they need to see you sometimes.

The doctor was pretty straight with me, she told me what to watch out for. It was Dr. Lester, you remember her. They think I'm doing really well with the transplant stuff. I'm allergic to raspberries now, just like Darwin. But they will

338

keep watching me for a long time. I could get infections, or there are tons of other delayed things, complications. I'm not getting them, but I could, I have to make the plans. My eyes too, I could get cataracts, you have to wait for a couple of years before you know.

It's all scary but I'm not dead, that's the bonus. Or it could come back. Maybe I'd rather head to Fort McMurray and have our own lives, but I don't get to choose that one. I have to stay where I can get help if I need it, and I've got Bertrice to go to, who's been really great.

I've got disability coming in now, and I have started back to cleaning a couple days a week and we are managing okay. So this letter is not to ask you for any more help of that kind and I hope to be able to repay you some of the money I know you laid out on us one of these days.

But I know Darlene and Trevor and specially Pearce really miss you and would like to spend some time with you once in a while, if that would be okay with you.

Hoping that you are well,
Yours sincerely,
Lorraine Gage

The stove light flickered gently in the night-silent house as she was writing all this, and she sat for a few minutes listening to the kitchen clock's delayed, inconstant tick. She read it again. It was a good letter. She tapped the pages together on their edges, and folded it neatly in thirds, and then reached for Clayton's lighter and set the edge on fire. The smell of burning paper was somehow pleasant in her nose. She carried the burning brand over to the sink. Then the smoke alarm screeled over her head, and she dropped the letter and grabbed a tea-towel to wave the smoke away from the ceiling before everybody woke up.

She would have to try another way.

Clary's cold settled in her head, making everything grim. She had developed an annoying purple splotch in her field of vision, like an amoeba. At first only a floating mark, it grew until it took over most of her right eye's sight. She lay in bed one bright morning, afraid to open her eyes. The night before she had stayed up late, doing her taxes, trying to sort out which expenses she could claim. No charitable donation receipt for practical efforts. By the end of it she hadn't been able to see straight, even around the blotch.

Right eye open. There it was, still. She would have to go to the doctor. Mrs. Zenko offered to come with her, but Clary laughed it off and said she'd be back by lunch and would stop in and tell her what they had said. Hughes was away; his vacation replacement sent her straight to Emergency. At Emergency they sent her to neurology on the seventh floor. It was a brain tumour, of course, and it would be inoperable.

The nurse said it would be an hour's wait, so Clary went down to the lobby for a bottle of water.

When the elevator doors opened she could see Paul Tippett coming across the lobby. She pushed 7 again, and the close-door button, stabbing it, but he slid his hand between just as the doors were closing, and when they obediently opened again he saw her.

"Clary!" he said, his face brightening in absurd increments, like a tri-light bulb.

She kept her own face stiff.

"Are you— Who are you visiting?" he asked, that fear in his voice which taints everyone who spends too much time at the hospital. Mrs. Zenko? Moreland's heart? Even Clary felt a clutching claw.

"It's only me," she said. "I mean, I'm here for myself."

He got into the elevator. "I'll go with you."

She did not want to talk to him. "Do you have time?"

"How high are we going?"

She laughed, and it made her mouth feel strange. The doors opened on 7. Paul went with her to the flotilla of chairs in the waiting room. He steered her to one beside an end table, and perched himself there.

"What's going on?"

She explained about the purple blotch. He listened, but said nothing.

"It's the strangest thing," she said, calming down in the face of no reaction. "I can see around it, and I can see through the other eye, but all I can think about is what's behind the purple. I'm moving my head all the time to try to see what I'm missing." She turned her head even as she was speaking. It didn't hurt at all, just lurked there, purpling. "It's like a stain on the world—a stain on my view, my way of—" She broke off, embarrassed.

"I broke out in a plague of blisters," he said.

She couldn't help it, she laughed. "I know! I looked up shingles on the computer at the library. I always thought they were minor, but they sound terrible, you must be in a lot of pain."

"It was more Exodus than Revelations. They're almost gone."

They sat in silence for a moment. Clary was swept with disappointment, sitting beside him, for the failure of their happiness. Of every happiness, every hope. Ridiculous, she thought. Everything was.

"Why do you keep going to church?" she asked him.

"Paycheque."

She laughed, but turned her head away. Because he had dodged her question, Paul saw. He shook his head to clear it. No need to be anything but honest with her.

"I have the relationship with God that some people have with alcohol. Something in me is always crying out *God! God!* the way other people's hearts pant for a drink."

She looked at his face carefully, to see if he was being flippant. "Sounds destructive."

He almost asked what she longed for herself, but remembered. Pearce, and Trevor and Dolly. *Flap-mouthed fool.* Talking about God—did he have to flare like an oil well?

The elderly neurologist peered into Clary's eye with different machines, booked her for an MRI two months ahead, and asked her twenty questions, to no great effect. Paul sat beside her as if he was her husband, praying silently in a constant flow, a storm sewer running under his thoughts.

"Well," said the doctor, giving up. "It will either get bigger, stay the way it is, or go away. It will probably go away. If it does, please phone and cancel the MRI." That was all.

Clary thanked Paul. She put out her hand and he held it for a moment: not just shaking hands, she thought—some contact, some reconciliation. That they could be friends, at least. He was kind, and she loved his hands. She closed her mind to the rest of it, to desire or hope, and walked away down the corridor. Too many times in this hospital, too many times down hallways, always to no purpose. She couldn't even be sick successfully.

It went away two days later.

To prevent himself from phoning Clary, Paul worked on the homilies for Maundy Thursday and Good Friday. *Lent like a prairie fire, burning off the dead material on top, but leaving the metre-long roots,* he wrote in his black scratch. *Burning off extraneous outer / that we are attached to but need to lose...* His belabouring of metaphor never failed to surprise him. He could use Hopkins in every sermon, or Rilke, but of course nobody wanted that. They wanted his own clumsy stories and the way he rode a thing to death, because they could understand that. *What I do is me: for that I came,* fair enough. *I say more: the just man justices... Acts in God's eye what in God's eye he is—Christ. For Christ plays in ten thousand places...* But he would not try again the solemn mass where he undressed the altar, the knocks to signify the hammering of the nails into Christ's hands and feet. There had been too many comments last year. Sheer Merton: *Suddenly there is a point where religion becomes laughable. Then you decide that you are nevertheless religious.*

Clary thought she had better talk to Paul. He had left a message on her phone to say he wanted to bring back the carpet. Giving away the damned carpet was the only good deed she had done that was not a blunder, and she was not taking it back. He would be at church all day, because it was Good Friday. She went to church, late, and stood outside the inner door listening, the wood of the door cool under her hand. Maundy Thursday, Good Friday and Easter had been her mother's favourite part of the church year, a hugely dramatic time of mourning and then a concomitant (and to Clary's mind, equally over-dramatized) awakening joy; Clary had only felt detached. Standing at the back of the church alone, she was ashamed. How could she not have valued, even for that one week each year, her mother's ecstatic spirit? Her lovely mother, gone from the earth. The only good reason ever to have gone to church was to be with her mother, she thought.

342

Paul was quiet, as he must be on Good Friday. Last Good Friday she had not known him at all. She looked back at herself then: self-contained, sad, lonely, desperate to be good for something more vital than looking after an old woman.

"We enter this yearly process of being abandoned by God," Paul was saying, ending the homily, as Clary cracked the heavy door open and slipped inside. "But not without hope," he said. "Although we become immersed again in the misery of betrayal and death, we know the end of this story, and our awareness of God grows within us."

It surprised her that he talked so freely in a sermon, never condescending, when she knew him to be shy and stiff in real life. How could she criticize his foibles when her own were so large and identical? He was, however, the one clear-eyed witness to her heavy-handed charity, and her humiliation. And the one whose opinion mattered most to her. Even remembering the rocking raft of his bed, the phosphorescent waves, there was no way back to being with him. In fact she thought she hated him.

Everything around her sank, tides pulled the ocean floor away, unreliable sand. She had stayed in the shadows of the side aisle arches, and she stepped quietly backwards, making sure he did not see her, until she could duck out the side door and go home. Good Friday was no day for talking.

47. Triumph

*N*oise outside woke Dolly. Not loud: the eaves-drop sound of her parents talking on the front step. She pushed the covers back and got up. The bunk bed creaked and shifted, like it never had at Clary's house, but Trevor did not stir. Dolly went quietly to the window and leaned against the window screen, the sharp metal squares graphing her forehead.

Their bedroom looked out on the front here, instead of onto the back yard like at Clary's. She could see the driveway and Darwin's old car that was theirs now, that he'd left for them when he took Fern to Vancouver, so her dad could give back Clary's mother's car. She missed the Dart. She leaned her elbows on the windowsill and listened. The screen door opened and closed, her mother going inside for something. Her dad sat sideways on the top step, one foot lounging down. She could see the smoke he blew out, and smell it, mixed with beer. Quiet for a Saturday night. Maybe it was really late. The street lamp a few doors down buzzed, a different sound than the crickets but slightly the same. No other noise but a motorcycle puttering down the road. The night smell of the pavement was black and wet, like it had rained, but it had not.

The motorcycle slowed, ran softly up the driveway at their house, and stopped. The man pulled off his helmet. It was Darwin, sitting on that big tattered motorcycle. He had long leather pant legs tied over his jeans.

"Hey," he said. "How's it going, Clayton?"

Her dad rustled his back on the side of the wall but didn't stand up or go down to meet Darwin. Dolly could not call out herself, because tomorrow was Easter eggs, and she was supposed to be asleep, not listening at the window. But she was tired of her dad not liking Darwin. The motorcycle had the word *Triumph* on it.

"Going okay," her dad said, finally, after a couple puffs on his cigarette.

Darwin walked up, still slow, not barging in. "How's Lorraine?"

Her dad laughed, meanly. "Took you long enough to ask. Where you been?"

"I go where the wind goes," Darwin said. He laughed too, but like he meant it. He leaned on the stair-post at the bottom of the steps and unbuckled his side straps.

"What you been doing?"

"Oh, you know, establishing justice on earth."

"Butting in." Dolly could see her dad's hand grind his cigarette out on the step. His hand looked white and small. His skinny wrist stretched far out of his jacket cuff, that old blue mark on his wrist-bone showing.

Darwin lifted his head and looked straight at her window. "Nice night," he said. She was pretty sure he couldn't see her, but she waved anyway, to show somebody was glad to see him.

"You're getting here late enough."

"A long ride through the mountains," Darwin said.

"Got your bike back, eh? Have a beer," her dad said. He shoved the beer case with his foot, scraping it across the concrete with a snow-shovel noise.

"How's Lorraine?" Darwin asked again.

"She's fine. She's working, my boss's wife got her a couple days cleaning here and there."

"She ready for that?"

Dolly waited for her dad to say something, but he didn't speak.

After a pretty long time he did.

"How's Vancouver?" he asked Darwin, his voice too loud for the night.

Darwin shrugged his shoulders and smiled.

"Been a while since I was out there—you see Garvin and those guys? Juice and Shayla and them?" Her dad laughed some more, like at a dirty joke. Dolly laid her head down on her arm, straightening out her legs one in front of the other as if she was an Egyptian, and gave her forehead a rest from the metal lines of the screen. She thought about that ad of the boy on the bus, and how his face shone the way her dad's used to.

At the doorway of the kids' room, checking on them, Lorraine heard Clayton say all that about Vancouver, about Shayla Morton and Garvin, that scary creep. She left her hand lightly on the doorknob, not moving a molecule, and watched Dolly bending down her head. Too much for Dolly to have to hear. She probably remembered Garvin from before.

Darwin said he'd heard they were around.

Clayton popped open another beer. "Yeah. While you were out there, I was thinking. Maybe I'll drive out there myself in the summer."

He was going to leave—even Dolly would be able to hear that.

Never mind, Lorraine thought. The middle of her body felt empty. She was not even mad, she just wondered, if she had to quit working, how long the disability would last. She did not think Moreland would kick her and the kids out. The pay-out for the Dart had come in March and she'd kept it, marked *egg whites,* in the freezer. $2,500 would see her and the kids through a couple months.

She could make him stay, if she wanted to. But maybe it would be a relief not to have to look after him. She was stronger now, it would be okay. She backed away from the door so Dolly wouldn't know that she'd heard, and wouldn't have to worry. And so she could go out and hug Darwin, and be peaceful because he was there, for however long he would be.

Dolly waited till her mom was gone, and then curled back up in bed.

She dreamed that Darwin came in and kissed her good night, leaning down with his jacket smelling of smoke, but not cigarette smoke. Wood smoke and hides being tanned. *The one who forms the mountains,* the soundtrack in her dream said in a rich, manly voice, like if church was a movie ad.

Late as it was, Paul was still at his computer trying to finish the sermon for Easter morning. Darwin's foot on the porch brought him down the stairs at a gallop, knowing who it was—he had to pause before he opened the door, not

346

to seem crazily eager. But restraint flew away as Darwin stepped forward to meet him, like brothers meeting in the wilderness.

"Where are you staying?" Paul said.

"Crashing here a couple days, if you don't mind?"

Paul pushed the door wider and took Darwin's duffle bag. "I've been pining for company," he said. "Clary and I fell apart, it was my fault."

He hadn't thought that consciously before. Lisanne had not been his fault, but Clary was.

"Things change," Darwin said. But did that mean they changed from perfect to imperfect, or that they could change again?

Early on Sunday morning Clary answered the phone without checking to see who was calling, which she hadn't done for months, and it was Grace.

"We're back," Grace said.

Clary couldn't think what to say.

"Welcome back!" Grace said, prompting her. "Hawaii was hot, Vancouver was rainy, we've been back for a while now but we were pretty taken up with Fern's news."

"I'm glad to hear your voice," Clary said finally.

"We're guessing you're mad at Moreland for letting them have the duplex," Grace said, her voice not changing at all from normal. "That was all a pretty big shemozzle, her getting better. Might have been better if she had died after all."

"No!" Clary said, the *no* torn out of her without thought.

"Well, exactly. And they needed a better place than that slum over north there. So I don't think it was Moreland you were mad at."

"Grace, don't lecture me."

"I wouldn't attempt to. Pot calling the kettle black anyway because I'm as mad as a fist myself. Fern here is about to have a baby any day, and it appears that she's planning to keep it and live out here with us, in the absence of an actual husband."

There was a short silence. Grace leaving time for Clary to put it all in order; Clary thinking about how sleepy Fern had been in January. If it was Darwin's baby, wouldn't Darwin stay with Fern? He had left one child already. Was no one any good?

"Don't worry, it's that shithead Jack from the U of S again. She met up with him in October when she went out there, no matter what anyone said, and he was back in town at Christmas when she figured out about the baby. And I guess he's the one who broke Darwin's nose, too. So she's spent a few weeks thrashing things out with him and his family, but he's sticking with the new girlfriend instead, she's richer. Fern says she's over him, whatever that means. Apparently Darwin got him to sign papers relinquishing the baby, so at least we won't have them breathing down our necks—him not suing over the broken nose might have helped with all that. But I'm fifty-six, here, I'm not that interested in a baby."

"Fern will be fine," Clary said. "She was wonderful with the children—"

How long since she had said *the children*?

"Well, I know that, but it's a different thing to have your own. But all we can do is stay calm."

"When is she due?"

"Oh, not till July, I'm exaggerating."

"When it gets to be too much for you, come to town, I've got a nice quiet house now. I need to talk to Moreland—I'm sorry I haven't talked to you both, but I was—"

"Fit to be tied—I bet you were. After all you did for them."

"No, no, it wasn't that—" But of course it was.

"It's that Clayton. He's prickly."

"They have their own family. I was just a stop-gap."

"Mm-hm."

"But I miss them." She hadn't said that, even to Paul, even when she was still talking to Paul. "I broke up with Paul, too. 'Broke up'—that sounds so teenagey."

"What on earth did you do that for?"

Clary sat down in a kitchen chair. Since this was going to take a while.

"I don't know, Grace. I was mad. I don't know."

"Well, you may not want my advice but I think you've lost your mind."

"No, I don't think so. His wife had just left, he was still in pain. He couldn't even talk to me. He only quoted poems to me all the time." How childish she sounded!

"I wish Moreland would quote a poem or two," Grace said. "Were you hard on him?"

Clary did not answer.

On Easter morning she tried again to talk to Paul, again thinking church might be the most natural place, while half-conscious that she was somehow sabotaging any hope of real conversation. Maybe it would be comfortingly familiar to go to church on Easter, sing *Alleluia*. Even if it was all hooey.

Watching the women laugh and jostle each other as they stood for the annual Easter Hat photo in the garden after church, she thanked God (or the vacuum of Nature) that she had not worn a hat, and that she had no responsibility in the parish. No need to be friendly, as she would have had to be as Paul's wife, or whatever they might have become. No bounden duty and service for her. All these women must know that she and Paul had been— whatever they had been. But none of them said anything, not this time. They might be protecting her, the way one or another would come and talk, would shift her attention this way or that, away from Paul, or break the line of sight. She didn't know why she had come. Now that he had mentioned the carpet she could hardly meet his eyes, for the images recurring.

She could not come back to church, it was impossible.

April Anthony had outdone herself: an Easter cake with coloured eggs in toasted-coconut nests. Trevor would love that cake. Clary was dying for a piece of it herself, suddenly hungry after a long Lent. She could see Paul's head bobbing above someone's hat as he nodded, being a careful priestly listener. He was full of flaws, an irritating combination of self-deprecation, self-importance and self-consciousness. He was emotionally spent. And so was she. She loved his nose and his dutifulness.

The question she asked herself, watching fascinated as Paul's head appeared and disappeared behind the ribbon-swooped, straw-boater-based confection on Mary Tolliver's head, was this: What was her liability? How much of all this was her fault, and how much did she owe, or could she expect, in compensation?

48. Things change

*I*t was on the kitchen calendar when Clary turned over to May. Trevor had written the wobbly red letters in January: *The Bug Play.* When the 10th came around Clary was at school anyway, and she thought she might as well walk down to the gym. Fooling herself into thinking she was fooling herself.

The music teacher had worked all term with them. Caterpillars, army ants, ladybugs: each genus had its accompanying song. Two Grade 3 girls did a swaying, in-folding dragonfly dance while the children sang. Trevor's firefly song was at the end of the program: "Things Change." His class trooped in and arranged themselves in rows, and a teacher by the door turned the lights off. Each firefly had a flashlight.

> *At times, things may look dark.*
> *Some days you've lost your spark…*

Their little voices were so sad. Very few of them could keep from wandering off key. The flashlights flickered in the darkness. She remembered her father reading her a *Pogo* comic strip, the firefly explaining that when the light was lit, they'd locate the ladies; when it was dark, they'd sneak up. Her dear father, laughing while he read it to her. As dead as anything, now.

...there's one thing very clear:
Things change! Things will change.

That old metamorphosis rag, Clary thought. *Plus ça change,* she said to herself, proud of her detachment. She looked around the audience, seeing the fathers and mothers as little children themselves, part of a long undulating chain of children. And the children parents of their own children, soon. Nothing ending, *Things Change* really meaning they don't.

A mother behind Clary was heaving loud sobs. She couldn't hold her video camera still; its red stability light was flashing, on and off, like a firefly.

We grow, we're not the same.
Your life will change, and it will set you free!

Clary knew what made the parents around her cry, more or less openly: that everything must grow and change and—rather than being set free— must die, all these children too. We die, they will die, their children will be dead. We resist mourning, because we know we will have to mourn soon enough, and the resistance makes us weep. *Their greenness is a kind of grief—* she thought that was Larkin. Or Dylan Thomas? She needed Paul to tell her.

Turning to leave, she saw Lorraine standing at the back with Pearce on her hip. Impossible to tell from that distance if she was crying or not, but she was smiling, anyway. Her pointy, crooked teeth showing, her dark eyes crumpled, her thin arm strong around Pearce. He had never sat so solidly on Clary's hip. He had grown.

Clary turned away and tried to calculate which door she could get to fastest. Did Lorraine even know that she worked at the school? She would think that Clary was there spying on the children. Everything was so awful.

Then Lorraine was beside her, and Pearce saw her. He jumped in shocked surprise, and threw his arms out toward her, crying, "Clah! Clah!"

She didn't know what to do—she couldn't reach back to him, she couldn't ignore him. Her breasts hurt. This was the most pain she had ever felt.

"Hey, Clary," Lorraine said, sounding happy. "Hold Pearce while I go give Trevor a hug?"

Without any more fuss than that, she transferred Pearce over and dodged through the crowd to find Trevor, not looking back. Pearce's arms went around Clary's neck, and her arms around him, and they were quiet in the middle of all that crowd. He smelled so good.

"Where's my mom?" Dolly asked, coming up from the Grade 4 rows.

"She's here," Clary said quickly, in case Dolly might think she had stolen Pearce. "She's gone to congratulate Trevor."

"I didn't mean she would leave," Dolly said, her nervous eyes darting around the crowd. "I was just worried about her."

Of course her mother would leave, Clary thought. Was leaving, like everybody was; would walk away from her and be gone. It was a butterfly life, not permanent, no-how. Might as well make the best of it. Pearce tugged at Clary's arm to be put down. He wanted to run to Trevor.

He said, "Re-ev, Re-ev," with his mouth pushed out as if that would help to call him gently, his voice giving it two notes.

"He copies that from you," Dolly said.

Clary put Pearce down and let him run. She kissed Dolly's cheek and said, "I've missed you all very much."

Then she darted off through the milling children to keep sight of Pearce. It was all right, Lorraine had him; she swooped him up and settled him on her hip again, and they waved to Clary, and they were gone.

Mrs. Pell staggered down the alley pulling the big beige suitcase she'd got at the Goodwill. The zipper was tetchy but she had Clayton's pliers in her purse if it gave her trouble.

She'd had to wait twenty minutes for a bus. Poor service early on a Saturday. She ran through the supplies in her head: peanut butter, vienna sausages, quilt, pillow, fleece nightie, the old Niagara Falls playing cards. Her pills. Bank card. Socks, other pants, white sweater. It beat the basement at the duplex. She got a tight, nasty feeling in her chest when those goddamn kids bugged her. The noise played on her eardrums like tom-toms, not that she could hear what any of them were saying.

Mrs. Pell leaned on the door-post and fumbled with the sticky catch, but she had the trick of it pretty quick.

Dusty in there. She rolled the big case in. Clary was simple, it was Mrs. Zenko she'd have to watch out for. Always prying, like Sally Caslo back in Bonner, when Clayton was two and Lenny Gage hadn't left yet. Sally happening along the one time she lost her temper and took into Clayton, calling the district nurse on her. Like it was an accident—she'd been lying in wait, peering out her window waiting for an argument and scuttling over, cockroach hearing the can opener. Like that old bitch in Brandon telling her off. What was that about? Something sly—to get a memory back you had to pull at it like a hank of wool, teasing out whatever was caught in there. Lights. The power was still on out here, that was good. Mrs. Pell wandered around the workshop, her mind drifting from Brandon back to that place over the store on Main where she'd lived with Lillian Parr, to Lillian's brother in the middle of the long, baking-hot night while Lillian worked the late shift at the midway, sawdust on the floor. The floor slid sideways to Lenny Gage, and backwards down all the men on that slippery slide until she hit the side of her head with her closed fist and skipped the needle over a groove to her sister Janet. She spread the tumbling-blocks quilt on the bed.

Clary looked out the kitchen window and watched Mrs. Pell pacing back and forth, silhouetted against the blinds. She should do something, but what would be best? Ignore her, tell Lorraine, call social services, call the police— It all went downhill from *ignore*.

Paul would know what should be done with a wandering old woman. Lorraine could come and get her. But she didn't need to call anybody, Clary knew what should be done. She made a cup of strong coffee with too much cream, found a set of clean sheets and a couple of towels, and went out into the pearly morning air.

Long after Mrs. Pell had turned out her lights that night, Darwin drove up on his motorcycle. Clary was out on the grass in front of her flower beds, looking at the veronica and wondering if she was letting it choke, if a little attention earlier in the year might have done wonders. She turned when she heard the bike, and was surprised when it stopped at her house. Then not surprised, when the rider took his helmet off and was Darwin.

He unstrapped a case and brought it across the grass. "Few things she didn't pack," he said, smiling with his huge open face, like the sun in the evening.

"Anything she'll need tonight?" she asked, being as casual as he was.

"Don't think so."

How tall he was. "I'll leave it outside her door, then," Clary said. "How did you know she was here?"

"Dolly told me. But where else would she be?"

Clary nodded.

"Want to go for a ride?"

She looked at the motorcycle. "Is it safe?"

"Hardly." Insulted that she might think so.

He left Mrs. Pell's bag on the porch, handed Clary the other helmet, and showed her where to put her feet. He swung the bike around, started it and rolled over the edge of the driveway as if it was the edge of the world, and away with a growl down the never-ending street, outwards. It was late enough that there was no traffic, and early enough in the year that there were no bugs. Only the crickets swinging on their creaking hinges, audible above the motor. The pavement slid away beneath them. Clary hung on, her arms halfway around his broad, flat back, and gradually found that she could straighten her spine and sway with the bike as he went around the last corner and headed south past the racetrack and the museum, past Early's where Moreland always went, and out into the night country.

The bike glided on, up and down the unexpected hills. Darwin did not talk, but he pointed once to a coyote standing by the side of the road and up, another time, to the bright spill of stars. He slowed at a long banking arc in the road, and around the blind corner Clary gasped to see a throng of deer spread out along the road. The noise of the motorcycle set them leaping into the grass, tails flashing.

Darwin swung around and headed back into the city, the lights spread out like a diamond necklace on the horizon. The lights swelled up into town again, the noise of the bike dulled, and they went swooping along under the street lamps, down her own street again, home.

He idled the motor and let the kickstand take the weight. She undid the helmet and found her head all in one piece. She went up the steps, her legs a bit unsteady after all that hanging on with her knees.

"Good work, with Mom Pell," he said.

"Thanks," Clary said. "Thanks for the ride."

"Any night," he said. He rolled around in a circle again and vroomed off. She stood and watched him go, his balance unwavering. Like a gyroscope upon the earth.

49. Ascension

On the 24th of May, Darwin phoned Clary in the morning to say it was hotter than hell already and why didn't she come out to the river with them for a picnic? "Bring the old lady, if you don't mind," he said.

It was a PD day, no school. She thought about it. "Are you asking Paul, too?"

"Already on board."

She looked out the kitchen window. Mrs. Pell was in the garden, sitting in the wooden rocker, but she looked movable. She'd been hunkered down in the workshop for two weeks and must be feeling safe by now, Clary thought, the way a turtle brought home from the store needs a while to acclimatize. "What can I bring?"

"All taken care of. Come right now."

But she had been to the river before. She brought all the chocolate she had in the house, and two large thermos jugs of water. They were heavy to lug across the meadow, once she had parked by Darwin's old green car that he'd given Lorraine, and the Triumph parked beside it. Mrs. Pell was no help, of course. She stumped off, carrying her folding chair. Not talking today. Fine.

Paul drove up while Clary was working out the best way to carry the jugs, and Mrs. Zenko got out of Paul's car, holding her ancient aluminum cake-carrier with the black Bakelite handle. What kind of cake might be in there?

"Did Darwin ask Paul to bring you?" Clary asked, hugging her. Why had she not thought of it herself? She was such a rule-follower.

Paul was climbing out too, empty-handed. "I thought of it on my own," he said. He took a thermos from Clary. "Hey, he said not to bring anything!"

"It's only water. You can't have too much water. And Mrs. Zenko disobeyed too."

"Darwin called me yesterday," Mrs. Zenko said, tying the arms of her sweater around her waist. "So I'd have time for baking. My, it's hot!"

"That's how transparent I am in my independent thinking," Paul said.

It was hot for May, but the trees still held their first bright green. The tall new grass was green too, springing through last year's brown and gold. A bird sang, invisible, cheerful, as they wandered along the half-beaten path, swinging their burdens. They found the track down the riverbank and crossed the fast-running stream to the first of the sandbars. Clary and Paul forded the water in their sandals, helping Mrs. Zenko to cross by the rocks. This early in the season, and a Thursday, there was nobody out at the river.

"It's Ascension Day, did you know?" Paul asked them. "It's unlucky to do any work today."

"What a good excuse," Mrs. Zenko said.

"Not till next week, for you Orthodoxers," Clary said.

"I'll take the day off then too."

Across the sandbanks and scrubby bushes they could see a little fire burning on a stretch of beach, heat spirit rising from the wood-coals.

Darwin raised an arm to greet them, and the children ran over the sand. Pearce scrambled down from Lorraine's lap. She was sitting in a black cloth folding chair, wrapped up in a jacket, but her dark hair, grown in, was blowing loose in the wind. She looked happy, waving both her hands at them.

Clayton was crouched at the water's edge with a beer, maybe fishing; Mrs. Pell already arguing with him about something, her mouth snapping at a distance. Clary sighed to think of her.

357

Pearce smacked Clary with a quick flowery kiss and pulled Mrs. Zenko away to show her the river. Then Trevor reached them, and stood in front of her, eyes strained, and Clary sank down on her heels in the sand.

"It's been so long since I've talked to you, Trev," she said, putting out her hand to touch his arm. "But I see you all the time at school," she said, at the same time as he said, "I see you all the time..." He leaned forward gratefully onto her knees.

"It's nice to see you," she said, holding him tight. Not saying that she had missed him, in case that made him feel guilty. He hugged her back.

Dolly took Clary's other hand to bring her to the fire. "Even when it's hot out, the fire is nice," she said. "Like a camp."

Lorraine stayed folded in her chair, looking cautious, but she put out her hand as Clary got close, and Clary took it: the same hand to hold, the long fingers, but with more strength.

Clary sat on a nearby rock, one of a few arranged around the fire. She smiled at Lorraine (who she had worked hard for, after all, and was very happy to see alive), and made herself glide through that membrane she could never pierce, and just talk. "You look so good," she said. "Even better than that day at the school play."

"Thanks for coming," Lorraine said. All she needed to say. "Nice to have a party with everyone. All we need is Fern and them."

"They're coming," Darwin said. "Takes longer from Davina, but they'll get here."

He was digging in brown paper grocery bags and called Dolly to help him hand out paper plates of sandwiches. Plate after plate of crustless tuna and salmon sandwiches, cut in triangles. Mrs. Pell said she didn't like fish and took her chair into the willow grove in the middle of the island, where she fell asleep with her hat on. Clary bit into a tuna sandwich with parsley around the cut edges, wondering if Darwin might have stolen them from somewhere— the United Church come-and-go tea for Edith and Willard Stepney's 75th, for instance, which she ought to take Mrs. Zenko to this evening. The Stepneys had owned the store between her father's hardware store and John Zenko's jewelry store. They'd been old even then. The window of time when you could do anything was so brief, Clary thought. The Stepneys had probably had all kinds of ideas of what they would accomplish, not including spending the last twenty years sleepwalking in the seniors' lodge. Good sandwiches. Darwin was laughing at her again. She screwed up her nose at him and had another. Salmon this time.

"I have half a mango here somewhere," Darwin said, rummaging through the supplies again. He hauled out a large bag of fruit, every kind, each one perfect. Dolly washed them at the water's edge and brought an orange to Lorraine and a ripe, medieval-perfumed pear to Clary. The orange sprayed a smarting arc when Lorraine bit into it to start peeling. Orange and pear, mixed with fire-smoke, wound and twined with the wind in their hair.

The children wandered along the shoreline eating sandwiches. Mrs. Zenko and Pearce walked more slowly, bringing treasures back to show Lorraine and Clary as they sat chatting carefully about nothing much—the heat, and school, and how it was to be working again.

Lorraine did not talk about anything that was on her mind: Clayton, money, or the slightly painful lump just over her left pelvic bone. That was most likely just a swollen lymph node, left over. She was not going to worry about it. The stress-acid that flooded through her arms and legs could run out on the sand and seep away, today. Every day. No more useless worry. She told Clary a funny story about the spectacled kid at one house she was cleaning, who came racing home early to tell her how amazing it was to find his clothes in the right drawers for a change. "His system made sense to me," she said. "He's a neat kid, tidy I mean, but the rest of his family, wow! I just start at one end of the house and do what I can. His room is a little sanctuary."

Clary listened with one layer of her mind while another breathed in the pear and checked Lorraine carefully for physical clues. She seemed tired, but calm.

"You look great," Clary said again. "You look ordinary. I'm so glad."

Lorraine nodded. "I'm good," she agreed, not having to work to convince Clary of it. She believed her.

"Gifts to the blind or the lame on Ascension Day will be rewarded with wealth," Paul said, walking with Darwin at the water's edge. "Eggs laid on this day never go bad, and bring good luck if placed in the roof... Clouds appear in the shape of the Lamb of God, and rain collected on Ascension Day is good for inflamed or diseased eyes."

"Does your head hurt, with all this stuff flapping around inside it?"

Paul half-laughed, feeling sorry for his monkey mind.

"You could choose to forget," Darwin said. "Pain, resentment, religious trivia…"

"But eggs in the roof, maybe that's what I need. Better than bats in the belfry, flap-flapping…"

"How are you doing?"

"Oh, the best I can. Keeping on with my work, doing my duty, making my visits," Paul said. Not a very noble recitation. "I don't know what more I can do."

Darwin stretched his arms up, flaring up, to the sun flashing in the blue-white sky above them. "Why not be totally changed into fire?" he asked. Then he danced his fingers around and laughed his head off.

Dolly wandered away from her mom and Clary, letting them look after each other. Mrs. Zenko was there for Pearce, and Trevor liked to be alone outside, although he always wanted her to be with him at school. She swung her arms out wide and twirled in a circle on the empty sand, wanting to be dizzy, to be in orbit around herself. She stopped, and staggered, and felt the vortex of the world whirling around her. But her legs braced her stable on the earth, even though it was just sand. She was wearing her gypsy skirt that Gran had bought her at the Sally Ann store. When she whirled it flared way out into the air. Her dad had said not to wear it to the beach, keep it for good, but her mom had said why not? This *was* good. She had her bathing suit on underneath and she tucked the skirt up into the waistband when she wanted to wade. When she ran through the dunes and the grass, the skirt flew out behind her and whipped in the wind, a blue-green swirl like imaginary water. Not like this river water that was all colours, clear over the rocks, brown in the shadowy deep channels, racing along grey-blue in the rapids. She splashed through the shallows and ran down the long wet sandbar in the middle of the river, like a movie of a beautiful girl running on a desert island.

Absent-mindedly following Dolly's running footprints, not noticing where he was going himself, Paul found Clayton blocking his way at the brink of a cut-away bank.

"Beer?" Clayton asked him, dangling the last can from an empty net of six-pack plastic.

"No, no thanks," Paul said.

"Good, 'cause I don't think Darwin brought any and this is my last one."

Paul laughed. "Kind of you to offer, then."

They walked along the shore for a while.

"You know Clara pretty well?" Clayton asked.

"Pretty well," Paul agreed.

"You think she'll help out with the kids again?"

Paul nodded.

"Thought so. She likes them, eh?"

"So do I," Paul said.

"Yeah. You're her boyfriend?"

"No," Paul said.

"Huh! I thought you were."

Paul shook his head. "We're friends," he said.

Clayton laughed. "Right." He bent for a stone and threw it far into the river, the motion strong and fluid. Paul could see the athlete he might have been.

Drifting on the dunes on the other side of the sandbank, Trevor watched the birds landing on the water. Geese, crook-winged seagulls, birds he didn't know. When they landed on the water they followed no path. Even the huge white pterodactyl pelicans could come and go without leaving a trace. Around one spit of land he could see a mile down the river, nobody else in the world. Ahead, a long slender vase of a blue heron stood on a driftwood stump.

He stopped still. No thoughts, nothing but clean empty space in his head. Then he turned around and walked back, his feet quiet on the sand. The funny little running birds left stick-man footprints on the sand so you could follow them back to the nest, but you would not because it would scare them. Trevor followed along one birdfoot trail and it led him straight to Darwin at the edge of the water.

He looked at Darwin's feet, and then up at his face.

"Let's go in," Darwin said.

It was hot, hot, and the water was running along warm over the shallows. They were all half wet from wading already. He and Trevor went in first, but Clary followed with Dolly, holding Pearce's hands between them. Lorraine stood on the shore, and Dolly waved back at her, beckoning. Mrs. Zenko came and put her arm around Lorraine, the light wind whipping up her short hair, the same length as Lorraine's. Silver and black; to Clary they looked like a time-lapse photo, thirty-five and seventy.

Darwin grabbed Pearce and swung him around, first into the air and then flying, diving under the surface and back up again, like a bird, Clary thought, a sea-bird used to the waves. Pearce was laughing, not at all scared. Trevor splashed deeper with Dolly until they stepped off the edge of a submerged sandbar and went under for a second—but Darwin grabbed them up and held them, one in each arm.

Downriver, Paul raised his arms in exaggerated alarm and waded into the water toward them. Clayton looked like he might follow, but his mother was calling from her willow-bush hideaway, wanting him to fix her chair, and he turned aside.

Clary cleaved through the water in Paul's direction. His face looked free, almost happy. This was the first time she had seen him happy in months—and even then, she thought, it had been dark at the time.

"Please, I don't want that carpet back!" She was desperate, suddenly, never to have it back in her house.

"No, no, I want to keep it," Paul said. "But I thought I should offer—"

Rising out of the water right behind them, Darwin hooked his foot in the back of Paul's knees, collapsing him into the water, and then pulled Clary in and under and up again, and gave her a big kiss. Then he sloshed away, back to the kids.

It was a relief to be wet all over. Clary took Paul's hand and pulled him into the current with her, in up to their waists. The river married them under the surface, the same water flowing through them.

"I will talk," he said. "Myself, my own words."

"Don't do anything different, I want what you, I mean you as—what you are. Except not to be worried, or fearful."

Oh, is that all, he thought. Well then.

"You smell good," she said. They fit together well. A driftwood stick floated by and Paul hooked it for a prop to brace them against the river current, stronger in this channel here.

"Look at them all, how big they are," Clary said, seeing the children from a perspective-creating distance. Pearce was up to Mrs. Zenko's sweater-hem already.

"Can you be friends with Lorraine now?"

"Yes." She stood straight, legs strong in the sweeping water, the sand carving away under her feet. "But I don't think I can go to church any more. That might be hard on you."

He nodded, looking down the river. "Well, you'll have to be—not be fearful either."

She touched his arm, his skin. Pretty well, she loved him.

"Did praying save her? One night, I thought my prayers were working. But they didn't work for my mother."

He poked his stick into the deepest channel, making it deeper. "I don't know," he said. "Why people die, when. I can't believe in a preordained arrangement, with death at the soul's most opportune time—or in a crafty, secretive God hunched over the plotting table in a war-room universe."

He pulled the stick downstream, winding it along, and the water followed the stick. "We're in the world. I think we are subject to the world, while we're here, and that God waits for us. That's all I can say."

"Not that prayer has no purpose," he added after a minute, looking up at her. "How could I say that? I pray constantly!"

"Yes," she said.

She bent down her head to see the shining rocks under the wavering prism of the current. Paul looked at the sky, where God was not. Or was. Mauve-tinted shafts in bright hot blue. That window opening in the sky, in the clouds: always a vision of the country of heaven.

Trevor straggled along the water's edge, maybe lonesome. Paul turned and followed down the sandbar after him. *Away grief's gasping, joyless days, dejection.* There was a beacon, wasn't there, an eternal beam? *World's wildfire, leave but ash...* He sprinted ahead, tagged Trevor and raced him back to the fire.

363

Darwin rustled his paper bags and brought out more fruit and bags of chips, and Clary remembered the chocolate, which had melted but could be squeezed out of the wrappers straight into their mouths.

Dolly lay on her back on sand beside the umbrella shading drowsy Pearce. Above them, clouds moved over the blue. "Like a bunch of sheep," she said to Pearce. "Look! Bouncy legs, and wool!" He moved his head lazily to see around the umbrella, and pointed his finger up into the sky, but she was not sure he was seeing the same sheep she saw. Two people could never look at the sky the same way.

After one more sandwich Clayton stood up and gave his plastic net to Darwin to stick in the trash bag.

"I'm taking Mom back to town," he told Lorraine. "She's beat. These guys'll give you all a ride, right?"

Mrs. Pell was grey and sullen under her cotton hat. She had hardly spoken all afternoon. Clary and Paul said they had room for everyone, between them.

Clayton bent down to kiss Lorraine. The brim of his baseball cap got in the way; he took it off. His pale forehead under the springing hair caught her off-guard, and she kissed him back fondly.

"Later," he said.

She smiled at him, as free as ever. "See you," she said.

He turned away from them all and went back across the streams and the rough grass with his mother. Clary looked after them. Both short, one stumpy, one skinny. She'll be in a nursing home within the year, Clary bet herself, for some comfort. She poured a big glass of water for Lorraine, and one for herself. She sat in Mrs. Pell's abandoned folding chair, and let those two go.

People had drifted away from the fire. Heat still rose off the sand in wobbling waves. Near Mrs. Zenko, watching in her chair, Trevor and Pearce lay flaked out on the dune with red faces—burnt? Clary checked, but they were just red from running. Lorraine squeezed more sunscreen onto both their hands and they slathered the boys again, making them jump with the sudden cold.

"Paul needs some too, look at his neck," Lorraine said, pointing to where he and Darwin stood out in the streaming current.

"Not Darwin, though, he's impermeable."

Lorraine gave her the sunscreen and said, "What a good guy Paul is, eh? Good thing, you need some reward for taking in Mom Pell."

Clary turned her head to look at Paul. "I was—he wants to try again."

"Better get some sunscreen on him, then."

Dolly had a good big stick. She'd taken it from Pearce when he was going to poke Gran with it, and he ran off after a bird. She dragged it along the sand. It made a fine line. Swinging around in a big circle on this swath of smooth sand, she drew a huge circle on the sand, as far around as the tip of the stick could reach. She jumped outside it and stood looking at it. Her mom stopped by her and looked too.

"Looks like the world," her mom said. She borrowed the stick and sketched in continents quickly, not real ones, but to make it look more like a globe.

"Put us on," Dolly said.

Her mom drew a couple of people in the middle of the world, their arms around each other's waists. They looked sturdy, standing there together.

"Me, put me," Trevor said. He had a stick too, but Dolly batted it away, so their mom could do him.

"Let him," Lorraine said. "It's okay, it's just sand, we can smooth it over if we want."

Trevor drew himself beside the taller figure. A stick boy, waving his hand.

"That's really good," Lorraine said. It was, too, it had a weird look of Trevor. "Who else needs to go on?"

"Put Clary," Trevor said, standing back to let her do it. "And Pearce."

Lorraine added Pearce to the little group, and put Clary farther north, but facing towards them. She looked up and saw Clary and Paul talking in the water, both gazing over the river in the same direction, so she put Paul beside Clary. Might as well, whether or not. Just sand.

"Gran?" The children nodded, and she drew a sitting woman way south, in an antarctic zone, looking down. This was good. She drew in Mrs. Zenko— nice little portrait, she thought—over to the east, with her arms out, a jar in one hand and a loaf of bread in the other. The kids knew her right away.

Dolly went to the other side of the globe, and said, "Fern, and More-land, and Grace." Lorraine added them, all standing together, a barn behind them, off to the west. Then Trevor wanted Mrs. Ashby on there somewhere, and Dolly thought of Mrs. Haywood and Francine, and the southern continent filled up pretty fast. They didn't put names, but you could tell who people were by who they were standing beside, mostly.

Ann Hayter: but there was nowhere to put her. Nobody knew where she had gone. There ought to be a moon, Dolly thought, and she drew a small one six feet away, and secretly put a little dot there for Ann. Her old Keys Books guy could be there too, he could look after Ann way out there on the icy moon.

Darwin came over to see what they were doing. He walked all the way around the circle, inspecting the people.

"Darwin!" Dolly poked her mom.

She drew in a chair at the north pole and sat Darwin in it.

"I got a good view from here," he said.

"And Dad," Trevor said, but his mom didn't draw him.

"I'll put him on the moon," Dolly said, and she drew a man standing on the moon, looking both ways, towards the world and away.

Lorraine looked at the man on the moon and laughed, and said, "Dolly, you are getting to be a good artist. That looks so much like your dad!"

"He has a hard time deciding," Trevor said.

Fern appeared over the edge of the horizon in the glowing early evening, Moreland and Grace in matching Hawaiian shirts carrying a big cooler between them. Fern's stomach was the first thing anyone could see. She was the full moon in the daylight sky.

"Pretty pleased with herself for a fallen woman," Darwin said.

Lorraine and Clary both went to meet her. How soon it must be! She was so huge! Fern kept laughing while she told them all the details of rolling baby acrobatics and no sleep, and she said right away, "The father's not interested, did Mom tell you? So no male role model, but I'm thinking my dad might be good for that, take another kick at the can, get it right this time."

Moreland had gone straight to the fire and was building it up.

"We brought marshmallows," Grace said. "Breaking the rules, I know, Darwin! And pop. And a few hot dogs—hey, I brought a pitcher of that lime-ade with strawberries we used to like, Clary, remember? We never did have any out at Clearwater."

"With the vodka or without?"

"Oh, without, without, because of Fern, but Moreland may have some up his sleeve. I brought blankets, too."

Grace and Clary set them out around and helped Moreland tend to the fire in case the children got cold when the sun went low, although now at eight it was still high and brilliant.

Dolly took Fern with her to see the world in sand, and she drew Fern's stomach, round as an apple, sticking out of her stick front. That made Fern laugh. Dolly thought maybe Fern would name the girl Darlene if it was a girl. Or her middle name—Rose—that would be good.

Mrs. Zenko had taken her cake out of the cake-carrier finally. Spice, Lady Baltimore, coconut… Clary craned her neck to see what kind: burnt sugar with burnt sugar icing, Clary's favourite. How could she, after an afternoon of sand-wiches and chips, be so eager for a piece of cake? The burnt taste in the cake matched the fire, complicated on the tongue. Not bitter, exactly. Scorched. Once burnt, twice shy; but she did not want to be shy, she wanted to be with people.

Vestal in her white sweater, Mrs. Zenko handed around cake, bending to each person in turn. Mrs. Pell and Mrs. Zenko had both worn white today. *My mother and your mother were hanging out clothes, my mother punched your mother, right in the nose—what colour was the blood?* Clary's mother's blood always had to be blue in that game. Mrs. Zenko and Mrs. Pell would both be red. Soon enough, because they were getting old, their blood would still. Mrs. Pell and Mrs. Zenko in their white sweaters—who would be dead first?

Clayton ran by the duplex and left his mother dozing in the car while he packed a few things. Then he took her over to Clary's place and helped her lever herself out onto the sidewalk.

There was Clary's other car, sitting there wasting. What did she need two cars for? She was so crazy about Lorraine and the kids, let her contribute something.

"You still have that extra key I got cut for Clary's mom's car?"

She dug around in her beige purse and found it, on the old Playboy keychain.

"Don't come running to me for help," she said.

"Yeah, as if."

To prove him wrong, she pulled out her wallet and peeled apart the secret lining, and filched out four hundred-dollar bills.

"Don't say I never did nothing for you," she said.

He put the money in his pocket. "See you," he said. He threw the keys to Darwin's old beater through its window. Couldn't get far in that.

Then he walked ahead to where Clary's mother's car was parked—well over onto the old screamer's property line, right in front of his house. Clary could get away with it, just not him. Typical. He adjusted the seat to suit his legs again and drove away.

Lorraine sat with her back against a log, wrapped up in a blanket with Trevor on one side and Dolly on the other, telling them a nighttime story about camping with Rose. Clary held Pearce while he cried for a sand-scraped knee and for it being late, and no bottle left out here to comfort a tired boy. She rocked him slightly, slightly, the way he liked, slowing down as slowly as a cloud moving in a windless sky. At last her mind was not noisy with wanting, and her heart had satisfied its longing.

"Okay, I'm on my way," Darwin said, standing up.

They looked up at him, surprised. Dolly and Trevor stood too, protesting. They let the blanket fall, but Lorraine folded the ends around herself, knowing Darwin.

"Drive safe on the way back to town," he said, and walked up the bank. Dolly could still see his hand waving at them for a while, above the haze and smoke.

It was colder, now it was getting dark. Moreland had built the fire up into a huge bonfire that snapped and spun sparks up into the night sky.

Paul took the stick they had drawn the world with and drove it deep in the heart of the fire to light it, then made patterns in the darkening air with the burning brand, red shapes that hung for a moment in their vision.

"*I do not care about religion, or anything that is not God,*" he said. Then he looked guiltily at Clary—but perhaps psalms would not count as quoting. She smiled at him. She had soothed and quieted Pearce until he slept, as peaceful as a child sleeping in its mother's arms.

Mrs. Zenko, sweet and tidy on the wild night shore, wrapped the wings of her sweater around the children to keep them warm while the others began to pack up, leaving that place, ready for the short walk back to the cars.

Acknowledgements

*I*n case one of Paul's quotations is tickling at the edge of your mind, here are the poets, in order of appearance. Philip Larkin, Dylan Thomas, Isaac Bashevis Singer (The Spinoza of Market Street), Emily Dickinson, Hebrews 13 ("entertaining angels unawares"), e.e. cummings, Stevie Smith at sad length, Gerard Manley Hopkins, Rilke, Hopkins again (and not for the last time), Dylan Thomas rhapsodizing on beer and then on whiskey, Flann O'Brien (on the aftermath of beer and whiskey), a drunken approximation of Michael Polanyi's ideas on tacit knowledge, William Carlos Williams, Amy Lowell, Shakespeare, St. Paul's Letter to the Romans, Thomas Hood, Alfred Noyes, Shakespeare again, W. B. Yeats ("so great a sweetness flows"), Pablo Neruda, Song of Solomon, Hopkins again, Matthew Arnold, Ted Hughes's cheerful little ditty called Lovesong, Hopkins (again), (and again), Thomas Merton, Hopkins one last time on the riverbank, and finally Psalm 131.

Dolly's books are *The Children Who Lived in a Barn*, by Eleanor Graham (now in a beautiful re-issue from Persephone Books in England), *Mistress Masham's Repose* by T.H. White (pretty widely available, but there's a nice edition, with the original drawings by Fritz Eichenberg, one of the great illustrators and printmakers of the 20th century, from New York Review Children's

371

Collection), and a cheap old edition of *Vanity Fair*, with front pages missing and a red board cover that reddens your hands if you read it in the bathtub.

Clary only thinks in poetry once (and it is Philip Larkin, as was her first instinct, not Dylan Thomas). She remembers *Pogo*, the seminal 50s comic strip by Walt Kelly, now available in reprinted collections. I've seen the charming *Bug Play* performed, but have been unable to locate the author or composer.

Thanks for financial support to the Canada Council and the Alberta Foundation for the Arts. For his generous and fearsome clarity I am always grateful to Peter Ormshaw. Thanks for her manifold gifts and cleverness to Freehand's Editor, Melanie Little. Thanks to Sara O'Leary, the ethereal companion, and to Jeanne Harvie, the constant reader. To Glenda MacFarlane, who also knew Binnie, for Clearwater and many other things. (Apologies to the real Clearwater Lake, which is a lovely little lakeside resort and nothing like the scrubby place described here.)

Thanks to doctors Thyra Endicott, Nora Ku and Jill Nation for help with cancer. And to Azana Endicott, too late.

Thanks to Rachel and Will Ormshaw, research and development. Thoughtful advice: Timothy Endicott, Jonathan Chute, Derek Dunwoody, Greg Clark. Early training: my dear father, Orville Endicott. I should add that the parish and diocese described here bear no resemblance to any on earth, and that no true bishop would ever wear suede shoes.

For their shining example, I am indebted to Bill and Violet Ormshaw. Thanks are due to the Senior Belts: Steve Gobby, Jeanne Harvie, Susan Kelly, Lee Kvern; to Wendy Agnew for drawing the world with me; to Connie Gault for her reading; and to Sarah and Mark Wellings, for time alone. Thanks to Bonnie Burnard and CBC Radio for the push: an early version of the first part of this book was commissioned for broadcast on *Festival of Fiction* in October 2000 and August 2001.

Thanks also, as always, to my lovely mother, Julianne Endicott.